NEWPORT BORO

Z26

006

D1348260

ADAM LOVEDAY

Kate Tremayne

HEADLINE

Copyright © 1999 Kate Tremayne

The right of Kate Tremayne to be identified as the Author of
the Work has been asserted by her in accordance with the
Copyright, Designs and Patents Act 1988.

First published in Great Britain in 1999 by
HEADLINE BOOK PUBLISHING

10 9 8 7 6 5 4 3 2 1

All rights reserved. No part of this publication may be
reproduced, stored in a retrieval system, or transmitted,
in any form or by any means without the prior written
permission of the publisher, nor be otherwise circulated
in any form of binding or cover other than that in which
it is published and without a similar condition being
imposed on the subsequent purchaser.

All characters in this publication are fictitious
and any resemblance to real persons, living or dead,
is purely coincidental.

British Library Cataloguing in Publication Data

Tremayne, Kate
Adam Loveday
I. Title
823.9'14 [F]

ISBN 0 7472 7481 9

Typeset by
CBS, Martlesham Heath, Ipswich, Suffolk

Printed and bound in Great Britain by
Mackays of Chatham PLC, Chatham, Kent

HEADLINE BOOK PUBLISHING
A division of the Hodder Headline Group
338 Euston Road
London NW1 3BH

www.headline.co.uk
www.hodderheadline.com

To my husband Chris – with love

Acknowledgements:

A special thank you to my agent Teresa Chris for making my dream come true.

Also for the support and encouragement from Jane Morpeth, Amanda Ridout, and Andi Sisodia at Headline . . . and Yvonne Holland.

To my friends, Verity Reynolds, Karen Vincent, Caroline Elderfield, June Tate, Jan Henley, Carey Cleaver and Pamela Fieldus for always being there and understanding when I need you most.

Chapter One

1787

The spear of lightning which split the night sky revealed the threat of the impaling rocks at the base of the Cornish cliffs. White spray rose high as a church spire, then subsided into a boiling cauldron in a devil's dance capable of wreaking death and destruction. A native of this coast, Adam Loveday knew the toll storm and rocks could take upon even the greatest galleon.

The frigate reared and pitched. Adam worked in the fore topsail rigging, the ropes supporting his bare feet abrasive as glass from the icy rain. He rode the wave. His body, attuned to the swell of the sea, was perfectly poised and balanced, whilst around his head and shoulders the tattered fore topgallant writhed like a nest of striking vipers. Muscles, strengthened by five years in the navy, corded and contorted in agony as he lashed the remnants of the sail against the yardarm.

The rain flattened his dark hair and moulded his short seaman's jacket and white breeches to his lithe form. He was aware of the score of sailors alongside and above him; each man battling with the elements to save the ship.

Another flash of lightning showed Adam that the frigate was finally turning from the rocks. Yet the danger was far from over, there was still the headland to clear.

They should never have come this far inshore. Returning to Plymouth after eighteen months in the Mediterranean, the HMS *Goliath* had been hailed by a revenue cutter to help pursue two fishing vessels suspected of smuggling. The vessels had been tiny dots on the horizon and they had chased them for an hour before the storm struck at nightfall. By then they were beyond Plymouth. The smugglers could hide in any of a dozen coves. Their cargoes of brandy, tea and silks stowed in waterproof kegs, would be jettisoned and weighted with stones to reside beneath the sea until it was safe to retrieve them. Pursuit was not only pointless, it would endanger the frigate. The coasts of Devon and Cornwall had been graveyards for hundreds of ships over the centuries. Now the wind was driving them dangerously close to the headland protecting St Mawes and Falmouth harbour. The officer of the watch, Lieutenant Francis Beaumont, was in his mid-twenties and inexperienced, and had sneered at Adam's earlier warning.

'You are impertinent, Mr Loveday. Do you question my judgement? Or are you in sympathy with these lawless smugglers? I've heard it said all Cornishmen turn a blind eye to the King's law where smuggling is concerned, to serve their own base needs.'

Adam clenched his fist and swallowed the insult. It was not easy. At twenty, his temper could still triumph over caution, especially on matters of his pride or injustice. Lieutenant Beaumont was conceited and his arrogance was hard to stomach. Although Beaumont had become a midshipman at thirteen and had been promoted to lieutenant at twenty-four, he was incompetent. His navigational skills were adequate but he had no real understanding of the sea or the changes of weather. He had less understanding of men, and judged any inferiors in rank with the tolerance of a farmyard bull.

His anger controlled, Adam regarded the man, who was shorter than he by four inches. The narrow face of Beaumont was pinched even tighter by his sneer. A powdered wig sat on the lieutenant's head like an oversize cauliflower, making him look ridiculous rather than dignified.

There had been countless such remarks from this officer during the voyage. Each was a deliberate taunt which struck at Adam's pride in his family or his homeland, It had taken all his self-control not to retaliate.

Since leaving Gibraltar, Captain Rawcliffe had been confined to his cabin with gout. The crippling pain made his unstable temper volcanic. Beaumont, with the advantage of seniority, ignored Adam's warning about the weather, jeering, 'Frightened of a bit of wind and rain, are you, Mr Loveday? Take three men and unfurl the topgallants. We'll board those confounded smugglers and press them into service.'

'With respect, sir, I beg you to reconsider.' The courtesy almost choked Adam when he yearned to teach the arrogant bully a lesson. Seven men had been put to the lash under Beaumont's orders during the voyage, two of which had died.

To Adam's mind Beaumont represented the worst elements of a naval officer. He was the favoured grandson of Admiral Algernon Beaumont, and constantly bragged of his family connections. He treated anyone below him in rank with contempt, whilst he toadied to his superior officers. Adam despised him. Soon, he vowed, Beaumont would answer for the insults over the last months. Adam expected his commission to lieutenant to be awaiting him at Plymouth. Owing to another confrontation with Beaumont at the start of the voyage, Adam had been denied earlier promotion.

'So you do question my judgement, Mr Loveday?' It was another challenge.

'You are the senior officer on duty. But as a native to these shores I know the weather and the sea. Within half an hour I hazard the storm will be upon us. The wind is easterly and it is freshening. There is a smell about it.'

'A smell!' Beaumont scoffed. 'What old wives' tale is this? The sky is clear. Do you think my grandfather became an admiral by harking to such nonsense? It is perhaps why your uncle remains a mere captain.'

Again Adam battled not to lose his temper at this further insult. It was more important to keep the HMS *Goliath* safe.

His naval career had started when he was fifteen, aboard a warship commanded by William Loveday. He admired his uncle because he instilled discipline without resorting to the unnecessary cruelty common on so many ships. Adam was proud of his naval heritage. In every generation a Loveday had served his country and many had lost their lives at sea.

Forcing deference into his voice, he declared, 'There will be a storm. The fishing smacks will take refuge in a secluded cove. And these shores are notoriously treacherous.'

Lieutenant Beaumont stepped closer, his expression haughty. 'Your opinion was not asked for, Mr Loveday. Get aloft and unfurl the topgallants. We will make the most of the freshening wind to catch those blackguards.'

Further protest was useless. Adam could not refuse to obey a direct order. His courtesy title of *Mister* was a sham, a concession to his genteel birth. He and the other three midshipmen on board had no more rights than the ordinary seamen, and were worked to exhaustion.

Adam had a wisdom beyond his years about the local weather. From the age of five he had loved the sea. Whenever his grandfather put one of the vessels built in the family shipwright's yard through its sea trials, Adam had accompanied him. Yet the navy had not been Adam's choice as a career. He would have preferred to work as a shipwright. He had fought against joining the service for years, which was why he had not become a midshipman until he was fifteen, when many men of naval families joined as young as eleven. His father had finally lost patience with the constant fighting and rivalry between Adam and his twin, St John, and Adam had been ordered into the navy.

He'd accepted the decision with philosophical grace. Trevowan could never be home to both himself and St John; there was too much rivalry between them.

After three years sailing with his Uncle William, who was commander of HMS *Neptune*, Adam transferred for this last voyage to HMS *Goliath*, a move that had shown him all that was bad about the navy. Captain Rawcliffe had no regard for the suffering of his

3

sailors. Three press-ganged men had jumped overboard, unable to face the unremitting misery of poor food and floggings. Beaumont was as ruthless as the captain. On several occasions Adam had been punished when he intervened to stop Beaumont beating senseless the young cabin boy, Billy Brown, over some minor incident.

Adam's courage had earned him Beaumont's hatred. The long and dangerous hours of exhausting tasks that he carried out with vigilance served to provoke the lieutenant to greater endeavours to break his will. From the start of the voyage, Beaumont, newly promoted from midshipman himself, had been jealous of the easy way Adam had won the respect of the other officers and also the seamen.

The sea was in Adam's heart and his blood. He excelled in his navigation and ship's management classes. He could climb the ratlines to the crow's-nest faster than any man on board.

Life as a midshipman was hard. Throughout the day and night he was on duty for each alternate four-hour watch and never able to snatch more than three and a half hours' sleep at a time. Scrubbing decks, mending sails, polishing the brass fitments were as much a midshipman's duty as training in navigation, gunnery and ship's management. Yet Adam thrived on it.

The present storm permitting, they would dock at Plymouth on the morning tide and he would be at Trevowan before evening. Thoughts of home and the comfort of Trevowan had sustained him through the blistering heat and torment of being becalmed during a Mediterranean summer, or half frozen and clinging to a masthead during storms.

Now, with the shredded canvas furled, Adam edged back along the yardarm. His lungs burned from his efforts. The pain in his shoulders was numbed by the icy sting of the rain. Thank God the headland was now behind them and the worst of the storm seemed to have passed. Every officer, except the stricken captain, was now on deck to bring the ship under control. The first lieutenant had been furious at being roused by the storm to find HMS *Goliath* in danger through the incompetence of Beaumont.

A violent gust flattened Adam against the rigging, then an ominous crack above him made him leap across to the ratlines. The main topmast had splintered and fallen to the deck, crushing a sailor. Another seaman, his legs snared in the rigging, was dragged with it. The man's scream was cut off when he landed head first on the deck. A heavy block and tackle swung like a pendulum, threatening to decapitate any man within its range. It was crashing against the ratlines perilously close to the unconscious figure of Seth Wakeley. Seth was hanging upside down. His body was suspended with his legs hanging through the ropes of the ratlines. It swayed with each pitch of the ship. From its angle one of his legs was clearly broken.

Adam began to climb to rescue him. Keeping one eye on the block, which swung unnervingly close to his head, he shouted for assistance. A sailor descended from above and helped to support Seth's weight. Adam withdrew his knife and slashed at the ropes which held Seth's broken leg.

He glanced down and saw a tangle of rigging and the broken mast with its sail hanging over the side of the vessel. Sailors swarmed over it, hacking at the ropes to release the mast. Its weight was causing the ship to list and was affecting the steering. If a wave hit them amidships, they could capsize. As it was, the ship was already veering towards the rocks. There was no sign of Lieutenant Beaumont. A scan of the deck showed Adam two men struggling by lantern light with the helm.

Twice he had to duck to avoid the swinging block. Once it caught him a glancing blow on the shoulder. The pain was excruciating. There was no longer strength in the fingers of his left arm. Fortunately, Seth was now free of the rigging. The only way to get him safely to the deck was for Adam to carry him over his shoulder.

The weight of the man added to the searing agony of Adam's injury. Each step stripped energy from his legs. His knees buckled and threatened to pitch both himself and Seth to the deck, still some thirty feet below. He willed himself to find the strength he needed and blotted out the debilitating pain.

With relief he lowered Seth on to the deck, to be taken with the other injured and treated by the ship's surgeon. For another hour, until the storm died away, Adam worked to clear the decks. The first glimmer of dawn was visible on the horizon when the ship's bell rang, announcing the change of watch.

Adam went below decks to check on Seth and the other wounded men. He was met by a scream which iced his blood. The surgeon was bent over a figure who was held down on a table by two men. The unmistakable rasp of a saw and the stench of blood churned Adam's stomach. There was a thud as the lower part of a leg was tossed on to the blood-splashed floor. The sizzle of a hot cauterising iron and the accompanying smell of burning flesh made him pray for the poor wretch who was suffering such torment. Amputation was the only way of preventing gangrene after a bone had been fractured.

It was Seth. The man had a wife and four children in St Austell. How would a one-legged man support them? Seth was one of the ship's carpenters. He should never have been sent aloft. Once his leg healed he would be capable of working again, but many employers would be prejudiced against a cripple when there were so many able-bodied men to choose from.

Although weary, and his bruised shoulder still stabbing with pain, Adam spoke with each injured man, offering them encouragement. Barty Owens, a young midshipman, called down to him to report to the captain.

5

'The old man is apoplectic over the ship being demasted,' Barty grimaced. 'None of it should rebound on you. Lieutenant Matthews knows Beaumont is responsible.'

Even so, facing Captain Rawcliffe's rage after such a gruelling watch was disconcerting. As Adam descended the stairs to the captain's cabin, there was an enraged bellow from Rawcliffe.

'Incompetent idiot. You damn near lost my ship. You are a disgrace to your rank, Mr Beaumont. Thanks to your stupidity we limp into port like a wounded cur. No self-respecting captain arrives at his home port demasted. Get out of my sight. You will never sail on my ship again.'

Adam stepped back as the fiery-faced lieutenant emerged from the cabin and stormed past. Billy Brown, the cabin boy, was walking carefully down the stairs carrying a jug of steaming water for the captain to wash and shave before they entered port. Beaumont blundered into the lad, knocking the jug from his hands. The hot water spilled over Billy's fingers, causing him to scream. It also splashed Beaumont's white breeches. With a snarl he lashed out at the boy, pushing him headlong down the stairs and then proceeded to shout and kick at his prone body.

'Dolt! You could have maimed me.' He kicked Billy in the ribs.

Adam pulled him off the sobbing boy. 'Don't take it out on the lad. You pushed into him.'

Beaumont rounded on him, his nostrils flaring and eyes glittering with fury. 'Get your hands off me, Loveday. I could have you flogged.'

'You have not the stomach to fight me man to man.' Adam positioned himself between Beaumont and the cabin boy. 'Get up, Billy, and fetch some more water for the captain.'

The boy scrambled away, his puny body bent as he cradled his side. Adam held Beaumont's enraged stare.

'I am reporting you for striking an officer and for insubordination, Loveday. That will put paid to you becoming a lieutenant this year.'

'That accident was your fault. And I never struck you.'

'But I say that you did. It is time you learned to respect your betters.'

Adam lost his hold on his temper. 'You are an arrogant bully and an incompetent fool. You nearly lost the ship because you were too pig-headed to listen to advice. You have had this coming a long time.'

He jammed his fist into Beaumont's stomach and brought his knee up to his groin as he doubled over. The powdered wig fell off and Adam pushed Beaumont's close-cropped head against the panelling of the corridor. 'That was for Billy and all the times you have bullied and beaten him, and for the men maimed or killed through your stupidity.'

'You will pay for this, Loveday,' Beaumont fumed.

'What the devil is all this commotion?' Captain Rawcliffe demanded.

6

The dishevelled state of Beaumont and his blackening eye spoke for itself. How much had the captain seen or heard? They could both be court-martialled for fighting.

'Mr Loveday, I would have your report on the incidents during your watch.'

The captain made no other reference to their brawling even after Adam had stepped into his cabin. Adam reported everything as it had happened.

'You are familiar with these waters. Did you not warn Mr Beaumont of the dangers?'

'I did, sir.'

'Mr Matthews informs me that you saved a man's life when his leg was broken at no little danger to yourself.' When Adam did not reply, Rawcliffe fixed him with a sharp stare. 'There will be no blame attached to yourself for this regrettable incident. In fact I will be recommending to the Admiralty that you receive your commission as lieutenant for our next voyage, should it not already be awaiting you.'

'Thank you, sir.'

'You are a fine officer, Mr Loveday. But there must be no dissension between officers on board ship. Guard that temper of yours.'

Instead of returning to his hammock, Adam was drawn to the ship's rail. With England at peace, the navy held little interest to him. He had joined the navy when the war of American Independence was at its height. He had spent a year in the Indian Ocean following the threats of the French to destroy the East India Company, which had come to nothing. Then in 1783 the Treaty of Versailles was signed and all hostilities ended. The present voyage had been in the Mediterranean patrolling from Gibraltar to Malta.

It had been an inglorious voyage: dysentery and scurvy rife on board, and no action to alleviate the boredom.

Adam's mood changed as HMS *Goliath* neared the waters of Trevowan Cove. The sight of the steep granite cliffs were a balm to his anger. The wind was now against them, the sea rising in a heavy greyish-green swell. The blue glimmer of dawn revealed the tall chimneys and high gables of his home. Homesickness smote him. He had always loved Trevowan and its land. He had not realised how desperately he would miss them during his voyages.

The knuckles on his hand whitened at the power of his emotions. The sea made an exciting mistress but his dream was to roam it free as captain of his own ship, not shackled by the prejudices and constraints of the navy.

Yet Trevowan was even more a part of him than the sea. How could he ever come to terms with losing it as his home, as one day he must?

Chapter Two

Adam crouched low over Solomon's neck as the chestnut gelding pounded along the cliff top above Trevowan Cove. He could hear the hoofs of St John's horse several yards behind him. He blocked out the pain in his bruised shoulder as he laughed and urged the horse to greater speed. He was bareheaded, his long dark hair tied back in a queue. The wind was exhilarating as it stung his cheeks. Overhead the sky was overcast, the tarnished silver clouds low on the horizon. The sea was streaked with purple, kingfisher and jade, and the breakers as they crashed on to the dark rocks were crowned with virginal whiteness.

This was the Cornwall Adam loved: wild and untamed, unpredictable and majestic. A glance over his shoulder showed that St John had fallen further behind and was struggling not to lose his tricorn hat in the wind. Adam turned north towards the Loveday shipwright's yard on an inlet of the Fowey river, and slowed his pace.

'Must you always ride as though your life depended on it?' St John complained, joining him.

'I have little time on land before I must rejoin my ship. You have become a sluggard whilst I have been away.'

His brother's face was flushed and the thick line of his brown brows were drawn together in displeasure. There was already a thickening about his waist; St John had always been stocky. No one would ever take them for twins. There was two inches difference in their heights, and at least two stones in weight, with Adam the shorter and lighter. Even their colouring was dissimilar.

Adam had inherited his mother's dark skin and raven hair from her French parentage, though his eyes were the blue green of the seas he roved. St John, with his heavier features and brown hair and paler blue eyes, was the image of their great-grandfather, Arthur St John Loveday. He had been a shipwright who had seduced and married a wealthy young widow, Anne Penhaligan, the mistress of Trevowan. He had used her money to start the Loveday yard. Despite the employment he had brought to the area, he was a tyrant, disliked by many. He fathered eleven children on his long-suffering wife. Only one, George, had survived to inherit when the old man died.

St John scowled. 'Sluggard be damned. Between the yard and the

9

estate I have precious little time to take any ease or pleasure. Father works me harder than any one, and I receive a pittance for my pains.'

Adam glanced at his brother's long embroidered waistcoat and braided ruby velvet jacket. They alone would have cost half his year's wages. St John was a dandy, his clothing more fitting for a soiree or dining with neighbours than riding the dusty Cornish lanes. Adam wore black breeches and a tan leather jerkin over his full-sleeved white shirt.

'You have responsibilities, St John. Father expects no less a commitment from you than he does from himself.'

'Father takes it all too seriously. What use is inheriting a fortune if you work longer hours than your servants and have no time for pleasure?'

Anger burned through Adam at his twin's attitude. 'There's many a wastrel who put pleasure before duty and brought a family to ruin.'

St John gave a harsh laugh. 'Spoken like a peasant. As heir to Trevowan I shall do my duty by marrying a wealthy heiress. Estate and yard overseers are paid to make the estate and business profitable, or suffer the consequences.'

'The consequences will be your ruin,' Adam retorted. 'No overseer will work with the same vigilance as a master.'

There was a malignant glitter in St John's eye. 'Since you hold duty so dear, perhaps I should employ you when I am master of Trevowan.'

The intentional barb, although familiar, was still painful. Adam foresaw the future of Trevowan as bleak once St John became its master. Fortunately their father, who was in his mid-forties, would live for many years. By the time he came to inherit, St John may have curbed his extravagant ways.

Yet resentment flared. St John was unworthy to be Trevowan's heir. Three minutes' difference in ages had robbed Adam of his inheritance: the home he loved and the shipwright's yard he had been obsessed with since childhood.

All his life he had been taunted by St John that he was the heir and Adam the pauper. It had festered into rivalry. He had been mocked on the day of their birth. The cord around his neck had prevented him coming naturally into the world first. The doctor had delayed too long; his mother was already dying when the Caesarean was performed and St John drawn first out of the womb. The birth had taken everything from Adam, even the beautiful mother who was only eighteen years old.

Yet it could not take his dreams, nor his pride in his family's heritage. St John was too pleasure-loving to manage Trevowan and make it prosper. Adam would make his own fortune in the world. He could never work beside St John, that was why he had entered the navy.

10

Once he became a captain the wealth of the seas would be his to reap. Never would he acknowledge that his twin was his master. He had too much pride.

Yet there was a part of him which refused to relinquish his dream of being master of Trevowan and the Loveday yard.

Trevowan will be mine. The words pounded through his mind to the drum of his gelding's hoofs as he sped along the narrow lanes towards the boatyard, St John again trailing behind. The hedgerows, festive with their hawthorn berries and wisps of old man's beard, were a blur of red and grey. At a brow of a hill Adam reined in to gaze down at the inlet. The rhythmic hammering and grating rasp of a two-man saw, cutting planks from a tree in the sawpit, quickened his heartbeat.

He surveyed the river bank and the activity of the boatyard. The smell of tar and freshly cut wood mingled with the tang of the river. Secure in a wooden cradle was an almost completed fishing smack. The men were caulking the hull by forcing tar between the wooden planks to make the vessel seaworthy. The dry dock held a twin-masted sloop having the weed and barnacles scraped from its bottom before repainting. There was also another keel laid down, the skeletal ribs partially fitted. It was larger than anything Adam had seen previously in the Loveday yard. His experienced eye visualised it completed. It would be the size of a brigantine or frigate.

This was the type of vessel he had dreamed of building and owning. On his last leave he had shown his father the plans he had drawn up for just such a ship: an armed merchantman with trim lines for greater speed than those currently favoured. It was a project he and his grandfather had discussed during the months before the old man died.

A lump of pride swelled in Adam's throat and he swallowed against it. Such a vessel would raise the status of the boatyard. They may even win orders to build the fast packet boats plying out of Falmouth, or a warship for the navy.

Another scan of the yard caused him to frown. Surely there should be more men at work. Two men pushed the arms of a capstan to raise a plank on the pulley on the port side of the bow. Of the four pulleys, one at each corner of the scaffolding, it was the only one being worked. At least one other team of men should be busy on the stern. There was the clang of a hammer on anvil from the blacksmith's forge, for the yard produced its own nails, but there was no sound of the scrape of adzes and planes in the moulding shed.

Even the row of eight labourers' cottages looked partially deserted, with just three children playing outside and only four lines of washing hanging out. More troubling was that three of the single cottages used by the shipwrights looked storm-damaged and had been left unrepaired. Over the forty years of the yard's existence a small community had

11

been built up. One of the houses had been converted to a kiddleywink, selling both ale and general provisions, named the Ship Inn.

The tall, slender figure of his father was outside the stone cottage which served as his office, talking to Ben Mumford, the overseer, when the brothers entered the yard. Adam's excitement at the sight of the new ship dispersed his fears that the business was in any difficulty. He leaped from his horse, firing questions at his father.

'Why did you not write and tell me you were building such a vessel? Who is it for? What is its tonnage? Is she to be a merchantman? Will she have three masts or two? And the . . .'

Edward Loveday put up his hand to stop his younger son's questions but his eyes showed his pleasure and affection. 'Come inside and look at the plans.'

St John yawned and sauntered ahead into the office. Edward called after him, 'A consignment of logs was floated down river and needs securing. See to it. Though you are hardly dressed for such work. You do not come here to sit in the office all day.'

'We were supposed to be calling at Traherne Hall but Adam insisted on visiting the yard first.' St John re-emerged, looking petulant. 'You were the one who insisted we spend more time together whilst he is on leave.'

He stalked off towards the jetty where the logs where being hauled out of the water by pulley and stacked on the shore, and the other three went inside.

Belatedly, Adam greeted Ben and shook his hand. 'How long have you been working on the new ship? She looks a beauty.'

'Aye, I thought you'd like her.' Ben scratched his bald pate and tilted his head to look up at him. 'We laid the keel last Lady Day.'

'That's nearly six months. She hasn't progressed far. Is there a problem?'

'That be for the Master to say.' Ben excused himself to supervise two men working on the deck of the fishing smack.

Adam dragged his gaze reluctantly from the merchantman, his mind racing with questions for his father.

Edward beckoned him over to study the plans laid out on his desk. Unlike St John, his father was dressed for work in a grey broadcloth coat and breeches. His greying brown hair, which had receded in two arches either side of his brow, was tied back with a black bow.

Adam gasped at the plans. 'But that is my ship. Those are the ideas Grandpapa and I spoke of.'

His father nodded. 'I was impressed with them.'

'So who has commissioned the vessel?'

'Sit down, Adam. The ship will be yours. Your Great-uncle Amos died last year – he was a widower and without children. He left you and St John legacies which are held in trust until you both are twenty-one. It is not a fortune but enough to build and fit out the ship you have always wanted. I have arranged with the lawyers that money will be taken from the estate as a loan against your legacy.'

Adam wiped a shaking hand across his chin. 'It is several years since I saw Great-uncle Amos. I had meant to visit him in Liskeard on my last leave. It was kind of him to bequeath me his money.'

'The money will secure your future.' He regarded Adam with a resigned air before continuing, 'I realised after our talks during your last leave that navy life would not suit you for much longer. Your Uncle William agreed. Querying orders from officers you believe incompetent has already resulted in disciplinary action. The ship will be ready and fitted out for you in the next eighteen months. I cannot spare men to work on it full time. And I suspect you will want to oversee what work you can to your own specifications.'

Adam was stunned. 'I do not know what to say. The navy holds little joy for me. I would rather captain my own ship.'

'I had hoped you would use her as a merchantman, but you will need backers for your first cargo. I expect you to stay in the navy until she is ready.'

'I have experience enough to captain her. There is more profit in privateering than as a merchant adventurer.'

'And more risk,' Edward cautioned. 'Our family has prospered from it in the past. And also suffered great loss. It was not so long ago that my younger brother Hubert was killed taking a Spanish ship which was supplying the rebel American colonists. Also, for such a venture to be a success England must be at war to claim an enemy prize. Without letters of marque from the government, it is piracy and a hanging offence. England is at peace. The days of buccaneering are past.'

'Aye, aye, sir.' Adam stood to attention and grinned. 'You are right. But times change . . .' He gazed out of the window at the keel, and a thrill of excitement made him laugh aloud. 'I can tolerate another year in the navy knowing I will one day own a brigantine built in our yard. There are no finer ships.'

Edward nodded but his manner remained reserved. 'Your legacy will not stretch to arming the vessel as a privateer. You must find the money for that yourself. No man became rich saving their navy pay.'

Nothing could diminish Adam's pleasure. Life as a captain-owner of a privateer held more lure than the constraints of the navy. Stories of Drake and the great Elizabethan buccaneers had filled his childhood. They were his heroes. If he could not have Trevowan, such a life would be some compensation.

'There is one more thing.' His father remained serious. He touched his fingers together and put them to his mouth before explaining, 'St John was informed that the ship has been commissioned by a private buyer. He will be told the truth in time, but if he learns I have so favoured you he will expect a similar sum loaned against his own legacy. It would be squandered on gambling or pleasure within a few months. I wanted to ensure that you could make your way in the world.'

Overwhelmed, Adam clasped his father's hand. 'Thank you, sir. The ship will be named *Pegasus*. Now I would look over her. And work on her every day during my leave.'

'Starting tomorrow. Today your brother expects you to accompany him to Traherne Hall. He is making a concession to you as Henry is your friend, not his. Extend an invitation for Sir Henry to dine with us this evening. You will have much news to impart to him, though even to your friend the ownership of the *Pegasus* must remain a secret.'

Edward watched Adam run to the scaffolding around the brigantine and talk animatedly with Ben Mumford. Edward rubbed his clean-shaven chin. He had not been entirely honest with Adam. The money for the brigantine was raised against Adam's legacy, but it had been the need to keep the yard looking prosperous and thereby attract new orders that had driven him to start work on the vessel. Years of peace had brought a lull in the shipbuilding trade. He had been undercut in a bid to build three of the new packet ships sailing from Falmouth. It had been two years since they had built a vessel over sixty tons. In the meantime, the Trevowan estate had suffered bad harvests. Times were hard for all the landowners.

His gaze turned upon four horses dragging a log to be stacked at the rear of the yard. Later it would be stripped of its bark and left to season. St John was nowhere in sight. More tailors' bills had arrived from Truro last week, the creditors demanding money or they would take legal proceedings. And there were also St John's gambling debts. Edward had cut off his allowance after the last time he was forced to settle a gambling debt of two hundred pounds. St John then borrowed money from the ne'er-do-well young gentry set he called his friends. The boy would bankrupt him. There were three of his markers to be repaid.

With Adam's future security now assured, it was time St John's future was settled. Marriage would cool his wastrel ways. St John must face up to his responsibilities or face the consequences.

14

Chapter Three

It was an hour before midday when the twins approached Penruan village, the nearest to Trevowan land. Adam was in such good spirits he had allowed St John to pull ahead as they rode.

'A guinea I reach the Dolphin Inn first,' St John shouted from his advantage of several lengths lead. 'We shall have a sup of ale before visiting Traherne Hall.' He raced off before Adam could respond, gaining further yards.

Throughout their childhood competition had been fierce between them. St John had used his strength to bully Adam, but the slighter built boy had never conceded, even when he was overpowered and beaten. By the age of seven Adam, although wiry, triumphed over St John in agility and ingenuity, and it was he who was usually the victor.

Penruan village was already in sight. It was at the head of a steep coombe which opened into the sea. The slate- or thatched-roofed cottages were spread around the horseshoe shape of the harbour arm in haphazard fashion, or perched on a rocky outcrop. They were mostly constructed of granite to withstand the violent storms of the Channel.

The fishing fleet was moored along the quay, the receding tide leaving some of them tilted on the mud. The air was heavy with the reek of fish. Adam had forgotten how pungent the smell could be. It clung to the work sheds and houses, and permeated the clothing of the fishermen's families.

A clatter of female voices drifted from the cleaning sheds as the fishermen's wives and daughters gutted and salted the catch, or packed the fish into panniers to be taken away by jowters, who were the travelling fish salesmen.

Adam drew level with St John as they reached the first of the houses. By the time they were forced to slow their pace in the steep, twisting narrow lanes, he was a length in front. The Dolphin Inn was in a small cobbled square opposite the tall-towered church and at the far end of the village to the gutting sheds. When Adam dismounted in the inn's yard he was several lengths ahead of his brother.

Adam threw the reins and some copper coins to Mark Sawle, who, at fourteen, was the youngest of the landlord's children. St John scowled and cuffed the lad's ear for not moving fast enough as Adam entered the taproom first.

The interior of the inn was dark, being poorly lit from just two small windows. The low-beamed ceiling made the air oppressive from the smoking fire in the grate and the fug of tobacco smoke rising from the fishermen's clay pipes. The inn had been built from timbers salvaged from a wreck a century ago. Its supporting beams were dissected with morticed holes and the once whitewashed walls were now brown with age.

'Welcome back, Master Loveday,' Reuban Sawle called from behind the bar. He was short and thickset like a wrestler, with a craggy face and a wispy grey beard hanging down his chest. 'Here be a glass of brandy to warm you.' He waved aside Adam's money.

Adam was immediately surrounded by several villagers greeting him.

'Careful, Reuban,' a fisherman joked. 'Bain't like you to be so open with your purse strings. Mine be a brandy as you're so generous.'

'You can go to the devil or buy your own,' Reuban grunted. 'This bain't no alms house.'

'Let there be a brandy for every one,' Adam declared. He grinned across at his brother, who stood surveying the taproom, clearly resentful that no one had acknowledged his presence. 'St John is paying from the guinea wager I have just won from him.'

With poor grace St John tossed the money on to the bar and withdrew to a quiet corner. Several dour glances followed him. Why did St John antagonise these people? Clem Sawle, the oldest of the Sawle brothers and the most headstrong, deliberately jolted St John with his shoulder when he passed.

'How is the pilchard catch this year?' Adam enquired. It would be a lean year for the villagers if the pilchard catch failed.

'It have be better and it have be worse,' Alf Rundle, an elderly fisherman, observed. The fishermen rarely told you if the season had been profitable. They were a hardy breed of men, their livelihoods reliant upon the capricious dictates of the sea and weather.

Adam spoke briefly with each man, enquiring of his family and recalling past escapades with the younger men he had played with as a youth. When he joined his brother, St John's face was white and pinched with anger.

'It does not do to mix with these men. Some of them are our tenants.'

'We have known them all our lives. Courtesy costs nothing. They are good men.'

'And we are gentlemen. If you choose to forget that, I do not. Familiarity is misplaced. Next thing you know they will be up at the house, cap in hand, pleading poverty after a bad season's catch and expecting their rents to be waivered. Unlike you I have my position as heir of Trevowan to consider.'

Again the pompous retort was a deliberate reminder that St John would one day lord it over his twin. It cut through Adam as jaggedly as a rusty-edged saw. He turned away to conceal the anger in his eyes.

Last night Adam had given his word to his father to do nothing to provoke any rivalry with his twin. St John had no such scruples. Each time he returned home it was harder for Adam to accept St John was the future master of Trevowan. The years Adam had spent at sea had taught him a great deal, especially about officers who abused their power. St John showed every sign of becoming such a man. It did not bode well for the people of Trevowan or the Loveday yard.

His attention was caught by a young woman approaching. His eyes widened with surprise. Eighteen months had changed the plump, hoydenish daughter of Reuban Sawle. Meriel, at sixteen, had an hourglass figure and her waist-length, blonde hair curled with wayward abandon. The wide-spaced blue eyes were bold and inviting, and her pouting lips full and sensual.

'Why, it be Master Adam come back to us.'

There was a teasing light in her eyes which captivated Adam. As she came closer he could smell the scent of lavender. She was dressed in a red skirt which was split at the front and secured back over the hips to reveal a green and white striped petticoat. A tight black-laced bodice nipped in her waist and accentuated the fullness of her breasts under the white linen blouse.

'Meriel!' He was stunned at the transformation in her. 'You have become a beautiful woman. You must have a string of beaux willing to court you.'

She shook back her hair. 'I've given my heart to no man.'

Her gaze was appraising. Adam found it exciting. For years Meriel had trailed around after her brothers and made little secret of her preference for Adam's company. He had good-naturedly included her in some of their less boisterous exploits, whilst regarding her as a nuisance to be tolerated. Now there was a challenge in her smile when she added in a husky tone, 'Perhaps I've yet to have the right man come courting. You've been away a long time, Adam.'

'And will be at Trevowan for three weeks before I must rejoin my ship, which is in dry dock after storm damage.'

You'll not be wanting to waste a moment of your time then.'

There was a lift to her arched brow. His throat dried. The invitation she was offering was clear. Meriel was too beautiful and vivacious to resist. Their stares held in understanding and charged expectancy. Then the mood was broken by Clem grabbing his sister's arm and pushing her back towards the living quarters.

'What you be doing dressed up like a duchess? Ma needs help in the kitchen. You'll get that Sunday finery soiled.'

Meriel glared at him. 'I'm no kitchen skivvy. We pay Tilda to help Ma.'

'I know what you're up to,' Clem snarled. 'Now get that finery off and get about your work.'

'I don't take orders from you,' Meriel retorted, the swell of her breasts rising above her low-necked blouse.

When Clem raised a hand to strike her, Adam stepped between them. 'Meriel meant no harm. Are we not all childhood friends?'

Clem rounded on him, his fist clenched. 'And what would a Loveday want with the friendship of an innkeeper's daughter? Nothing honourable.'

'You insult us both,' Adam countered, but there was a warning in his voice. He did not want to be fighting on this leave. Clem was an old adversary. They were evenly matched, although Clem was four years older. For a long moment Clem weighed Adam's level stare and his gaze lowered first. Even so, Adam realised he would be taking a dangerous step by getting entangled with Meriel. But a glance at her lovely face was enough to convince him it was worth it.

He scanned the room and noticed that Clem's brother Harry was missing from the gathering. Harry would not miss a lunchtime drink unless he was up to no good. 'Where is Hal? Not still out fishing, is he?'

'He be taking the cart to Truro for supplies.'

'And he was supposed to take me,' Meriel announced. 'I wanted some ribbon for my hair. It be market day. He took off with that no-good slut Hester Moyle.'

Adam guessed Harry's business in Truro. Four years ago, to get Adam's attention, Meriel had shown him the false bottom in the Sawles' cart. In it would be stored smuggled silks, tea and kegs of brandy for sale in the town. The Sawle family, together with others in the village, were known for their free-trading, as they referred to their smuggling. Reuban was reputedly their leader. Everyone turned a blind eye. Even Edward Loveday had a keg left in the stables whenever Trevowan Cove was used as a landing place.

'It seems a pity that Meriel is all dressed up and has nowhere to go,' Adam teased.

Clem's bearded jaw jutted forward. 'She bain't going nowhere. There be work to be done, not jaunting.'

'But I want to listen to Adam's adventures,' Meriel pouted, and eyed Adam boldly.

St John glowered at his twin. He had enjoyed the hostility towards Adam sparking from Clem. It was not until Meriel fawned over Adam that St John became incensed. Adam's interest in her made St John realise how lovely she had grown. But the wench had ignored him. Antagonism stirred his rivalry. As he studied her, he puffed out his chest with self-importance and pulled the frilled cuffs of his shirt over his wrist. He would impress Meriel with his elegance. He took a

18

silver snuffbox from his pocket and sprinkled some on the back of his hand. With a deft movement he sniffed it. Some grains struck the back of his throat, sharp as nettles, and made his eyes water.

There was an amused glitter in Adam's eye at St John's discomfort. Damn him. Adam as usual looked unkempt, his shirt half undone, the ruffle hanging loose to one side. And those black breeches were indecently tight. A lock of hair curled over his brow and his face and hands were stained mahogany from the Mediterranean sun. He looked like a damned pirate.

Arrogance dispersed St John's ire. Cavorting with a village trollop lacked finesse. Besides, he had a pretty widow for a mistress living in Fowey.

A delighted shout made St John turn to the door, and his mood again darkened. Sir Henry Traherne had entered the inn and clamped his arm round Adam. His round boyish features were flushed with pleasure. Locks of ginger hair had escaped its ribbon and corkscrewed around his ears in tight curls. To his cost St John knew that Henry's slight frame was deceptive. When as children St John had picked a fight with him, it was himself who got the black eye, as Henry ducked under his guard and agilely avoided his punches. St John did not care much for the fellow.

The Traherne estate was on the far side of Penruan. The Traherne tin mine had built the estate's fortune, but now it was all but worked out, and Sir Henry was in debt to a half-dozen of the county's bankers.

'Adam, I learned you were home this morning.' Henry slapped him on the back. 'I rode to the yard and was told you were here.'

'We were about to visit Traherne Hall.' Adam returned his friend's greeting with equal fervour. 'Father asked me to invite you to dine this evening. I was sorry to hear that your father died last winter.'

'He had been ill for some time.' The laughter left Henry's eyes.

Adam and Henry took their tankards to join St John.

'How is the mine?'

'We have just struck a rich lode of tin. Did you hear that I am to marry?'

Adam's eyes widened with surprise and he laughed. 'You must be smitten to wed so young.'

'I am marrying Roslyn Druce.'

'Good God, man!' St John broke his disgruntled silence that the two men had been seemingly unaware of his presence. 'The woman is a shrew and several years older than you.'

'But if you love her . . .' Adam countered, angered by his brother's rudeness.

Henry downed his ale. 'Her dowry will keep the mine open and pay for the machinery to drain the new level and work the new lode. It should also pay off the creditors.'

Adam was sorry that his friend had taken such drastic action to safeguard his home and mine. Arranged marriages were commonplace. But he had an uneasy feeling that Roslyn Druce, although comely enough, had too spiteful a tongue to bring his friend happiness.

St John glowered at the two friends. They bored him. He glanced round the room. No one was paying him any attention.

He got up to leave, his exit unnoticed by the friends, who were talking earnestly. He had a far better way to spend his afternoon – in Fowey with the widow Judith Kempe. But he was tiring of her. She was too demanding of his time and purse. It would be diverting to steal Meriel from Adam and show his superiority over his brother. The notion, once rooted, flared to an obsession without thought of any far-reaching consequences.

Chapter Four

When Adam returned to the Dolphin Inn the next evening it was already dark. The taproom was empty and he skirted round the building to enter by the kitchen as he had done as a boy. The room smelled of the fish stew, which constantly simmered in a cauldron over the cooking fire, awaiting any needy customer; and of yeast from the rising dough of tomorrow's bread in a covered bowl.

Sal Sawle was seated in a rare moment of ease in the wooden rocking chair by the fire. In her lap was a pile of thick hose which she was darning for her sons. She looked up at the sound of Adam's footfall, and her wrinkled, rounded face broke into a smile.

'Master Adam, Reuban said you were home. I was sorry to have missed you when you came by yesterday.'

He strode to the hearth and kissed her cheek. 'I met with Sir Henry Traherne or I would have come through. How is my favourite lady?'

Sal giggled. 'Shame on you, Master Adam. You always did have a silver tongue.'

'Not where you are concerned, Sal.' There was genuine affection in his voice. 'I have not forgotten how you tended my cuts and bruises when I got into scrapes in the village.'

He propped himself on the edge of the scrubbed kitchen table. 'I saw the fishing smacks sailing out to sea. Where's Reuban or Mark? The bar was empty.'

'Mark is at sea with his brothers and Reuban is about his own business.' Her evasive stare remained on the socks in her lap. 'Anyone who wants a pint know they have but to call.'

It was a warning not to enquire into Reuban's affairs. Adam had a great respect for this woman whose life was far from easy. She worked like a slave. When the bar finally closed at night she cleaned it ready for the morning. No matter what the time of the early tide she would rise to greet her returning fishermen sons with a hot meal. At three and forty, Sal's back was rounded, her body swollen from fourteen pregnancies of which only five children had survived. Her eldest daughter, Rose, had run away from the harsh life with a travelling player from the harvest fair. Once Sal had been as beautiful as Meriel. Now her grey hair was hidden under a mobcap and three of her teeth were missing, the result of Reuban's drunken rages. In recent years,

21

Clem and Harry had protected her from the worst of Reuban's temper.

Sal studied Adam, her expression sobering. 'You haven't given up an evening when you could be carousing to talk to an old woman. Since the boys are at sea, it be Meriel you'll be after. In the last year every unattached man in the village, and some that bain't so unattached, have pursued her. She'll have none of them. Got her sights set high, has that young madam. But you and I know that no gentleman is going to marry an innkeeper's daughter, however pretty she be.'

Her stare intensified and Adam shifted uncomfortably. He was saved from answering when Meriel herself sauntered into the room.

'I thought I heard your voice, Adam. Ma, why didn't you tell me we had a visitor.'

'Happen he came to see your old Ma,' Sal said perversely.

Meriel wore her everyday clothes of a russet wool skirt, black laced bodice and white full-sleeved blouse. Her blonde hair was unrestrained and curled over her full breasts.

'I had no chance to speak to Sal yesterday,' Adam answered. He had been rash coming tonight, drawn by his need to see Meriel again. He withdrew a length of emerald ribbon from his jacket. 'We met a tinker on the road and you mentioned you needed some ribbon. Please accept it as a gift.'

Meriel reached out her hand, her smile enticing. 'Why thank you kindly, sir—'

'She'll do no such thing,' Sal interrupted with a sternness Adam had not heard in her voice before. She took a pottery jug from a shelf hung with saucepans and shook out some copper coins. 'We pay our way no matter how kindly your intentions.' Sal slammed the pennies on the table. 'There'll be no gifts given to my daughter by any man other than family or her future husband. She has her reputation to consider.'

Meriel twirled the ribbon around her fingers, then touched it to the side of her mouth and smiled. 'The ribbon is lovely. It was thoughtful of you—'

'Was you wanting some ale, Master Adam?' Sal interrupted. Tension was building in the kitchen and her stare had narrowed with suspicion.

'I am meeting Sir Henry this evening. I should be going.'

He bowed to both women and left, hoping that Meriel would find an excuse to follow him. Outside the door he heard Sal ordering her to fetch her shawl from the bedroom.

Sal took the shawl from her daughter, noting the speed with which she had returned and her flushed cheeks. 'You be rushing headlong for a fall, young lady. Men like the Lovedays want only one thing from a girl like you and it bain't marriage.'

22

'What would you know about men like the Lovedays? You settled for the life of a drudge. I never will.'

There was sadness in Sal's eyes as she watched her daughter flounce out of the kitchen. She knew the price of loving unwisely. She had guarded her secret well. Clem wasn't Reuban's child. He was the son of a naval lieutenant whose family owned an estate in Devon. Sal had met him in Falmouth where her father had run the Crown Tavern and she had worked with her two sisters.

Like Meriel she wouldn't believe her lover would play her false. Jamie said he loved her, otherwise she'd never have lain with him. She'd been his mistress for two months when she fell pregnant. When he'd learned of her condition he'd abandoned her. To hide her shame Sal had quickly married Reuban, who delivered the illicit brandy to her father's cellar. Reuban had been asking her to marry him for more than a year.

If Reuban suspected Clem wasn't his he never let on. But the viciousness of his drunken beatings was loaded with accusation. She bore it stoically. Many would have thrown her out once her shame was suspected.

She shook her head. Meriel thought she was clever. She'd come to a bad end, that girl. And cause havoc while so doing.

Meriel ran towards the stables in time to see Adam trotting out into the square. She stamped her foot in frustration that she had been unable to waylay him. She had seen the desire in Adam's eyes as he'd looked at her, and a thrill of expectation held her in its thrall. She had loved Adam Loveday for as long as she could remember. She had thought it a childhood infatuation and behind her, but upon seeing him again her emotions were thrown into turmoil.

She was both elated and annoyed with herself. Many men had pursued her and she had remained aloof and in control, which had served only to increase their ardour. It had been a game to her, proving that her looks and figure were her fortune to catch a wealthy husband.

She was in no mood to return to the inn and be subjected to one of her mother's lectures, or given some endless task. Reuban was at a meeting with his business partner, Thadeous Lanyon. The man owned a rival inn, The Gun, the pilchard drying sheds and the general shop. He also acted as agent and banker with the merchants in Guernsey, where the goods to be smuggled to England were purchased. Yet Lanyon was feared more than respected in the village. Too many men were in his debt.

Meriel shuddered. A widower of three months, Lanyon had recently turned his amphibian stare upon her. Several times when in his shop, he left his ledger desk at the rear of the premises to sidle up against her. Dismissing Moira Bray, his servant, his hands brushed Meriel's arm or leg as he served her. His touch repelled her. Used to the unwanted advances of local men, Meriel knew how to put them in their place. Yet the scathing set-down she had given Thadeous Lanyon brought a lascivious glitter to his eyes which left her uneasy.

The evening breeze was fresh but, in her restless mood, Meriel scarcely noticed it. The sky was clear of clouds and the moon almost full. She loved to watch the moonlight on the water, and rather than return to the inn, she decided to walk to the headland beyond the harbour wall.

Halfway across the square a male voice called her name. Her heart leapt. It was Adam. Had he doubled back in the hope of seeing her? The voice came from within the shadows of the church lych-gate. With a glance over her shoulder to ensure that her mother was not spying on her, Meriel ran towards the church. The dark silhouette of a figure detached itself from the shadows but as the moonlight fell on the man's face disappointment smote her.

'St John, why are you hiding in the churchyard?' The twins' voices were similar enough to have confused her.

'Waiting for a chance to see you, my pretty.' His voice was low and coaxing. 'I have a gift for you. Something elegant to match your beauty.'

Meriel was intrigued. She had no money of her own and Reuban was miserly, providing her with the bare essentials in clothing. St John held up his hand to the moonlight. From his fingers dangled a pair of scarlet stockings of the finest wool. Meriel's eyes widened with delight. She had never possessed anything so fine and was instantly determined to have them.

Even so, she was wary of his intentions. 'I could not accept such a gift.' Her manner was coquettish and her voice heavy with reluctance. 'It would be immodest.'

'How so, when they are given as a token of the esteem in which I hold you?'

She still hesitated and, knowing of the rivalry between St John and Adam, she did not want St John bragging to the brother she preferred. 'Then why do you not come openly to the inn? Do you think my affections can be bought?' She allowed her anger to show. 'I have a regard for my reputation, even if you do not, sir.'

Meriel's reputation was important to her. She had no intention of remaining in this remote fishing village all her life. She would never end up a drudge like her mother. She wanted a life surrounded by every comfort: jewels, velvets, a grand house and a host of servants. She dismissed the limitations of her birth. She had wit and beauty. This last year she had come to know how men lusted after her. So far she had kept herself pure. Her maidenhead was her greatest treasure. She had no intention of wasting it on a handsome face. It would be bartered for a wedding ring and then only to a man who could provide her with the life she craved. She had faith that Adam Loveday would carve his own wealth and destiny. Unfortunately, it could take him several years.

'How sadly you wrong me. I have the greatest admiration for you.' St John did not let his irritation show at her prevarication. He had purchased the stockings in Fowey and had expected her to fall into his arms with gratitude. He had sought her out in secret after Clem's earlier threats in the bar, wishing to avoid a confrontation with her ready-fisted brother. Perversely, her manner whetted his appetite to conquer her and win her from Adam. For that triumph he was prepared to be patient.

His expression was contrite. 'I had no wish to offend. The purchase was made on impulse. Now what am I to do with these?' He laid the stockings on the seat beside the lych-gate. 'They are of no use to me. Perhaps some passing maid will take a fancy to them and think fortune has smiled on her. I bid you good night, Mistress Sawle.'

He bowed and took her hand to lift it to his lips. Meriel snatched back her hand and walked away, her head tilted at a haughty angle. When she heard St John ride away she ran back to the lych-gate and retrieved the stockings.

Her mind was busy calculating. Adam had always been her favourite but St John was the one who would inherit the family property. This autumn held a world of possibilities for her. And she was a woman determined to make the most of them.

Chapter Five

The sight of Trevowan in the afternoon sunlight made Adam bring Solomon to a halt before he entered the stables. The house nestled in a protective fork on the side of a wooded hill. Its three stone gables and tall chimneys were set against an azure sky. Drifting in from the sea were rain clouds that billowed like a galleon's sails. The golden lichen on the wooden roof shingles was interlaced with the green of ivy which had overtaken the west wing. Each of the dozen mullioned windows reflected the mixture of sun, blue sky and pewter clouds so typical of a Cornish sky. The porticoed front door was open. It was only ever shut on the wettest and windiest days.

Adam regarded his home with pride and pleasure. The stone-built house was as weathered as the moss-edged flagstones that led to the door blending in with the landscape and nature. There was solidity and permanence about its structure, despite its being less than ninety years old, which made Trevowan seem as enduring as the granite on which it had been built.

His possessive gaze scanned the coach house, stables and rambling single-storey outbuildings which were set at a right angle to the house. Some of the shingles had slipped in a storm, and the black and white paintwork was peeling. That surprised him; he had never known the estate to show any neglect.

The moment of disquiet passed. As always the sight of his home brought a lump of emotion to his throat. Trevowan was an unostentatious and comfortable gentleman's house. Adam loved its simplicity of lines. Behind the stables there was a walled kitchen garden. At the rear, elm trees planted by his great-grandfather formed a crescent protecting the neat lawns, shrubbery and hedges from the worst of the wind. The garden at the front of the house was laid in a formal pattern of low hedges with flagstones sweeping in a circle around a low fountain of Neptune riding a chariot pulled by dolphins. Beyond the hedges was a wide sweep of cliff-top where the crash of waves against the rocks of the cove was a serenade he never tired of hearing.

His adventures at sea paled into insignificance. This was where he belonged. Yet one day he must leave and make his home elsewhere.

Adam began to unsaddle Solomon himself. The stable, with its smell of horses, straw and leather, was an integral part of his life at Trevowan and sadly missed during his months on a naval frigate. There were ten stalls for the family hunters as well as the carriage horses. He was surprised to see that Rex, his father's horse, St John's mount, Prince, and one of Aunt Elspeth's mares, Bracken, were missing.

'Master were called away sudden.' The stocky figure of Jasper Fraddon appeared behind Adam. The head groom, who also acted as gamekeeper, shook his head. The once-barley-coloured hair was shot through with grey and cropped short below his ears to form a frizzy halo around his ruddy features. He took Solomon's bridle from Adam. His face lined as an ancient oak, he looked stern. 'Six cattle have gone missing from the long field. Reckon it be those Jowetts from Bodmin up to their rustling tricks again.'

'Could not Isaac and Dick Nance deal with it? Father said the Rivieres have arrived from France.' Adam had been irritated that his father had called him away from his work at the yard. His time there was precious. 'They were not due until next week. But it will be good to see my mother's family again.'

Jasper shuffled on his bandy legs. He had worked at Trevowan since before Adam was born and was plain-speaking without being disrespectful. 'Master expected you an hour past. Those Jowetts have been stealing our cattle for months. He wants them brought to justice. Not that he'll catch them. They got more bolt holes on that moor than the wiliest fox.'

'Looks like I have missed out on some exciting action,' Adam grinned. 'It is time the Jowetts were bought to account for their crimes.'

'The day they all hang won't be soon enough. Murderers and thieves, the lot of them.'

The Jowetts were not the only lawless band in the district, Adam reflected as he hurried towards the house. Smuggling was a way of life and often highway robbery took place on the moors. There were even rumours that a recent shipwreck had been the work of wreckers. He shuddered. It was the bloodiest and most evil of crimes. Fortunately there had never been any ships lured on to the rocks near Trevowan.

He entered the house by the side entrance near the kitchen and gun room. A second door led into the hall with its black and white marble flooring with a sun-ray pattern. From the middle of the hall a divided staircase swept upwards to the east and west wings. Five rooms led off from the central hall. The sound of his boots resounded on the floor and he heard voices in the green salon. After two days of rain, the country lanes were rutted and puddled and his clothing was splashed with mud. He really should change before presenting himself to his relatives.

The booming voice of Claude Riviere hailed him.

'*Bonjour,* Adam.'

Adam paused by the door of the saloon, with its pale green Chinese wallpaper, and was shocked at the change in his uncle. His stout figure had become thin and his cheeks were sunken. An unnaturally high colour was emphasised by the elaborately curled bagwig. Last winter he had been ill for some months.

'Uncle Claude, this is a wonderful surprise. How fortunate that I am on leave for your visit.' He and St John had spent four summers with the Riviere family in Paris during their youth. Claude Riviere was a silk merchant and agent for several companies in England. Edward Loveday's friendship with Claude, which had started when they were both young men and visiting Bristol, had led to Edward's travelling to Paris. There he had met, Marie, the sister of Claude's fiancée, and had fallen in love and married her. After Marie's death Louise Riviere had insisted that the family ties remained strong.

Adam spread his hands in a gesture of apology. He had been at the yard since first light working on the keel of the *Pegasus* and his workclothes were out of place amongst the delicate French furniture and elaborately draped green velvet curtains. 'Forgive me, I must change.'

'That can wait. Let me see you, my boy,' his uncle insisted.

'What brings you to England?'

'Business,' Uncle Claude answered. 'As you know a quarter of the fine silks and materials I export are sold to England. I must visit my agents in various cities, including London. And is it not too long since our families were together?'

Adam clasped his hands in greeting, then kissed his aunt's cheek. She was dressed in blue silk with a diamond necklace at her throat and her black hair powdered. At seeing his younger cousin, Lisette, reclining on the cream brocade chaise longue, Adam held up his hands in mock astonishment.

'This cannot be Lisette? You are quite the young woman.'

'She is fifteen,' Aunt Louise reminded him.

Despite his words, to Adam Lisette still looked like a child dressed in adult clothes. She was petite, her skin translucent against her dark hair and huge eyes. Her health had always been delicate. Her small, oval face was whitened with powder and her dark hair piled high with curls in a style too old for her years. Her immature figure was encased in a stiff stomacher. Overcome with shyness, she lowered her gaze to her lap.

He made an extravagant bow to honour her new-found maturity. 'How lovely you have become. I trust the voyage has not tired you, Lisette.' He spoke in French as the last time they had met she had known only a few words of English.

'I am well, cousin,' she replied in the same language. Her cheeks

29

flamed with heat and her gaze was riveted upon her fingernails, which Adam saw were chewed to the quick.

Lisette stood up and curtseyed to him. Although she wore two-inch heels and her hair was curled in a style to add more height, the top of her hair barely reached his shoulder.

'How long are you staying?' Adam addressed his aunt.

'We are in Cornwall for two weeks. Our stay in England will be for a month—'

Uncle Claude interrupted, 'Etienne will be taking over our business next year and I have always believed in personally knowing our agents in England.'

Adam glanced around the room. 'Where is Etienne?'

'He was restless after the voyage and coach journey from Plymouth,' Aunt Louise replied. 'He has gone riding with St John. I asked them to wait for you to join them.'

Hence the missing horses. The absence of his cousin did not trouble Adam. Etienne was three years older than the twins, and on their last visit to the Rivieres' home, he had been self-opinionated and a braggart. Uncle Claude was a wealthy man who could not refuse his son any indulgence.

There was the sound of a stick tapping across the floorboards and the tall, formidable figure of Elspeth Loveday appeared. She was leaning on her cane, her pince-nez low on her hooked nose. 'That Winnie Fraddon is getting above herself. She has taken on Sarah Nance to work in the house now there are four extra to cope with. I told her four is not an army. In Mother's day we had a house full of guests at least once a month.'

'And several more staff,' Adam appeased. 'There is only Winnie and young Jenna Biddick. And you can be an exacting taskmistress, Aunt Elspeth. Sarah always helps out.'

'I will not have the standards lowered, or my authority questioned.' Elspeth sniffed and turned a stare, as piercing and unblinking as an owl, upon her nephew standing before her in his work clothes. She jabbed her stick at him. 'My salon is not a place for such attire. Look, you have muddied the Persian carpet.'

'It is our fault,' Aunt Louise defended. 'We were so eager to see him, we wouldn't let him change.'

Elspeth was unmoved. She was ten years older than Edward and had never married. After the death of Adam's mother she had taken over the running of the house, performing her duties with cold efficiency – the same coldness with which she regarded her family. The only time Adam had seen Aunt Elspeth show any sign of affection was towards her horses, and riding with the hunt was her sole pleasure. It had not dimmed after the accident three years ago which had injured her hip.

30

Subjected to her formidable stare Adam withdrew to change. When he reached the curving staircase there was a scampering of claws on wooden floor at the back of the house and high-pitched barking. Sabre, his father's wolfhound, bounded towards him with Barnaby, Adam's ageing liver and white spaniel, sliding beneath the wolfhound's legs. Adam greeted them warmly, ruffling their ears.

'Get those wretched curs out of the house,' Elspeth demanded from the green saloon. 'I never have any trouble with them when Adam's at sea. Wretched boy, encourages them.'

Adam ordered the dogs outside. When he descended the stairs after changing his clothes, he found Uncle Claude pacing the hall. From the kitchen Elspeth's voice was strident as she gave more instructions to the servants concerning the evening meal.

'Your aunt and Lisette are resting. Edward has been called away by Isaac Nance, your estate bailiff, I believe. Something to do with some cattle taken last night.'

Adam nodded. 'The thieves will be the Jowetts from Bodmin Moor. Not that there'll be any trace of the animals near their farm. The moor holds many secrets and only a foolhardy man ventures too far from the road if they do not know the terrain. The bogs are treacherous.'

Claude beckoned to Adam, his expression grave. 'I would have a word with you while we have a moment to ourselves.' He led Adam into his father's study, where he paced the floor in a way which made Adam uneasy.

Two walls of the study were lined with books, another contained a large carved chest which held duplicates of all the plans of the ships built in the yard. After several moments, Uncle Claude halted and studied his nephew intently.

'Has your father mentioned the letters we have exchanged throughout the summer?'

Adam shook his head.

'Good. It was something I wanted to discuss with you personally. This visit may be my only chance.' He tapped his chest. 'Another attack like the one I suffered last winter may well kill me. I want my affairs put in order.' He looked weary and was breathing heavily. 'It is why our visit coincided with your leave.'

He sat down on a chair and indicated for Adam to be seated opposite him. 'I have to know that Lisette will be safe. There is much unrest in France. Queen Marie-Antoinette is hated and the King is unpopular. The price of bread is rising and the poor go hungry. Supporting the war in America against your King, and then the attack against the East India Company, has cost France dear. Of course, it was to weaken your navy, but France is now heavily in debt. Now the burden of extra taxation falls on the people.'

'I can understand their anger if the people are hungry.'

31

'*Mon Dieu!*' The King will not listen to his counsellors, who advise him to tax the nobles and clergy. Even an absolute monarch risks his throne if he tries to overthrow the privileges of those classes.'

Claude wiped his sweating face with a large handkerchief. 'I fear for the future of France. And my Lisette, my dearest child . . . what will become of her?'

'Is it truly so bad, Uncle?' Adam was aghast.

'Hunger and poverty are surly bedfellows. The decadence of the court is there for all to see.' He shook his head. 'The unrest in Paris is growing.'

'I am sorry to hear this. Why do you fear for Lisette? You are a man of wealth and influence.'

A bony hand was raised to silence him, but it was some moments before his uncle spoke. His sunken cheeks were ashen, the once-bright eyes now rheumy. Adam's unease increased.

'Your aunt and I have a great fondness for you. It has always been our wish that our two families again be linked. It would make us very happy if you would consider Lisette as your bride.'

Adam jolted upright in the chair. 'You honour me but . . .'

Claude Riviere waved his protest aside. 'You are young. Not yet ready for marriage. I understand. I ask only that you think upon it. Lisette will be well provided for. Her dowry of ten thousand livres will enable her husband to establish himself in business. Your father wrote of your desire to be a merchant adventurer. For that you need capital.'

Adam was now the one to pace the room. The rheumy eyes burned into his back. 'I am honoured at your proposal, sir. But Lisette is so young. I have nothing to offer her. It will be years before I am captain of my own ship.'

'Your father would not be averse to your bride living at Trevowan.'

Adam felt stifled. Although it was usual for parents to arrange their children's marriages, Adam resented that his father had not consulted him. 'You have discussed this with my father?'

'Of course. He is agreeable to the match but wishes it to be your choice.'

Sweat broke out beneath Adam's cravat. As he swallowed, the material tightened against this throat like a noose. Family pressure would be great. Marriage was something for the future. The distant future. And to a woman he loved. He searched for excuses, unwilling to offend his uncle. 'We are cousins. Such a marriage would be frowned upon.'

'Louise was your mother's half-sister. The relationship is not so close. And cousins wed all the time.'

'Lisette is Catholic. I am Church of England.'

'A compromise can be reached providing that Lisette is allowed to practise her faith. Your mother was a Catholic.'

Adam still couldn't believe his uncle was serious. 'But I do not love her. Though I am fond of the girl.'

'Few marriages within our station are love matches. They are for convenience and mutual benefit.'

There was a finality in his uncle's voice, making it clear that he and Edward Loveday approved of the match.

'Have you discussed this with Lisette?' Adam still hoped for a reprieve.

'Lisette agrees. I know with you she will be happy.'

The sensation of being trapped persisted.

Claude nodded in understanding at his nephew's silence. 'I will not press you for an answer now. However, it would grieve me should Lisette be wed to the suitor of Etienne's choice, for all the man has a title. Lisette is too precious to be delivered up to an ageing roué. Etienne sees the marriage as a means of winning the patronage of wealthy courtiers.'

The blackmail was subtle but it was still blackmail. Lisette was so sweet and gentle. 'Surely you cannot intend to marry Lisette to a degenerate, no matter what his title?'

'I would not. But Etienne is set upon it. And if I was not alive to prevent it . . . ?' He shrugged fatalistically, but kept his gaze steady upon Adam. 'A betrothal contract between yourself and Lisette can be drawn up to be effective either upon my death, or upon Lisette's eighteenth birthday – whichever is first. It would give me great peace of mind.'

'I need to think upon such an honour. Please allow me some time . . .' Adam retreated from the room, his mind in turmoil. Lisette was a child compared to Meriel, with her sultry beauty. Meriel set his blood on fire and tormented his sleep with erotic dreams. Lisette roused only sympathy for her plight. Yet Lisette was a gentle girl who was easily hurt. And she was family. Family duty and loyalty was not something Adam found easy to ignore.

An inner battle raged and he walked from the house towards the cliffs. He climbed down the jagged rocks to the water's edge of the cove and sat staring out to sea.

The light was fading and the wind chilled him. Duty hung like a millstone around his neck. He remained there, searching for an omen to help him make his decision. None was forthcoming.

Eventually he rose stiffly and walked back towards the rocks. A movement caught his eye and he froze. To the right of him was an outcrop of rock with a fissure wide enough for a man to squeeze through into a widening cave. Meriel stood poised and waiting. Her creamy profile was exquisite. She was beautiful, unforgettably so. Yet there was also something else about her which intrigued men. It

33

was not easily apparent – you had to watch closely and many men never saw beneath the beautiful shell. There was about her a resolution, a ruthlessness capable of cruelty. Such a face belonged to Diana, the goddess of the hunt, or Morgan le Fay, notorious for her beauty and treachery.

Yet he desired her with a craving which defied reason and overrode the noble concepts of loyalty and duty.

As Adam approached, ensnared by her allure, her blonde locks blew wildly around her head like the snakes of Medusa's hair. The vision was fleeting, and its omen went unheeded.

Chapter Six

A n hour later Adam returned to the house and was confronted by his father in the hall.

'Where have you been? Our guests are waiting to dine.'

'Your pardon, sir. I had much to think on. I walked to the beach and did not realise it had become so late.'

Edward regarded him with a sigh. 'You have put Elspeth in a taking. Did Claude speak to you? Is that what you needed to think upon? What have you decided?'

Adam's thoughts were in turmoil. How could he consider marriage to Lisette when he knew himself to be falling in love with Meriel? For all her brazenness in seeking him out, she had allowed him no liberties apart from a kiss. Yet even as she denied him, and scolded him for treating her as a woman without virtue, there was a beguiling promise in her eyes. Adam had cursed her for a tease, but with desire skewering him, he could not shake her from his mind.

'It is a decision which is too important to be rushed.'

His father's eyes flashed with annoyance. 'I did not think I needed to remind *you* of family loyalty. St John yes, but not you.'

The rebuke stung. 'Then have St John wed Lisette.'

'Claude has chosen you and the girl is agreeable. Besides, I have other plans for St John. It is time he assumed his responsibilities.' The set of his father's jaw was uncompromising. 'I expect your agreement to this. Anything less would not be honourable.'

It was unlike his father to make such an ultimatum. That troubled Adam. It also sparked his anger and a streak of stubbornness. Although aware of family duty, he would act as his conscience dictated and not be pressurised.

'There you are, you wretched boy,' Elspeth piped shrilly. 'Now you have deigned to join us, we can all dine.'

The intervention allowed him to avoid answering his father, but there was a stiff set to his shoulders as he entered the oak-panelled dining room hung with portraits of his ancestors. The family were seated. From Lisette's fiery cheeks and Etienne's glower it was obvious that his father's words had carried to them. The only empty chair was between Lisette and Uncle Claude. His uncle's face was flushed as he downed one glass of claret and poured himself another.

35

Etienne was seated directly opposite Adam.

Although his cousin's dark hair was unpowdered and drawn back into a neatly curled queue with a wide bow, his brocade jacket and breeches of buttercup yellow edged with gold made even St John's burgundy silk look dowdy. Adam held out his hand to his cousin and it was taken in limpid fingers as two maids hurried forward to serve the soup.

'I hope you enjoyed your ride, Etienne,' he said. 'Aunt Elspeth likes her horses spirited. They are all a handful.'

Etienne fixed him with black, hooded eyes which gleamed with hostility. His wide mouth was compressed into a thin line and his olive skin was stretched taut across prominent cheekbones. A long bony nose with a point above the nostrils reminded Adam of a washerwoman's peg.

St John laughed. 'He was on Bracken and the bracken was where he ended up when she bolted after being startled by a hare.'

'Bad luck,' Adam commiserated, although he had never found his cousin's company amiable. Etienne was a conceited fop and clearly since they'd last met had not changed.

'Bracken doesn't like to be ridden by men,' Elspeth observed. 'None of my girls do. Men are too rough by half. My girls need a gentle hand. Bracken has never thrown me.'

'And which of your little darlings broke your hip, Aunt?' Etienne sneered.

The loud thwack of Elspeth's fan rapping Etienne's knuckles was followed by his yelp of pain. The force of the blow had knocked the silver soup spoon from his hand and it landed in St John's lap, leaving a greasy stain on his cream breeches. He protested volubly but his voice was drowned by Elspeth's angry retort.

'Insolent boy!' Two ruby pebbles of colour appeared in her pallid cheeks. 'That fool Penwithick collided with my mare Griselda as we took a hedge together in the hunt. The man rides with the finesse of a hunchback on a bullock. I was lucky poor Griselda suffered no more than a strained fetlock. The idiot could have caused her to break a leg and I would have had to destroy a fine horse.'

'You had a lucky escape yourself, Elspeth,' Louise said with concern. 'You could have been killed. Is your hip dreadfully painful?'

Elspeth gave an unladylike snort. Ignoring Louise's remark she ordered Sarah Nance and Jenna to clear the dishes and bring in the next course, of lampreys. To dispel the tension Edward filled the wine glasses.

'A toast to this happy reunion. May it lead to a greater understanding between our families. I am sure that is Adam's wish also.'

The implication was clear in his words: he expected Adam to marry Lisette.

Uncle Claude drained his third glass of wine, leaned towards Adam and patted his arm with affection. His voice was slurred. 'It has ever been my desire for our families to be united, nephew. I am delighted that you have accepted Lisette as your bride. Let us drink to the happy couple.'

'No I—' Adam's protest was lost in the babble of congratulations.

He felt his throat seize up with shock at his uncle's declaration. Was the man drunk? He had agreed to nothing. Aunt Louise had risen from her seat and flung her arms around him, talking excitedly in French. 'I am so happy.'

Edward raised his glass. 'A toast to Adam and Lisette.'

Adam was paralysed by horror. Even Aunt Elspeth was chuckling and congratulating Lisette. St John glared at him; his brother had stolen the limelight again and would pocket a decent dowry into the bargain. Etienne was white-lipped with fury. There were tears of joy in Lisette's eyes as she gazed at him.

Adam scuffed back a lock of hair which had fallen over his temple. 'There has been a mistake. Uncle Claude is under a misapprehension.'

The colour drained from Lisette's cheeks and with a cry she fled the room.

'How could you be so cruel, Adam?' Aunt Louise remonstrated, before hurrying after her daughter.

'Are you to wed the girl, or not?' Aunt Elspeth demanded. 'I will not countenance you playing fast and loose with the child's affections. It is clear she adores you.'

'Nothing was decided,' Adam defended himself.

The room was now silent. His father and uncle looked condemning; St John was smirking at his discomfort and Etienne hid his satisfied smile behind the wine glass pressed to his lips. Aunt Elspeth rose painfully to glare at her nephew in disgust.

'I will not remain in the same room as a man who would jilt an innocent girl. There is no greater coward or scoundrel.'

Her cane rapped loudly on the wooden floor as she made her exit. At least her anger was justified. Elspeth had been humiliated when she was jilted by her betrothed a week before her marriage. The man had left the district without word to her and she had heard nothing from him since. According to Edward, the experience had turned the once-loving and generous-hearted woman into the embittered shrew woman she was today.

'What have you got to say for yourself, Adam?' his father demanded. 'Your conduct is disgraceful, You have broken that sweet girl's heart.'

Adam turned to Uncle Claude. The injustice of their accusations broke through his numbness and anger surfaced. 'Sir, you are aware that I agreed to nothing.'

Claude shrugged and slumped back in his chair. His stare was accusing. 'I may have been overhasty. But would you deny a dying man the wish to see his daughter secure and happy?'

Etienne banged the table with his fist. 'Lisette has a suitor. A marquis, no less. Have you lost your wits to wed her to a man who has no fortune? She will live like a peasant.'

'No wife of mine would live like a peasant.' Adam was goaded to defend his honour.

'Trevowan is large,' Edward interceded. 'Adam's wife and family will always have a place here.'

'The marriage to the Marquis will make our fortune,' Etienne stormed.

'We are not poor.' Uncle Claude sat forward, his face as red as the claret in his glass, his breathing laboured. 'You forget yourself. Leave us, Etienne. This is for Edward, Adam and me to decide.'

Etienne stood up and glared at Adam. He stormed from the room, followed by St John, who had been dismissed by Edward.

Adam paced to the fireplace and hooked his thumbs over the waistband of his breeches before addressing the older men.

'I do not love Lisette. It would be wrong to marry her.'

'You would condemn her to a life of misery with the Marquis,' Uncle Claude said with a catch in his voice which was uncomfortably close to pleading. 'She will be his fourth wife. All have died young. There is a coldness to the man which repels me.'

'Think of family duty and loyalty,' Edward reasoned. 'Does your uncle ask so much? What have you against her?'

'Nothing. I am even fond of her.'

Uncle Claude sighed. 'There is someone else?'

Adam did not answer and it took all his willpower to hold the two men's condemning stares.

'Who is she?' his father rapped out. When Adam remained silent, Edward added, 'I see . . . a light of love of no consequence. And for her you would turn your back on family honour and loyalty.'

Adam could feel their censure. Guilt kicked him. His uncle was a proud man. Illness had made him vulnerable. And his father expected him to do his duty. He loved and respected these two men. How could he live with himself if he failed them?

'Very well, in the circumstances I am compelled to agree to the match. But on the conditions mentioned earlier. We will not marry until Lisette is eighteen.'

'Unless I die before then,' Claude amended. 'We will celebrate the betrothal in style before we leave Cornwall.'

The invitations were sent out. At Uncle Claude's insistence and expense there was to be a ball at Trevowan the following week. There would be a banquet, and a string quartet for dancing in the entrance hall for the gentry. A barn was being cleared for the estate tenants, the villagers of Penruan and families of the men working at the shipyard. A fiddler would provide them with music for the country reels, and an ox would be roasted over a spit. Already six extra servants had been engaged to help with the cooking and preparations.

Aunt Elspeth's querulous demands had twice reduced Winnie, the cook, to tears and Aunt Louise had become the unofficial peacemaker between the two women.

Adam resented having to spend so much time away from the shipwright yard and his work on *Pegasus* to entertain Lisette. To compensate, he rose before dawn and arrived back at Trevowan at midday, having learned that Lisette rarely left her bedchamber before noon.

'Her delicate health precludes too strenuous activity,' Aunt Louise explained. 'The doctor has advised she must rest each morning.'

Lisette had always been cosseted by her parents. Twice as a young girl she had almost died. Louise, a doting mother, had become overprotective in matters of her daughter's health. Lisette was not permitted to ride. Her only exercise, when not shopping in town, was a gentle afternoon walk in the gardens providing that the weather was clement.

It made entertaining her trying for a man as active as Adam, especially when he considered that her constitution appeared robust, despite her frail appearance. Once her initial shyness was overcome he discovered she had a keen wit and was a skilled player at both backgammon and chess. For the moment Adam did not dispute his aunt's strict regime over her daughter. It suited his purposes. His time spent in the yard was precious.

St John was not so industrious. He delighted in the chance to stay away from the yard with the excuse of entertaining Etienne. Etienne had not hidden his displeasure at the betrothal and St John resented so much attention being paid to Adam. Two days ago they had ridden into Truro and had not returned. Since Lisette was also in the habit of retiring early, Adam took the opportunity to slip away to Penruan to see Meriel.

He received a cheerless welcome from Sal when he walked through the back door into the dingy, low-ceilinged kitchen of the Dolphin Inn. He ducked his head beneath two smoked hams suspended from the rafters. By the door were three rabbits hanging up, waiting to be skinned for the pot.

Sal looked up from kneading dough for tomorrow's bread, her dimpled arms and apron smeared with flour. 'Meriel is spending the evening with friends. What would you be wanting with her?' she accused. 'You've a fiancée at Trevowan now, I hear.'

'I need to talk with her.'

Sal shook her head. 'Leave Meriel alone. Reuban and Clem won't take kindly to you calling on her. Clem won't stand for Meriel bringing shame to this family like our Rose. He can be a violent man.'

'I am not afeared of your husband nor of any of your sons.' Adam held her gaze, affronted by the threat.

''Tisn't right for you to be seeing Meriel and you bain't welcome here if that be your intent.' Sal turned her back on him and thumped hard on the dough, punching it with her fists in a rare show of anger.

Adam left the inn but sat on the lych-gate seat opposite, hoping that Meriel would appear. The tall square tower of the church and the surrounding yew trees sheltered him from the wind. There was no sign of Meriel that night.

It was the same two evenings later. He had been battling against his desire to see her. All day a need to explain his feelings had been gnawing at him. It had destroyed his pleasure in his work on the *Pegasus*, and Lisette's company had been a trial. He could not stop comparing her childish naïvety with Meriel's womanly charms, her timidity with Meriel's zest for life. His betrothal was to be celebrated in three days. He knew it was wrong to go to the village, but Meriel's image beckoned, firing his blood and destroying his judgement.

Adam guessed that hearing of his engagement, Meriel was angry and avoiding him. He felt guilty that she had learned of his betrothal from another, so soon after he had pledged his affection for her. He had to see her to explain.

Tonight the inn was full. It was not fear of the Sawle brothers which stopped Adam from entering; it was a need to protect Meriel from their wrath. They would be as unsympathetic to a meeting as Sal. Skirting the building, Adam saw no sign of Meriel through any of the windows.

He realised that after so long away at sea he knew little about her present life. Yet somehow he could not see Reuban allowing his daughter to roam the village streets alone at night.

He sat under the lych-gate to wait. After two days of rain the afternoon had been sunny, and now a mist was rising from the land. It swirled down from the trees on the hills each side of the coombe and chilled the air. Adam pulled up the collar of his jacket. As the cold penetrated his clothing, his patience was tested that Meriel remained elusive. He also began to feel foolish at acting like a love-lorn schoolboy.

He was on the point of leaving when a light appeared in an upstairs window. Meriel's figure was outlined against the panes. Adam tossed a pebble against the windowpane. She started back, then looked down where Adam now stood in the light of the porch lamp of the inn. He gestured for her to join him. Although her face was in shadow he was left in no doubt of her anger. The inner shutter was banged shut, blotting out the light. Short of calling out and risk being overheard by the drinkers in the bar, Adam decided to let her anger cool.

Meriel leaned on the windowsill, her brow against the shutter. Her body shook with sobs. How could Adam so betray her? He had been so loving in the cave. He said it didn't matter that she was the daughter of an innkeeper. Her beauty had captivated him.

He had not spoken of love but the ardour of his kisses had convinced her that she had stolen his heart. She had been overjoyed, her love for him blossoming from her earlier infatuation. In his arms she had forgotten her interest in St John. Adam was the lover she had always dreamed of. The lover she wanted. The lover she was prepared to wait for.

Within two days her dreams had been blasted. The village buzzed with the gossip of his betrothal. Her nails gouged her palms, the pain echoing the agony which swelled in her heart. He had played her for a fool. She had tried to hate him. It had been impossible. This was the third evening he had come to the village. She had seen him in the shadows of the lych-gate but had been too angry to meet him. Could it be that his betrothal was not as it appeared? Adam was the most honest man she knew. That had made his betrayal the harder to bear.

She willed her mind to be calm and to think rationally.

How could she have got it so wrong? She had been convinced that Adam was falling in love with her. There had been more than desire in his eyes. No man looked at a woman as he had done if he was not in love.

His handsome image filled her mind. Her pain turned to determination. She was not so easily defeated. Adam had wanted her. Adam *did* care. She was not going to lose him without a fight.

With devious intent she saw the wisdom of not confronting him with accusations. The rumour in the village was that Adam would not marry for another three years. His cousin was still a child. Meriel smiled, her eyes narrowed and calculating. A great deal could happen in three years – three months, even three days.

41

Chapter Seven

The guests began to arrive two days before the ball. Edward's eldest sister, Margaret, and her husband, Charles Mercer with their son, Thomas, had travelled from London. Aunt Margaret, despite the arduous week-long coach journey, was soon supervising the clearing and decorating of the barn. Edward, Charles and Claude were closeted together and the four male cousins, at Thomas Mercer's suggestion, were practising their swordplay by the fountain.

In England it was still common for the sons of gentry to wear swords, and the fencing schools remaining popular haunts. Adam practised whenever he could, knowing that in a sea battle, if a ship was boarded, proficient swordsmanship could mean the difference between life and death. And although duelling was banned, competency with a sword could also save a traveller's life on the highway or walking the darkened streets of a town at night.

It was a warm morning, the sun dispersing the last of the mist from the tops of the hills. The leaves were beginning to turn golden and soon the first of the autumn gales would shed a carpet over the hills and woodland. Adam would be at sea before then. He must return to Plymouth in five days.

Etienne, in a ruffled shirt open at the neck, strutted about the courtyard swishing his rapier from side to side. In France only noblemen and King's officers were permitted to wear swords, but Etienne, with ideas of grandeur, had insisted that he attend a fencing master.

The other men stripped off their waistcoats and Adam paired with Thomas Mercer. Thomas was ten years older than Adam, his figure very tall and slim. He had pushed back his short wig, exposing a band of close-cropped blond hair. He bent his knees several times before bringing his rapier to *en garde*. His grey eyes sparkled with merriment, their corners lined from his habitual laughter.

He struck a more theatrical pose. '*Once more unto the breach, dear friends, once more;*'.

With a grin Adam countered with another line from *Henry the Fifth*: '*Follow your spirit; and, upon this charge Cry "God for Harry! England and Saint George!"*'

'Then let us do the great bard proud,' Thomas added. 'May your sword match your agility with words . . . I say, coz, that is rather a fine sentiment. I must remember it. It will work well in my new play.'

'And have you met with success in the theatre?'

'What do those fools in Drury Lane know of new talent?' Thomas patted his wig and raised a finely plucked brow. 'And in truth it is deuced difficult to find the time to write. Father keeps me at the bank until nine of an evening. If it was not for my good friend Lucien Greene, with whom I now share rooms, I would not commit a word to paper.'

'You have left home then?' St John asked. 'Lucky dog. Living the high life, are you?'

'Not exactly,' Thomas shrugged. 'Lucien is a poet. His friends come round for readings of their work or we discuss a play.'

St John snorted in disgust. 'Good waste of a man's freedom, that.'

'Actors and playwrights are no better than vagabonds and scoundrels,' Etienne sneered.

Thomas started forward, his sword pointed at Etienne. For all his theatrical posturing he was quick to take affront. 'You may answer to my sword whenever you please.'

Adam intercepted Thomas's blade with a flick of his own. 'This is a morning for sport and pleasure. You are to be my partner, Thomas. Would you deprive me of pitting my skills against yours?'

The men broke apart and although Thomas glowered at Etienne he did not pursue the matter. Etienne laughed maliciously and taunted St John as they began to circle each other. The first clash of steel put to flight the dozen doves sunning themselves on the stable roof.

Adam was surprised at Thomas's skill. He had believed his cousin to be something of a fop, always bewigged and fashionably dressed, as befitted his role as a banker. His long slender hands and fingers were those of an artist. Adam stared briefly at his own rectangular hands. They were strong and capable, whether for using a sextant for navigation or planing a length of ship's timber.

The courtyard rang to the rasp of metal, the deepening breathing of the men and the stamp of their feet. An occasional grunt of exertion accompanied the banter as each acknowledged the other's skill. Etienne had St John in retreat and there was a shout of triumph as St John's sword clattered to the flagstones.

The contest between Adam and Thomas was close. While Thomas relied upon speed, dexterity and a furious assault upon his opponent, Adam was equally fleet of foot and hand. For ten minutes the men fought without break: circling, retreating, advancing; neither gaining the advantage. Sweat was running down Thomas's face and his shirt clung damply to his shoulders. Each breath was laboured and his movements began to slow. Adam, used to the rigours of naval life, was not even breathing heavily. Finally Thomas was too slow in recovering from a lunge and Adam's blade slipped under his sword to rest lightly over his heart.

Thomas laughed and held up his hands in submission. 'A fight well won.'

Etienne snorted. 'Adam has skill enough to pursue the life of a pirate, which will no doubt be his future as a privateer. My sister's name will be shamed by such exploits.'

'Steady on!' St John blustered. 'The Lovedays have pride in their name and position.'

'The Rivieres are honest merchants. We do not resort to roguery to make our fortune. But then what else can one expect from an Englishman.'

Etienne made a pass with his rapier at an invisible opponent, his black eyes malicious as they regarded Adam. Since his arrival Etienne had been spoiling for a fight, his arrogance fuelled by his anger at Lisette's betrothal to her cousin.

Adam had put aside his own antagonism towards the marriage. He had three years before Lisette would be eighteen, and in the last days Uncle Claude had recovered from the debilitating effects of their journey and looked hale enough.

'You forget your manners, Etienne,' he said, his temper sliding dangerously.

'It is not for the likes of you to teach me them,' Etienne bristled. With deliberate provocation he slowly circled Adam so that the sun was directly in his eyes.

Adam side-stepped, keeping the sun out of his vision. 'Were it not for the laws of hospitality which prevent me from insulting you, or using arms other than in friendship, I would say that lesson was long overdue.'

The black eyes narrowed with scorn. 'You use hospitality as an excuse. Are you craven?'

Thomas strode forward. 'You go too far, Etienne.'

'This is about Lisette, is it not?' Adam declared. 'You have made it clear you resent the match. Let the matter be settled now.'

'No!' St John protested. He had enjoyed Etienne provoking Adam and would have relished the Frenchman besting his twin in a sword fight. But the mood had turned unpleasant. Etienne was out for blood. 'What if one of you is hurt? Papa will be furious.'

'A contest of skill will prove who is the better man,' Etienne answered, taking up a position so that the sun was again in Adam's eyes. 'On your defeat you will refuse to marry Lisette.'

Adam kept all emotion from his expression but his voice was scathing. 'I cannot, with honour, agree to such terms. It will ruin Lisette's reputation and cause a scandal. Besides, you have yet to prove that *you* are the better man.'

'That will be my pleasure. *En garde!*' Etienne snapped, his sword raised and ready.

'No good will come of this,' Thomas groaned. 'Stop them, St John.' But his words were lost amidst the impact of swords.

Within seconds Adam knew they were evenly matched. Etienne produced some fancy footwork and wrist movements Adam had not encountered before. His own success came with greater agility and strength. A subtle movement of his body left Etienne's sword point inches from its intended mark, and his rapid counterattack was to his advantage.

The protests of St John and Thomas turned to cheers of encouragement as they caught the excitement of the fight. After a dozen passes Adam was beginning to feel a tightness in his chest. He had been given no time to recover from his bout with Thomas while Etienne had been at ease for several minutes. But there were signs that Etienne was tiring too. His lunges were erratic, the thrust behind the blade weaker as his arms and legs tired. The arrogance in his eyes was now bleak with murderous intent. Adam knew he would not be spared if Etienne could sink his blade into his body.

Adam's guard blocked each attack, his blade lethal as it darted in search of a weakness in his cousin's guard. Although Adam was breathing heavily, his stamina did not fail him. He pressed Etienne into retreat.

When the two sword hilts locked at shoulder height, Etienne snarled, 'You shall never have Lisette. I will see you dead first.'

'The contract was signed last night by your father and myself. Accept it with good grace.'

'Never.'

They broke apart. Adam seized upon Etienne's slow recovery and sliced his blade beneath his guard. The point of his sword pressed against his cousin's throat.

'Concede,' he demanded.

Etienne's eyes glittered with malice. A dangerous tension emanated between the two men. St John gave an embarrassed cough.

'You are the victor, Adam.'

Adam lowered his sword, aware that he had earned his cousin's hatred. He stepped back and turned as he heard the rumble of carriage wheels. St John and Thomas were also distracted.

Pain seared Adam's arm. He stared down to see a rip in his sleeve and a spreading stain of blood. 'A reminder that nothing is resolved between us.' Etienne spun on his heel and marched away.

The three remaining cousins stared at the bloodied arm. There was a shout of disapproval as a battered coach drew to a halt. Adam covered his wound with his hand. The portly figure of the Reverend Joshua Loveday lowered himself from the coach. His face was puce with fury above his parson's cassock. 'That whelp needs horsewhipping. I saw how he struck you.'

'The wound is slight.' Adam clamped his hand tighter over the torn flesh to stem the bleeding.

'The intent was vicious. He will not escape a piece of my mind. "Answer a fool according to his folly, lest he be wise in his own conceit" – Proverbs. Papist or not, he shall heed the Good Book.'

'I would rather nothing was said,' Adam insisted. 'If Uncle Claude learns of this it will upset him. His health is not good.' He also did not want knowledge of his wound upsetting Lisette. There was no point in stirring up further trouble within the family.

The diminutive figure of Aunt Cecily stepped from the coach and pushed Adam's hand away to inspect his arm. 'This wound needs attention. You must attend Dr Chegwidden.' She then addressed her husband. 'A sermon may be all well and good for the man's soul, but Adam is right. Let it be done in private.' She turned to her three children as they alighted. 'Not a word of this, or it will be the worse for you all.'

She turned her cheek for Adam to kiss. Her short stature, plump figure and short-sighted way of peering at people reminded Adam of a pigeon. But this pigeon had sharp talons when it came to administering discipline. It was she and not Joshua who ruled their roost.

Cousin Japhet, three years older than the twins, winked at Adam. He was a handsome, large-framed man, his black curling hair the rival of any gypsy's. There was a sparkle in his hazel eyes which hinted at roguery. The thin moustache he favoured gave a sardonic twist to his lips. 'Just say the word and we will show that damned Frenchie how an Englishman avenges treachery.'

Adam shook his head. 'This is my problem alone.' He greeted his other cousins. Hannah's dark locks were copper tinted. She was a young wife and heavy with her first child which was due next month.

'Dear Adam, I must introduce you to darling Oswald. That wretched navy kept you away from our wedding.'

Adam kissed his vivacious cousin and held out his hand to Oswald Rabson, who owned a farm in Joshua's Parish of Trewenna. Rabson was in his mid twenties and had been courting Hannah for three years. He had commanding, regular features and had been considered something of a hermit before he had met Hannah, rarely being seen in the villages or town. He was retiring in manner and speech and it surprised Adam that Hannah had chosen to wed such a dullard. Yet once their engagement had been announced he had changed; though never verbose he attended every social gathering with his fiancée.

'You look radiant, Hannah,' Adam said, noting that the mischievous sparkle always in her eyes was now tempered by tenderness as her

47

gaze fell upon her husband. 'I do not need to ask if you are happy. It shines from you.'

'I recommend marriage. I wish you the same happiness with Lisette that I have found.'

A thin bony hand was then jabbed towards him and he surveyed his cousin Peter. 'Pious Peter' he had been nicknamed when they were children. Still little more than a youth, Peter studied Adam with a primness which was disconcerting. 'That knave deserves a day in the stocks for the way he attacked you.'

Adam laughed at his virulence. 'Pious Peter has become Peter the Prosecutor. There is a time to settle scores and much can be said for knowing when to turn the other cheek. Would you have dissension in our family when so many of us are together for the first time?'

St John was leading the family into the house. Hannah was teasing him, their laughter easing the tension in the courtyard.

Thomas held out Adam's jacket. 'If you are to have your arm tended we should leave now. It will rouse less comment if we go together and we will be back in time to dine.'

'Uncle Joshua, will you tell Father that Thomas wished to see the *Pegasus* and we have ridden to the yard? There is a retired surgeon I can visit. Dr Chegwidden in Penruan is not known for his discretion.'

At the parson's frown, Thomas added, 'We are not asking you to lie for us. I do want to see the *Pegasus*. And Father is insisting I return to London with him in two days.'

'It is a long journey for such a short stay.'

'Papa refuses to leave the bank for too long.' Thomas looked disappointed. 'Mother is staying on for a few weeks. It is arranged she will return to London with Squire Penwithick and his good lady next month.'

Joshua did not follow his family. Instead he drew Thomas's sword from its scabbard and faced Adam. 'A trick your grandfather showed me. Draw your sword and prepare to defend yourself.'

Adam did so with amusement. He had expected a lecture from a parson for fencing; instead he was being given a lesson, but then Joshua had never been a staid or sermonising servant of God. It had shocked the family when, at the age of twenty, he had declared he would attend a seminary. After a wild youth, when he had run away to London for three years, Joshua had returned to Trevowan amid rumours he had killed a highway robber who waylaid him on Hampstead Heath.

Joshua proceeded to show Adam a double feint with a lightning wrist movement. It disarmed his nephew with a jolt of pain in his wrist.

'Your grandfather reckoned that saved his life on several occasions. Practise it regularly. Even though still illegal in his day, duelling was not uncommon over a lady's honour. Your grandfather had a roving eye before his marriage.'

He tossed the sword back to Adam, who stared after his uncle in amazement. 'Father never said you were a swordsman. And from your skill I would say you use a rapier often.'

'Japhet caught me practising a few feints last year and insisted that I teach him. We practise weekly. Neither your aunt nor the parishioners would approve, so it is our secret. Now get your wound treated before Edward discovers your injury.'

Recalling his position as spiritual guide, he added, 'Not that I condone the sword as a weapon other than used in defence. Take care you watch yourself where Etienne is concerned. The devil is at that young man's shoulder.'

Chapter Eight

By the afternoon of the ball all the family had gathered at Trevowan. Uncle William was also on naval leave, his ship, HMS *Neptune*, having docked at Falmouth. He had arrived an hour ago. Every room in the house was in chaos.

The men were ill at ease amidst so much domesticity, and eagerly sought diversion as the neighbours began to arrive. Another thirty guests were expected and both the dining room and winter parlour were lined with tables laden with refreshments. Some guests had travelled many miles and would be sleeping the night, so rooms and bedding had to be aired for them. Truckle beds were brought down from the attics, and the male cousins were sharing rooms to accommodate everyone.

Elspeth had been patrolling the house since daybreak. Nothing missed her inspection. 'Those cakes should have been finished an hour ago, Winnie.' Elspeth worked herself into a frenzy. 'Where's your husband, Jasper? I told him to get more chairs from the attic to be put in the hall.'

Winnie groaned and rubbed a podgy hand across her sweating brow. Two cooked salmon were on the table and she was straining melted butter through a muslin cloth to clarify it. Nora Tonkin, the wife of an estate worker, was stirring grated nutmeg into a mixture of milk and wine heating on the large cooking range to make syllabub. Nora's mother-in-law, Meg, was humming toothlessly, deaf to Elspeth's orders, as she rolled out pastry. There were three generations of Tonkins on the estate, living in two cottages. Nora's seven-year-old daughter, Fanny, looked sullen as she plucked another chicken to go on the roasting spit.

'Jasper has got the chairs down,' Winnie said. 'He be out back giving them a polish.'

'Where's that lazy slut Jenna?' Elspeth was relentless. 'She should be helping you. There are pies still not made. If she is flirting with Dick Nance again I will—'

'I bain't responsible for Jenna,' Winnie cut in. 'I got enough to do with me own work.'

Elspeth limped to the larder and inspected the shelves of cooked meats waiting to be sliced. Her face was pinched with pain. She had been up since five, harrying the extra servants taken on in the last two days. The smell of freshly cooked pies and tartlets did not placate her. The guests would be arriving in three hours and there was still much to be done.

Louise entered the kitchen, looking calm and serene. 'Stop fretting, Elspeth. The barn is ready. Hester is laying the cloths on the trestle tables. Dick Nance is setting up the cider barrels for the villagers. You should take a rest before our guests arrive.'

'How can I rest?' Elspeth flared. 'The servants will stand round gossiping and nothing will get done.'

Winnie banged down her copper saucepan and folded her plump arms over her pudding basin breasts. Strands of greying blonde hair, which had escaped her mobcap were plastered against her shining face. 'Gossiping, indeed. Bain't we all working our fingers to the bone? For two days every woman from the estate has helped out. Do we get a word of gratitude? Do we get so much as a word of praise? Not a word!'

Elspeth and Winnie were old adversaries, the role of mistress and servant tempered by more than twenty years of familiarity. Winnie had come to the house as cook in 1766, the year Elspeth's mother had died and Edward had married. Five years later Winnie had married Jasper Fraddon. Her meals could tempt the most jaded palate, and many a guest had tried to lure her into their employment. She remained loyal to the Lovedays, but regarded the kitchen as her domain and resented any intrusion from Elspeth. Elspeth was a mistress who felt it her duty to interfere.

Winnie eyed Elspeth with resignation. Even she knew when her temper could take her too far. 'Everything will be ready in time. Not one of us wouldn't feel shamed if Master Adam's grand day wasn't a credit to Trevowan.'

Elspeth banged her stick on the flagstones. Every servant was at once wary. She took a long look around the kitchen, noting the array of dishes already prepared. The pain in her hip was agony. It felt it was being torn apart by hot pincers. All the bloodletting and purging she had endured from Dr Chegwidden had given her no relief.

Louise put her hand on her shoulder. 'Please rest Elspeth. You will make yourself ill. There is ample food.'

Elspeth nodded. For all her criticism, which was made sharper by her pain, she knew the long hours these women had laboured. 'You have done well, all of you.'

As she turned to leave, the pain in her hip attacked. She gave an involuntary gasp and leaned heavily on her cane. Her face was ashen when she straightened. Louise fussed around her in an irritating fashion. Then she saw a tall, slim young woman enter the kitchen. The woman did not live in Penruan and it took a moment for Elspeth to recognise her. She was dressed in a dark green, square-necked gown of linsey-woolsey, a large apron covering the skirt. Her brown hair was partly hidden under a white linen square, from beneath which a thick plait hung down to her waist.

'Polglase, isn't it? Senara Polglase.'

'Yes, ma'am.' There was no subservience in the woman's manner. Her poise was as assured as it was graceful. Neither was it arrogant. There was something disconcerting about the serenity of her green-flecked hazel stare.

A month ago Elspeth's mare Bonnie had slashed her leg when jumping over a wall. Elspeth had been walking the mare back to Trevowan when Senara Polglase appeared.

Elspeth remembered old Nathaniel Polglase, a rough-and-ready man with a quick temper. He had worked at the Loveday yard until drinking made him unemployable. A daughter, Leah, had moved away and his wife was long dead. Elspeth had met the Polglase woman, Leah's daughter, close to where she lived with her mother and sister in the isolated cottage by a stream.

Senara had returned to her cottage and produced a poultice for Bonnie, then cleaned and tended her wound. It was obvious that the mare would damage her leg if she continued to walk back to Trevowan. Senara had offered for the mare to be stabled there until the wound healed. Elspeth was reluctant to leave Bonnie but had finally agreed.

She had visited Bonnie each of the three days it took the mare to recover. The initial long walk back to Trevowan had made her hip torture, and the rides to visit the mare had aggravated the pain. On the first visit, before she left Senara had pressed a jar of unguent into Elspeth's hands and a pouch of herbs to be sprinkled in a hot bath. The pain had eased. The young woman's medicine was more effective than Dr Chegwidden's bloodletting and leeching.

'Bonnie recovered quickly. You would never know she had been so recently injured,' Elspeth said with a rare smile, which turned quickly to a grimace of pain. She stumbled.

Senara was at her side to steady her. Her voice was soft so only Elspeth would hear. 'You are in pain. You should rest or the day will be spoiled for you.'

Annoyance flashed in the older woman's eyes at her presumption. Then another onslaught of pain sent a shudder through her frail body.

'Let me help you,' Senara offered. 'I noticed yesterday you were in pain.'

Louise pushed Senara away and, hooking her arm around Elspeth's waist, propelled her towards the door. 'Now I insist you lay down.'

Elspeth flinched from the pain of her jarred body. She struck Louise on the wrist with her cane. 'Confound you, leave me be.'

Winnie called out, 'If you be in pain, I'll make a posset and you can take those drops Dr Chegwidden left.'

'Polglase will attend me,' Elspeth ordered, and held out her arm for Senara to take.

Senara was uncomfortable at feeling the servants' gazes on her. Her mother and sister had returned to Cornwall three months ago. Previous experience made her wary of others' interest and she gave only vague answers regarding her former life. Until witnessing Elspeth Loveday's pain she had avoided drawing any attention to herself. It had served her family ill in the past. Three days' offer of work and a growing need for money had brought her out of the isolation she preferred.

As they reached the foot of the stairs three men appeared. They were dressed in open ruffled shirts and breeches. Each was holding a rapier in his hand and their faces were flushed with exertion. Senara had seen the three cousins before. Two of them were dark and handsome, their looks roguish and dangerous. The other was delicate, almost feminine in his mannerisms.

She cast down her eyes, distrustful of men of their rank. The young handsome ones were best avoided.

'Aunt, what ails you?' Adam Loveday joined them.

'Elspeth will not rest,' Louise complained. 'She is being stubborn. Now her hip pains her.'

'I never wanted all this fuss,' Adam confessed. 'A quiet family dinner would have sufficed.'

'The ingrate will suggest jumping over a bonfire for the wedding service next or some other heathenish ritual,' Elspeth retorted. 'It is too many years since Trevowan had cause to celebrate with a grand ball.'

There was a smothered sigh from Adam which caused Senara to glance at him. For a man celebrating his betrothal he looked far from happy. So the match was not of his choosing. A sense of foreboding smote her. She had seen his fiancée who was young and spoilt. But also vulnerable. This man emanated virility and masculinity. It was so potent she involuntarily took a step back. Whipcord muscles were outlined through his shirt. He was a man of action: fearless, ruthless. An adventurer. His eyes were as turbulent or enticing as the sea. With that cinnamon-hued skin and dark hair, it needed but a gold earring in his ear to complete the image of a buccaneer. Yet his fine bones had a delicacy. Here was granite encased in velvet. A man capable of tenderness. A man of passion.

The marriage was doomed. Passion would destroy this man.

The insight shook her. Often she sensed the destiny of a person. It was a curse she had tried to banish and failed.

'And where has this beauty been hiding?' The other dark-haired

54

man slid his arm around Senara's waist.

She slapped it aside, her eyes blazing. 'Keep your hands to yourself, if you please, sir.'

'A wench with spirit. Fine sport indeed. Your beauty would steal any man's heart.'

'If you want sport, keep to your fencing,' Senara turned on him. She despised his type. They thought all women were fair game. His handsome looks masked something sinister deep within. The teasing charm was meant to hoodwink and posed a persuasive threat.

'Japhet, leave the girl.' Elspeth prodded his chest with her cane though her words were gritty with pain. 'I will not have the servants molested. Out of my way, all of you.'

She hobbled on to the first stair, the hand becoming a steel claw as it gripped Senara's arm. Her frail body shuddered when the pain tore through her as she heaved herself up another three stairs.

A hand on Senara's shoulder eased her aside. Adam lifted his aunt in his arms and carried her to her room. Senara hurried after them.

'Put me down. You wretched boy, I will not be manhandled this way. Put me down, I say.'

The smooth silver ball atop her cane struck Adam's arm and he faltered on the top step. She had hit the sword cut which was still painful after receiving a dozen stitches, and he clenched his teeth as he overcame the agony. He laid her on the counterpane of her tester bed, saying, 'Shall I send for Dr Chegwidden?'

'Stop fussing. I shall rest for an hour and be fine. Go to our guests and keep your cousins out of mischief. Especially that Japhet. For all he's the son of a parson, Japhet has the devil in him.' Suddenly her voice sharpened. 'There's blood on your arm. Did that devil's cub spike you whilst fencing?'

Adam walked to the door. 'It was a scratch and not done by Japhet.'

The harsh edge to his voice sent a shiver through Senara. The undercurrents in this family disturbed her. She kept her head bowed until Adam Loveday left the room. Whilst she tended Elspeth she was questioned about her knowledge with herbs. Her answers were evasive. When the old woman dozed, she knew it was time to take her pay and leave this house.

She sensed danger swirling around her. The house was filled with tensions; they permeated the wainscotting and panelling. Storms were brewing. Hatreds swirled, lying in wait in the shadows and recesses.

Her spine prickled. Safety lay away from this place. The need to escape was strong and frightening in its intensity. Tonight was a full moon, a time once revered by the ancients when magic could be performed, or the seeds of destruction manifested.

* * *

As twilight settled on the celebrations the house was lit by over a hundred candles. A violin quartet played behind the banisters of the first-floor landing. Later dancing would take place in the spacious square entrance hall.

Adam graciously received congratulations from the guests in the green saloon, where the furniture had been pushed back against the walls to allow everyone to mingle freely. Already the room smelled of beeswax from the candles in the crystal chandelier and gilded wall sconces. Heavy perfumes and hair pomanders masked the rankness of stale sweat which rose from the expensive silks and brocades of the guests. Adam stood beside Lisette and, with her arm linked through his, her timidity left her.

Her appearance had surprised him. Her hair had been powdered and dressed high. Diamonds glittered at her throat and her panniered dress was of a deep rose pink which flattered her pale complexion. In her happiness an angelic beauty radiated from her. There was excitement and adoration in her gaze, which was constantly upon him.

How could he not feel a glow of warmth in return? She was so trusting, so innocent. That delicate loveliness, so fragile and ethereal, roused his chivalry. Her profile was as dainty and perfectly proportioned as a cameo. Her midnight eyes studied him with a mute appeal, pleading that there would be happiness in their union. He could not find it in his heart to deny her. In the company of such blossoming beauty it was easy to believe that all augured well for their future.

The moment came for Adam and Lisette to lead the guests to the hall for the first dance.

'Such a delightful couple . . .' Aunt Margaret dabbed at the corner of her eye with a lace handkerchief. 'I despair of Thomas ever settling down. He pays no heed to any of the eligible women he is introduced to.'

'Time enough yet,' Elspeth consoled. 'To my mind Adam is too young. And how will Lisette cope with her husband away at sea for months, if not years?'

'She will have her children to occupy her,' Margaret said. 'They are to make their home at Trevowan, are they not? Perhaps St John will have a bride by then.'

Louise Riviere rapped her son on the arm. 'Do not scowl so, Etienne. Adam is Lisette's choice. Be happy for her.'

Etienne did not answer and sipped his brandy as he watched his sister dancing. A set dance was in progress. Lisette was gliding gracefully as she weaved in and out of a line of dancers. When she joined Adam and they linked hands to pivot slowly in a circle, her adoring gaze churned the bile in her brother's gut. How dare she defy him? In England he was impotent to do anything about this match, but once they returned to France . . . That would be a very different matter.

Chapter Nine

At the end of the dance Adam led Lisette from the floor. 'We must not neglect our other guests, my dear. The villagers will expect to wish us well.'

Lisette hung back. 'Must we? It is so much more pleasurable here. And I have already met so many strangers.'

'Who all adore you.'

'It is your duty, child,' Elspeth reminded her at overhearing her words. Elspeth was in good spirits and her limp was barely perceptible. She was the only older woman present who wore no powdered wig but had chosen a silver spangled turban to cover her head.

Adam squeezed his fiancée's hand. 'They are our tenants and Trevowan has always been host to fêtes for the villagers of Penruan,' he gently reprimanded. 'The people will be charmed by you.'

'Of course they will. Now do your duty child,' Elspeth added. 'And if you see that Polglase woman, tell her I am again beholden to her.' She slapped her side. 'My hip has never felt better.'

All the cousins – except Etienne, who preferred to play cards in the room set aside for them – accompanied the betrothed couple to the barn. Adam approached Sir Henry Traherne before leaving the dancing. He had seen little of his friend during the evening. His fiancée, Roslyn Druce was a dour sentinel at his side, demanding all his time and attention.

'We're putting in an appearance in the barn for half an hour, Henry. Will you join us?'

Before Henry could answer, Roslyn spoke sharply, 'Certainly not! Henry's place is with me. I will not mix with the lower orders.' Roslyn was tall and thin. Dressed in amber silk and adorned with the family emeralds she made an imposing figure. Although no great beauty, she had a comely face, except for when something displeased her. Then her expression hardened, her thin lips were drawn back over large protruding teeth and the lines about her mouth grooved with a harridan's bitterness.

With a resigned shrug Henry complied with her wishes. Hannah who was passing by them on Oswald's arm laughed at Roslyn. They had been friends since childhood. 'Ros, you will miss such fun. Were I not *enciente* there is nothing I enjoy more than a country reel.'

Roslyn sniffed. 'I have often despaired of you, Hannah. I would have thought marriage would have given you a greater sense of decorum.'

'There is time for that once I reach my allotted three score years and ten. I do declare I shall join Adam and Lisette.'

'I will not hear of it,' Oswald was aghast. 'You have danced too long as it is. You should now rest.'

'While I am strong enough to continue with the morning milking I am strong enough to dance. Oswald, I am no paper doll. Lisette will feel more at ease if I am with her.'

Roslyn remained stiff and disdainful, raising a brow at Lisette. 'Pray do not keep your charming fiancée with the common people for too long, Adam. She must get to know those who will one day be her neighbours. I am sure we shall be great friends.'

Adam again had reservations. Roslyn liked to manipulate people and Lisette, with her timidness, was vulnerable.

When they entered the barn a cheer greeted the couple. Lisette flinched at the noise and pressed closer to Adam for protection. More than sixty people were inside, the sound of their heavy boots thudding on the hard-packed mud floor loud as they danced an energetic reel. Others clapped to the rhythm of the fiddler or shouted to make themselves heard.

Aware of Lisette's nervousness, Adam stayed close to her. Hannah was enthusiastically dancing with Oswald, though her face was becoming red from the exertion. When Japhet or Thomas partnered Lisette in a dance he was free to mingle with his guests. It was expected of him to dance with at least three of the women.

On entering the barn he had seen Meriel surrounded by several men. Their gazes had locked. Then she had turned away, her face animated as she flirted with Dick Nance.

'That one is a beauty,' Japhet said, elbowing past St John. 'Meriel Sawle, is it not?'

'And as brother of the betrothed it is for me to claim the first dance.' St John barged in front of his cousin to whisk Meriel into a country reel.

Japhet lifted a brow as he contemplated the revellers. 'Now where is that ravishing wench I encountered earlier today? She was attending Aunt Elspeth. Have you seen her?'

'She does not appear to be here,' Adam replied. 'The family keep themselves very much to themselves.'

'A woman of mystery.' Japhet fingered his moustache. 'How intriguing. Such a beauty should not hide herself away.'

Adam frowned. Japhet was a womaniser and could be relentless in his pursuit and conquest. Then he discarded the women. Adam had taken little notice of the Polglase woman, his mind clouded both by images of Meriel and guilt that he felt no more than fondness for Lisette. It had made him doubly attentive to his fiancée.

'There are pretty women here aplenty to fall for your blackguard charms, Japhet,' he taunted.

'There are indeed. And fine sport for the choosing.'

Meriel was flirting with St John but suddenly her mood changed and she looked displeased at something he said. She flounced away from him and was caught round the waist by Japhet who swung her into the dance. St John started forward his fist raised in anger. Thomas ran to restrain him. St John shook off his arm and stormed out of the barn.

Witnessing the scene, Adam was gnawed by jealousy. Meriel cast him a sidelong glance during the dance and there was triumph in her eyes. She was deliberately goading him, torturing him for his betrayal. He turned away to hide his pain. So great was his infatuation and torment, he wanted to tear Meriel from Japhet's side and run away with her. God help him, he could not forget her. His need for her was all-consuming.

'That wench is trouble,' Thomas said. 'She delights in the way St John and Japhet are competing for her attention.'

Hannah, who had finally agreed to return to the house, paused by Thomas at his words. She watched the threesome with amusement. 'That scheming little fortune huntress would be a handful even for Japhet. She will run rings round St John.'

'It is unlike you to malign another, Hannah.' Adam was stung to respond.

'She has always been a sly one. What Sawle is not? I would rather she did not get her claws into one of my family.'

'I must mingle with our guests.' Adam retreated behind a mask of hospitality. He danced with Sal, who was quick to praise Lisette and his good fortune. Later he danced with Sarah Nance and Lucy Mumford, who was married to Ben from the boatyard. Though he never glanced in her direction, Meriel's presence taunted his senses. Her laughter rose above the music mocking him. Mocking his choice of bride.

St John returned to the barn and he and Japhet were rivals for dances with Meriel. Japhet also danced with the prettiest of the village women. Thomas danced twice with Lisette and had partnered Winnie Fraddon, but mainly he seemed content to watch the proceedings from the door.

To Adam's delight he saw Lisette join the reel with Isaac Nance and then Ben Mumford. Later, seeing her dancing with Harry Sawle, he kept a concerned eye upon her. At the way the villagers had taken her to their hearts she had overcome her nervousness. Outside the formal atmosphere of the house, she was laughing and vivacious. Her childish innocence charmed him. At the end of the dance with Harry she did not seek out Adam but stopped to talk with Jenna Biddick,

61

who was the maid appointed to her during her stay. Jenna lived in the village and was introducing her to Hester and Annie Moyle, the daughters of the village chandler.

This was a side of Lisette Adam had not expected and it cheered him. He supped deeply from a tankard of ale, his throat parched. The air in the barn was dusty from the dancing. Although it had been swept and dampened down, it had been impossible to remove the fine straw dust. The vigorous dancing had added to the forming haze. Sweating, shiny faces reflected the pale light from the tallow lanterns set around the beams. The dancers threw up long shadows against the walls. In the darker recesses, the older villagers nursed their tankards or clapped to the rhythm of the fiddler. Adam was about to join Lisette when Meriel came to stand before him.

'I've danced with all the Loveday men, am I to be denied the company of the man in whose honour this dance is held?'

'The pleasure is all mine.' Relief flooded him that she was no longer angry. The dance was sedate by country standards, giving them time to talk. 'I'm sorry if—'

'No apologies, Adam.' Her voice was all sweetness. 'I wish you happiness. Is not your fiancée rather young?'

'Her father is ill. He wanted her future settled.' He caught himself up, annoyed that he felt the need to explain.

The dance took them away from each other and on her return Meriel smiled. Her eyes sparkled like moonlight on the sea, their expression deep and fathomless. She was at her most provoking, acting aloof, while every subtle movement of her body enticed him.

'I have tried to see you and explain.' Conscious of inquisitive eyes upon him, he glanced around as they again parted and then returned to their place in the square set. Sal and Clem Sawle were frowning in their direction. Lisette was now dancing with Thomas and waved gaily to Adam.

'Yes, I am owed an explanation.' She regarded him archly. 'But not now, with so many eyes upon us. Later, in say an hour. Come to the cave.'

'I cannot abandon my guests.' He cursed the dance which separated them.

Meriel did not look at him when she was again at his side. 'You rejoin your ship in a few days. Time is short. I do not know when else I can get away.' Her voice was low, throaty and irresistible. 'Clem is suspicious, but even he will not expect you to meet me this evening.'

She moved in the dance and the fullness of her breasts touched his arm, searing his flesh through his velvet jacket. A sidelong glance through her lashes held so much promise that his throat dried with longing.

The offer was as tempting as it was dangerous. The smell of her skin was intoxicating. The wine he had drunk was heavy in his veins. He could not shake off the memory of her kisses in the cave. He wanted her. It was madness. But he could not resist the spell she had woven. No man could.

The dance ended and before she turned away her hand brushed against his thigh. 'I shall be waiting.'

Adam saw that Japhet was leaving the barn with Hester Moyle on his arm. Harry Sawle was slumped in a drunken stupor over an upturned keg which had been used as a table.

Clem grabbed Meriel's arm and propelled her away. 'Stay with your own kind and stop acting like a harlot. Thadeous Lanyon is angered that you have not danced with him.'

'I don't like the man.'

'Then you'd best set about liking him and more. The Lovedays will bring you nothing but sorrow. Lanyon is looking for a wife. You'll be the richest woman in Penruan.'

'And the most miserable.'

Clem tightened his hold to a bruising grip. 'Stay away from the Loveday men. Or it will be the worse for you.'

To allay her brother's suspicions, she danced with Thadeous Lanyon. Somehow she managed to suppress her shudders as his fingers, dry as scales, held her hand. He pressed his body close to her, his paunch rubbing against her breasts. She stamped on his toe and although he no longer crushed her, she had to endure his frog-like eyes ogling her cleavage.

'Your father has done me the honour of permitting me to call upon you,' he said, moistening his fleshy lips. 'I shall look forward to furthering our acquaintance.'

'You will find I am my own woman and not my father's chattel, Mr Lanyon.'

'Which is why I would wed you,' he cooed salaciously. 'Enjoy your flirtations tonight. You hunger for wealth and position. And I am a wealthy man who would reward your beauty well. All Penruan will envy me my bride.'

'You presume too much, sir.' Gagging on her anger, Meriel spun on her heel and almost collided with St John. The other Loveday men had returned to the house.

'I could not leave without another dance from the most beautiful woman present. I chanced to notice that you are wearing red stockings. So you accepted my gift. They could not grace a trimmer ankle.'

This was safer ground she could handle. Flirting with Adam's handsome brother was a pastime she enjoyed. It was only the attention of ugly men she could not stomach. 'You mistake the matter, sir. These were no gift. Someone had carelessly mislaid them and they came into my possession.'

'Come outside,' he demanded. 'You have no interest in these clods.'

'Clem would flay me. Look how he hovers. It is too risky.'

'How am I to see you? It is impossible at the inn.'

She had not expected such ardour. 'A man as ingenious as yourself will find a way,' she taunted, hoping that St John's attentions would spur Adam's jealousy. There was scant time to win the man she loved.

The dance ended and when St John rejoined his family, Meriel ignored the other village men who vied for dances, and sought out her father. Reuban was propped against a roof support, supping a quart of ale.

The cider she had drunk made her bolder. 'I will not be in when Thadeous Lanyon calls. The man is a lecher.'

'He be wealthy.' Each word was delivered as though a threat. Reuban thrust his face close to hers, his breath reeking of onions and beer. 'He'll not see any of his wife's family starve, come a hard winter.'

'I will not be sold. When I marry I shall choose my own man. If Thadeous Lanyon was anybody in this community he'd be up at the house not here. Despite his wealth, the gentry shun him. His father was a cattle thief hanged at Bodmin.'

'Thadeous is respected by the villagers.'

'Because most of them are in debt to him.'

'Exactly. Your brothers included.' A malicious smile twisted his lips. 'You'll do as you're told, my girl, and that's an end to it.'

Meriel spun away from him, her heart thumping with fear. If Clem and Harry were in debt to Lanyon, they would do everything in their power to force the match. She knew they were capable of cruelty. They would starve or beat her into submission. Neither would they let her run away. They would not let her repeat the shame her sister Rose had brought upon the family.

Reuban stepped close, his breath hot and menacing against her cheek. 'Lanyon has a mind to wed at the end of his mourning year for his second wife. That be in three months.'

The warning was clear. To calm her panic Meriel went to the makeshift bar for another glass of the strong cider. Three men were in a stupor on the floor at her feet. As she drank the cider, a sense of desperation overwhelmed her.

The meeting with Meriel unsettled Adam. Lisette's adoring gaze had become irritating. Also she clung to his arm, several times knocking the sword wound. It was as painful as a tooth abscess, the pain only slightly lessened by the brandy he was drinking. Now they were in the house, she expected him to remain at her side. Her lack of maturity was making her pettish. She was tired and wanted him to sit at her side in a quiet corner. Guilt at his intention to slip away and meet Meriel made him edgy. As the time neared he was restless to escape.

'We must mingle with the guests. You have hardly spoken to Henry's fiancée, Roslyn. Or her mother, Lady Druce. Look, Squire Penwithick and his family are beckoning to you.'

'Please, no more strangers,' she simpered. They had been conversing all evening in French. 'My head is in a whirl with so many new faces and names and my English is so poor.'

'Everyone adores you.'

She put a hand to her head. 'It is so hot in here and the violins are making my head ache. Could we go on to the terrace for a few minutes?'

Adam checked his impatience. Lisette did look flushed. She plucked a glass of champagne from a passing maid and drank half of it rapidly. She had been drinking steadily all evening. Adam took the glass from her. 'That is lethal stuff. We cannot have you getting drunk.'

She giggled as he led her out on to the terrace. 'I do not need champagne to make me happy when you are at my side.'

Lisette released his arm and walked to a part of the terrace wall which was in shadow. The full moon was unveiled from earlier cloud and cast a silver pathway across the sea. Coloured Chinese lanterns had been placed around the Neptune fountain and the gentle cascade of its water was barely audible above the music and conversation within the house. She giggled again and turned to face him. There was a defiant tilt to her chin.

'Everyone does not adore me, Adam.'

He laughed. 'They are enchanted.'

'No. You are not enchanted. You act so gallant, but I think you are not happy that we marry.'

Inwardly he groaned. He had been a churl, obsessed by his need to see Meriel. In the last hour he had neglected Lisette and her feelings were hurt. He stood at her side and put his hands on her shoulders. 'I am content. You are my pretty cousin, whom I have always adored.'

Her face, powdered and painted to look a woman's, turned up to his. He could see her only as a child who was uncertain of her future.

'Adam, I would like very much for my fiancé to kiss me. Is this not the custom in England?'

The initial shock at her forwardness was banished at the wide-eyed innocence in her eyes. The French were a romantic race and as a child, Lisette had been full of tales of chevaliers and their fair maidens. With a rakish grin he planted a light kiss on her cherub lips.

To his surprise there was scorn in her tone. 'Etienne said the English are poor lovers, cold-hearted and without passion. I have seen French sweethearts kissing. They embrace and cling together as though buffeted by a storm.'

His pride was ruffled at her words. This time he crushed her against him and kissed her with a thoroughness intended to right the slur upon all Englishmen. When she drew back unsteadily to gasp for air, his tone was mocking. 'Now, mademoiselle, if you are content that your brother is misinformed, we must rejoin our guests.'

'Oh, can we not kiss again?' Her disappointment was obvious, drawing a laugh from him.

'Our guests must be entertained.' A clock was chiming the hour when they re-entered the house, reminding Adam he must soon meet Meriel. Lisette's flirting was forgotten. In his preoccupation with getting away from the party, the ardour and experience of Lisette's response to his kiss had scarcely registered.

They were waylaid by Squire Penwithick, who was Adam's godfather and a Member of Parliament. He was as imposing and hearty a character as Falstaff, and chucked Lisette under the chin. With a wink to Adam, he stated, 'Pretty wench, my dear boy. Much happiness to you both. A moonlit terrace is a place for romance. I will not ask you how two lovers of different nationalities communicate.'

'My French is fluent enough after my visits to Paris.'

'Rum goings on in France by all accounts. Must be a worry to your uncle.'

'How does Parliament view the situation there?' Adam asked.

'With concern. Marie-Antoinette would do well to curb her extravagance with so much poverty amongst the masses.'

Lisette,who could understand more English than she could speak, was indignant. 'What is this talk of poverty? Our Queen is beautiful, yes? Many are jealous of her. What do you English know?' Her mouth quivered and she was clearly upset. She stamped her foot and her eyes sparkled with tears.

'James, for a politician you have no tact. The girl has taken offence,' his wife, Dorothy, remonstrated. She guided Lisette back to Louise and Elspeth, who held court with another half-dozen women by the hearth.

Adam was relieved at Dorothy's intervention. He was feeling the strain of the evening, and Lisette's outburst was embarrassingly childish. The glimpse of the coquette on the terrace had vanished.

Captain William Loveday had joined Adam and the squire in time to witness her outburst. He stood out from the other guests in his naval uniform. He looked concerned. 'Lisette is young. Too much excitement. I must also congratulate you on your promotion to lieutenant. It has been agreed by the Admiralty, so I heard at Plymouth. Yet Edward says you will not stay in the navy.'

'Is that so?' Penwithick said. 'It is a worthy career.'

'But not suited to us all,' Uncle William observed. 'You hav~ of my brother Hubert in you, Adam. He was not at ~ constraints navy life enforces. Too much his own m~ his thirst for independent adventure and ac~'

admiral. I am a dullard compared to him; I like routine and an orderly life.'

'I would prefer life as a merchant captain and I will have my own ship.' He nevertheless was delighted at his promotion.

'I had not realised Edward would so provide for you.' Uncle William looked askance. 'Or is it to be a wedding gift from Riviere?'

Belatedly Adam realised the brandy had made him indiscreet. 'Neither my father nor uncle will provide the money for this venture.'

'And I have a feeling you will succeed in your aims, Adam,' Penwithick said with a laugh. 'Ambition and a thirst for adventure has made many a man rich. But as it will be some years before you wed Lisette – will you be spending much time in France?'

'I had not considered. But naval duties would make that difficult.'

The dancing had set his injured arm throbbing and he took another brandy from a tray carried by a maid. Its warm glow dulled the ache. As quickly as he could he made his excuses to his uncle and godfather.

It was time to meet Meriel. He moved slowly through the guests until he reached a side door. Then, waiting until he was unobserved, he made his escape.

The fresh air momentarily made his head reel. He had consumed a great deal of wine and brandy this evening. He inhaled deeply to regain control, then hurried through the garden. Luckily the sky was clear, the moon full; and his route was illuminated enough in the dark.

When he arrived at the cave it was empty. He paced for several minutes, fearing Meriel had been unable to escape Clem's vigilance. The sound of falling stones bouncing past the entrance of the cave alerted him. It was followed by an unladylike oath.

Meriel was crouched by the entrance, rubbing her ankle. 'I think I've sprained the wretched thing.' The words were slurred and as she straightened her figure weaved tipsily. She giggled. 'Aren't you going to carry me inside?'

Adam swept her up, ignoring the ache in his arm in his joy at holding her close. He carried her to where a funnel of moonlight entered the cave. His kiss was passionate and eagerly received. Then with a sob she pushed him away.

'Nay, you play me for a wanton. You told me you cared. You lied. You knew you were about to be betrothed.'

'I did not lie. It is you I care for. I marry Lisette out of duty.'

'And what of me?'

He pulled her close. 'I would cherish you always.'

She was stiff in his arms, her eyes bright and accusing. 'Yet you would cast me aside for a child.'

'It is you I adore.'

Her beauty and sensuality made him physically ache to possess her. Sensing this, she smiled. She was a seductress artfully ensnaring him. A woman meant for loving, silently offering him fulfilment beyond his wildest dreams. .

'Do you love me, Adam?' Her voice was nectar, her lips parted.

The pliant curves of her figure drove his body past restraint. 'You know that I do.'

His kisses silenced further questions. Meriel was no longer coy; a madness seemed to have possessed her. She was all he had dreamed of, but even so, the proof of her virginity was a sobering shock.

Tears spangled her cheeks when he drew away from her. His passion sated he was consumed by remorse. Meriel was no light-of-love to be treated thus.

'I never meant for this,' she murmured. 'Why did I drink so much? I was angry with you. And frightened I would lose you. This must change everything. You love me?'

She searched his face, the contours hollowed by the moonlight. It was as handsome and unreadable as a statue. Fear gripped her. Dear God! She could not have misjudged him. Adam was a man of honour. He would not abandon her now.

There was no reassurance in his eyes. His face was taut with tension. Horror and despair seeped into her heart. Had she miscalculated and made the greatest mistake of her life?

Adam stepped back, appalled at her words and shamed by his actions. 'I love you, but how can it change anything? I am bound to Lisette. I have given my word.'

Chapter Ten

'St John, I will not pay your debts. And there are your bills from tailors, bootmakers, and a gunsmith for a pearl-handled pistol. What possessed you to such extravagance?'

St John lounged on the chair opposite his father in the study of Trevowan. Adam had ridden to Plymouth that morning and the Rivieres had left at noon to travel to Bristol. After so many days of leisure and entertainments the house was morbidly empty. His father had seemed in good spirits during the celebrations but now his face was dark with anger. St John bristled with indignation. 'I cannot appear in public dressed as a pauper. I have my position to uphold.'

Edward rose, his knuckles white as he gripped the edge of the pitted Jacobean table he used as a desk. 'Your position! What, pray, is that? A dissolute! I expect you to work to improve the profitability of the estate and yard. Not gamble the proceeds away. Would you see us ruined?'

St John was startled by the violence of his father's attack. He was used to these lectures but the debts were always paid. Now there was a sinister threat behind his father's words which alarmed him.

Edward stared at his elder son and cursed his misfortune that St John and not Adam had been the first-born.

'Are you blind?' he raged. 'We have had no orders at the yard for months.'

'There is the merchantman.'

'Which is a special concession taken on to attract new customers. There will be little profit in it. We are a small yard compared to many. Competition for new trade is fiercer than ever. Since your aptitude in the yard is so poor you were entrusted to bring in more orders. I do not send you to Plymouth and Falmouth to take pleasure in a gaming house, but to seek out new orders. Your growing reputation as a wastrel reflects on the family and on our business.'

'You have agents to find new customers.' St John straightened, his unease mounting.

'We have never relied solely on the agents. Our finances are not unlimited. Any new vessel we build requires vast expenditure before we are paid. I must insist that you live within your allowance. These gambling debts alone exceed your quarterly allowance. This time they will be settled but your allowance will be stopped until they have been covered.'

'You cannot leave me without funds!'

The contempt in his father's eyes shook St John. 'I will see you rot in debtors' prison before I lose the yard because of your wastrel ways.'

'If I do not visit my usual haunts rumour will spread that the yard is failing,' St John blustered.

'Then inform your friends you intend to mend your ways. That you are interested only in building the finest ships, not gaming and wenching with fops.'

St John's face contorted with fury but his father countered his outburst by declaring, 'You are not my only son. Adam loves the yard. You must prove to me that you are worthy of your inheritance, or I shall disinherit you in favour of your brother.'

'You would disown me!' he croaked. He rose and staggered back as though he had been mortally wounded. 'Think of the scandal. Our reputation would be lost.'

'Your conduct is the only scandal in this family.'

The two men glared at each other. Under that forthright and accusing stare, St John quailed. He nodded agreement. His father did not make idle threats.

As St John turned to leave Edward spoke again, less harshly this time.

'Heed your brother and consider taking a bride. If you are wise she will bring as her dowry the money we need to tide us over when business is slack or customers have yet to pay.'

A deeper fear iced St John's spine. 'Are our circumstances so dire?'

'That depends upon your expectations for your future. You know your duty.'

Edward sawed his hand across the back of his neck. It was knotted with tension. He could no longer ignore his misgivings concerning St John. His son was weak and too easily led by unsuitable friends. Edward felt he had been lenient for too long. They could no longer afford for St John to shirk his responsibilities.

It was a problem Edward had been wrestling with for the last year. Tradition had been the backbone of his life and it did not sit easily with him to break it. The eldest son always inherited both Trevowan and the Loveday yard. It had been stipulated in his grandfather's will. The fortune of the family home and business were locked together. It was their strength. Separate them, and bad harvests or a drop in shipbuilding orders could destroy them all. Yet both yard and estate were only as solid as the man who governed them. Time and again Edward had made allowances for St John's youth. Time and again he had been disappointed. It was hard to acknowledge that his heir was a wastrel with no grasp of business affairs.

This was St John's final chance to prove himself. Too much was at stake to allow him any more failures.

'Sawle, my good fellow, I trust this is not an inopportune moment to call.' Thadeous Lanyon boomed from the taproom.

Meriel froze in sweeping the kitchen floor. Earlier that morning she had seen Adam ride through Penruan to rejoin his ship. It would be months before he returned. Her heart felt it was breaking. Now she had to endure Lanyon's company. It was unbearable. She threw the besom into a corner and whipped off her apron. Panic made her fumble. She cursed the tangle of strings which halted her flight. Wriggling the apron down over her hips, she stepped out of it and hurled it on to a table. Anger flushed her cheeks, but fear was uppermost, dashing caution aside.

A glance towards the washing line showed her Sal and Tilda, struggling against a stiffening breeze to lift the dry flapping sheets from the line. Meriel bolted across the inn yard and through the stables to escape into a side street. Her pace did not slow until she reached the headland rock. There she sat out of sight of the village. She could not endure another session in Lanyon's company. This was the second time he had called in a week.

The first she had been unable to escape. She had been forced to sit with him in the parlour, accompanied by Sal and Reuban. Harry was tending the bar and Tilda was left to prepare the family meal. The minutes had crawled by like snails. To avoid direct conversation, she had picked up one of Clem's shirts which needed the cuff restitching.

'There be no need to do that,' Sal reprimanded, knowing that Meriel loathed sewing and the stitches would have to be unpicked as unfit for Clem to wear.

Meriel tossed the garment aside and gazed out of the small window. Sal kept the conversation flowing, interceding when Meriel's absent stare left a question unanswered. Reuban was close-lipped by nature and replied only when spoken to.

'Meriel, are you away with the pixies, child? Will you answer Mr Lanyon?' Sal finally snapped.

She replied curtly, turning her head away, unable to bear those frog eyes leering at the outline of her breasts. When Lanyon left, she rose to flounce out of the room. The leather of Reuban's belt stung her shoulder. She covered her face as several more blows lashed her shoulders and back.

'That be enough, Reuban.' Sal thrust her large body between them. 'You'll end up scarring her. Lanyon won't want her then.'

Reuban pulled Meriel's hair, the pain stabbing like needles through her skull. 'That be a taste of what you'll get if you don't speak prettily to Lanyon when he calls.'

Today she had escaped, but how many more times could she avoid him? Her heart was heavy as she stared out to sea. Her mind was filled with memories of Adam. She had not seen him since they had stolen away from the ball. His parting words had cut her deep. She had been so sure of her hold over him; had gambled everything to win him. The way he had left his fiancée to come at her bidding had proved that he loved her. Yet he had treated her shamefully.

Why had she drunk so much cider? It had made her reckless and given her a sense that she was invincible; that her beauty could ensnare any man she wanted. And how she had wanted Adam!

With impatience she wiped away a tear. Adam would not rescue her from the drudgery of the Dolphin Inn. Never again would she allow her emotions to rule her head. Never again would she lose control.

Somehow she had to escape Reuban's tyranny. She would drink poison before she endured Lanyon's vile touch. There had to be another way.

The return to naval duty was onerous. Adam's thoughts were with the *Pegasus*. The heaviness of frustration weighted him. It was in his blood to trim and plane the timbers. The touch of smooth golden oak as seductive as a woman's form. The *Pegasus* was his dream and should be fashioned by his hand and created under his supervision.

When he reflected upon his leave, it was only the hours spent in the shipwright's yard which gave him a sense of wellbeing and fulfilment. It was the one place he felt in control of his life, and even that was transient. The Loveday yard could never be his.

Then there was Meriel. Thoughts of her induced tangled emotions which ranged from elation to deepest guilt.

Now as he stood on the quay at Plymouth, he quashed the temptations at Trevowan which lured him from his duty. He narrowed his eyes as the sunlight dappled the *Goliath*'s tall side with dancing reflections from the water. The gilded figurehead in Roman-style armour beneath the bowsprit carried an out-thrust sword. The giant Goliath was open-mouthed, roaring his challenge to his enemies. The paintwork was fresh on the frigate's sides and the new mast and rigging erased all traces of the storm which had battered her.

The last of the provisions were being loaded. The smaller casks of salt pork, salt beef and ship's biscuits were rolled up a gangplank into an open hatch. The larger barrels of fresh water and beer were hauled up on pulleys, then taken down to the hold and stowed by hand. There were also crates of fresh fruit, which helped prevent the scurvy, being stowed aboard. It was a disease he had witnessed too often. It began with a swelling in the gums which then spread to the limbs. The sailors died bloated and in agony.

Adam cast a last glance across the Tamar, the county boundary. The Cornish side of the river was lush with trees, some already with their leaves turning to the red and golds of autumn. It would be several months if not longer before he returned to his home.

Remorse again smote him. He should have spoken to Meriel before he left. Yet what would it have resolved? It could not have eased his longing for her. She was the first woman he believed himself to love. Yet he could hardly ask her to wait for him. His eyes narrowed with the pain of his longing: the thought of her in the arms of another man was crucifying.

Adam went below to stow his sea chest. With the rank of junior lieutenant he shared a tiny cubicle with another officer. Between their hammocks was a gun carriage, the partition affording privacy would be removed when the order was given for the decks to be cleared for action.

'Good to have you aboard, Mr Loveday,' his companion boomed as he languished his spare, gangling frame against the gun carriage. 'So we share a berth.'

'Casford, you old devil. It's good to see you.' Of all the officers on board Casford was the one he liked best.

'Congratulations on your promotion. That will put Beaumont in a taking. He only kept his post because Admiral Beaumont pulled his weight at the Admiralty. Anyone else would have been court-martialled for incompetence. Instead, Beaumont is strutting like a peacock.' Phillip Casford tapped his long thin nose. 'Last I saw of Beaumont he was cussing the day you were born and has vowed to make your life hell. He is still senior to you.'

'Beaumont can go to the devil. He is an ass and a bully, the worst kind of officer.'

'And with an admiral as a grandfather, he can ruin a young lieutenant's career.'

A piercing note on a pipe called everyone to leave their duties and attend the arrival of Captain Rawcliffe on board. As Adam came on deck he scanned the faces of the assembled men. Many were familiar. The cabin boy, Billy Brown, gave him a cheeky smile. After his ill-treatment Adam was surprised he was again serving. Many lads deserted in port. But then Billy was an orphan and at least on ship he did not starve.

Another twittering of pipes heralded Captain Rawcliffe stepping aboard. His stocky figure was topped by a bicorn hat with a tall cockade. He paused to inspect his officers.

'Why are not the stores secured by now? There is grease spilled on the decking. I want it holystoned until it is spotless. Who is the officer of the watch?'

Lieutenant Beaumont saluted. His new tailored uniform fitted him like a snake's skin. Captain Rawcliffe glowered at him. 'The *Goliath* limped into port looking like a bedraggled beggar, Mr Beaumont. She will sail out immaculate as a queen at her coronation, or I will want to know why. I shall inspect her at the end of your watch.'

A stain of red branded Beaumont's cheeks as he shouted orders. The new midshipman, Mr Winsett, a lad of only twelve years, had joined the ship yesterday. When he did not move fast enough Beaumont kicked out at his ankle. The boy crumpled on the deck with a howl of pain.

'Still picking on those who cannot retaliate?' Adam snapped. With Beaumont on board, Adam expected and was prepared for trouble.

Three weeks later they were off the Azores, the sky and sea dark and turbulent with an impending storm. Adam came on deck early for his watch. Beaumont was bellowing at the new midshipman. 'Mr Winsett, get aloft or I'll flay you until I see if your spine is made of bone or jelly.'

The boy was forty feet up the ratlines and frozen with fear. Adam signalled behind Beaumont's back for a sailor aloft to encourage the boy.

'Leave him alone, Trotter,' Beaumont shrieked.

The midshipman inched upwards but halted after another two feet. Lieutenant Casford joined Adam for their watch and muttered, 'What is that boy doing aloft?'

'Blubbering are you, Mr Winsett?' Beaumont continued to shout. 'We will see how you blubber when your hide comes off your back. Move yourself.'

It was obvious the boy was too terrified to move. The ship was rearing in the heaving swell. The bell rang for the change of watch. Adam addressed Beaumont. 'Order the boy down or I go up after him.'

Beaumont drew his thin lips into a sneer. 'Move yourself, Winsett. I ordered you to the crow's-nest. There is no place for milksops in the navy.'

'The boy is terrified,' Adam intervened. 'Order him down.' He stared up at the terrified figure. Fear of heights was something many seamen had to overcome. Once in a storm Adam had been paralysed up in the topgallants. Encouragement from an old seadog had saved his sanity and his life.

Beaumont ignored him and Adam rapped out, 'Get yourself down here, Mr Winsett. Your watch is over.'

'I'll report you for this, Loveday,' Beaumont snorted. 'As senior officer . . .'

Adam kept his gaze on the young boy. 'Trotter, Smith, assist Mr Winsett back on deck.'

When the seamen hesitated, Casford ordered, 'Do as Mr Loveday says. I am the senior officer on duty for this watch.'

The men helped Winsett down. The boy was hysterical when he reached the deck. There was blood on his hands where the rough ropes had cut into them as he clung on in terror.

'Go to the ship's surgeon; he will tend your hands,' Adam said kindly. He also noticed a dark bruise on the boy's neck where it looked like he had been half throttled, and on the back of his hand were three raw burn wounds. One of Beaumont's nasty punishments was to hold a midshipman's hand over a candleflame.

'Winsett is a coward,' raged Beaumont. 'He should be whipped, not played nursemaid to.' In his anger he hit out at the boy, and from the way Winsett flinched it was not the first such beating Beaumont had given him. 'A snivelling coward, that is what you are, Mr Winsett. You are a disgrace to the navy and to your name.'

Adam deflected Beaumont's hand by striking his arm with his fist. 'The sea is rough,' he raged. 'An inexperienced boy should never have been sent aloft in such conditions.'

There was a cry from Smith. As Adam spun round he saw the seaman dart towards Winsett, as he ran away from them to leap on to the rail of the ship. Before Smith could reach him Winsett threw himself overboard. In those rough seas there was no chance of his survival.

Adam rushed to the place from where the boy had jumped. He gripped the ship's rail and searched the heaving sea. There was no sight of Winsett. Anger burned in him at the unnecessary waste of a young life.

Casford rounded on Beaumont. 'Report to the captain, Mr Beaumont. I shall give him my report at the end of the watch.'

'This was your doing, Loveday. If you had not interfered I would have ordered the boy down.'

'The boy would be alive but for your bullying.'

Beaumont's hand went to his sword hilt and there was murder in his eyes. A sharp warning from Casford reminded them both of the penalty for an officer drawing a sword against another in anger. Beaumont stormed from the deck.

'You have made yourself a dangerous enemy there, my friend,' Casford warned. 'He is out for your blood but fighting with him will earn you a court martial.'

Adam's expression was grim. 'That will not stop me if he oversteps the mark again.'

Chapter Eleven

St John rode away from Trevowan in a foul mood. Without his allowance he was condemned to months of drudgery. How could he face the Honourable Percival Fetherington and his friends without the means to sit with them at cards? Yet he dare not risk his father's censure again.

Since he had to pay in kind for his debts, it was time others reciprocated. Meriel had taken the red stockings, a sign that she was not averse to his attentions. He needed a diversion to compensate for the curtailment of his usual pleasures.

Fortune smiled on him at discovering Meriel sitting on the rock which formed the headland of Penruan Bay. She was staring moodily out to sea, and started at the sound of his horse's hoofs. Recognising him, she relaxed.

'This is an unexpected pleasure, Meriel. Are you not usually busy in the inn at this time of day?'

'Father has business. I'd rather keep out of his way.'

'And your brothers?' He didn't want Clem blundering upon them. The fisherman was the type to strike first and ask questions later. It was beneath St John's dignity to brawl with the lower orders.

'Harry be looking after the bar, Clem mending his nets.'

St John dismounted from Prince. 'What brings you out here? You looked unhappy. If it is in my power to remedy that, I am your servant.'

'And how would you banish my megrims?' She leaned against the rock, her breasts thrust provocatively forward. Her blonde hair ruffled in the breeze, her eyes were taunting and speculative. 'With more gifts of red stockings to win my affections? I am not so cheaply bought.'

'Your beauty places you above the common woman and should be treated thus.'

He then ran his finger along her neck. When she did not pull away, he smiled. Yet when he would kiss her, his lips met cool air. She had moved out of reach.

St John curbed his impatience and edged closer. Again she avoided his embrace, but there was mischief in her eyes, encouraging him.

'You have no regard for my reputation, sir.'

'A kiss is all I ask.'

'And when did one kiss not lead to another?'

'A pleasure doubled.' St John caught her close. Her mouth was parted, the lips moist and inviting. His mouth covered hers. She did not resist, the softness of her body moulded to his with a sigh of compliance.

'Now I have you,' he chuckled.

Breathless she broke away, her eyes bright and challenging. 'You have my lips, not the woman.'

Nimble as a water sprite, she skipped on to the headland track and began walking back to the village. A trill of teasing laughter was blown back to him on the wind. The swing of her hips beckoned like a beacon.

Prince had wandered off and was grazing, and St John lost precious moments catching the horse and mounting. From his position in the saddle he saw Meriel almost at the first of the whitewashed village houses. The Dolphin Inn was on the far side of the horseshoe harbour. He could waylay her yet.

A commotion broke out in the narrow street as he drew level. The high-pitched squeal of a piglet, which ran between his horse's feet, unnerved the hunter. Three ragged boys chasing the swine yelled with laughter as one dived after the piglet. Prince rolled his eyes and reared. By the time St John had brought him under control, Meriel had disappeared from sight.

Disgruntled, he made for the Dolphin. He was in time to see Thadeous Lanyon leave. Meriel was standing under the faded painted sign by the doorway and she bobbed a deferential curtsey to the smuggler's banker. Reuban had his hand on her shoulder. It was unlike Reuban to make any display of affection in public. They disappeared inside the taproom.

St John acknowledged Lanyon's greeting as the man passed him. The merchant was renowned as a miser and it surprised St John to see the newness of his coat and rich embroidery on his velvet waistcoat.

When he entered the inn he was served by a surly Clem. Reuban did not appear in the taproom for some time and when he did his face was dark with anger. The atmosphere became oppressive. St John had come to the village for diversion. Meriel's teasing and evasion had soured his mood. When she made no attempt to enter the taproom, he cursed her and left. She needed teaching a lesson.

Mark Sawle was not in the stable when St John wanted his horse. He tightened the girths and was about to lead Prince into the yard when he heard a sob from the far stall. That end of the stable was in shadow, but he saw the hem of a russet skirt similar to the one Meriel had been wearing.

Meriel was curled on her side. The back of her blouse was ripped and streaks of blood soaked the rags.

'What in the name of heaven has happened to you?' He peered

closer and saw dark wheals and bruises across her arms.

She lifted her face. Her hair was matted with straw and plastered to her cheeks by her tears. Apart from a graze along her jaw, her face was unmarked.

'Who did this? Was it your father?'

She nodded but kept her head bowed. 'Go away. I'm ashamed to be seen like this.'

'You should be inside so Sal can tend your wounds. Can you stand?'

He put a hand to her elbow and helped her rise. Still her face was averted. Gently he put his finger to her chin to raise it. Despite her pain, her eyes sparked with anger.

'I hate him. I hate this place.'

'Why were you beaten?'

'Because I disobeyed him.' Anger strengthened her voice.

'Had he seen us together?' St John felt queasy. Was there a risk to his own safety?

She laughed caustically. 'I would not obey his wishes.'

Relief that he would not next face Reuban's wrath roused his pity for her plight. He assumed a false bravado. 'Would that I had come to the stables earlier and stopped him.'

'You would have risked his anger for me?'

He cloaked himself in self-importance. There was a dawning respect in Meriel's eyes which increased his bluster. 'I would have taken my whip to him to save you from pain.'

'You would risk so much for me?' Briefly, her fingers rested on his chest and he could feel shudders passing through her body. She drew a jagged breath and straightened. 'If father sees us together it will be the worse for me.' Her gaze lifted to meet his, and rising on tiptoe she kissed his mouth. Her tongue flickered like quicksilver across his before she drew away. 'Thank you for your kindness, St John.'

'I shall await you by the church in two evenings' time an hour after dark. Come to me then?'

'How can I?'

'You are a resourceful woman and I shall have a trinket for you.'

She made no promise but he had seen the speculation in her eyes. She would be there. He watched her stumble across the courtyard to the kitchen. There was a wail from Sal. As he rode out of the inn yard Sal's voice was sorrowful. 'You brought it on yourself, girl. You're a fool to go against your father's orders.'

And he heard Meriel's enigmatic reply: 'I know what I'm doing Ma.'

How in the space of a few weeks could so many things go wrong in her life? Meriel fumed. The protection of childhood had been brutally peeled from her. She had been so sure of her own destiny and power.

She had believed she could control her life now she was a woman. But womanhood had brought with it bitter lessons of a woman's status. One of insignificance in the eyes of men, especially her father. Her desires were unimportant. Their greater strength would always triumph.

How that rankled. She had a keen mind although her education was scant. She had more ambition and the wits to achieve success than her brothers. Her sex was a barrier she found hard to accept.

Womanhood had brought with it shackles she resented. If she had seen her looks as a way to win her fortune, so had her father. He would sell her to the highest bidder in marriage and thus secure his comfort in old age.

Thadeous Lanyon called each evening for an hour. Sal chaperoned the meeting. Meriel was mutinous but complied, though she all but choked on the polite conversation she was forced to endure. A broken little finger was the reward from rebelling against Reuban's orders a second time.

Desperation drove her into St John's arms. She had considered running away, but having no money, and the certainty that her father and Clem would hunt her down, stopped her. St John was her only hope.

Twice Meriel had managed to meet St John in the churchyard, but never for more than a few minutes before Sal or one of her brothers was calling for her. Tonight the cart had been taken from the stables: the Sawle men were engaged in landing a cargo for the free-traders. Unfortunately most of the fleet were in the harbour and she did not expect St John to come to the village tonight. Time was slipping by. When Lanyon had left earlier she had overheard her father say that it would all be settled by Christmas. He could only be referring to her wedding. She would not allow that to happen.

St John was restless. Stuck at Trevowan, he could not shake Meriel from of his mind. Even though it was drizzling he saddled Prince and rode to Penruan. The taproom of the Dolphin was deserted and in darkness except for a single candle on the bar. He led his horse to the stables and noticed the cart was missing. He grinned. Reuban was up to his smuggling tricks again. The coast was clear.

When he approached the back of the inn he was surprised to see the shutters closed. A crack the size of his thumb in their wood showed a yellow light. To check that neither Clem nor Harry was within, he peered through.

The kitchen fire was glowing red, banked high against the chill of the late autumn night. Sal was asleep over her darning. The chair opposite her was empty. Then a movement caught his eye and he stared in amazement.

A beer barrel was upended by the fire and from out of it appeared Meriel's head and bare shoulders. It took him a few seconds to realise that the barrel improvised as a bath and that she was soaping her hair. She had obviously taken advantage of the absence of her menfolk to bathe.

Transfixed, he watched as she ducked her head to rinse the suds and wrapping a linen towel around her hair rose up out of the water. Her body in the glow of the fire was as golden as sunrise. High full breasts swung sensuously above a narrow waist. He bit his lip to stop a groan of exquisite agony at his need to suckle at the rosy nipples. When she rubbed the towel across the flare of her hips and exposed the pyramid of golden hair, he laid his cheek against the wet windowpane, fighting a raw desire which caused the blood to thunder in his ears.

He smothered a groan and eased the tightness of has lace stock with a shaking hand. He gave her several minutes to dress, then tapped lightly on the kitchen door. It was opened a crack.

'What are you doing here, St John?' Meriel asked.

'I had to see you. It has been days since our last meeting.'

'I could not get away.'

She glanced over her shoulder and St John saw that Sal was still sleeping. Meriel slid through the door and closed it silently behind her. Her blonde hair was touselled and the warm smell of her freshly soaped skin assaulted his senses. She drew back, looking embarrassed. A hand pulled at her damp hair. 'I look a mess.'

'No, you are beautiful.'

He kissed her, holding her tight to prevent any resistance. She continually teased him and permitted him only the briefest of kisses at their meetings.

Tonight she was different: softer and more submissive. He was beguiled. 'Come into the stables.'

'Ma could wake and find me gone. I dare not.'

'I would risk everything for you tonight.'

With his arm still tight around her, he drew her, unprotesting, to the stables. A lantern burned on the doorway to light their passage. Once inside he kissed her roughly, the weeks of pent-up passion driving him to a frenzy. When his hands slid under her skirts to explore the milky softness of her thighs, she gasped and wriggled in his hold.

'No, St John. I will not be your doxy. Taken then forsaken.'

She strained back against him, the lantern light playing over her naked breasts which he had freed from her blouse. His blood was at fever level. 'You would never be that.'

He kissed her neck, murmuring soft words of coercion. She permitted him to kiss her breasts but, when he demanded more, gave a sob of anguish. 'I will be ruined. Shamed. I could not give myself to a man who did not love me. Say you love me, St John.'

'Of course I do,' he placated, promising anything to end the torment she was creating.

'Then say it.' Her hand was splayed against his chest her body tense and ready to flee.

'I love you,' he mumbled, his lips hot against her breasts as he hoisted her skirts to her waist. Taking her hand, he pressed it against his tumescence. Her palm was jammed against their two bodies, its touch rousing him to the edge of insanity in his need for release.

The minx was no easy conquest. He played the gallant to seduce her. She acted the coquette one moment, an outraged maiden the next, but the sting of rebuke was always softened by throaty laughter.

They lay on the freshly laid straw of an empty stall, her body offering silent promises, only to withdraw them. His frustration was torment. The need to possess her filled his senses and mind. Persistence and strength finally won. Her struggles were confused with the writhing throes of pleasure until he gained the shuddering blessing of relief.

He rolled away from her and readjusted his clothing. The outside lantern made visible the paleness of her naked figure on the straw. It was her eyes which shocked him. Eyes which were no longer sultry, coy or teasing. They were bright, feral, and filled with cold-blooded triumph.

Chapter Twelve

The smell of evil carried on the wind. It was as rancid as Satan's breath. It also struck as much fear into the hearts of stalwart sailors.

The horizon was clear. Captain Rawcliffe, on the poop deck with Adam, hawked and spat over the side. 'Slavers. The stink stays in your nostrils for days.'

A half-hour later they were heaving to a hundred yards from the stricken slave vessel *Swan*, out of Bristol. She had hoisted the British Jack but most of their crew looked foreign. The mizzen mast was snapped in half and they were rudderless.

'Ahoy there. Do you need help?' Lieutenant Casford shouted into a mouthpiece.

It was obvious that they did, but the laws of salvage were complex. A captain would earn the anger of the owners of a stricken ship if he surrendered the value of the cargo without the condition of the vessel being in peril. Since the *Swan* was listing badly, without assistance it looked unlikely she would reach port.

A dialogue began between the two vessels. The captain, first mate, carpenter and bosun, together with a dozen members of the crew of the *Swan* had died of food poisoning ten days ago. They carried four hundred slaves and more than a quarter had already perished. They had sailed from the Gold Coast and were bound for Barbados. The squall which had damaged her had also loosened the ancient timbers of the hold and she was taking in water faster than the bilge-pumps could cope.

Captain Rawcliffe viewed the vessel with distaste. 'Damned slavers are the scum of the sea. But she's British and it wouldn't do for the Frenchies to claim her. Mr Loveday, you are best equipped to assess the damage. Go aboard and then report to me.'

A longboat took Adam and two other officers aboard. He gagged and put a kerchief to his face.

'Ain't too sweet are we?' a seaman, with a face as wrinkled as a walnut, wheezed. 'But yer get used to it. Thought we were gonners till we saw yer sail.'

Adam ignored him and hurried below, determined to get off this hell-ship as soon as possible. Hell-ship was right. Below decks the stench clawed at his throat and nostrils, and smarted his eyes. Vomit, mixed with excrement and urine were bad enough, but the press of unwashed and diseased bodies in an airless deck was noisome beyond endurance. The suffering of men, women and children shackled to wooden platforms with just enough room to lay flat turned his stomach. Some of the dead were still manacled to their neighbours. He averted his eyes from the slaves, appalled at the cruelty and their misery. For surely although their colour was different and their cultures considered primitive they were still human. They were treated worse than cattle. A glance into any of their faces showed the starkness of pain and fear. It was no wonder the Abolitionists were so fervent to end the trade.

He worked quickly, assessing the damage and the repairs needed. When he finally came on deck, his stomach betrayed him and he vomited over the side. He ordered the dead slaves to be removed before further disease spread. To his mortification the bodies were hurled into the sea, without ceremony or holy service as though they were disposing of a plague of rats.

When he stepped over the entry port of *Goliath*, Beaumont had replaced Casford on watch. 'Puking like a milksop, Mr Loveday,' he sniggered. 'Couldn't take it, then?'

'Thank God I had no stomach for those sights. Only a fiend would be immune.'

Adam reported to Captain Rawcliffe, who nodded in satisfaction. 'If we tow the *Swan* will these repairs keep her afloat until she reaches port?'

'Yes, sir. I am surprised she survived the squall,' Adam added tersely. 'She was unfit for the high seas before she left the Gold Coast.'

Later in the wardroom, as they dined, Beaumont taunted Adam. 'I hope you did your work on the slaver well, Mr Loveday. From salvage each officer will receive a percentage of her value.' Beaumont rubbed his hands in anticipation. 'Could be a tidy sum if they do not lose any more of the cargo to disease. Good fortune, is it not?'

Adam had not given any thought to the payment of salvage. The money would help finance the *Pegasus* but the money was tainted by suffering and that sat ill with him. How could good come from the profits of such evil?

Meriel was frightened. St John had been avoiding her since that night in the stable. Six weeks had passed since she had seen him. She had been unable to seek him out with her brothers watching her. The pressure to accept Lanyon's proposal was growing. Another beating had left her weak and nauseous. Hidden by her gown, her back and arms were a mass of bruises.

Today was Sunday. This afternoon Lanyon was coming to the Dolphin and Reuban expected to make the wedding arrangements. The thought brought Meriel a return of queasiness as she entered the church for the morning service. She hoped the Lovedays would be in attendance, although they usually attended the service in Joshua Loveday's principal parish of Trewenna church in the next valley.

Throughout the service she felt Lanyon's frog-like eyes on her. The church was decorated with holly, and a nativity scene was laid on a table by the pulpit. Meriel was wrapped in a thick cloak against the cold but she could not stop trembling. Fate was overtaking her. She had staked everything on St John being smitten by her surrender.

In her misery, the sermon was a jumble of incoherent words to her. There was not a muscle in her body which was not sore from Reuban's beating. It was hard to breathe without agony tearing across her bruised ribs.

Hatred festered towards her family, Lanyon and also St John. The way he had used her had made her feel cheap. His abuse had been the greatest of all and she vowed to make him pay for what he had done. At the last moment she had protested against his complete possession of her. His strength overpowered her struggles. There had been no tenderness. She was just another woman to him. He should have been her saviour; instead she was again forsaken.

Her breathing became faster until she panted like a hind at bay. Images blurred and distorted before her eyes. Lanyon's figure across the aisle seemed to loom towards her: his bulging eyes leering, his hands reaching to paw at her body. She was going to be sick. Her stomach lurched in a spasm as she pushed her way to the end of the pew and ran to the door. Outside she leaned shakily on a gravestone. Her eyes refocused and the engraved words 'Repent Thee Sinners' made her cry out in despair. Frantically she gulped for air as her senses again swam and her knees buckled. Her brow struck the corner of the gravestone as she crumpled on the grass.

The acrid stench of burned feathers stung her nostrils and she gasped and opened her eyes. She was in the kitchen of the Dolphin. Sal, Reuban and her brothers were ringed around her like avenging gargoyles.

'Why are you putting yourself through all this, Meriel?' Sal said, her voice trembling with distress. 'You'd always aimed high in marriage. Thadeous Lanyon is a wealthy man.'

'He be old and repulsive.'

'He can give you everything you ever wanted,' Reuban bellowed.

'You'd turn me into a whore for your own greedy ends.'

Reuban raised his hand to strike her. Sal interceded. 'Beating won't solve anything.' Hands on hips, she regarded the pale face of her daughter. 'You'd be honestly wed. And it be more than time.'

Meriel never cried but now she burst into tears. Sal ordered the men from the room. 'I'll make her see reason.'

'This has to be settled, child.' Impatience harshened her tone.

'It would be worse than whoring.'

Sal snorted. 'Rather late in the day for that excuse, my girl. This bain't the first time you've been sick this week. Or tearful. Tell me the truth, girl.'

A worm of fear wriggled in Meriel's gut.

Sal gripped her hair and jerked her head back, her face bleak with fury. 'There were no bloody cloths of yours to be washed this month. If the sickness didn't also tell me, there are other signs a mother knows. They are in your face. Who is the father of your bairn, Meriel?'

The last was said quietly but the words hovered in the air with menace.

'There has been no man.' The fear rose up, threatening to stifle her.

'None that we've been aware of unless it be Adam Loveday. He be at sea. You'll be wed to Lanyon soon as can be arranged. Time enough to convince him and the community that the child came early. There'll be no shame brought to this family.'

Meriel held her mother's stare without flinching. There had been moments she feared she could be with child. In her determination to shape her own destiny she had refuted it, blaming the beatings for the lack of her usual bleeding.

'Adam was betrothed on his last leave. Do you take me for a fool?'

'Aye, but it was sudden like, and not of his own choosing. Not from the way he were looking at you.'

The now familiar nausea bubbled up from her stomach and she lurched forward. Sal shoved a chipped pottery bowl under her head.

When she pushed the bowl away, she said hollowly, 'It wasn't Adam Loveday.' She burst into tears. 'It was St John. He forced himself on me. I were too shamed to speak out. His sort don't wed the likes of us, you've said so yourself.'

Clem slammed open the door. 'I heard all that. St John will wed her or die. Lanyon is no fool. He won't pay money to a family who foist a bastard on him.'

Sal rounded on Meriel. 'You and your damned high-and-mighty notions. I dare say you led him on. But what be done can't be undone.'

'It'll be sorted, Ma,' Clem vowed, and strode out of the kitchen, yelling for his father.

'Get to your room, girl,' Sal ordered. 'No good will come of this. No good at all.'

St John trotted along the country lanes from Fowey. It was an hour past dawn and he was drowsy after being turfed from Judith Kempe's bed. Frost coated the hedgerows and skeletal branches of the trees, the sky a threatening grey haze mottled with sulphurous patches. There was an eerie absence of birdsong. The biting December wind made him shiver and he pulled the collar of his greatcoat higher. With little else to do of an evening, he frequently visited Judith at Fowey. She knew how to soothe a man's spirits. Judith was several years older than he, and had been his mistress for a year. She was a widow, well dressed and discreet, giving St John set evenings when he may call upon her.

He disliked these early morning rides but he had abandoned his pursuit of Meriel. That look in her eyes had alarmed him, but perversely it had also excited him. She was a dangerous minx. Having taken her, he should have long forgotten her. Why did her wildness stimulate him in such a way which made him hunger for her? She had been no compliant conquest. That was what made her different. The wench still had the power to rouse his desire.

The memory of possessing her made his recent nights with Judith pale into insignificance. Judith was too eager to please. While that was gratifying, it left an unfulfilled yearning to be appeased. If it had not been for Meriel's brutish brothers he would have sought the girl out. But Clem was capable of breaking every bone in his body. Even that fear could not shake the need to tame and dominate Meriel. Perhaps he had been a fool to deprive himself of so much pleasure. After all, Clem was nothing but a common fisherman, illiterate and uncouth.

An image of Meriel standing on the headland rock, her expression sultry and seductive, heated his blood. By God he would have her! She was worth the danger. He could outwit the Sawles. He savoured a feeling of triumph as in his imagination he tamed Meriel's wildness, hearing her call out his name in the throes of passion.

Slowly through his daydreams filtered the awareness of danger. It began with a prickle in his neck, then spread to a writhing within his stomach. He huddled further in his greatcoat, and pulled his tricorn low over his eyes. Ahead figures detached themselves from the hedgerow. St John withdrew his pistol from the saddle holster. There was something about the attitude of these men which was menacing. They were not walking on their way to work, but were stationary and spread across the road. Their hats were low over their eyes and woollen mufflers were wrapped around their mouths.

His spine tingled with the growing awareness of danger. He decided to wheel Prince around and gallop away. As he turned the hunter's neck, Clem and Harry Sawle appeared out of the hedgerow ahead of him. Clem was holding a blunderbuss which he aimed at St John's head.

'Drop your pistol, Loveday,' Reuban Sawle demanded from behind him.

The chill was chased from St John's body by a rush of hot stinging fear. He glanced at the two groups of men, judging whether he could make a dash for it. Reuban held two pistols. Harry was uncoiling a bullwhip.

'What is the meaning of this?' St John blustered. He raised the pistol, pointing it at Clem, convinced that Reuban would not risk him shooting his son. The other men he vaguely recognised as Sawle cousins from Polperro.

'Don't be a fool, Loveday,' Reuban warned.

Harry flung out his arm and suddenly the whip coiled around St John's waist. A sharp jerk dragged him sideways in the saddle. Two men snatched at Prince's bridle and two more pulled him to the ground. The pistol was knocked from his gauntleted fingers with a cudgel.

'This is an outrage, Sawle,' St John gasped. 'You won't get away with it.' A fist slammed into his stomach, doubling him over.

'You do right by us and we'll do right by you.'

'To hell with you,' he grunted through his pain.

Two kicks, to his kidneys and groin, robbed him of speech. Reuban stood over him, his feet planted either side of St John's head.

'Meriel be carrying your child.' A boot thudded into his ribs. 'Even a Loveday won't bring shame on us and ours. You will wed her.'

Through the red mist of pain St John felt real terror. These men were capable of killing him. 'My father will never permit the marriage,' he managed to gasp.

'It bain't him we're asking,' Reuban sneered. 'We got us a parson. With witnesses it will all be legal.'

Clem pushed the wide barrel of the blunderbuss in front of his face. 'You know the choices.'

Chapter Thirteen

The ceremony was performed in a freezing church by a parson who could scarcely stand, he was so fortified with brandy. Each vow from St John was forced out at the prod of a pistol to his ribs. Meriel's own voice trembled, not with fear but with excitement at the temerity of her actions. She knew the Loveday family would not easily accept her. Neither did she care. She had their name and as wife to Edward's heir she would have the position she had always craved.

Their names were entered in the parish register with Clem and cousin Roland making their mark as witnesses. An hour later they had been escorted to Roland's tithe cottage on the outskirts of Squire Penwithick's estate. St John, still with a pistol levelled at him, had been forced up the stairs and the door of a bedchamber locked behind the bridal couple.

Clem stood outside the door and jeered, 'You can take your pleasure with her or not, makes no difference. As a married couple you'll spend your first night together. The child will be proof that you bedded her.'

Imprisoned and humiliated, St John flung himself away from Meriel to glare out of the window. Meriel understood his anger. She had achieved her heart's desire to be wedded to a gentleman and was prepared to make the best of it.

'I be sorry this has come to pass. I kept being sick in the mornings and Ma guessed my trouble.'

St John did not answer, his resentment swathing the room. She lit the fire, which had been set in the grate, from the single candle provided for them. Her stare kept hovering between St John and the double bed which dominated the room. The faded patchwork quilt looked grubby. It had been Roland's parents' bed, both of whom had died in it, and her cousin had not married. Sal had prepared the room but, after witnessing the ceremony, had returned with Reuban to the Dolphin.

The sight of the bed made Meriel nervous and she viewed it with distaste. St John had forced himself on her in the stable and given her no pleasure. Now her husband had total rights over her and she wondered if she could bear such intimacy. An alternative life was also unendurable. Sal would have cast her out and even to save herself from living off the Parish she could not have wed Thadeous Lanyon. The mere thought of his body lying next to her brought another rush of nausea to her throat.

She swallowed it with difficulty. Far better to have wed St John. He at least was young and good-looking. If she had to bear his passion to reap the rewards as his wife then she would not shirk her duty. Once their son was born, her power would be supreme. Until then she still had to be accepted by his family. And from his manner now, also by St John himself.

She removed her cloak. Underneath she was wearing her Sunday best scarlet skirt with its green and white underskirt. The bodice was low cut. Since her pregnancy her breasts had become larger and were pushed high by her corset. She poured herself and her husband each a tankard of ale from the pitcher left for them. There was also bread and cheese for them to eat.

Before handing St John his tankard, she pulled the pins from her hair and fluffed it out around her shoulders. Her beauty and body were her only assets; she would use them to her advantage. She pressed the tankard into his hands and sat on the edge of the bed.

'I know you must hate me. That is what is so hard to bear. I thought you cared for me. You were so kind when Pa beat me. He's beaten me several times since to tell him who fathered my child. I was hoping you would come to me. I was frightened. Pa wanted to kill me and the bastard I carried. Ma stopped him.' She rolled back the white sleeve of her blouse and held out her purple mottled arm. He did not even glance at it.

'Ay, you are right to hate me,' she murmured. 'I was nothing to you. Your words of devotion were false. They meant nothing.' Her temper surfaced as her own indignation and pain at his treatment overrode her intention to be meek. 'You saw me as a whore and that is how you used me. Damn you! I did not make this child alone. Did I not beg you to stop? You would not heed me. Now we both must suffer the consequences.'

At her accusations he rounded on her. She recoiled from St John's torrent of abuse. He cursed her family, vowing vengeance upon them. As she heard it all, her colour mounted dangerously high.

'No trick was too low for you to use to seduce me,' he spat. 'By some unholy witch's trick you knew I would visit that night. That's why you brazenly bathed in the kitchen, knowing I would see you. You planned it all.'

That he had spied on her bath was something she had not known, and it infuriated her. 'Lecher! How dare you spy on me, then accuse me of setting out to trap you? If your brains were anywhere but in your groin I would still be a virgin.'

The tankard was still half full and in her fury, she flung the contents in his face. It darkened his brown hair and dripped down his nose and chin on to his stock.

'Bitch!' His hand shot out, striking her cheek, and she fell to one side on the bed.

In an instant she sprang upright, and her hand had returned his slap with such force he staggered back against the wall. Her body followed the impetus of her hand and her eyes blazed. She had taken too many beatings from Reuban to have her spirit broken by her husband.

St John grabbed her wrists as she struck out at him a second time. He forced them down. Both he and Meriel were breathing heavily. In her struggle her blouse had slid off her shoulder and exposed several of the bruises from Reuban's last beating. St John stared at them and then into her eyes. Some of the tension left him.

She remained still, holding his glittering gaze with proud defiance. Subtly his expression changed. She was close enough to feel his arousal and knew that despite his anger and resentment that he still desired her. The power of that knowledge was exhilarating.

Her lips parted. If he made love to her, he could not seek a means to put aside their marriage. He appeared to be fighting his emotions, but his eyes had darkened. She swayed against him, her breasts pressed provocatively against his chest. When he inhaled sharply, her voice was seductive. 'St John, do not hate me. I am as much a victim of my brothers as you.'

A barely perceptible shudder passed through him and his heavy-lidded gaze was hungry upon her breasts. She knew he was going to kiss her. She had won.

Their lips were a finger's breadth apart when Clem coughed harshly on the far side of the door. St John tensed and stepped back from her. 'I will not be tricked a second time. My father shall see that this is no marriage. Your brothers can lock us in here until kingdom come but I will not consummate our marriage.'

He sat down on the rag rug and turned his back on Meriel. He steeled himself to blot out her movements. The bed creaked as she lay down. 'Good night, husband. It is your choice that you do not spend tonight in our bed. Our marriage is legal. The floor must be hard and cold. Come let me warm you.'

St John groaned. Her words were torture. His senses were tuned to the smell and presence of her. She had not undressed but in his mind he vividly recalled the perfection of her nakedness. Was she witch or siren? Whatever she was, she would be his damnation if he surrendered to his need for her. His father had accused him of weakness. Tonight he would be strong. It was lies. They were not married. He would not allow his lust to jeopardise his freedom.

It was no jubilant wedding party which arrived at Trevowan the next day. The Sawle men trudged in silence each side of two riders on the horse. Meriel, at Reuban's insistence, was riding pillion behind St John on his gelding. He sat stiff-backed, holding himself away from her figure.

Her husband had not looked at her since Clem had unlocked the cottage door and ordered them to mount Prince.

Clem smirked. 'Whole village knows Meriel's been missing these two days. They'll draw their own conclusions when you ride through Penruan together.'

'My family will cast her out and you will be thrown in gaol for abduction. You have overreached yourselves.'

'Your family will accept her,' Reuban snarled. 'Otherwise you'll be found washed up in Penruan harbour. I don't make idle threats.'

The murderous eyes were without mercy. St John knew he was beaten. He leaned towards Meriel, his whisper harsh. 'You will get no joy of this, madam, that I promise.'

That threat did not trouble Meriel. She was Mistress St John Loveday and carrying Edward Loveday's grandchild. Nothing could change that.

They entered the main hall at Trevowan. When St John tried to seek out his father, Reuban stopped him. At the sound of voices Aunt Elspeth limped from the parlour.

'Where the devil have you been these last days? Up to no good, I warrant.' Her gaze scanned the group and suspicion hardened her face. 'What is this intrusion, nephew? Why are these people here? If they have business Isaac Nance will see them at his cottage.'

Reuban Sawle dragged off his battered slouch hat and cuffed Clem's arm for him to follow suit. 'It be a matter of family business, ma'am. You'd be wise to summon Mr Loveday.'

'I am no one's lackey.' Her withering glare fastened on Reuban and his family.

St John cleared his throat, his expression as stricken as a man awaiting the gallows drop. 'Aunt, it would be as well if you informed Father we are here. I was married to Meriel Sawle yesterday.'

'What knavery is this?' Elspeth shrilled, jabbing her stick at St John and Reuban Sawle. 'It must be a lie. A wicked lie.'

'Go fetch Mr Loveday,' Reuban became surly, addressing Elspeth as abruptly as he would Sal.

Elspeth's cane descended upon his head. She was quivering with rage. 'How dare you come into my house making demands?'

Meriel hid a smile behind her hand at the way the old dragon was putting her father in his place. As yet Elspeth's wrath had not descended on her. She was prepared for it and thanks to Sal had an ace up her sleeve. She surveyed the hall, noting the marble floor and large crystal chandelier. There were some pretty gilded chairs along one wall and a heavy carved chest which looked so old it should have been relegated to the attic fifty years ago. She had heard the landed gentry liked to hang on to their old relics. There was no accounting for their strange ways. You would think with all their wealth they would follow the latest fashions.

Red-faced with anger, Elspeth picked up a silver bell and rang it. Jenna Biddick appeared from the kitchen and yelped in fear at encountering so many incensed expressions.

'Kindly inform Mr Loveday that there is a matter requiring his attention,' Elspeth ordered. 'Then summon Isaac, Dick Nance and Jasper Fraddon.'

'Bain't no call for that,' Reuban declared.

'Do as I say, Jenna.' Elspeth limped to a chair in the hall and sat down with both hands resting on the silver top of her cane. When her haughty glare alighted upon Meriel it was cold and hostile.

A lesser woman would have quaked. Meriel did not lower her gaze. They were to be left standing – treated as insubordinates. It was one insult Meriel was prepared to let pass. The old harridan would not intimidate her. Had she not been the wronged party?

At the sound of Edward Loveday's approach, Elspeth rose. 'We will adjourn to your study, brother. This is a grave day for Trevowan.'

Edward frowned as he regarded his son. At seeing Meriel, the lines furrowed deeper across his brow. He stepped back to allow the Sawle family to file into his study. Elspeth seated herself by the fire and Edward stood by his desk. The Sawle men shuffled uneasily in Edward's presence. St John stepped forward, his pale face working with pent-up emotion.

'Truly, I had no choice. You have to believe me, sir. They overpowered me and threatened me at gunpoint.'

Edward glared at Reuban. 'These are serious allegations. I could have you thrown in gaol for threatening my son.'

Reuban tipped back his head, his eyes hard with no trace of servility, though Edward was respected in the village. 'Your son was married to our Meriel two days past. He dishonoured her and she carries your grandchild. We have righted the wrong done to us.'

'Under such conditions the marriage would not be lawful,' Edward observed.

'It were all legal. We made sure of that. Service was performed by Mr Lugg at St Catherine's church at Polmasryn.' Reuban stuck his thumbs in his belt. 'It but needs for you to recognise the union and we will go peaceably.'

'Do not threaten me, Sawle,' Edward raged. 'You have used force upon my son. For that I could have you arrested.'

'Ay, you could. If you want a scandal to set Cornwall afire with gossip. Meriel be pretty enough to turn any man's head. Thadeous

93

Lanyon has offered for her. She couldn't go to him bearing another man's child. A Loveday child.'

'A scandal is inevitable,' Elspeth retorted. 'No Loveday would marry out of their class. And the manner of it will make us laughing stocks. This is blackmail. Throw them out, Edward. And that strumpet with them.'

Meriel bit her lip to stem a retort. She had resolved to be meek and allow the men to settle the matter. To be drawn into an argument with Elspeth Loveday would show her in a bad light. She must impress Edward Loveday with her humility and dignity.

She saw Reuban glower at St John's aunt but his words were addressed to Edward Loveday. 'Your son bain't the first to marry below his class. Sir Horace Prideaux married an actress, and her once mistress to a royal duke. There's no scandal attached to Meriel's name. She'll bring no shame to you or yours.'

'I've never heard such—' Elspeth began. A sharp glance from Edward silenced her.

'What have you to say, St John?' He rounded on his son. 'Does this woman carry your child?'

With Clem's threat hammering in his brain, St John had no choice but to put on a brave face. 'It is possible.'

Elspeth banged her cane on the floor, working herself up into a fury. 'That strumpet has used the oldest trick there is to snare a rich man.'

Meriel swallowed her anger. One day she would be mistress of Trevowan; she could afford to be magnanimous. When she faced Edward Loveday tears formed in her eyes. 'Our love was wrong. The consequences fearful. But St John was man enough to stand by me, knowing he would face your anger.'

Elspeth snorted. 'With a gun at his head, it sounds like. I will not stand for it.'

'Can you not be merciful?' Impassioned, Meriel threw herself at Elspeth's feet.

'Nay, there be no need for that,' Reuban said, shifting uncomfortably.

Meriel knew men were ill at ease with a woman's hysterics and used them to her advantage. Her cheeks were awash with tears but as she stared into Elspeth Loveday's eyes her own were glittering. In a voice so low only Elspeth could hear, she murmured, 'Goodwife Warne were cousin to my ma. They had no secrets from each other before Goody Warne died.'

The flicker of shock in the older woman's eyes was barely perceptible. Sal had known Elspeth would create problems. To protect her daughter she had broken an oath of secrecy.

With surprising strength Elspeth shook Meriel's clinging form away

94

and stood up. 'Edward, I leave you to judge the matter. I will not stand for a scandal.' She leaned more heavily than usual on her cane as she limped from the room.

The silence which followed her departure was weighted.

Edward cleared his throat. 'I cannot say this day has brought me anything but disappointment and pain. In the eyes of God St John and this woman appear wed.'

'They are that. It were all done legal,' Reuban stated.

'Then I have no choice but to accept the marriage. Though whether my son's conduct makes him fitting to remain my heir is another matter. That we will discuss later.'

He glared at Reuban. 'It will be announced that your daughter and my son eloped and married without my permission. Meriel may visit her family whenever she wishes. It is inconceivable however for you to expect to be received here. Or to expect any favours or remuneration from this match.'

'We but sought to protect her honour,' Reuban growled, 'though Lanyon had offered a handsome sum of money to wed her before this disgrace befell us.'

'There will be no payment from me, or further communication with your family. You will agree to my conditions, or I shall disinherit St John, and your daughter will find herself homeless and married to a pauper.' Edward walked to the door and opened it. 'Now get out.'

He waited until the Sawle men left before addressing the couple. 'The room next to St John's chamber will be made into a parlour for you. You may join the family at meal times but not otherwise unless invited. It will be for you, St John, to teach your wife the social graces. I will ask Elspeth to sort through the attic for dresses which can be made suitable for your wife to wear. A dressmaker will be engaged to do the alterations.'

'Sir, now I am wed, my allowance—'

'Since you have no care but for your own gratification, it is time you learned the truth. Trevowan is heavily mortgaged and so is the yard. Had you chosen a wealthy bride you could have saved the estate and yard. Now, because of your actions, we could be bankrupt.'

St John paled and staggered back. Edward advanced on him, his fury erupting. 'You will receive only what money you have worked for. To that end you will concentrate half your time on the estate. The three fields by the river will be put under the plough and sown by your own labour. Whatever profits they produce will provide your income.'

Meriel was aghast. Edward turned to her. He remained angry but his manner was cool and courteous. 'Madam, you will at all times deport yourself in a manner befitting a Loveday. My sister is mistress here: she will inform you of your duties. Extra help is always needed in the buttery and preserving room. They are tasks the Loveday women have always performed with diligence.'

There was no warmth in either of the men's faces. This was not the riches and comfort Meriel had envisaged.

Chapter Fourteen

Adam returned to Plymouth in April. Torrential rain lashed the deck as they entered Plymouth Sound and the grey stone wall of the Citadel was a ghostly outline through the gloom. The usually noisy and bustling quayside was subdued. Even the seagulls had ceased their cries. Only the disgruntled orders of an officer on a nearby frigate, driving the soaking sailors to stow the cargo, rose above the drumming of the rain. It was a gloomy welcome.

Chilled after his last watch, which had ended with their docking, Adam made for a tavern and a warming measure of rum. His leave was short and he was eager to return to Trevowan and inspect the work done on the *Pegasus* in his absence.

There was no slackening to the rain as he left the quayside of Devonport. The streets were all but deserted. Those abroad were hunched in greatcoats or oilskins, heads bent low and paying no heed to their neighbours. The gutters had become streams to be waded through or leapt over: a dead bird was washed along with rotted cabbage stalks, frayed bits of rope and indistinguishable harbour debris. A few beggars squatted in the porch of a church, and two dogs, their ribs showing under their coats, fought over a dead rat. The narrow streets bordered by tall stone warehouses were dark and forbidding. High above Adam's head a windlass danced like a hanged man from the gables of a chandler's shop.

Adam turned a corner, leaving the quay to enter a street of shops.

'Buy a wooden doll for your daughter, sir. A horse for your son.' A man with a wooden leg rose up from out of the doorway of a derelict building. Adam ignored him. The voice was harsh with pleading, 'Then for the love of God, good sir, spare a penny for my wife and children. I lost my leg at sea in the King's navy. No one will employ me.'

Something in his piteous tone moved Adam and he drew a few coppers from his pocket and tossed them to the old tar.

'Bless you, sir.' The man hobbled forward. Two small heads with hollow cheeks emerged out of a threadbare blanket to stare up at Adam. 'Why, it be Mr Loveday!'

Adam tipped back his tricorn where water trickled down before his eyes. The voice was familiar but at first he did not recognise the man. When he shifted on his peg leg, Adam exclaimed, 'Seth Wakeley!

I am sorry to see you in such straitened circumstances.'

'Who wants to employ a one-legged man? I look after the two youngest kids while the wife works in the laundry with the elder girl.'

Adam was shocked at his appearance. Seth could not be more than his late twenties but was as haggard and stooped as an old man. His once-muscular body was thin as a hoe. 'You had four children.'

'Nipper died while I was in hospital. Missus got turned out of our lodgings in St Austell and had to live on the street. He got a fever. There will be another arriving in two months.' He shook his head. 'I don't know what's to become of us.'

It saddened Adam to see Seth reduced to such penury. He had been a jovial sailor and was a skilled carpenter. In his spare time he had whittled toys for his children out of odd pieces of wood. He saw one of the waifs clutching a wooden horse. The child's cheeks were flushed with fever and he began to cough.

Seth turned in anguish and picked up the child. There was a tear in his eye as the wracking cough refused to subside. 'You don't know of any work do you, sir?'

At Adam's embarrassed silence, Seth hobbled back to the shelter of the doorway. 'I shouldn't have asked. Not from you. You saved me life. That be debt enough.'

'Where are you living?'

'In a derelict warehouse which don't have much of a roof. Sometimes I can earn a few pence helping out on market day or selling a toy I've carved from a discarded piece of wood.'

Adam wanted to help Seth. Before his disability he had been obliging and hard-working. Adam did not like to see a man like that reduced to begging. He picked up a wooden horse which was exquisitely carved. The face was lifelike and the muscles defined on its legs and body. 'I cannot promise but there could be work at our family shipwright's yard.'

'Anything would be a godsend, sir.'

'The yard is up the river from Fowey. There's a cottage needs repairing. If you were to put it in order, I am sure my father would not expect much in the way of rent. I must speak to him first. Where can I send word at the end of the week?'

'You can leave word at the laundry in the next street where my wife works.'

'I will let you know one way or the other. The decision must be my father's.' He took a silver crown from his pocket and flicked it to Seth. 'Get the child some tincture for his cough and some hot food for your family.'

Adam turned down a side street to an inn where he intended to hire a horse for his return to Trevowan. As he approached, there were raised angry voices from within. The press gang of eight men and an officer emerged into the street. Two semi-conscious men were being dragged between them, their legs buckled under them and knees scraping on the cobbles. One was singing drunkenly, barely aware of his predicament, the other was writhing and struggling.

'No. No!' he sobbed. 'Me ma sent me to bring me gran to live with them. Gran be ill. Needs help. Ma! Pa! Help me!'

It was a voice Adam recognised. What was Ned Holman doing alone in Plymouth? He was the son of Dan and Betty Holman, tenant farmers on Trevowan. Although over thirty he had the mind of a child. Ned was so slow-witted he would be more danger on a ship than use.

'Looks like we have got ourselves a crybaby here. It's the navy which needs your help,' a ferret-faced sailor sniggered, and struck Ned across the head with a cudgel.

Adam intervened. 'That man is of no use to you. Let him free.'

The officer's face was shielded by the peak of his bicorn hat pulled low on his brow to protect him from the rain. Now the man's head shot up, his whole manner stiff with affront.

'Who the devil . . . ? By God, *Loveday*. This is none of your concern.' Lieutenant Francis Beaumont glared at him.

'That man comes from our estate. He is a simpleton and given to fits. If you had looked at him properly you would have noticed his withered hand.'

'He'll still have his uses,' Beaumont snapped. 'There are three other frigates in port and the choice of pickings is slim. We lost eighteen men on the last voyage.'

Beaumont was one of the few officers who relished the duty of press officer. The lieutenant was still out of favour with Captain Rawcliffe and his leave had been curtailed until the press gang had raised their full complement of men.

'You cannot in decency take this man.' Adam was angry and hostile. He hated the press gangs and the dirty work they did. It was an unacceptable face of naval life, but, if a ship was not to sail short-handed, a necessary evil. 'There is another week before we sail. He is unfit for duty and a danger to the crew.'

'You take too much upon yourself, Lieutenant Loveday,' sneered Beaumont. 'On your way, men.'

Adam blocked their passage. The rain had stopped but its droplets ran off the sailors' hair on to their necks and faces. 'A man with the falling sickness is a curse on a voyage. Do you want to risk that?'

The sailors looked uneasy. Beaumont was senior to Adam and capable of making their lives miserable if they disobeyed him. Yet still they hesitated.

Beaumont was red-faced with anger. 'I'll have the lot of you whipped for insubordination. Take him along.'

He swivelled to face Adam, his sword half drawn. 'Stand aside.'

99

Adam stood his ground, his own hand resting on his sword hilt. Ned was a part of Trevowan. Adam had a responsibility to protect his tenants, especially someone like Ned. 'The man is unfit for duty.'

'Are you questioning my authority? Damn you, Lieutenant Loveday. It is time you answered for your insolence.'

The sword hissed from Beaumont's scabbard. Adam flicked his cloak over his shoulder and drew his sword. A weak sun was pushing its way through the clouds. The first clash of steel juddered along Adam's arm. He parried the lunge and countered. The tip of his sword flashed past Beaumont's neck, slicing the thick collar of his uniform. Beaumont swore and sidestepped. Adam was faster. His opponent's blade could get nowhere near him.

Again Adam's blade danced lethally close, this time ripping Beaumont's epaulettes.

'You bastard. You'll pay—' His threat was cut short as he slithered on the wet cobbles and made an awkward recovery.

One of the sailors laughed.

There was a manic gleam in Beaumont's eyes as he attempted an impassioned lunge. Adam sidestepped, twisting his wrist to turn Beaumont's sword aside. His own blade hovered against his opponent's heart. It had been an unevenly matched contest.

'Throw down your sword!' Adam demanded. 'You wouldn't last two minutes if you drew this against an officer in battle. Though I dare say it impresses the ladies and you have used it to bully many a civilian.'

He signalled for Ned to be released. The simpleton was gibbering with fright and there was foam at the corners of his mouth. As the press gang released him, his body landed on the ground and jerked spasmodically.

'Stand back.' Adam knelt at Ned's side. Remembering how he had once seen Betty Holman deal with one of her son's fits, he checked that his tongue had not rolled back down his throat, then thrust the hilt of his dagger between Ned's teeth.

The superstitious sailors backed away with horror on their faces. More people were on the streets now, some of the older citizens complaining of yet another drunken brawl and cursing the disruptions brought to their town by the navy.

'We want none of his likes on our ship,' declared the ferret-faced man.

Beaumont stood up. The white linen breeches of his uniform were smeared with black rainwater from the runnels. He scowled at the press gang. 'I want ten more men before nightfall. There will be no grog or leave until they are chained and on board.'

The sailors dragged the remaining press-ganged victim away. Beaumont snarled at Adam. 'I won't forget this, Loveday.'

Adam watched him march stiffly away and enter another tavern further down the street. Ned groaned, his face cut where he had fallen. Adam took a hip flask of rum from his pocket and pressed it to the man's mouth.

'Drink it, it will help revive you.'

Ned coughed and knocked away the flask. He sat up, staring round in wide-eyed fear.

'They have gone, Ned. You are all right. I will see you get home safely.'

With a loud sob the man flung his arms round Adam's knees and wept. Gently disengaging Ned, Adam was aware of several grinning faces peering from the tavern windows, drawn by the commotion of the fight.

He helped Ned to his feet. 'Did you come into Plymouth by cart?'

Ned nodded. 'Ma told me to get Gran. Gran's been ill. She's gonna live with us now.'

'I will come with you. It will save me hiring a horse to return to Trevowan. At least the rain has stopped. It would not do your gran any good riding in such weather.'

Ned gripped his arm. 'You won't tell Ma what happened? It'd upset her.'

Adam knew Dan and Betty were strict Methodists and didn't hold with drinking. From Ned's unsteady gait he had drunk more than his fair share before the press gang took him.

'I will not mention it, but I want your promise you will not go in the waterside taverns of Plymouth again.'

Although Ned nodded vigorously, Adam doubted he could keep a promise for long. Like the child he was, he would soon forget the dangers.

Adam arrived at Trevowan when the family were at their evening meal. The great hallway was lit by two candle sconces, the great crystal chandelier used only when guests were present. The familiar smell of beeswax, faint cooking smells and woodsmoke from the fires were like a welcoming embrace. He put a finger to his lips to silence Winnie Fraddon, who was carrying a large soup tureen into the dining room. 'Give me that,' he said, taking the tureen. 'I want to surprise them.'

'Anyone for soup,' he announced. The surprise was turned upon him at seeing Meriel dressed in blue silk and seated beside St John. Inadvertently he started and the hot soup splashed on to his hand. He hurried to the table to pass it to the maid, Jenna, to serve. Meriel looked haunted at his entrance. 'Good Lord, what are you doing dining here?'

Elspeth's fork clattered to the table. St John's surprise turned to a supercilious grin. His father leapt to his feet and slapped his younger son affectionately on the back, ignoring his puzzled question.

'You were expected last week. Thank God you are safe and well. We have had some bad storms this spring.'

'Gales off the Scilly Isles blew us off course.' Adam skirted the table to kiss Aunt Elspeth's cheek.

'Bad weather for hunting,' she observed, patting his hand. 'Glad you have returned safe. But your coat is wet and you have come into the dining room without shoes.'

'They were muddy, Aunt. I will change after I have eaten. I am famished.'

The initial greetings over, he crossed to the blazing fire in the black marble fireplace to warm himself as Jenna set a place for him at the candlelit table. No one had answered his question about Meriel and the atmosphere was strained. He took a moment to settle his own composure, then with a lift of his brow he turned to Meriel. She was not looking at him and fiddled with her knife.

St John gave a dry laugh. 'Bit of a shock for you finding Meriel here, I warrant. Had an eye on her your last visit before Lisette ruined your chances. Have you no congratulations for us?' St John studied Adam with a mocking smile. 'We were wed last December.'

'Married . . .' Adam stared at Meriel. There was a blush creeping up her neck into her cheeks. He kept his own face impassive. So much for Meriel's declarations of love. She had betrayed him and chosen the richer brother. His temper soared and bile rose to his throat. It wasn't enough that St John would one day have Trevowan and the boatyard. He had stolen the woman he loved. What amazed him was that his father had permitted the wedding.

He looked askance at Edward, who, guessing his unspoken question, shrugged.

St John gave a brittle laugh. 'Did I not say that the better man would win this beauty's love?'

'So it was rivalry which was behind your conduct.' Elspeth pursed her lips. 'The fool got her with child and the Sawles forced him to wed her.'

That explained much. But it was a double treachery. Meriel must have accepted St John's advances within a month of his sailing, Adam calculated. He studied them both. Meriel was sullen. A sign of her displeasure. St John behind his bravado looked ill at ease, and glanced nervously at his father. Edward was concentrating on breaking off a piece of bread. Only a vein pulsating at his brow showed his anger and displeasure. This marriage had caused fireworks and the aftermath was still unsettled.

Adam clicked his heels together and bowed with exaggerated formality to Meriel. 'Congratulations. May this marriage bring you both the happiness you deserve.'

Understanding his mockery, Meriel lifted her gaze to bore into his. He was unable to hide his contempt. She paled and fainted into St John's arms. His twin flushed and apologised.

'Take her to your room,' Elspeth commanded. 'Her manners still leave a great deal to be desired. One does not make oneself the centre of attention at the dining table.'

Adam forced himself to appear normal. He answered his father's questions, albeit rather stiffly, and each mouthful of food was like dry sand to swallow.

He was convinced that Meriel did not love St John. And he despised his brother whose spite and weakness had so compromised their family. He only wished Meriel's betrayal was not so hard to stomach. He saw her now for the calculating creature that she truly was. The couple deserved each other.

Chapter Fifteen

'Once *Pegasus* is seaworthy I shall leave the navy, sir.' Adam faced his father in the office of the shipwright's yard. 'I have the experience to captain her.'

'You need capital for your first voyage. Unless you intend to wed Lisette sooner than anticipated, and claim her dowry.'

Adam shook his head. He had arrived at the yard early this morning, eager to see the new work on his ship. His father had joined him an hour later. By midday St John had still not appeared. Adam strove to master the anger he felt towards his twin. His temper had been on a short rein since his return to Trevowan. 'When I marry I will have the means to support my wife, not live off her income.'

'Commendable, but how will you raise the capital? With things as they are I cannot help you this year.'

'I could raise a loan using the ship as security. A run or two to Guernsey or France will set me up.'

'Free-trading!' Edward looked pensive. 'You would not be the first Loveday to be involved, but the patrols are more vigilant now. If boarded, the ship will be seized and auctioned. Smuggling is a hanging offence. I cannot give my approval of this venture. Those days are behind us, Adam. Your ship will not be ready for another year. Bide your time. You are better off in the navy until then. The atmosphere here is—'

He broke off and shrugged. His stare was piercing as he regarded Adam. 'You and St John are spoiling for a fight. Is it because of Meriel? Was she the reason for your reluctance to marry Lisette?'

'She had taken my eye. It is St John's manner. His gloating. What has he got to be proud of? Damn him, it was his duty to marry well. If Meriel set her cap at St John then she has got what she deserves. I feel nothing but contempt for the two of them.'

A strong April wind had whipped the river to a dull pewter and the leafless trees added to the air of barrenness. Apart from the *Pegasus* there was only one other boat, a small skiff, in the yard being built.

'Are there no orders on the books, sir? I have never seen the yard so forlorn or forsaken. Does St John do nothing? He must face up to his responsibilities.'

'Since his marriage he is working long hours, spending more time on the estate than here.'

Edward took out the plans of the brigantine and spread them on the table. 'He has not your foresight in matters of the yard. The sea is not in his blood as it is in ours and was in your grandfather's.'

'Yet he will inherit?' The words were punched out as his frustration surfaced. 'If the yard was mine I would—'

He bit off the words. He wanted to help his father, but resented that ultimately it would be St John who reaped the rewards of his labour. Yet why should St John inherit? What did he, Adam, need to do to prove to his father that he was the more worthy heir to the shipwright's yard. 'Sir, do you agree that the yard needs new lifeblood to save it from ruin? Orders for the brigantine have been slow and she is an expensive ship to build. We need a smaller, more popular vessel.'

'Fishing smacks have always been our mainstay.'

'We need something new. The customs men are using a new design of cutter. There are only a few in service at the moment, but they are the fastest vessels I have seen.' His enthusiasm drove him on. 'I have made some rough sketches and calculations. I could draw up plans. The hulls have to be strong to carry an array of canvas and are clinker-built, giving them stability and speed. They can operate in all weathers and the design can be adapted from say forty-five to a possible two hundred tons. They are the vessel for the future.'

'Such potential,' Edward said with keen interest. 'But the cost of such an investment is high. I was relying on orders for the brigantine.'

'These cutters could save the yard.'

'Mumford is a good master shipwright but he has no experience of these vessels.'

'I can build one,' Adam said with confidence. 'I want to save our family business. But I want to be the one who inherits it, not St John.'

'The eldest son always inherits both the estate and business. They have always been bound together.'

Knowing how strict his father could be about family traditions, Adam said with passion, 'And in the past the eldest son has been a shipwright like grandfather and yourself. St John will still have Trevowan. Sir, you have many years ahead of you. We must move ahead with the times. I would see the Loveday yard as the greatest on the south coast.'

'And you believe these cutters will make it so?'

'Am I not prepared to stake my future on it?'

Edward rubbed his chin. 'You spoke as passionately about being a merchant adventurer.'

'Because I thought that was the best I could aspire to. I ask for two or three years to prove to you how important these cutters will become to our yard.'

'I have to consider this. The yard has always supported the estate. That is why they are bound together.'

'St John will bring the yard to ruin. I cannot believe you want that. Grandfather bought more land. Surely Trevowan, managed as a farm, can support itself.'

'I cannot see St John as a gentleman farmer,' Edward declared. 'His marriage is proof of the rivalry between the two of you and the damage it can wreak. St John will never accept these terms.'

'Can you see him making this yard a success?'

'He could have a son who shares our love for the yard.'

Adam could not answer that.

Seeing his anger, Edward conceded. 'I shall bear your ideas in mind. They require more funds than I can raise at the present time. I had to lay off another four men.'

Adam realised his father would not commit himself further. And he had made a promise which had yet to be honoured. 'Ben Mumford told me. It makes this difficult for me to ask, but in Plymouth I met a sailor who served on the *Goliath*. He lost a leg because of an officer's incompetence, and with a wife and four children is reduced to begging on the streets and they are homeless. He's a good carpenter.'

Edward looked wary, prompting Adam to add, 'I said there was a possibility he could have one of the cottages which need repairing. He would do any odd job you asked of him.'

The sound of his father's fingers drumming on the desk was his only reply, then a heavy sigh. 'He is welcome to do up the cottage using any wood in the yard, but as for work . . .' He shook his head. 'I could not take him on when I have laid off men I have employed for years. The only other work available close by is farm labouring. With one leg who will take him on? He is better off in Plymouth.'

'Then let him work on *Pegasus*. We have no one skilled enough to do the gilded carvings on the ship's stern and it will need a figurehead. I will pay his wages. It will be hard to get a finer craftsman than Seth. And if the *Pegasus* is to be the flagship for future orders, everything about her appearance is important.'

Edward regarded his son with a mixture of amusement and exasperation. 'The cottage is there if this carpenter wants it. If he repairs it, and the other buildings damaged by last year's storms, he can live there for a peppercorn rent.'

Adam picked up his tools from the corner of the office but before he could leave, his father delayed him.

'St John's marriage did not please me. At least Meriel's manners have improved and, despite her conduct last night, she knows how to conduct herself in company.' He shook his head sadly. 'Apparently Thadeous Lanyon intended to wed Meriel. Unfortunately last year I raised a one-thousand-pound loan with Lanyon. He has called it in.

107

To meet it I am going to London to arrange another loan.'

'Had this loan anything to do with my legacy and the money needed to build *Pegasus*?'

'I would have repaid that and the interest when you came into that money at twenty-one. And I do not regret the risk.'

'But the legacy is payable in two months.'

'Lanyon wants his money without delay. The estate is also heavily mortgaged.' Edward stood up, stroking his chin as he paced the small room. 'I want an end to the bad feeling between you and St John.'

Adam's anger towards his brother only added to his father's problems.

'Let me draw up some plans for the new cutters before you leave for London. You can also take the plans of the *Pegasus* with you,' Adam insisted. 'Contracts for two such ships will clear your debts.'

'Those plans are your property, not mine.'

'Then I give them to you. I do not want the Loveday yard to founder any more than you.'

'Thank you, Adam. I will take them on the condition that any orders from them must result in a commission for you.' There was a lighter tread to Edward's step as he went to lift the plans from the oak chest. 'We will ride this crisis and emerge triumphant.'

Adam spent the day working on the plans for the cutter. He stopped when the yard ship's bell sounded for the end of the day. He strolled outside to ease the tension in his body from long hours of inactivity. The crimson and gold of the sunset turned the wooden beams of the *Pegasus* to a rosy sheen. Gazing at his ship his tiredness ebbed. In its place was satisfaction and exhilaration. The six gunports along each side showed the vessel's capabilities to defend itself.

He breathed deeply, relishing the smell of the cut wood and the salty tang of the river inlet. It was easy to visualise the *Pegasus* fully rigged, with sails billowing as it ploughed through a distant sea. If he closed his eyes he could feel the power of her beneath him, the quick response of the helm to his hands. To be master of such a ship would be a good life if he was denied the ownership of the yard. But for now he was shackled to the navy as reluctantly as any pressed sailor.

By the time Adam approached the four tithe cottages on the Trevowan estate the moon was bright in the sky. The cottages were built in a crescent shape, with vegetable plots between. Two of the families who lived there, the Nances and the Fraddons, worked in the house and grounds. The other two cottages were rented by the Holman family and the Tonkins, who helped on Trevowan farm. Three generations crowded into the house of Silas and Meg Tonkin. There were their three sons, Paul, Baz and George. Paul had married a woman from Liskeard, Nora, and they had three children.

Paul had left home when they'd married and worked in Wheal Fortune before it closed, along with so many of the tin mines in recent years. His family had moved back to share the cramped cottage with his parents and brothers last year.

Both the Holmans and the Tonkins rented a couple of fields and shared a cow byre, which held two milk cows. They each had three pigsties set further back from the houses. To one end of the cottages was a communal duck pond and each household had its own chicken coop. As Adam was passing, on his way home, a fox was sniffing round one of these, agitating the hens inside.

A door opened, Betty Holman waddled out and, hearing the squawking of the hens, aimed a stone at the fox.

'Ger away, you rotten bugger. Dan get your gun. That blasted fox be at our hens again.' She gave a stifled scream at seeing Adam riding along the track. 'Master Adam, you fair sent my wits abegging. But I be wanting a word with you.'

He waited for her to come closer. Betty was a large woman with a round homely face which had never known beauty. Yet for all her size and plainness she had a caring way which lent dignity to all her actions.

'How can I be of service, Betty?'

'Service you've done already. Ned told us how you saved him. He were took with bad dreams last night, raving and yelling, and it took an age to calm him. I can't thank 'ee enough. Reckon you saved his life and stopped my heart from breaking. I bain't never letting him loose in Plymouth alone again. He'd been drinking, hadn't he? He would'na own to that. But I know he'd been drinking.'

'I cannot say,' Adam soothed. 'He looks a strong man and the press gang . . .' He paused and continued heavily, 'Well, they take any man they can. If Ned had not had that fit, my intervention would probably have come to nothing.'

'You be too modest, Master Adam. You saved my boy's life.'

Adam coughed into his hand to cover his embarrassment at her impassioned tone, then bade her farewell. Aware that the family were to dine with Sir Henry Traherne he galloped the rest of the way home, left Solomon at the stables and hurried to his room to change. The carriage had been brought round to the front of the house and Aunt Elspeth was impatiently pacing the hallway.

'There you are at last. You should have been ready a half-hour past. Get yourself along into the carriage. Your father has disappeared into his study. It is more than body and soul can stand to get the men of this household together at the same time.'

She rapped on Edward's study with her stick. Eventually the three of them were settled in the carriage.

'Drive on, Fraddon,' his father ordered.

'Are St John and Meriel not joining us?' Adam commented. 'Has

109

Roslyn and her family refused to accept her?'

Aunt Elspeth set her lips into a prim line. 'Meriel is not ready for society. Her manners have improved prettily, but they are not yet second nature to her. I will not be embarrassed in front of my friends. Also, she has to learn not to give herself false airs and graces. After the child is born will be time for her to join our family in public.'

Adam fell silent. Since his father did not dispute Elspeth's words, it was clearly their way of punishing the couple. St John would resent having his pleasure curbed and Meriel would not be happy at being excluded from a social gathering. Yet the punishment was light. Many men in his father's position would have disowned his son. None the less, St John had much to do to win his father's favour.

Chapter Sixteen

Traherne Hall was a square, redbrick mansion built in the reign of William and Mary. The casement windows each had carved pediments, and the formal garden of low box hedges was segmented by the straight gravel drive. It was on the outskirts of the small village of Trelynn, whose church was one of Joshua Loveday's parishes. The Traherne estate was twice the size of Trevowan, and a coppice marked the boundaries of the two properties. To reach the hall the Loveday carriage negotiated narrow lanes and entered through ornate gilded iron gates set in a twenty-foot-high brick wall.

Tonight's gathering included the Traherne family, the Lovedays of Trevowan. Joshua and Cecily Loveday, Hannah and Oswald Rabson, and Squire Penwithick and his wife.

Adam was greeted warmly by his friend Henry, now married to Roslyn Druce, but when he would have drawn Adam into conversation about his latest voyage, Roslyn approached with a brittle smile. She clung to her husband's arm and commandeered the conversation towards the improvements she had made to her new home since their marriage.

Adam surveyed the dining room, which still smelt of paint and new plaster. The ceiling had been given a wide plaster border of pink-tinted rosettes, and gilded scrollwork was interlaced between decorative blue plaques depicting Greek gods and goddesses. The family portraits had been removed and replaced with landscapes placed strategically between Corinthian pilasters. Over the fireplace was a carved gilt-framed mirror. The effect of the room was rather too ostentatious for Adam's taste.

'It is most impressive,' he complimented, aware that Roslyn was waiting for his response.

'Ros has plans for the grand saloon which will be begun in the summer,' Henry added as they took their places at the table.

Roslyn made a great show of spreading her ruby taffeta skirts as she took her place at the head of the oval table. Adam had been placed in the centre, three places down from Henry, who continued to bombard him with questions about his last voyage. Henry frequently asked the advice of Oswald on matters of husbandry and the two seemed to have formed a close friendship since Adam was last in Cornwall.

Hannah also kept up a steady conversation with Roslyn and her younger sister, Gwendolyn. When Adam had a chance to intersect her chatter, he said with a laugh, 'Motherhood has not changed you, Hannah. You are more lovely than ever.'

She waved aside his compliment with an impatient gesture. 'I am happier than I have ever been.'

'And how is Davey? I must come and see my new cousin.'

'He thrives, as does the farm.'

'Where you work too hard,' Roslyn observed.

Hannah laughed. 'I am no lady of leisure like yourself, it is true. But I enjoy my work on the farm. The quiet life suits me.'

'Unlike that rakehell brother of yours,' Roslyn said with spite. 'Japhet is the talk of Truro. Lord Fetherington challenged him to a duel over a woman they say. Fortunately Fetherington was persuaded by his friends to apologise to Japhet so no blood was drawn.'

'Japhet cannot be responsible for the wildness of every young buck in town,' Aunt Cecily defended her son. 'He has been told of your return, Adam. We see little of him these days now he has taken rooms in Truro, but he will not miss a chance to visit with you.'

'And how is Peter?' Adam felt prompted to enquire of his youngest cousin, although he had little liking for the youth. 'I had thought him old enough to join such gatherings.'

'He is shy and is so much younger than you all. He feels more comfortable in the company of his books.'

'He is not so shy when it comes to preaching to his betters,' Hannah observed with a brittle laugh. 'The tyke gave Oswald a lecture for not attending church last Sunday because one of the cows was ill. Also he as good as called the young Polglase woman a witch for saving our plough horse when he had colic. And it had taken me all my time to persuade her to help after Aunt Elspeth told us how the girl had cured her mare, Bonnie, and her.'

Adam chuckled. 'And no doubt you sent him away with his ears ringing.'

'Ears ringing! I could have wrung the pious monster's neck,' she had lowered her voice and shot her father a furtive look. 'Papa should be more strict with him. Give me Japhet's carefree ways any day.'

'Adam, you were telling us of your voyage,' Squire Penwithick bellowed along the table. 'I warrant there were adventures, were there not?'

'Do tell us all,' Hannah enthused. 'How many ladies' hearts have your broken? Did you encounter pirates? And the ports . . . Were they exotic?'

'Naval life has none of the glamour you would credit to it,' Adam answered her teasing.

Uncle Joshua also plied him with questions until Roslyn gave a theatrical sigh.

'Really, Henry, one would think nothing of interest had happened in your own life the way you hang on Adam's words.' Her voice rose to dominate the conversation. 'Our marriage was quite the most spectacular event in the county.' This aside was meant for Adam, who had been at sea and had missed the celebrations.

'Indeed, my dear,' Henry said with unusual patience. 'But I doubt Adam would be interested.'

Roslyn gave a superior sniff, 'I dare say it did not cause the sensation of his brother's wedding. And that must have been such a disappointment to you, Mr Loveday, that you did not officiate at your nephew's nuptials.'

Cecily gasped and put her hand to her mouth. Elspeth glared at Roslyn, but her retort was forestalled by Joshua. 'I had the honour of performing the blessing in Trewenna church. I believe you chose not to attend Lady Traherne.

Her smile faltered and she turned to Elspeth. 'Such a pity St John's wife is indisposed this evening. Her condition no doubt. How many months is she? Seven is it?'

'You never did have much of a head for your schooling,' Elspeth returned, 'though I would have thought you had mastered your numbers.'

Henry had whitened and rapped out, 'They have been wed but five months. You are indelicate, my dear.'

Undeterred Roslyn persisted, her thin face becoming animated. 'It must have been a shock to you, Adam. There was talk in Penruan that you and St John were rivals for the woman's favours.'

'The malicious extent of gossip never fails to amaze me,' Adam was driven to remark.

A giggle from Gwendolyn, Roslyn's sister, earned her a sharp retort from Lady Druce. She was an amiable woman and a widow of three years. Her daughters' legacies were tied up in marriage portions, but after the expense of two seasons in London, Gwendolyn, who was older than Roslyn by three years remained unwed. Her mother despaired that, at twenty-seven, Gwendolyn would ever make a match, although Lady Druce diligently applied herself to the task of matchmaking.

'St John has my sympathy,' Roslyn continued with a prim twist to her lips. 'That Sawle woman was out for his fortune. I will not receive her.'

Hannah stood up. 'Then you will find your home the scarcer of our company. If my cousin's wife is not welcome then I, and I am sure all my family, will not impose ourselves upon you.'

'Merciful heavens, Roslyn!' Lady Druce threw up her hands in horror. 'How your tongue runs away with you. You insult our friends.

Of course Meriel will be received.'

Henry dabbed at his mouth with his napkin as he regarded his wife along the length of the table. 'I am sure Roslyn spoke in haste. Please be seated, Hannah. There is no question that St John's wife will be received by us.'

Roslyn returned her husband's stare with frosty silence and, as Hannah sat down, Edward enquired of the King's health from Squire Penwithick who had recently returned from London.

The tension in the room eased, though Hannah was pointedly ignoring Roslyn.

Adam sat between Gwendolyn and Alice Penwithick, who was married to the squire's son, Lance. Alice was as timid as Gwendolyn was shy, and any conversation with them was hard work. Lance was a thin, studious man, eight years older than Adam. He managed the Penwithick estate in his father's absence, but his main passion was Celtic archeology. He spent all his free time examining the ancient stone sites and burial grounds on the moors.

Lady Druce sighed dramatically. 'Henry, it is such a disappointment for Gwendolyn that none of your unattached friends is present.'

'They had prior engagements,' Henry replied.

'And what about you Lance? Your friend, that delightful Mr Chapman who was staying with you when we last dined at the Manor – I thought he showed an interest in Gwendolyn.'

Lance cleared his throat and peered short-sightedly across the table. 'Mr Chapman is a schoolmaster. He has not the means to support a wife.'

'Gwendolyn is well endowered.' Lady Druce sniffed. 'A schoolmaster, you say? That is not suitable at all.'

Then she homed in on Cecily and Joshua. 'That son of yours is a gentleman. I thought he would be here to welcome his cousin home from sea. Is it not time Japhet settled down? He could do worse than Gwendolyn.'

Joshua spread his hands. 'Nothing would please me more should Japhet's eye be taken by the lovely Gwendolyn. But I have no influence with my son regarding his affections.'

Hannah clapped her hands, her eyes bright with mischief. 'Gwendolyn would be a perfect wife for Japhet. Do you not agree, Roslyn?' She knew her friend had once been infatuated with Japhet, who had shown little interest in Roslyn. She was still angry with Roslyn for insulting her family.

'Japhet does not strike me as the marrying kind,' Roslyn retorted.

Gwendolyn sighed. 'Mama, I would like to feel I could dine with our family without making some young man uncomfortable that you are intent upon matchmaking.' Gwendolyn spoke with such rare verve that her mother and sister stared at her in astonishment. Her freckles and pastry-coloured complexion stained to a raspberry hue and she hung her head to fidget with the silver lace on her sleeve. 'I wish they would leave me alone,' she muttered. 'It is obvious that Japhet would never look at such a plain Jane as myself.' Her rush of colour betrayed her emotions.

Adam was used to the effect Japhet had on women. They seemed to adore his roguish charm and looks. And Japhet never could resist flirting with any woman. No doubt he had set Gwendolyn's heart aflutter using her as no more than a momentary diversion at some house ball or supper.

Under cover of an outbreak of conversation, he whispered to her, 'Japhet knows a good woman when he meets one.'

To his astonishment Gwendolyn laughed. 'Then there is the rub: your cousin has a reputation for a certain type of woman . . . of a kind one could not describe as good.'

Adam found himself warming to her. There was more to Gwendolyn than he had believed. She had humour and spirit. He smiled. 'Your mother means well. She would see you happily wed.'

'No, she would not. She acts the matchmaker. It was obvious that Mr Chapman had no interest in me or was suitable. And as for Japhet . . .' She broke off and lowered her head to hide her blush. 'She would have a fit of the vapours if a man of his reputation called upon me. Mama would rather I remained an old maid and be her constant companion in her declining years. I do not mind that. It is the hypocrisy which I hate.'

Dorothy Penwithick leant forward. She was the squire's second wife and, in her mid-forties, a decade and a half younger than her husband. It was also her second marriage and she had produced no children. She was a good-natured if frivolous woman and given to decorating herself with patches. A comet and two stars chased each other across one cheek and two large hearts, one by her eye and another by her jaw were also displayed. She clapped her beringed hands together with excitement. 'The dear squire has engaged some strolling players to put on a play for us next week. I do hope you will all attend. It is arranged for Tuesday.'

'A play! How delightful,' Elspeth replied.

'It would be a pity if St John's wife could not attend.' Roslyn watched with pleasure the annoyance on Elspeth's face. 'It is a rare treat to have players in the district.'

'I believe St John took her to see them when they put on two plays in Penruan last week,' Edward answered smoothly. 'Her attendance will, of course, depend upon her health.'

Lady Druce signalled frantically to Roslyn, who realised that her own bladder was uncomfortably full after being seated for almost three hours. She announced with ill grace, 'Ladies, let us adjourn to the parlour and leave the men to their port and brandy.'

A footman brought the decanters to the table and was dismissed by Henry. Whilst the port was passed around Adam leaned across to his friend, saying quietly, 'How goes married life? I am sorry I missed your wedding.'

'Roslyn is not as bad as her bite. At least I no longer rattle around this house on my own. It gives her pleasure to entertain. I am content.'

'I am pleased for you.'

The other men were listening to Penwithick discussing matters in Parliament. It was over four years since Pitt had ousted Fox as Prime Minister. 'Pitt remains open to the need for reform within Parliament. He is set on maintaining peace and building the economy.'

'Does this younger Pitt have any of his father's popularity?' Edward asked. 'He is still raw behind the ears, is he not at eight and twenty? Do you approve of his policies, Penwithick?'

'I do most heartily. The man has a flare for rhetoric. And, of course, the King's approval.'

'Therefore he is hated by the Prince of Wales,' Henry laughed. 'Fox encouraged the Prince's extravagances.'

'The scandals of the Prince are an embarrassment to the King,' the squire replied. 'Not least his marriage to the Fitzherbert woman.'

The talk was of politics until Adam was moved to enquire, 'And what of the Bill to abolish slavery? We came across a slave ship off the Azores. I have seen many unpleasant sights in the navy but none as inhuman as on that ship.'

'It is being debated,' Penwithick declared, 'but many are against it.'

'Reforms are needed.' Adam spoke with passion. 'With so many mines closing, there could be trouble next winter with the vast number of men out of work and their families facing starvation.'

'Edward, this son of yours would make a good politician,' Squire Penwithick enthused. His face was flushed from wine and port. 'We could have another Young Pitt in our midst.'

Joshua laughed. 'The squire is right. Would that Japhet used his talents more wisely.'

Adam shook his head. 'I have no ambition in those quarters. Being cooped up in Westminster would not suit me. There is too much talking a point to death and not enough action.'

The squire chuckled. 'Aye, you have the looks of a buccaneer of old. It is part of our Cornish blood.' His expression sobered. 'Edward said your last port of call was La Rochelle.'

'Our stay was brief. We put into harbour for two nights. The captain was negotiating the release of four British prisoners held there.'

'Were they smugglers?' Henry enquired.

'We were told it was the crew of a privateer which had been

116

shipwrecked after being blown off course in a storm. A ransom was demanded.'

There was a general mumbling of dissent. 'We are supposed to be at peace. The damned French get above themselves,' Squire Penwithick barked. 'How did you find the mood of the French people? Reports are that the country turns more against the King with each day.'

'Insurgents rouse the populace from the market squares. Every extravagance of Queen Marie-Antoinette is relayed and exaggerated.'

'Too many nobles seek only self-aggrandisement at Versailles and forsake their people in the provinces,' said Squire Penwithick.

'Quarrelsome race, the Frenchies,' Henry observed. 'If they are warring amongst themselves, at least they are not at war with us.' He winked at Adam. 'More is the pity for you. There are riches in overpowering an enemy ship and promotion to captain is faster during a war than in peacetime. And there is none to beat the British navy.'

'Time we joined the ladies, gentlemen,' the squire reminded them. He guided Adam away from the other men. 'The government needs the ears and eyes of men who can appraise a situation. Talk with me some more before you return to Plymouth.'

He followed the others, leaving Adam intrigued.

It was late when they left, and Aunt Elspeth snored as she dozed in the coach on the journey home. Although Adam had been up since dawn, and the work in the yard was strenuous, the fresh air the stimulating company and conversation had given him a feeling of light-headedness. By the time they reached Trevowan he found himself wide awake and restless. Had there been moonlight he would have chanced a ride along the cliffs. But there was no moon, and such a ride would be foolish and dangerous.

His father and aunt went straight to their beds and Jenna Biddick, who had waited up for them, was dismissed for the night.

Adam removed his boots and, carrying a three-branched candelabra, strolled through the house. His leave was short and he wanted to breathe in the atmosphere of his home before he was exiled from it for another voyage. It could be more than a year before he returned again. Next month he was twenty-one and on his return from his next voyage he would leave the navy. Barnaby, roused from his sleep, padded beside him, his ageing step slow and companionable. As a youth Adam had raced through these rooms with the spaniel barking excitedly at his heels. Sabre remained contentedly by the glowing embers in the hearth.

He paused to study the portraits of his ancestors in the panelled dining room, then lingered by an ormolu clock he had seen his grandfather wind every week during his childhood. A favoured figurine

117

of his grandmother's was picked up and tenderly replaced. He entered the peacock room or morning room which overlooked the rose garden. It was his favourite room and he held the candle high, its light flickering over the yellowing wallpaper with its blue and red peacock design. The wallpaper had been chosen by his grandfather and put up to welcome his bride to her new home over fifty years ago. Adam hoped it would not be touched during his father's lifetime. Its familiarity was endearing and cosy in a way Roslyn's pristine painted and gilded plasterwork would take decades to achieve.

Still the restlessness persisted. The grandfather clock in the hall chimed midnight, its loud ticking the resonant heartbeat of the house.

The chill in the rooms finally penetrated Adam's clothing. The fires had long since died down. He had turned towards the stairs when the sound of a soft footfall in the west wing drew his attention. Meriel appeared at the top of the stairs. Before he could speak, she put a finger to her lips and ran down to him. Her thin cotton nightgown billowed behind her, and the fullness of her curves and long slender legs were outlined in her haste. Her hair was loose and he had never seen her look so lovely.

Forbidden memories of her flooded his mind and his hand shook, spilling the wax of the candle onto his ruffled cuff. 'Meriel what are you doing up so late?'

'St John is away.' She pulled him into the parlour. 'He rode out after your family left this evening. He's ridden to Fowey to join his old drinking companions. He won't be back before dawn.'

'Then he serves you ill by his neglect.' Adam's anger over the marriage surfaced once more.

Meriel shrugged. 'What right have I to make demands on his time?'

'You are his wife. He should honour you.'

'The marriage was forced on him as he did force himself upon me. There is no love between us.'

'Are you saying that he raped you?' His face twisted with fury. 'I could kill him for that.'

She put a hand on his chest. As she tipped back her head to gaze up at him, her golden curls massed around her beautiful face like a halo. 'Talk not of killing. At least he spared me the disgrace of raising a bastard. Oh, Adam, why did you return to sea? You know I have always loved you.'

The perfume of her hair and body assailed his senses. She moved closer, her hip brushing against his and the light from the candles illuminating the longing in her eyes. The heat of her skin burned through his clothing.

She smiled seductively. 'You are the only man I have ever loved. Thadeous Lanyon was pressing his suit and my father was insisting on a marriage. The man was repulsive to me. St John was a diversion

118

which went horribly wrong. We can be together whenever you are on leave.'

The enormity of her words raked him like grapeshot. He recoiled. Lanyon's spite in calling in the Loveday loans could ruin the family. When she moved closer, her lips parted to invite his kisses, he felt the rounded hardness of her swollen stomach. Her touch became repulsive. She carried St John's child. His free hand closed over her arm which she had wound around his neck, and he put her from him.

'We are on the brink of losing the yard because of St John's marriage to you. And you would dishonour him by making a cuckold of him with his own brother.'

He stepped back from her in disgust. Her loveliness no longer held him in thrall. He saw only the scheming enchantress who had brought his family to near ruin.

'Adam, how can you make it sound so sordid? You love me. I gave myself willingly to you in the cave and you were the first. Does that mean nothing?'

'Then I am as much to blame for the trouble brought upon my family as St John. I was wrong to give in to my passion.'

'No. It was not wrong. Adam, don't look at me as though you hate me.' She held out her arms in entreaty.

He was unmoved and put a greater distance between them. What he was feeling was very close to hatred. Self-loathing at his own weakness sat uncomfortably upon him. Meriel had used St John to escape a marriage which repelled her. Enchantress was an apt description of her cold emotionless beauty. She could make a man cast discretion and honour aside to possess her and she would feel nothing but her triumph in that power. He shivered, appalled at his insight. Even despising her, he could feel the effect of her beauty coiling around him like flames. It threatened to draw him into her spell – and damnation.

To step further back took all his willpower. 'The child is St John's? There is no possibility that it could be mine?'

She heard the tortured note in his voice. She had seen the disgust and hatred in his face as he assessed what was behind her words. When she stepped towards him, he tensed.

'Lanyon was not good enough for you, was he?' Adam ground out. 'Sal warned me about your ambition, madam. You sought to trick me into first betraying my betrothed, then abandoning her to marry you. But St John was the better catch. He is the heir of Trevowan. I am but a humble lieutenant with no prospects to support a wife for several years.'

'That is not true.'

'Answer me, Meriel. Is the child mine?'

The loathing in his eyes shook her. She had been so certain of

119

Adam's love; that his rivalry with his brother would ensure they remained lovers. Again she had misjudged the strength of loyalty which bound him to his family.

'What type of woman do you take me for?' Her indignation made her tremble. 'You prate of honour. You said you loved me and I believed you. I was the one betrayed by you and your brother. I was the one used to appease the lust of you both. How dare you accuse me of trickery?'

They faced each other, both breathing heavily. Adam walked to the door. 'I bid you good night, madam. You have made your bed, but I will not be the one to lie on it.'

If he had slapped her, she could not have felt more humiliated. Through eyes bright with unshed tears, she watched him take up the candelabra and stride away. Only when the point of light disappeared along the landing upstairs did she move. She shivered and drew a shuddering breath. The cold penetrated right to her heart, sealing it in ice.

Her marriage had fallen far short of her expectations. She was allowed no contact with their neighbours. Even her attempt to blackmail Elspeth by going to Edward with the knowledge she had learned about the older woman had failed to work. True, Elspeth had grudgingly accepted the marriage and even taken it upon herself to teach Meriel how to behave in polite society. Meriel was furious that Elspeth was adamant that she would not appear in public until the child was born. Tempted as she was to push the harridan further, Meriel knew when she had met her match. It would be foolish to make an enemy of Elspeth Loveday.

The child in her belly was her security that she could not be put aside, and St John could not restrain his desire for her. He was becoming more easy to manipulate. If the Loveday fortune was not all she had dreamed of, it was still a better life than being married to Thadeous Lanyon.

Yet Meriel did not count her blessings. She would not be satisfied until she mixed with the highest realms of Cornish society. Neither could she forgive an insult.

The humiliation of Adam's repudiating her love turned to rage. With that rage came the all-consuming need for revenge.

'Curse them, they cannot keep me caged like a cur,' St John fumed as he watched from his bedroom window as his family drove to Squire Penwithick's to see the play.

'Then go out, for you are poor company,' Meriel retorted.

'I have no money.'

She halted in brushing her hair. 'There are ways of getting money other than from your family. How do you think the fishermen survive through a bitter winter when the catch is poor?'

'You mean join the free-traders?' St John frowned.

'Why not?'

'I do not mix with common men. Or labour like a skivvy hauling kegs of brandy across the countryside.

'Then you will remain at the mercy of your father's purse strings. But it is not the fishermen handling the contraband who get rich, it is the men who invest in the goods. Like Lanyon and my father.'

'Reuban is hardly rich,' he scoffed.

'That is what he wants people to think. He's a clutchfist when it comes to spending money, but he has it in plenty locked away in an iron chest in the cellar.'

St John flung himself down on to a brocade chair. 'I have no money to invest.'

'Then get some. Work with my brothers for a half-dozen runs and build up some capital, or . . .' she paused, her eyes hard with cunning, '. . . or sell something to raise the capital.'

'How?'

'How do you think?' Her exasperation exploded at how thick-headed he could be at times. 'Sell something. This house is full of old things worth a pretty penny or two.'

'I could not steal from Trevowan. If Father found out then I would be disinherited. Everything would go to Adam.'

Meriel threw down the hairbrush and paced the room. Her nightrobe swirled around her in her agitation and each time she passed before the firelight her naked figure beneath was clearly silhouetted. 'How can you steal what will one day be yours?' She mastered her anger. 'If you don't want to sell them, then use them as security against a loan. And to be safe, don't go to someone who knows your father. Truro has many such bankers in the back streets.'

He still looked uncertain and she persisted with an encouraging smile. 'You can buy them back out of your profits. It will take longer to make your fortune but it can be done.'

St John shook his head. 'The risk is too great.'

'Faint heart!' she jeered. 'Take a few small items of silver which won't be noticed.'

'Aunt Elspeth would miss them.'

'Are there not valuables locked away? In a month they can be reclaimed and you will have the profits to reinvest. Isn't it worth a risk?'

She halted in front of the fire. Her proposition was tempting, as was her lovely body. She had been withholding herself from him in recent days and was always complaining that they never went anywhere. Yet the first weeks of their marriage she had been accommodating and eager to please. That was before his father's

121

restrictions had become harder to bear. Only once this month had she shown how generous she could be in her loving and that was after he had taken her to Truro to the playhouse. The admiring glances of men as they passed had taken the sting out of his marriage. She was beautiful and men envied him for possessing her. At seeing the way her golden hair tumbled over her shoulders to curl around her breasts stirred his desire.

He reached for her shoulders, feeling the heat of her skin through the thin material. But when he bent his head to kiss her, she stepped away. 'I thought I had married a man, not a milksop. My brothers aren't afeared to take risks and I doubt Adam would be.'

He grabbed for her and when his arms closed around her she did not pull away, neither did she yield. Her figure was rigid and her eyes blazing with contempt. 'Prove you are a man who knows how to shower his wife with riches and I will give you all you desire and more.'

She rubbed her hips against him, her lips parted and inviting. Desire hammered through his veins and he held her chin in his hands, staring down at her with a mixture of passion and loathing. He had resented the manner of their marriage, but her initial ardour had woven a spell upon him. He may revile her for bringing misfortune upon him, but when she played the seductress, he could not resist her.

'I will speak with your father,' he said.

'And the money?'

'There is some old silver plate in the attic. I will use it as you suggest.'

His hands moved over her body.

She laughed softly and drew him towards the bed. Tonight she would endure his caresses though they left her cold. Ever since Adam had taken her in the cave and abandoned her, she had not taken pleasure in any union, only in the power her body could wield over men.

Chapter Seventeen

A dam ran the gamut of his emotions during his leave. The pleasure had been stripped from it. It had been difficult to accept St John's marriage when he had believed himself in love with Meriel. Then had come his anger at his twin's lack of family duty by failing to wed a woman whose dowry would have solved their financial problems, his duty as he was the heir. After his confrontation with Meriel, Adam had felt guilt and shame. Even his joy in the *Pegasus* had paled on realising that the cost of the building materials was partly responsible for his fathers' debts. At least his legacy would be paid on his twenty-first birthday, and that debt would be cleared.

When a heavy shower stopped work in the yard that afternoon, to avoid Meriel, Adam rode over to Trewenna to visit Uncle Joshua and his family.

They greeted him warmly when he entered the Rectory parlour, though it was only four days since he had seen them at Traherne Hall. Aunt Cecily fussed over him. 'I declare you have grown two inches on your last voyage. But there is not enough meat on you. Navy rations are atrocious. I hope Elspeth is feeding you up.'

'It is hard work which keeps him lean.' Uncle Joshua put down his quill and covered his brass inkwell. He was working on a sermon at his desk in the corner. The room was plainly furnished, with a wooden settle by the fireplace and two Jacobean high-back chairs which had once been at Trevowan. The Rectory was not much larger than a cottage, containing a kitchen, parlour, three bedrooms, and an attic room for their servant. Joshua lived as simply as most of his parishioners.

His uncle chuckled. 'I suppose you spend all your time in the yard.'

'When you should be enjoying yourself,' Japhet had been lounging on the settle seat, one leg drawn up to his chin. 'Having paid my respects to my family, I was about to seek you at the yard. We will go into Fowey this evening. There's a pretty new barmaid at the George.'

'All you think about is wenching, brother. You shame us with your wastrel ways.' Peter scowled at him from a chair by the fire where he was reading a book in Greek.

'I will have you know, you pious little toad, that I work hard for my living.'

'Gambling is not making a living, brother. And as for your horse dealing, I should not wonder those nags were stolen, the company you keep.'

Japhet grabbed Peter by his collar and lifted him bodily from the chair. 'They were paid for fair and square. I am sick of your pious whining.'

'Japhet, leave Peter be,' Joshua demanded. 'And stop taunting your brother, Peter.'

Japhet gave his brother a rough shake before he slammed him down on the wooden chair. 'Just you watch your mouth.'

'Oh dear, why must you two always fight when you visit us, Japhet?' Aunt Cecily was near to tears. 'I see little of you and you always spoil your visit by fighting with Peter.'

Japhet laughed, scooped his tiny mother into his arms and planted a kiss on her cheek. 'I will be on my best behaviour.'

Her smile was doting as he kissed her again and put her back on the ground. For all his wild and reckless ways, Japhet adored his mother.

'I am fortunate to find you at home,' Adam said, 'now you have taken rooms in Truro.'

'For now – but I am thinking of going to London.'

'I wish you would reconsider,' Uncle Joshua said. 'Men like yourself go to London looking for adventure and most find only ruination.'

'You went to London when you were younger than me,' Japhet accused.

'So I know what I am speaking of.'

'I have no intention of coming back a parson as you did, sir, if that is what you fear.' His eyes were bright with mockery.

'It is no matter for jest,' Uncle Joshua declared. 'How will you make a living? You settle to nothing.'

'Have I ever come to you for money in recent years?' Japhet flared.

Joshua sighed. 'You dress and act a gentleman but you have no income. My stipend cannot stretch to an allowance.'

Adam studied his older cousin. Japhet looked drawn, and there were deeper lines about his mouth now than when he had last seen him. There was also the air of a dissolute about him.

Joshua regarded his son with sadness in his eyes. 'For your mother's sake curb your wildness. She worries about you.'

Japhet snatched up his tricorn from a peg by the door. 'I did not come home for a sermon, sir.' He slammed out of the house.

Cecily put her hand to her mouth and wailed, 'Go after him, Adam. I do not know what gets into him nowadays.'

Adam found Japhet saddling his mare. 'Had enough of their piety too? Come into Fowey. I doubt you have had much joy from your leave. Rather an upset at home was there not, with St John marrying

124

that tavern wench? You had a fancy for her yourself, I thought. You know your father threatened to disown St John over that marriage?'

'I did not know that.'

'He was in a rare taking.' He laughed, his anger rarely lasted, and when in his spirits Japhet was more entertaining than anyone Adam knew. 'I would have given much to have seen St John's face when the Sawle men confronted him. Abducted him, they did. It was marriage or his life, so they say.'

The way Japhet described it made the incident sound amusing. 'Trust St John to get himself in such a scrape.'

Japhet winked, his teeth white beneath his black moustache. 'I would have left the county rather than be tied to such a scheming baggage.'

'Let's not talk of it. What of yourself?'

'I will tell you over our ale in Fowey, and I wager you a guinea I bed that barmaid tonight.' He gave a deep infectious laugh. 'Come, cousin, tonight let us forget our cares. You can go on to the yard in the morning. A night's carousing is what you need to forget your troubles.'

Japhet would not accept his refusal and Adam allowed himself to be persuaded.

They spent an hour drinking and recounting escapades of their youth, with St John the butt of all Japhet's jokes. Halfway through the evening Adam left Japhet to relieve himself outside. When he returned to the taproom, he saw Japhet talking to two thickset bearded men. As Adam approached they slunk away. Japhet did not meet his cousin's eye.

'Was that two of the Jowett brothers? What are you doing talking to those cattle rustlers?'

'They mentioned there was a cockfight in town. Are you interested?'

Japhet was eager to attend. The barmaid he had been interested in no longer worked at the inn. 'Come, Adam, a cockfight will liven up the evening.'

Adam complied, although he was not fond of the sport. The cockpit was gloomy and crowded. The press of a hundred men and a few women, notably of low repute, jostled for space. A half-dozen lanterns hung above the circular pit, which was marked by straw bales. The sides of the room were in shadow. A fight was in progress and shrieks rose from the press of figures around the pit as they encouraged their birds. Gentlemen in velvets and lace rubbed shoulders with labourers in smocks, and unkempt fishermen. The three Jowett brothers were much in evidence, taking bets. Seven of the birds fighting tonight belonged to them.

'Keep your hand on your purse, coz,' Japhet warned. 'Many a pickpocket has prospered in this lair.' He pushed his way through the crowd to place his bet. Adam leaned against the wall. The unholy halo of light in the centre illuminated faces contorted by the fever of blood-lust.

Every time a Jowett bird went in the ring it won. Several times Adam saw Japhet stop to pass a word with one of the brothers. Once he was certain that Saul Jowett passed him a money pouch. Japhet moved among the crowd, talking to many of the men keeping a betting book. He also flirted with a red-haired woman accompanying a foppish gentleman who was gambling heavily. Twice the man had warned Japhet off and his cousin had laughed at him. When the next fight was in progress he boldly beckoned the woman with his finger. Adam shook his head in amazement as the woman followed Japhet and they disappeared outside. By the time her companion realised she had left him, the couple were nowhere in sight. Japhet returned looking pleased with himself and picked up his winnings from the fights he had not stayed to witness.

Adam was about to place a wager on the next Jowett cock to fight when Japhet put a hand on his arm and whispered. 'The other cock will win.'

'The Jowetts cannot be bested this night. The white cock is a fine bird.'

Japhet rubbed the side of his nose. 'It will not win. I am chancing all my winnings on its opponent. And the odds are ten to one.' He held up a fat purse.

Adam added his money to his cousin's. The fight was even when suddenly the Jowett cock began to stagger and after the next strike from its opponent keeled over. There was an uproar. Three-quarters of the gamblers had wagered for it to win. There were cries of foul play but with the Jowetts hollering the loudest that they had lost the most, a fight was avoided.

Adam was delighted as he pocketed his winnings. Japhet was making the rounds of several men to receive his winnings and was in high spirits. Adam saw Japhet goading the fop from whom he had enticed the redhead. The fop was one of the few winners in the last fight. As he approached, Japhet jerked his head towards the door.

'Time to go.'

It was two in the morning and Adam wanted to be at the yard at six, so he readily agreed. As they reached the door a cry went up. 'My hunter watch has been stolen. And my purse.'

'Mine too,' another voice yelled.

Adam glanced over his shoulder to see the fop Japhet had last spoken to searching his jacket for his own purse. 'So has mine,' the main wailed.

'No time to dawdle,' Japhet said, breaking into a sprint. 'Unless you want the beadle set on you for being an accomplice you had better run fast, cousin.'

Japhet was a pickpocket. Why did that not shock Adam as it should? He had always been stealing things as a child: a trinket from a stall at a fair, an apple from Lanyon's shop.

Japhet knew the Jowetts from Bodmin Moor. Had the last fight been rigged? Was that why he was so certain of the winnings? And all those wagers he had collected – was that the Jowett money he had paid out and received for them on the last fight? It seemed likely. If so, he mixed with dangerous company. The Jowetts were the worst kind of rogues.

Adam sprinted after Japhet, who was running towards where they had stabled their horses. As they galloped out of town, he shouted at his cousin. 'Damn you, Japhet, are you insane? You will be hanged if you are caught.'

His answer was a wild laugh. 'First they have to catch me. And who is going to suspect a parson's son? Especially when that parson is as well respected as my father.'

Chapter Eighteen

Troubled by Japhet's confession, Adam found it hard to concentrate on his work the next day. He was worried about Japhet. The drinking excesses of the previous evening had left a nagging headache which persisted through the afternoon. When work at the yard finished he decided that a long ride would chase away the megrims.

He allowed Solomon his head and they turned north at the crossroads leading to Penruan. He cut across meadows owned by Sir Henry Traherne and began to circle back towards the coast.

The high hedgerow bordering the lane opened up at a wood. In a clearing the group of travelling players was still camped. There were three caravans housing the eight players and a cart for the stage props. Three of the men sat round a smoking campfire and two women sat on their caravan steps gossiping; one preparing vegetables for a stew pot, the other mending a gaudy stage costume.

He slowed Solomon to a trot and had ridden some distance before he heard shouting ahead. It sounded like children, but there was a menacing ring to their voices which disturbed him. He called to Sabre, who was running through the undergrowth, to keep him beside Solomon. At seeing a group of a half-dozen youths, he recognised some as being part of the players' troupe. They were circling and chanting.

'Devil's cub! Freak!'

Adam halted. The boys had sticks and were beating a creature on the ground, taunting some hapless beast.

Sabre growled and Adam ordered him to remain at his side. The wolfhound's hackles were raised along his neck and back. 'You there,' Adam called, 'what the devil do you think you are playing at?'

The authority in his voice stopped the boys. When they saw he was alone they regrouped and continued. The pause had been long enough for the creature on the ground to give a mournful whimper and try to raise itself up. Then the blows and kicking were renewed. Adam was incensed. It was no animal they were taunting but a child.

'Stop that at once!' He dug his heels into Solomon's sides and sped towards them. Sabre bound ahead, snarling and snapping around the boys' feet. Adam's riding crop came down on the head of the tallest and stoutest lad. The youth's dirty face stared up at him, terror

129

in his red-rimmed eyes. The lad turned and fled.

Abandoned by their leader, his companions followed, chased by Sabre. Adam called the dog back. The bundle of clothing on the ground had wrapped itself into a ball, the frail figure shuddering with fear.

Adam dismounted. 'They have gone. You are safe now.'

Still the figure remained cowered. Adam stooped and put a hand gently on its shoulder. The answering wail was high-pitched with terror.

'I will not harm you,' he spoke softly as he would to a nervous horse. He could see enough to discern it was a young girl with brown hair. 'Those knaves have gone. You are safe. Did they hurt you? Let me see. There is no need to fear me. I would help you.'

Without warning pain flared in his cheek and he was knocked sideways. Putting his hand to his face it came away covered in blood. The youth he had struck with his crop was running back into the woods. There was a large flint stone by his knees which had hit him.

The pain in his face was agonising but the plight of the girl was more serious. She was crying inconsolably, her head tucked into her chest. 'Let me take you home. Your mother will tend your ills. Do you live far?'

As he spoke his hand slid down her back to lift her and take her home. The twisted spine with its small hump on one shoulder was obvious under her thin gown. She flinched as his hand moved over it.

The poor waif must often suffer such taunts merely because she was different. She could not be more than nine or ten. In places her dress had been torn, and bruises were already forming across her shoulders and ribs. 'I will not hurt you,' he soothed. 'You cannot stay here; the boys may return.'

She rubbed her eyes. Apart from the dirt where she had been pushed into the ground, her skin was clean and pink as a dog rose. She had a pretty elfin face with large doe-like brown eyes. With a smile which set his cheek on fire, Adam handed her a handkerchief. 'Dry your eyes.'

Her tears abated but every few moments her body continued to shudder with silent sobs. He pushed her straight hair back from her brow, saying softly, 'Let me take you home.'

She gave him a long scrutinising stare before nodding and pointing in the direction they should go.

Adam wondered if she was mute. 'Can you speak?'

She nodded. Sabre edged forward to sniff her.

'Heel, boy.' He was worried the large dog would frighten her further.

She put out her hand for the wolfhound to sniff and then lick. She rubbed the wolfhound's nose and he rolled on his back to have his stomach scratched.

'Are you not frightened of such a big dog?' he teased.

'He's not so big. You should see our Angel.' She rubbed Sabre's belly and he waggled his legs in the air in delight.

'What were you doing out here alone?'

'I heard the boys playing and wanted to see what they were doing.' She had a serious and careful way of speaking which made her sound older than her years.

Adam suspected the girl had few friends. The only place he knew in the direction she had pointed was a derelict cottage which had been built by old Nathaniel Polglase. Then he recalled the tall young woman who had attended Aunt Elspeth when her hip was especially painful. They must be sisters.

The cottage was in a remote spot, protected by the wood and granite hill behind it. It was close to a stream for fresh water, but as far as Adam knew the land belonged to no one. It was too inaccessible and poor quality to be workable.

Carefully he lifted the girl in his arms. 'You can ride Solomon and arrive home in style. What is your name?'

'Bridgit, but I prefer to be called Bridie.'

'Well then, Bridgit who prefers to be called Bridie, let us get you home and your wounds tended.'

The girl pointed to his cheek. 'Senara must tend your face. Do you hate me because those boys hurt you?'

Her mournful expression touched his heart. 'Of course I do not hate you. Those wicked boys deserve to be taught a lesson.'

Her eyes rounded in alarm. 'No. Ma doesn't like for us to call attention upon ourselves. It were my fault. I should've known not to go looking at them. Freaks like me don't fit in.'

She began to cry again and Adam mounted behind her and squeezed her gently, careful not to hurt her battered body. 'You are not a freak. You are a very brave girl.'

The shudders persisted and her body was beginning to feel unnaturally hot. They had travelled almost to the edge of the wood when he heard a woman's voice frantic with worry call. 'Bridie! Bridie, where are you?'

'That's Ma, she'll scold me proper for wandering away.'

A woman in a black dress and a bright red shawl ran into view. Her badger-streaked hair was pulled back in a bun which had begun to come loose. She stopped and put a hand to her mouth at the sight of Adam.

'Your daughter is safe, but she was being bullied by some boys from the players' troupe camped the other side of the wood. She is too shaken to walk. Permit me to carry her into your home. I am Adam Loveday of Trevowan.'

'That is kind of you, sir. She's been told not to wander off.' The face was smooth of lines despite her greying hair, and her grey eyes

131

were filled with anguish as she put up a hand to touch her daughter's knee. 'I thought she'd learnt her lesson. She's been hurt before.'

The woman continued to look up at him with concern. 'Heavens, sir, for your kindness in helping our Bridie, you've been hurt yourself. Senara will tend to you. My poor eyes are not what they were. Our home is this way, sir, if it pleases you.'

She walked at his side with a firm step. There was a proud tilt to her head and although her black dress was of stout serviceable material, it was not rusty with age nor showed signs of mending.

'Forgive my poor manners, sir.' She looked distressed. 'I was so worried they deserted me. I am Leah Polglase.'

'You are Nathaniel Polglase's daughter? Senara Polglase worked at Trevowan last year. My aunt spoke highly of her healing skills.'

'Miss Elspeth's mare was hurt last summer not far from here. Senara tended the horse. She is my daughter.'

Adam tried to piece together the information he knew of the family. 'I had not realised you had returned to the district.' He realised belatedly that she was using her maiden name. Had she not then married? That was no affair of his.

'I came back last August to make my peace with my father, but I was too late. He'd been dead for two years. It seemed a good place to stay for the winter.'

Leah, who was in her forties, was not what he had expected. He remembered Polglase as a rough-and-ready man with a quick temper. Leah had a quiet dignity. She could pass as the wife of a respectable shopkeeper. So why had she shut off her family from the world to live as hermits in a remote cottage?

They had reached the cottage. The ancient thatch, half of which had been stripped away in winter gales, was covered with a weathered and stained sail. It was the only sign of deterioration. The door and two small windows were freshly painted black and the outside walls had recently been limewashed. One half of what passed as a garden was newly dug. Behind it was a small stable with a donkey's head protruding over the door. Tethered beside it was a nanny goat, which was heavily pregnant, and a dozen chickens pecked at the ground for the last of the scattered grain. The cottage was bordered by granite rocks on one side and on the other by a clear water stream.

Adam dismounted and was about to lift Bridie down when a deep growl from Sabre was answered from close by. Anxious, Adam watched as a huge brindle mastiff bound into the yard.

He inadvertently took a step back. The dog was larger than Sabre and built with the solidity of a rock face. Stiff-legged, it advanced, yellow fangs bared and menacing. It was also the ugliest dog Adam had even seen. Both ears were ragged and frayed, and it had an eye missing; one side of its head was distorted so that it regarded him at a strange lop-sided angle. It looked like it had emerged from the deepest pit from hell. Adam reached for Sabre's collar. If the dogs fought, Sabre would be severely wounded.

'Down, Angel,' a woman's voice ordered. The dog obeyed but Adam kept a wary eye on it. From the far side of the stream a tall woman with earth-brown hair ran towards them. Slender and graceful, she crossed the stepping stones in the river.

'Bridie, where have you been? I've been searching everywhere for you.' Her scolding tone was cut short by a gasp of alarm. 'You've been hurt.'

Leah held out her arms for Adam to pass Bridie down to her. 'Mr Loveday helped her. She was set on by the children of those player folk in the wood.'

'Then I'll have something to say about that.'

'No, Senara,' Leah warned. 'Let it bide. We came here to find a quiet life.'

The young woman seemed to be fighting an inner battle, then spun on her heel and disappeared into the house. The mastiff followed with a final growl at Adam and Sabre. Senara had ignored Adam's presence. His injured cheek was turned away from her.

Bridie wrenched herself free from her mother's grasp and with a shuffling gait hurried after her sister.

'Your pardon, sir. Senara is headstrong,' Leah said with a perplexed stare after her elder daughter. 'Come inside. Senara will tend your wound.'

'Dr Chegwidden will see to it. The dogs could be a problem.'

She laughed. 'Angel is docile enough once he knows you are a friend. He won't attack your wolfhound unless provoked. Why not tether your horse and let Senara see to your wound? You cannot ride as far as Penruan without a great loss of blood. It be bleeding and staining your jacket. It should be soaked or it will be ruined. And besides that, a sawbones will leave your handsome face disfigured. Senara has a gentler hand and a herb balm to aid the healing.'

Adam looked down at his jacket and was startled at the amount of blood which had spread there. He put a finger tentatively to his cheek and felt the flap of torn skin.

'Leave it alone, you'll get it infected,' Leah scolded. 'Senara will tend you. It is little enough we can do after you saved Bridie.'

Adam was drawn to follow. The two women intrigued him. Senara was tending to Bridie's bruises. To his relief the mastiff was curled up by the fire.

'He won't hurt you,' Leah chuckled at Adam's wariness.

'Where did he get the name Angel? He looks anything but that.'

'Senara says he be our guardian angel,' piped in Bridie. 'She saved him when he was dying. His old master set him against the bulls and

133

one gored his face. He be as gentle as a lamb unless someone threatens one of us.'

The girl's torn dress and upper undergarments had been stripped off and she was seated on the table. Senara draped a shawl over her sister's deformed shoulder.

Adam shook his head. 'There is no need to hide it from me.' He smiled at Bridie. 'She has been a brave girl.'

'Happen she will need to be,' Leah said with bitterness. 'Poor mite has suffered enough already. Yet what else is in store for her? All people see is her poor twisted body, not the kindly soul within. Now take off your jacket and I will soak the blood from the shoulder in the stream.'

Adam handed it to her. Senara lifted the black iron kettle, steaming on a trivet hook over the fire, and poured water into a pottery bowl. Then, examining a row of pottery jars on a shelf, she opened one and sprinkled some dried herbs into the water before bathing Bridie's bruises and cuts. The girl did not make a sound though some of them were purpled and raised and must have been painful to the touch.

Adam stared around the interior. The cottage consisted of one room with a large straw pallet in a corner where all three women evidently slept. The room smelt sweetly, with bunches of herbs hanging from the rafters. There was little furniture: the table, a bench stool by the fire and a three-legged stool. A wooden blanket chest was placed under the window and held a painted pottery bowl and a jug containing a bunch of bluebells. Two shelves held an array of pottery jars, cooking utensils and two iron pots. There was also a colourful rag rug on the earthen floor and a besom and garden spade in one corner. A squawk drew his attention to the rafters. A magpie was preening its feathers, and in the darkest corner an owl slept with its head under its wing.

He laughed. 'You have quite a menagerie of pets.'

Bridie giggled. 'Senara saves them. We used to have a fox cub but when it was full grown Senara set it free.'

Adam noticed a potter's wheel in one corner, which explained the abundance of fine pottery, some with painted designs, piled on the floor and in use by the women.

'Which one of you is the potter?' he asked.

'That's Senara,' Leah said with pride, as she laid his coat on the settle to dry by the fire. 'The pots are sold in the market. She's built a kiln outside.'

'You also seem to have a great knowledge of herbs.'

'Some.' A wary note had entered Leah's voice. 'Now, Senara. Will you tend to Mr Loveday's cheek. Though the poor man will need your darning needle or be badly scarred.'

Adam was ushered to the bench stool while Senara examined his cheek.

'It is a deep and nasty cut. I must cleanse it.' Her manner towards him relaxed and he was struck by the luminous greenness which flecked her hazel eyes. 'Sir, I'm sorry you suffered such an injury when helping Bridie. It will leave a scar.'

Taking fresh water she tipped some more herbs into the bowl before bathing his wound. It stung slightly and smelt of moss. She then dabbed it with a balm taken from a small clay pot. 'That will deaden the pain while I stitch it. We've some brandy that will also help.'

Leah poured a measure into a horn beaker. At his querying look, she smiled. 'Senara often gets paid in kind for the pots she sells. Brandy is a good preservative base for some of her remedies.'

Adam was grateful for the brandy and clenched his jaw as Senara stitched his face. She was close to him and he studied her to take his mind from the pain. Her skin was smooth and creamy, although there were three tiny pockmarks just below her hairline by her ear. They did not mar her loveliness. He was fascinated by the way she caught her lower lip in white even teeth as she concentrated on her task. The smell of lavender rose from her skin and hair. Unusually her waist-length hair was drawn into a single thick plait.

Leah sighed and threw another log on to the fire. She rubbed her hands, which were swollen at the joints. 'At first, to make ends meet, Senara sold her pots at any house she came across. It is easier now she has the market stall. They be good pots and sell well.'

'I am sure they are. It is an unusual trade for a woman. The only potters I have known are men.'

'Men don't like it,' Senara said with anger. 'I had my stall turned over one week and all my pots smashed.'

'Where did you learn such a skill?'

Both women tensed, their manner again wary.

'Forgive my inquisitiveness,' Adam apologised. 'I do not mean to pry.'

'I was taught by a potter in gratitude for saving his wife and child from the smallpox.' Senara stated. 'To prevent further attacks on my stall I now say I be selling the wares for my father.'

'Even most physicians shun patients with the smallpox, it is so contagious and deadly.'

'I contacted it as a child. Leah's care ensured I survived and I was spared disfigurement.'

Adam rose from the bench; Senara had finished. Bridie was being cuddled by Leah. 'I hope the child suffers no ill effects from her ordeal.'

'Thank you again, Mr Loveday,' Leah smiled.

Senara said, 'Come back next week and I will remove those stitches.'

'I set sail in three days. The ship's surgeon will do it.'

'I fear there will be a scar but it should not be too disfiguring.'

Senara held out a small pot. 'Use this on it. It will heal quickly and stop the risk of any infection.'

He left the cottage intrigued by the air of mystery surrounding the two women and the little girl.

Senara rounded on her mother when she heard Adam ride away. 'Why did you tell him so much?'

'That man can be a good friend to us.' Leah regarded her daughter sternly. 'Three women alone need someone they can trust from time to time.'

Chapter Nineteen

'It's like a pirate's treasure cave!' Meriel exclaimed with excitement as she stepped through the door of the attic.

St John held a candelabra aloft. Elspeth was helping Joshua and Cecily with their charity work at their parish orphanage, and St John and Meriel had taken advantage of Edward's absence at the yard to explore the riches of the attic. The light wavered over a dozen leather trunks and four wooden padlocked chests. There were pieces of heavy Jacobean and Elizabethan furniture, notably several broken chairs in need of repair. Rolls of tapestries, which St John's mother had stored away as they were no longer fashionable, lay across the top of a dismantled tester bed. Against a wall several truckle beds, which were used as spare beds when required, were lined up on their sides. A pile of wooden toys, mostly ships and soldiers, were stacked in boxes.

Meriel ran to the coffers, lifting the lids to see what was inside. She sneezed twice as the disturbed dust tickled her nostrils. Most of the coffers contained old-fashioned clothes. One even held two limp and yellowing neck ruffs like the ones worn in the ancestral portraits. A carved crib and a chest of exquisitely embroidered baby clothes brought tears to her eyes.

'Our baby will be dressed like a lord.' She held up a fine lawn baby gown edged with lace. 'That old dragon Elspeth never told me there was so much.'

'The child is not due for four months. The silver is over here.'

She dropped the baby gown back into the chest and peered over St John's shoulder as he unlocked the chest with a key from a bunch he had earlier taken from his father's study.

'Did you put the gown back as you found it?' St John demanded, his voice tense with nerves. 'Something like that will alert Elspeth that someone has been in here.'

He lifted the lid of the chest and swore roundly. 'It is empty. Papa must have sold the silver.'

He dived at the next chest and his anger mounted to discover that also contained no silver. 'I cannot believe there is nothing left . . .'

'He wouldn't get rid of it all. There was silver aplenty when Adam was betrothed, so Jenna told me. She had the task of polishing it all. Look in the other coffers.'

The third one held some pieces but they were mostly cutlery. 'Even those will fetch something. What about the family jewellery?'

'The silver is one thing, but I could not risk the jewels. Besides, Papa keeps them in the Truro bank. Elspeth has only a few pieces she cares to wear.'

The fourth chest held a stack of pewter plates and jugs. Meriel sighed but was undefeated. 'So it's not the riches we hoped for, but it's better than nothing. You should raise at least thirty pounds. Reuban will accept that much as a partnership in a smuggling run.'

'It will hardly make us rich,' he scoffed.

She eyed him stonily. 'You plough all the profits from the first run back into the second and so on. Come the end of a year you won't be complaining at the rewards.'

St John rode to Truro without delay, and the pewter and cutlery were left as security against a loan of twenty-three guineas, redeemable in two months. Even so, St John was worried that his father would discover they were missing before they could be returned. Guilt made him avoid Edward when he returned from Truro and, pleading a headache, he kept to his room. It annoyed him that Meriel dined with the family, especially when he heard her laughter. Anger ground through him. Was she flirting with Adam? He was tempted to go to the dining room and drag her back upstairs. Halfway across the bedchamber he realised the absurdity of his actions.

He lay on the bed in a sullen mood and when Meriel came to bed cross-examined her about the conversation.

She laughed his peevishness aside. 'If you had the backbone to face your father you would have dined with us. It would have looked suspicious if both of us were absent.'

He took her roughly and she lay still and impassive beneath him. Her eyes stared up at him with contempt.

'Damn you, woman. Respond. Where's the pleasure in bedding a corpse?'

'I will not respond to an animal. Treat me as your lover and I will give you pleasure.'

Her disdain mocked him, made him feel inadequate. He drew back with an oath. Then as quickly her mood changed, her brow lifted to question, her voice soft, inviting. 'Be my lover, St John. I will not be used by any man to satisfy their base pleasure. Do I not deserve more?' Her hand moved over his shoulder to his cheek.

He groaned; his desire was greater than his anger and resentment. With her golden hair spread across the pillow she was entrancing and completely bewitching. He was enslaved.

He woke with a start in the middle of the night, his dreams of violent fighting with the revenue officers making him cry out. He was covered in sweat. What had he done by taking the silver and pewter? If he failed to make the payments they would be forfeit. Fear of discovery and failure gnawed at his conscience.

'What can go wrong?' Meriel reassured but she could barely contain her irritation that his restlessness had disturbed her sleep.

'Your father was distrustful,' he accused. 'He insisted I show my faith by travelling to Guernsey and dealing with the agents there direct. How can I be away three nights and Father not be suspicious?'

Meriel curbed her impatience at St John's worries. He needed careful handling or he would back out of this scheme to make them rich. 'You are worrying unnecessarily. Edward is talking about visiting your Aunt Margaret in London for a week or so. Elspeth has decided to go with him. It will have to be then.'

St John sat up and chewed on his nail. 'Reuban says I have to know what is involved. There is a cargo coming ashore tomorrow. I have to help with that or the deal is off. What if I am missed? With Father having cut off my allowance and threatening that this is my last chance to prove I am a fitting heir, this is not the time for me to cross him.'

'Reuban is testing your mettle. You will be back before dawn. No one is going to disturb us once we have retired for the night. I shall ensure that the terrace window is left unlocked once your father is abed. No one will suspect you are missing.'

He continued to look unconvinced. He did not like being pressurised. There was a queasiness in his stomach which threatened to unman him. What if the revenue men came upon them? He could be arrested. Then the whole tawdry business would become public.

Meriel knelt astride him, her hands becoming playful and encouraging. 'Stop worrying. My father and brothers have been evading the revenue men for years.'

She kissed him, but so deeply rooted were his fears that even her wiles could not chase them away. St John pushed her from him and rose from the bed. He poured himself some claret from a bottle he had taken from his father's cellar.

'You're drinking too much,' Meriel stated. 'You'll need all your wits about you tonight. Make a mistake and it won't be the revenue man you have to worry about, it will be Clem. Bodies have taken weeks to be washed ashore if any man crosses him.'

Was she trying to scare him witless? Men could be press-ganged or transported if they were caught smuggling. Meriel had a spiteful tongue and she was too fond of comparing him unfavourably to her brothers. And Adam?

His eyes hardened with resentment. Did she still have designs on his brother? The stab of jealousy was unexpected. St John could not bear the thought of Meriel with another man. Did he not know how well she could use her wiles to enslave a man's senses? Since his marriage he had stopped visiting his mistress. Even though he still despised Meriel for the mess she had made of his life, he could not stop desiring her. All women paled in comparison to her beauty.

Satisfaction swelled in him. He had bested his brother over Meriel and he knew Adam was too honourable to make a cuckold of him. Aware of his wife's impatience, he tried to make light of his fears. Too often his father complained St John did not show enough initiative in the business. Well, he would show him now. Meriel was right: he could make a fortune by investing in contraband. A pity he had to deal with gutter-life like the Sawles to achieve his aims.

He smiled to himself and drank the claret in one swallow. For now Reuban and Clem Sawle had much to teach him, but he envisaged a future without them and then great riches would be his.

The next morning St John's mood was optimistic and, even though it was a cold and blustery day, for once he did not mind going to work in the boatyard. His head was filled with thoughts of success of his new venture. Adam was there before him as usual. His twin could not seem to get enough of the place and devoted all his time to the merchantman they were building. Perhaps Adam saw himself sailing in such a vessel one day. St John laughed maliciously. There was not much chance of that. Adam would end his days in the navy with little to show for his life.

His twin was with Ben Mumford, and accompanied by a short man with a peg leg. How had Adam persuaded his father to take on such a useless workman? Seth Wakeley and his noisy brood of children had moved into an empty shipwright's cottage two days ago and the cripple had been busy repairing it.

St John glared at the man. As he stabled Prince, he could hear Wakeley praising Adam for his generosity and bravery in saving his life in a storm. It sickened him. Adam had always been a favourite in the yard amongst the workers, while he himself was shown respect only because he was Edward's son. St John resented that. He even resented that Adam had been chosen by Claude Riviere to marry his daughter. Her dowry would set Adam up for life. If things did not prosper at Trevowan and the yard, St John could find himself the one who was a pauper. Though after tonight that could all change.

He scowled at his twin. It sat uncomfortably with him that Adam was so much in favour with their father while he was in disgrace. It was unthinkable that Edward should disinherit him if he did not mend his ways. His hatred for his brother rose up. He would kill Adam before he saw him inherit Trevowan.

A naval sloop, tying up at the landing stage, drew St John's attention. Two officers stepped ashore.

140

'Is Lieutenant Adam Loveday present?' one demanded.

Adam stepped forward. 'I am Lieutenant Loveday.'

'Then I must ask you to accompany us. You are to answer before Admiral Hoxstead for conduct pertaining to your arrival in Plymouth.'

Edward Loveday had come out of his office and was marching towards the officers. 'What is the meaning of this? You are on private property, sirs. And trespassing.'

The senior officer ignored him, addressing Adam. 'I am Captain Bagshawe. We will escort you to Plymouth on the tide.'

'I need to return to Trevowan to change into my uniform,' Adam replied. 'I shall return in an hour. The tide is not yet full.'

St John concealed a smile of satisfaction. Adam was not so perfect after all. It sounded that he was in serious trouble.

'What is my son to answer for?' Edward demanded.

'I was not informed,' Captain Bagshawe responded.

'I reckon Beaumont has reported him,' Seth groaned. 'He saved some man from the press gang.'

'But that was Ned Holman.' Edward was incensed. 'The man is the son of one of our tenants. He is a simpleton and given to the falling sickness.'

Captain Bagshawe puffed out his narrow chest. 'My orders are to bring Lieutenant Loveday to Plymouth with all speed.'

Edward declared, 'I shall bring Ned Holman so your tribunal can see the man is unfit for duty.'

When Adam rejoined the naval launch he was uneasy. It was a serious offence for an officer to interfere with the press gang. There was also the matter of his fight with Beaumont. Had someone reported them? Duelling was forbidden between officers. It could lead to a court martial and disgrace.

So Adam was not leading such a charmed life as St John had believed. His father would not be so pleased with Adam now. Best of all, it means that their father would not be at Trevowan this evening when St John must join the Sawle men.

An hour after dark he met the Sawles and a dozen other men from Penruan in a cove two miles from the harbour. The cove was tiny, which made it harder for any revenue cutter of excise men on land to detect them. The wind had died away and a dense freezing sea mist swirled around the waiting smugglers. The village men conversed softly, making St John feel the outsider as they spoke of past runs and fishing catches. St John had expected Clem to be landing the cargo in his boat.

'Sometimes we meet the Guernsey agent's men at sea,' Clem explained. 'Sometimes they bring the cargo in. Other times we load in Guernsey. Depends.'

'Surely they won't land the cargo in this,' St John groaned, as he vigorously rubbed his arms to instil some warmth into his frozen limbs.

'Best weather for it. Less risk of running into unwanted visitors,' Clem grunted.

'But how can they find the cove?'

'Listen.'

In the distance the chimes of Penruan church clock struck the three-quarter hour.

'They get their bearings from that. It was a wise investment for Lanyon when he paid for the clock to be installed in the church tower.'

It was another hour before a muffled voice came from the sea. 'Ahoy there!'

St John's heart lurched with panic. What if it was the revenue men?

Clem cupped his hands and gave two seagull's cries. Another came in answer.

'That be the signal.' Harry Sawle prodded St John in the ribs. 'Get moving. We're not here to stand and gawp.'

The sound of oars was now audible. St John was shoved forward. Three rowing boats were appearing out of the mist. He gasped as the icy waves rose over the top of his boots. The men had formed a line to pass the goods along and be secured on the backs of horses and donkeys.

'Stay close to me, Loveday,' Bert Glasson advised. 'That way you won't get in the way of the others.'

Few words were spoken as the boats were unloaded. Several times St John was cursed when his cold hands fumbled with a package or keg. His back was soon aching and his arms felt wrenched from their sockets as he took the weight of a keg and passed it on.

Two of the boats had set back out to sea and the third was just pushing off from the beach when a cry went up.

'Revenue men!'

On legs shaking violently, St John staggered back to the shore. A wave more forceful than the others caught him off balance and he fell. The water crashed over his head. His clothes now weighted, he was dragged backwards in the undercurrent and he swallowed a mouthful of salty water.

He was choking. The water had entered his lungs. The sea roared in his ears as he fought to regain his balance. His legs had no grip on the shifting sea bed and his lungs were bursting. Then suddenly his head broke the surface. He gulped air and struck out for the beach. The shore was only a few yards away, but in his sodden clothing, with his boots filled with water and his strength failing, he was terrified of drowning. Another wave carried him forward and his knees rammed against a rock. He locked his arms around it and, finally able to put his feet on the bottom, heaved himself ashore.

142

He paused a moment to recover his breath.

'Give us a hand with this!' Bert Glasson shouted as he dropped the final keg. He was limping and clutching his thigh.

'Leave it, man, and save yourself,' Harry Sawle ordered.

Only then did St John realise that they were being fired upon. A shot whined past his head. He yelped in terror and fled towards the horses, ignoring Glasson. The Penruan men were running ahead.

'You can't leave, Glasson,' Barney Rundle yelled, and tried to drag St John back.

St John shook him off. Shots ricocheted off the rocks. A ship's cannon was being fired offshore and there were raised voices as the revenue men pursued the smugglers' craft. Despite shivering in his sodden clothing, sweat was pouring from St John's brow. His heart was pounding so hard he found it difficult to breathe.

He had reached his tethered horse when Rundle snatched his bridle. 'Put Glasson up behind you. He's been shot.'

Harry Sawle was half carrying, half dragging the smuggler. Reluctantly, St John helped Glasson. If any one of them was taken, they would all be implicated. The other smugglers were dispersing, most already lost in the mist. For a moment St John was disorientated. Then Penruan clock struck the half-hour and he wheeled in that direction. No more shots were fired towards the cove but they continued out to sea, muffled by the cloaking mist.

'That was close. Is it often like that?' St John forced out from his tortured throat.

Glasson did not answer. Fearing he was unconscious St John glanced back. The man's heavy-lidded stare was filled with contempt. 'You were scared witless, Loveday. We don't leave our own when they can be saved.'

'I nearly drowned,' St John blazed in self-defence. The fortune he desired from the trade would be robbed from him if he failed to prove himself to these hardened men.

'There be no place for cowards in our trade. Reuban will have something to say about this night.'

St John dug his heels into Prince's sides. 'You forget your place, Glasson. You and your father have come cap in hand to Trevowan begging for work often enough in a hard winter. Speak against me and they will find no more work at Trevowan.'

St John caught up with Reuban, who was leading six packhorses. 'Glasson is wounded. I will take him home.'

Reuban nodded. 'We'll talk tomorrow at the inn.' With that he trudged away.

St John resented the summons. It did not do for common men like Sawle to think themselves above him. But as St John watched the line of horses and donkeys, their backs piled high with kegs and packages of tea, coffee, brandy, silks and fine linens, his anger mellowed. Someone would make a grand profit from this night's work and in future he was determined that it would be he himself.

Adam stood before three superior officers headed by Admiral Hoxstead. He had lost an arm in battle with Turkish pirates off Cyprus, and was short of temper and short of stature, with bulbous eyes and a permanent sneer. He addressed each word to Adam's chest as he refused to crane his head to look up at him. The charges read out were for impeding a press officer and duelling. Both were serious offences.

Adam gave his report on the incident.

Admiral Hoxstead rapped out, 'The press gang works on the King's commission. You could be stripped of rank or cashiered for your conduct.'

'With respect, sir, the man in question is outside. You can judge his capabilities for yourself,' Adam declared.

Hoxstead nodded for Ned Holman to be brought in. Ned shuffled into the room. His hair had been parted in the middle and smoothed down with goose-grease. His large hands held his cap and his eyes darted wildly around the room. When he saw so many official-looking strangers, he began to gibber and edge back to the door. Edward Loveday, who accompanied him, spoke to Ned and, taking his arm, led him forward.

The fear was stark in Ned's eyes when a captain rapped out a question. Ned blinked and shook his head, too frightened to take the proceedings in. Three more times the captain questioned him, frightening Ned further, until he ran into a corner and hid his face in his hands.

'The man is an imbecile,' the admiral snapped. 'Get him out of here.' He waved a hand to dismiss Ned and turned to Adam. 'There is now the more serious charge of duelling with a fellow officer.'

'There was no duel, sir. It is forbidden.'

'An alderman reported that an officer in charge of a press gang duelled with another officer outside the inn where Holman was taken. You and Lieutenant Beaumont were the officers involved.' The admiral sat back in his chair. His black eyes and hooked nose gave him the appearance of a scavenging gull.

'Do you deny that you drew swords and fought?'

Adam felt his gut twist with alarm.

'How do you answer, sir? Did you draw your sword and engage with Beaumont? How came you by the cut on your cheek? Was it caused by Beaumont's blade?'

'It is a wound I received yesterday. Any ship's surgeon can verify it is a fresh wound.'

Adam stood stiffly to attention, masking his anger at these questions.

His naval career was at stake. If Beaumont had already answered these charges, had he tried to clear his name by accusing Adam of drawing a sword on him?

The admiral fixed Adam with a stare as sour as sloes. 'I have received a good report on your behalf from Captain Rawcliffe. Though he says that you and Lieutenant Beaumont have had disagreements in the past. Personal vendettas will not be tolerated. Answer the question, did you draw your sword on Lieutenant Beaumont?'

'Yes.'

'Then your conduct is a disgrace. You are stripped of your commission, Mr Loveday, and will spend three months in Admiralty Gaol.'

Adam clenched his jaw as a wave of fury overrode him. He forced himself to meet his father's eyes as shame engulfed him and he was led away under guard.

Chapter Twenty

L ondon was basking in late evening sunshine as Edward and
Elspeth alighted from the stuffy post chaise in the courtyard of
the Tabard Inn in Southwark. Edward had slept little in the ten days
since Adam had been taken into custody. He was angry, not with his
son, but at the circumstances which had brought Adam to this. He
would have acted the same way. There had been some satisfaction in
learning that Lieutenant Beaumont had been cashiered as witnesses
had claimed that he had instigated the duel. Once Adam's sentence
was served he would give him the money to buy himself out of the
navy.

Raising the money would be the problem. But he had Adam's plans
for the brigantine and sketches of the cutters. They could save the
Loveday yard.

The noise and press of humanity assaulted his senses. Ragged and
grime-encrusted beggars sidled up to them, demanding alms. A few
desultory tinkers, flushed by the heat, waved their wares in front of
them, their cries shrill as they vied for attention. A thin woman with
lank brown hair, her breasts pushed high by her corset, beckoned to
Edward.

'Looking for company? For the cost of a geneva or two, I'll give
you a night to remember.'

Elspeth sucked in her breath and lifted her skirts away when two
gin-sodden women lurched across her path. Three young children,
barefoot and in rags, cried pitifully as they tugged at the skirts of their
mother, who was in a drunken stupor.

'God spare us!' Elspeth groaned. 'The place is a cesspit of
humanity.'

Aware of the danger of pickpockets, having had his purse stolen on
a previous visit, Edward took his sister's arm and guided her into the
inn parlour. The landlord, seeing the quality of their clothes, hurried
forward to attend them.

'We are awaiting a carriage sent by Charles Mercer. Has it arrived?'
Edward asked.

'It has indeed, sir, an hour past. Have you travelled far? Can I offer
you some refreshment?'

Edward was inclined to press on and get to his sister's house but

147

Elspeth was looking pale and rubbing her hip, which must be paining her.

She took a coin from her purse and gave it to the landlord. 'There are three children outside, the mother is drunk. Make sure they are given a pie to eat. They look like they haven't eaten in days.'

'You cannot feed every starving child in London,' Edward said. 'You give most of your allowance to the orphans and needy children in Penruan.'

'Do I question how you spend your money, Edward?'

He knew the futility of arguing with his sister. 'Landlord, bring a cordial for my sister and your best Madeira for myself.'

'I will have a Madeira, Edward,' Elspeth intervened, as she limped across the room and massaged her hip. 'It is more reviving. But let us not tarry. I am weary and in need of a hot bath to ease the torment of my limbs. That fool driver hit every pothole between here and Truro. There were bedbugs in the mattress of the last posting house and I saw a louse drop off the head of that man who joined us yesterday.'

The journey to the Mercers' house was slow and equally tortuous. The press of carts, carriages and sedan chairs over London Bridge and through the City brought them to a standstill several times.

When a coal and beer wagon locked wheels, each driver refusing to give the other precedence, the coal sacks spilled on to the cobbles. Urchins appeared like rats out of a sewer, darting amongst the horses' hoofs and dodging the drivers' whips, to pick up the scattered coal and make off into dark alleyways. The drivers swore and raved abuse at each other.

Elspeth put her hands over her ears and groaned. 'How can anyone stand to live in such a rabbit warren? The noise . . . It's like Babel out there. Do they never cease their bickering and caterwauling?'

She was still complaining when she greeted Margaret. 'I must have more hair than wit embarking on this journey. Never again. I ache in every bone.'

'A bath will revive you, and we have entertainments planned for your stay: an opera and several plays; Vauxhall Gardens if the weather is kind. There are soirees, and Lady Greenwich is giving a ball.'

'I am no giddy girl to be entertained every night,' Elspeth remonstrated. 'We are happy to live quietly at Trevowan. I shall miss the riding.'

'We shall drive through Hyde Park on a dry day, or you could hire a hack if you had a mind.'

Elspeth sighed. 'Parading along Rotten Row is not the same, my dear.' At seeing Margaret's crestfallen expression, she relented. Margaret had never had more than a reluctant tolerance for horses, and had been physically sick after seeing her first fox killed. She never rode now if she could avoid it. 'Still, there will be decent horseflesh on Rotten Row to admire.'

'It is the riders who are there to be admired,' Margaret said drily. 'They parade to see and be seen.'

Elspeth laughed but there was a warning glitter in her eyes. 'Pray let there be no matchmaking from you on this visit. I am content as an old maid. Though I would not be a burden to my brother now we have Meriel to take up the reins of housekeeper at Trevowan.'

'Trevowan is your home and you are no burden,' Edward pronounced.

Margaret was concerned at the strain in her brother's voice. He looked tired. 'Is anything amiss, Edward?'

'There is no point in keeping it from you. It is Adam.' He related the events which led up to his son's imprisonment.

'But that is dreadful! Adam was defending himself against that popinjay Beaumont.' She poured him a brandy. 'All the worry over St John and now this . . .'

'Adam never was suited to the navy,' Elspeth observed. 'Too headstrong by half. As for St John – the boy is a trial.'

'Is Meriel settling into her new life?' Margaret asked.

Elspeth tutted. 'She would lord it over us all, given a chance.'

'Meriel is a credit to your training, in her speech and manners, Elspeth,' Edward stated. 'It is early days.'

Elspeth glowered at him. 'She is a scheming baggage. I do my duty to train her to be a fitting mistress of Trevowan. Since St John has demeaned himself so far as to marry a tavern wench, it is for us to make the best of a bad job. And that young lady has badness in her. You mark my words.'

'Crossed you, has she?' Margaret said. 'Two tigresses in one household cannot be easy for you to live with, Edward.'

He raised his hands in submission. 'I will not be drawn, Margaret. I dislike lack of harmony in my home. We must all be tolerant. Meriel may not be our choice, but by the time the child is born, she will be ready to enter into society.'

While Edward answered a question put to him by Charles, Elspeth leaned towards her sister and lowered her voice. 'It will take more of a man than St John to tame that wife of his.'

'I am sure you curb any unbecoming behaviour.'

Elspeth glanced at the men and did not reply until she was certain they were deep in conversation on the far side of the room. Her voice quivered. 'She has found out about my visit to Goodwife Warne. The woman was cousin to Sal Sawle.'

'Oh, my dear, that is terrible. Does Edward know?'

'No, thank God. But the minx has threatened to tell him.'

Margaret squeezed her hand. 'It was a long time ago. Perhaps you should tell Edward. He will not condemn you after so long. He is not like Father, who would have disowned you.'

'My shame was bad enough when Lionel jilted me a week before we were to wed. But at least I could still hold my head high with people believing I was the wronged party. That would not be so if it became known that I had been carrying Lionel's child. I could not bear the shame of it.'

Tears filled her eyes and she blinked them aside. For years her vulnerability had been hidden under her irascible temper. The pain and humiliation of Goodwife Warne's ministrations to rid her of that child had almost killed her. Neither had she forgotten the baby she had forsaken.

Guilt and accusation haunted her from the face of every child who looked her way. On countless nights her empty arms ached for the lost warmth and love of her baby, who now would have grown to womanhood. The misery had been so acute that she restrained from lavishing too much affection on the twins; a foolishness born of stubborn pride, for despite her reserve, she adored them both.

She drew a shaky breath and cast a nervous glance towards Edward, who remained engrossed in conversation. 'If you had not stayed on at Trevowan to comfort me after Lionel jilted me, you would not have discovered the truth. I swore you to secrecy then and I must hold you to it.'

'But if you fear Meriel will use it against you, surely it would be better for Edward to hear it from you.'

Margaret had been shocked when Elspeth had told her she was pregnant. Their father had been threatening to hunt Lionel Farraday down and horsewhip the blackguard. It had been a whirlwind romance when Lionel, a distant cousin of Squire Penwithick, had spent the summer with them. He was handsome but Margaret had not fallen for his charm, sensing something of a rogue about the man. He had the twinkle in his eye of a womaniser. But Elspeth was besotted. She was twenty-three and fearful she would end up an old maid.

A week before the wedding another acquaintance of the squire, who lived in Bath, was in the district on business, and had called at the Manor. Within an hour of his arrival Lionel Farraday had packed his bags and fled. It was left to the embarrassed squire to explain to the Lovedays that Farraday, whom he had not seen for several years, was already married to a much older woman who lived in Bath.

Elspeth had been inconsolable. The shame had changed her. She was no longer loving and carefree, and over the years became shrewish and embittered and never trusted another man with her affections. It was rumoured that Lionel Farraday had fled overseas to escape imprisonment for attempted bigamy.

'I have kept my secret buried so long,' Elspeth said with some force, and seemed to be recovering her stamina. 'Edward has worries enough.'

'Do you think Meriel is vindictive enough to tell others? That would be worse, if it became the gossip of the county.'

'Meriel is no fool. And would anyone believe her? For some twenty years my reputation has been impeccable. It would be my word against hers and I doubt Sal Sawle would back her up in such malicious gossip. I suppose she told her daughter to ensure that Meriel was accepted by our family. I can handle Meriel. For her to mix in society she needs my help and approval. I also watch the baggage like a hawk. If she makes one transgression, she knows I will again have the upper hand.'

'Seventy pounds is my share of the investment in the cargo.' With money in his pocket after disposing of the pewter, St John had been unable to resist the gaming tables and a night with his old friends. Luck had smiled on him. St John tossed the money pouch on the bar of the Dolphin Inn. It gave a satisfying heavy thud.

Reuban studied it. 'Lanyon be our banker. He must be informed of this.'

'I want no dealing with Lanyon. He takes a high cut of the profits. We are family now. We can do this together.'

'Lanyon also carries the debts if a cargo is lost.'

'But I heard Lanyon is being difficult since Meriel and I wed. He has other gangs working for him. How many times have you worked for him since our marriage?'

The innkeeper was impervious to taunts. 'It bain't just the money. Lanyon has the agents in his pay. He has the routes of distribution all planned.'

St John was sweating. He had not expected Reuban to be so stubborn. Neither had he realised that Lanyon was so involved with the smuggling in the area. Meriel had misjudged her father's involvement. Reuban was sly, but he did not have the wits to plan the distribution routes and find markets for the smuggled goods.

Reuban remained antagonistic. 'Don't think you can flaunt your money and expect all the rewards. There be trust to build. Between all parties.' Reuban's stare hardened. 'This be our livelihood. The rewards from one run are soon spent. We need a banker who'll not run out on us at the first lost cargo. Because that happens. Or one who'll find the heat too hot when the excise men come sniffing round.'

St John wiped his hands on his breeches and his stock was uncomfortably tight. He had been lured by the chance of making easy money. He did not want to lose it. 'Who does Lanyon sells the goods to?'

'He has contacts all over. Harry takes the goods inland; he'll know some of them.'

151

'Give me the name of the contacts and I will make the arrangements. We will sail to Guernsey and meet with these agents. Think of the greater profits.'

Reuban rubbed his chin. Lanyon had been cutting him out of his business since the wedding. 'We'll not do your dirty work whilst you take no risks. You take part in the landings and take your risks with the distribution.'

'When can you sail to Guernsey? I need to go while my father is in London.'

'In two days.'

St John held out his hand to shake on it. He did not intend to risk his life for long with the landings and distribution. Lanyon and others like him did not. But he knew if he was to make the profits he wanted, he had to know the distribution routes and agents used across the country. It would be dangerous but only until he became established. Then others would take the risk and he would reap the rewards.

Chapter Twenty-One

A dam paced his cell like a stalking panther, his mood as dangerous. After only two weeks of inactivity his incarceration weighed heavily on him. He was bored and resltess. They had allowed him books, and reading passed some of the time, but too often the cramped single cell became suffocating when his athletic body craved open spaces.

The hot weather did not help. The cell was stuffy and airless. He cursed Beaumont's arrogance and his own idealism for landing him in this mess. At least his father had understood his motives. Across the table were spread the detailed plans of a cutter. Apart from the sleeker-than-usual lines she would carry a large mainsail, double square topsails and a triangular jib forward of the mainsail.

Whilst at sea Adam had made hundreds of sketches of ships and their rigging, or the sailors at work. Now the bare walls of the cell and tiny window, which showed only a distant church spire and patch of sky, gave him no inspiration.

He longed to be working in the yard, feeling the smoothness of the wood as he planed it into shape, or his muscles straining as he hauled on a pulley to heave a timber into position.

He flopped down on the narrow plank bed and thrust his fingers through his long unbound hair. Patience had never been one of his virtues. Even on board ship, he could find the restrictions of navy life onerous.

He had ample time for reflection that his punishment had been deemed fitting to break his idealist fervour. No sailor had any rights as far as the navy was concerned. Adam had flouted naval law by questioning the suitability of a man taken by the press gang. How else were they supposed to get the full complement of men to man the ships, when conditions at sea were so appalling and the pay abysmal?

In recent months Adam had to come to terms with how naval law was at odds with his conscience. Duty pulled him one way, his own belief and lack of hypocrisy another.

A rattle of keys jerked his thoughts back to the present and he stood up. Any diversion was welcome.

'Visitor, Loveday,' the turnkey mumbled.

Squire Penwithick was shown into the cell. He placed a leather valise on the table. 'Rum do, all this. Sorry it had to happen to you, my boy.'

'Thank you, sir.' Self-consciously he picked up a black ribbon and tied back his hair. His shirt was crumpled and clung damply to his shoulders. 'It is kind of you to visit.'

'Not really a social call, my boy.' The squire seated himself on the three-legged stool and peered up at Adam through his spectacles. 'Sit yourself down, Adam. I cannot bear to have you looming over me like a siege tower.'

Adam sat on the bed, one leg bent as he studied the squire. Penwithick had been friends with his father since their childhood. Ill health had kept him in Cornwall for the winter and spring. Usually at this time of year he would be in London, performing his duties as a Member of Parliament.

'After you are released, what are your plans? You were dissatisfied with the navy before all this.'

'I shall buy myself out. I want to do more in the yard.' He picked up the plans he was working on. 'These are my designs for a cutter. They are the ship of the future.'

Squire Penwithick gave the plans a cursory glance, then raised a grey-tufted brow. 'Any plans to visit your fiancée and her family?'

Adam frowned. He did not like being reminded of his commitment to marry Lisette. There was another two years before he had to concern himself about that. 'Father needs my help in the yard. There is much to be done. I would see the *Pegasus* finished. I have no funds to spend time in France.'

'And no liking at being cooped up here.'

Adam sighed. 'None indeed.'

'This brigantine you are building at the yard – it will be yours, will it not?' He laughed at Adam's startled expression. 'Your father confided in me. How long will it take to complete?'

'With a full yard of shipwrights three months, but we have had to lay off workers, so it could be a year before she is fully rigged and ready to sail.'

'A privateer with free access between England and France, whose captain has a knowledge of the political situation, could be of great use to our government.' He studied Adam intently. 'There is a network of men with such easy access to the Continent and the right credentials who serve the government. I am in constant contact with Mr Pitt.'

'Are you saying you are part of an organisation of spies?' Adam whispered.

The squire nodded, his affected manner disappearing as he leaned forward and spoke in a low voice. 'A man such as yourself would suit our purposes well. Someone who is not afeared of danger and can handle himself in a difficult situation. It will be an easy task to settle this matter with the navy and gain your release on condition you go to Paris. The pay is good and all your expenses will be met.'

'I would not wish to stay in France indefinitely.'

'No, indeed not. We need someone who travels frequently between the two countries. Someone above suspicion. A man would be expected to visit his fiancée every four months or so. It is a perfect ruse. Unless you prefer to spend the next few months here.'

The prospect of adventure was tempting. 'How long before I can be released?'

'I already have the papers for your release, but you must be on the first packet to France without returning to Trevowan. You can be of use straightaway.'

Adam sprang up and clasped his hand. 'Then I agree.'

'We will discuss it further over lunch at the inn where I am staying. I will return in an hour to effect your release. You will be given ample funds to cover your expenses in Paris.' He tapped the valise. 'I took the precaution of getting Winnie Fraddon to pack some clothes for you.'

'Could we not have a quiet night without gallivanting out or your house being invaded by people?' Elspeth sighed as she descended the stairs with her sister to await the arrival of guests. 'I grow giddy with all this frivolity.'

'Tonight will be quiet enough. Amelia Allbright is dining with us, and Charles's brother and family.'

Elspeth regarded her sister with suspicion. 'This is the fourth time Mrs Allbright has joined us. That ghastly widower Gerald de Lacey will not be present. He has made no secret that he is looking for a third wife and is eager to be aligned with the Mercer money. He must be nearing seventy.'

'He is a business acquaintance and he is no more than fifty-five. That is not much older than you. He is wealthy and his wife will be mistress of a grand house in the Strand.'

'I told you I want none of your matchmaking. And I have no love for London or ageing roués. As for the Allbright woman, I suppose you have your eye on her for Edward.'

'Amelia is interested in Edward. They met last year.'

Elspeth entered the withdrawing room, with its gilded rococo carvings and delicate French furniture. Upon seating herself at the harpsichord and striking the first notes, she emphasised, 'Amelia Allbright may have set her cap at Edward, but I shall not be home if Gerald de Lacey calls again.'

'I shall never understand you, Elspeth. Many women in your position would be grateful for his attentions.'

Elspeth stopped playing and rounded on her sister. 'De Lacey is the size of two men and full of flatulence. Good Lord, my horses break wind quieter than he, and not so often.'

Margaret spread her panniered skirts and patted her domed powdered hair. She also could be stubborn when she considered she knew what was best for her family. 'He would refuse you nothing. He has a generous nature.'

'He can take himself to the devil.' Elspeth played a piece by Mozart, the erratic temo showing her agitation.

'Did you not even like Charles's friend Andrew McAllister? He is two years younger than you and very personable.'

A discordant chord ended Elspeth's playing. Her glare was outraged. 'He also has nine of the most ghastly and unruly children I have ever set eyes upon. If you are so fond of matchmaking why is it Thomas remains unwed? When he dines here he usually has a male friend accompanying him.'

'Those poets are always hungry. Do you think I have not tried to interest Thomas in a suitable wife? He can be tiresome, he is too wrapped up in his writing.' With a flutter of her fan Margaret changed the subject. 'Do you think Edward is interested in Amelia? He was paying her a great deal of attention at the play.'

'Edward is always charming to unaccompanied women. It means nothing.'

A feminine voice carried to them from the hallway. Margaret cast a knowing look at Elspeth. 'There she is and I can hear Edward is with her.'

The couple entered together. Amelia Allbright was a dozen years Edward's junior. She was tall with unpowdered, russet hair and a trim figure, and was pretty enough to have attracted several admirers since she became a widow two years ago. There was an independent streak to her nature which had stopped any hasty remarriage. Elspeth admired that. The diamonds in her ears and around her neck were not ostentatious, and her rose and silver gown, although of the richest brocade, was sensibly panniered and did not affect the ridiculous width fashion dictated. Her heart-shaped face was tilted as she listened intently to Edward's speech.

Clearly Amelia was taken with her brother. However, his easy charm appeared no more pronounced than usual; or was it? There was a softening to his mouth and the lines of worry which had deepened of late were less noticeable. They did make a handsome couple.

Another outburst of voices distracted Margaret. 'That is Thomas with his friend Lucien.'

The two men sauntered into the room. Elspeth blinked and readjusted her pince-nez as she regarded the resplendent glory of Lucien Greene. She had never seen such an Adonis, and that his frock coat and breeches were of vermilion added to his exotic air. He was some inches over six foot and his flaxen hair was unpowdered, although it was curled in a feminine way around his temples. He looked like he had stepped from a Renaissance painting. When she saw him preening the ruffles of his stock the name Narcissus sprang to mind to erase that of Adonis. And she was sure the man was wearing face powder and patches.

'Lucien is a poet,' Margaret raised her eyebrows as though that should explain his appearance.

'For a moment I wondered if he was a Lucy not a Lucien.' Elspeth again studied him through her pince-nez. 'Quite extraordinary.'

She was aware that Margaret was looking uncomfortable. Her sister leaned closer. 'We do not approve of Thomas's friendship with Lucien. But he is adamant. He even threatened to leave the bank if Charles objected.'

Elspeth turned her attention upon her nephew, who was fawning round Lucien as he introduced him to Edward. It was the first time she had seen Thomas act so gushingly. He could not be more attentive if the man were his fiancée. She agreed with Margaret that Lucien Greene was not a suitable friend for Thomas Mercer.

Whatever her opinions of the poet, he certainly was a lively and amusing conversationalist. He plied them with anecdotes of theatre life and had a scything wit when gossiping about which actress was bedding which lord or duke. Elspeth and Amelia found him vastly entertaining, though Margaret looked rather sour at all the attention her son's friend was gleaning. Charles did not seem at all impressed and kept turning the conversation to more domestic matters. Charles, who was usually always so courteous, clearly had little time for Lucien, and twice Elspeth caught him glance at the man with distaste.

When they withdrew to the music room where Lucien played several pieces for them, Elspeth leaned towards Margaret as they sat together. 'Is Lucien not married? He must be several years older than Thomas.'

'There is a wife somewhere in the country. Hampstead, I believe. They live separate lives and have no children.' Margaret then pointedly nodded towards Amelia, who was seated across from them. Edward was standing behind her chair, draping a shawl across her shoulders. 'Edward would have no more financial problems if he wed Amelia.'

Usually Elspeth dismissed Margaret's matchmaking but her interest was pricked. She found Amelia pleasant and intelligent company. She owned a fine set of carriage horses, which said much for her good taste and her wealth. Because of St John's rash and inappropriate marriage, Edward had been considering selling some of the land. He had even hinted that they could no longer consider the filly Elspeth had been interested in buying from Lord Fetherington. That was unthinkable.

Margaret sighed. 'I suppose Edward is too set in his ways. I cannot see him marrying again.'

'We will see.' Elspeth had a determined sparkle in her eye. 'He always had an eye for the ladies and though he has been discreet, there have been different mistresses over the years. He was very much in love with Marie, but she has been dead so long.'

At first Margaret thought she had misheard her sister's response. But there was an animation about Elspeth only normally apparent on the hunting field.

'So Mrs Allbright is a wealthy widow. How wealthy?' Elspeth enquired.

'Her husband owned property all over London – Belgravia, Mayfair, the Strand – elegant houses rented to noblemen and wealthy businessmen. He died of the typhus.'

There was more laughter from the couple. Margaret smiled indulgently. 'It is good to see Edward so relaxed.'

Elspeth nodded. 'A match would certainly put that upstart Meriel in her place.' It irked her that Meriel already saw herself as mistress of Trevowan, believing that as wife to the heir she had more right to the title than herself. Elspeth would happily relinquish her duties to a woman she saw as worthy. And how much worthier was Amelia Allbright than the strumpet Meriel Sawle.

A week after his interview with the squire Adam arrived at Versailles with some coded documents to deliver. His fluent French and dark colouring enabled him to pose as a Frenchman.

It was five years since he had last been to France and he was shocked at the poverty in many of the villages. The people were gaunt, their faces hardened by deprivation. The children were stick thin, their eyes overlarge in emaciated faces. The people had been taxed past their capabilities and endurance, and the crops were also failing. The price of bread was rising, and with it the numbers of beggars and vagrants.

The documents were sewn into the lining of Adam's jacket and were for Gaston Darnelle who worked as a footman in the palace at Versailles. Adam had been amazed how vast was the network of spies Penwithick organised. The squire suspected that someone within the network working in Paris was a double agent. Three agents in the pay of the British government had been murdered in the last two months. Each had had his throat cut and was found in the Seine. Penwithick wanted Adam to discover the man who was betraying his associates.

It took three weeks of meetings with various agents before Adam had any suspicions. A man going by the name of Jean Pierre Filbert had been seen with the murdered men on occasions before their deaths. Adam would have been surprised if, short and slight of build, Filbert was capable of overpowering the heavier agents. Many of Filbert's associates were insurgents. The back rooms of the taverns he visited rumbled with the voices of dissent against the aristocrats and the unjust taxes and high price of food.

Intent on discovering the truth, one night Adam followed Filbert to a gaming house in a narrow street with high gabled houses. As Filbert entered Adam was forced to flatten himself against the wall of a house as four linkboys carrying flaming torches ran ahead of a closed carriage which rumbled along the cobbles. It was followed by two panting sedan-bearers, who put down their burden outside the gaming house. The stout male occupant complained at the discomfort of the ride and threatened to dismiss his servants. He swaggered up the steps of the gaming house and one of the bearers spat on the ground, mumbling, 'Pigs like him will soon wallow in their own filth.'

A comment like that on its own meant little, but Adam had heard many such rumblings of discontent in recent days. More soldiers were visible on the streets than Adam had seen previously, breaking up any groups of men. The divide between the poor and the wealthy was more noticeable in Paris where many nobles visited from Versailles than elsewhere in France.

He entered the crowded gaming house. It was also a bordello. There was a tawdriness about the interior which repelled Adam. It was an old timber-framed building, poorly lit and reeking of cheap perfume. The furnishings were scuffed and the upholstery torn and worn. The clientele were mostly bourgeois, of the type who liked to emulate the few noblemen present. There was also a rougher element in attendance with whom Filbert seemed at ease. From the lingering odour on their clothes as Adam passed them, they were tannery owners, fishmongers or tripe merchants. Half-dressed, blowsy women, their exposed flesh unappetisingly grey from lack of bathing, sauntered amid the gamblers to entice them to accompany them upstairs.

Filbert was playing at the hazard table. Adam stood watching the play, and observing new arrivals and any signs of Filbert making contact with an associate. To avoid the unwanted attentions of the women he began to wager money he could ill afford. After half an hour a blonde courtesan, who had been with a customer, threw her arms around Filbert and they went to an upstairs room. These rooms led off from a corridor with an open balustrade overlooking the gaming tables.

A young girl was brought out to the staircase and paraded by the raddled madam of the bordello. They halted halfway down the stairs so that the girl was visible to everyone present. She was dressed in a shepherdess-style dress favoured by the Queen, except that no fichu covered her breasts. The small orbs were displayed, her nipples darkly roughed. The split front of the crimson dress was drawn back over a black taffeta underskirt and secured over her hips. Adam looked away in disgust. She could be no more than twelve. Loud shouts broke out amongst a half-dozen men as they jostled to get close to the girl.

'Our Monique is a rare jewel,' the madam crowed. 'She is for the connoisseur who values such beauty. For a man who values the worth of her inncoent charm.

An auction began and, as the bidding rose, the madam removed the girl's bodice to reveal the corset which pushed her small breasts unnaturally high. Then she pulled away the false front of the taffeta underskirt to reveal slender limbs in scarlet hose and black garters. A short chemise barely covered her hips. The men bayed like wolves over a carcass, their bids doubling in their lust for possession. The bidding reached a climax and there was a triumphant shout from a man in his mid-twenties who had outbid his opponents.

Adam looked at the face of the girl. Her eyes were wide open but without expression. It was obvious she had been drugged. The man who had won her was drawing her up the stairs to a room. From his rich attire he was a nobleman, his handsome face scored by lines of debauchery. The girl moved with the jerkiness of a marionette.

Adam turned his back on the proceedings. Filbert had not reappeared and Adam's losses at the table were mounting. He was down to his last livre when Filbert appeared on the stairs. A scream came from behind the door where the young girl had been taken. Several more followed. Then silence.

A man sidled up to Filbert and they spoke for several minutes. Adam then saw the stranger surreptitiously hand a money pouch to Filbert, who pocketed it and prepared to leave. Adam decided to follow the stranger. He excused himself from the card game and followed him into the street.

It was two in the morning. Scufflings from the shadows alerted him to the danger of footpads. Since only noblemen or military officers were permitted to wear swords in France, Adam had a dagger hidden in his boot. As he rounded the corner of the bordello another scream came from the house. A second-storey window was flung open and for a brief second he glimpsed the naked figure of the girl Monique on the ledge before she flung herself on to the cobbles. Her pale body lay unmoving in the light of the open window. Her back and buttocks were crisscrossed with whip and teeth marks. Her hands were bound together with a length of silk and the same binding was around one ankle. The girl had been tied up as that monster performed his atrocities upon her.

Adam swallowed the nausea which rose to his throat. The inhuman savage who had done this to her deserved to hang for his vile lechery. The man he was following was far ahead.

Adam hesitated as he drew level with the body. Her eyes were open and unfocused. He pulled off his gloves and stooped to put a finger to her throat. There was no pulse. She was dead. A tragic waste to a young life.

He stumbled away. The girl's face and the man's triumphant leering as he led his prize away haunted his footsteps as he hurried after his quarry.

They traversed the labyrinth of streets, passing close to Notre-Dame. The man disappeared down a narrow alleyway and, as Adam cautiously approached, he heard the hacking cough of a beggar in the shadows.

'Ah, Manigault, my friend. A few sous to buy some soup. I have not eaten in two days.'

Now Adam had the man's name he could make further enquiries.

Chapter Twenty-Two

It took Adam three weeks to gain enough information about Henri Manigault, who was a printer, to prove he was a double agent. The man was the son of a Jacobite who had brought his family to France to escape the persecution of the followers of Charles Edward Stuart after the '45 rebellion. His father and mother had died penniless within five years of their exile. Henri had been adopted by a French printer and his wife and had taken their name. Now in his fifties, Henry was an ardent revolutionary with no love for the Hanoverians on the English throne nor for Louis of France. To him monarchy meant repression. He gave information to whoever paid him highest.

Adam was appalled that his investigations revealed how rife the discontent was towards the monarchy in France. In the back rooms of coffee houses the whispers of rebellion grew more forceful.

Once the identity of the double agent was known Adam had been given strict instructions not to deal with the man himself. His name was to be passed to another agent known as Lizard, who was a professional beggar and pickpocket in the Montmartre district.

Six weeks after his arrival in France, Adam visited the Riviere family. This morning he had been seen by Uncle Claude when he was following Manigault across the square in front of Notre-Dame. He was hailed by his uncle, who was affronted that he was in Paris and not staying with them.

'I arrived late last night,' Adam lied. 'And took a room at an inn so as not to disturb you. Squire Penwithick had asked me to deliver a letter to a business acquaintance when he learned I was to visit Paris. I intended to call on your family this afternoon.'

'Then you will stay with us. Lisette has been pining for you, and your aunt will be delighted. What is your business in Paris?'

'To visit Lisette. I fear I have neglected her. I have left the navy and will be working in the yard. Papa suggested I made a brief visit to France first.'

Adam realised he would rouse suspicion if he did not reside at the Riviere house. Fortunately his investigations were coming to an end. Following Manigault had become a formality. There was a meeting he must attend in two evenings' time as he had infiltrated the insurgent's circle, passing himself off as a Frenchman who was equally incensed at the tyranny of the nobility. He would make excuses to get away from the family that evening. Then he hoped his report for Penwithick would be complete and he could return to England.

'Louise and Lisette are at home this afternoon. Lisette has recently been low with a fever but she has recovered now. Louise insists that she rests. There could be no better aid to her recovery than sight of her betrothed. Surprise them. I will be home early, but now I must hurry to a meeting. *Adieu*.'

The Riviere house was an elegant mansion of gold sandstone on the Rue St-Honoré. The maid, Blanche, who opened the door, had been with the Rivieres since their wedding. On recognising Adam she threw her apron over her face, her ample girth quivering in her excitement.

'*Oh là là!* Monsieur Loveday. Such a surprise. A delight, no? I will tell Madame and Mademoiselle you are here. They are in the saloon. We will surprise them, no? Maître Riviere is at the warehouse.'

'Blanche, who are you talking to?' Lisette called from the upper floor. 'Have we visitors?'

Her dark head appeared over the banisters and she let out a scream of joy. 'Adam! Maman, it is Adam!' She ran down the stairs and flung herself into his arms. '*Mon chéri*, I have missed you so much.'

When he would have kissed her cheek, he found her lips fastened like a limpet to his, and her arms wound around his neck as she pressed himself against him. The passion of her welcome astounded him.

'Is it really you, Adam?' Aunt Louise called from the upper saloon.

Gently Adam disengaged his fiancée's arms.

'Let me see you, Lisette. You have grown and are more beautiful.'

'It has been eight months. Have you missed me?'

'But of course.' He felt a twinge of guilt at how little thought he had given her. His eyes sparkled with mirth as he looked down at her. She was lovely, but still so childlike. Yet her innocence was refreshing. Last time he had compared her unfavourably to Meriel. Now it was her sweetness and freshness which put any comparison in Lisette's favour.

Aunt Louise was equally ardent in her welcome. 'I had no idea you were in France. You will stay with us, of course.'

'Thank you. I have left the navy and wanted some time to myself before I began work in the yard.'

The excuse sounded lame to him, but his aunt and Lisette accepted it without question.

'It will be so much better for Lisette when you marry that you are not at sea for months at a time.'

'But I intend to have my own ship,' he reminded his aunt. 'As a merchant captain I will still be at sea.'

'It is not the same. The voyages will not be for so long. You will be your own master.'

He did not dispute with her. If he was to engage in trade in the West Indies, Americas or the South Seas he would still be away for months.

'Your uncle is at the warehouse. He will be delighted at your visit.'

Lisette let out a shriek. 'Adam, your poor face. It is scarred. How dreadful. Were you in a battle?'

Adam touched the crescent-shaped line on his cheek. It had healed neatly but with his skin so swarthy from his open-air life, the scar was white against the darker flesh.

'Not a battle. It happened in Cornwall.'

'Were you attacked by a highwayman? Did you kill the rogue?' Lisette gaped in open-mouthed wonder.

'Hardly. It was nothing.'

'But how did it happen?' Lisette insisted.

Irritated by her persistence at something he felt unworthy of such attention he explained.

'How dashing and courageous of you,' Lisette cooed. 'Mama, is he not so brave and daring?'

Aunt Louise laughed. 'It was very noble of Adam but you are embarrassing him by making so much of it.'

'I think it is wonderful. I am so proud of him,' Lisette gushed. 'It is not so bad a scar. You are so handsome, Adam, you carry it well. Like a badge of valour.' She clasped her hands ecstatically to her breast.

Adam could see no glamour in the scar or the terrifying events of Bridie's ordeal. Lisette's shallowness annoyed him. He had seen too many hideously scarred seamen wounded by grapeshot, or more commonly splintered wood, either in a battle or a storm.

To change the subject he asked, 'Aunt, how is Uncle Claude's health?'

'He has been much better this summer. But I insist he rests more and does not have too many worries. It is anxiety and working too hard which caused his last attack.'

Lisette said, 'Etienne is supposed to be taking over at the warehouse, but since his marriage he spends less time there.'

'Etienne is married?' Adam raised an eyebrow at his aunt. 'When was this?'

'In June.' Aunt Louise replied. 'Did Edward not get my letter?'

'I have not been at Trevowan for some weeks. Who did he marry?'

'Such a match, you will not believe. He has wed the youngest daughter of the Marquis de Archachon. Unfortunately there is no money. Vivienne is the youngest of ten daughters. It has made a great difference to your uncle's business. Many of the nobles now purchase their silks and brocades from us.'

165

'Giving poor Papa much work,' Lisette said. 'We scarcely see him. If Papa is ill again it will be Etienne's fault.'

'Of course Etienne must spend time with his bride.' There was strain in his aunt's voice. 'Claude purchased a house for them. It is almost as grand as our own, except Vivienne finds it cramped after living in a château.'

'Without a dowry what has she to complain about?' Lisette said. 'I do not like her. She thinks we are beneath her.'

'We all need time to get to know each other better, my dear,' Aunt Louise looked displeased. 'It is early days.'

'How long can you stay?' Lisette pulled Adam down on to an elegant gilded and brocade-covered settee and linked her arm through his. 'I will be heartbroken if it is for less than a month.'

'I cannot stay so long. A week at most.'

'Shame on you, Adam.' Aunt Louise looked appalled. 'Lisette has been pining for you. I insist you stay a month. And now that St John and Etienne are married, it is not too soon to start making plans for your wedding. Have you decided whether it will be in England or France?'

Adam felt as though he had been engulfed in a sudden avalanche. 'It was agreed we would not wed until Lisette was eighteen.'

'Oh, that is nonsense!' Aunt Louise brushed aside his protest. 'It is not fair on Lisette that she sees so little of you. Why can it not be this September?'

'Because I will not wed until I have established myself in business and can support a wife.' The excuse sounded pompous to his ears and he hated the reluctance which made him speak out in such a fashion.

Aunt Louise gave an airy wave. 'Lisette's dowry is ample. You must not allow your pride to get in the way of love. St John did not. And I had always thought him the less adventurous one.'

'St John is heir to Trevowan. I have to make my own way in the world.' He struggled to keep his temper. 'It was agreed we shall wed when Lisette is eighteen.'

Lisette burst into tears. Aunt Lousie threw up her arms. 'Adam, how can you be so heartless? She is teased mercilessly by her friends that she has no lover courting her.'

'I cannot help that we live in different countries.'

'You have neglected her badly.'

Aunt Louise rose from her chair. 'I will leave you two to talk. I must give Blanche instructions about the meal and preparing your room, Adam. This is a delicate matter and must be resolved. I trust that in the circumstances Lisette does not need a chaperon.'

When Lisette continued to cry, he put his arm around her. 'Do not take on so. What sort of a man would I be if I was content to live off your dowry?'

'We would be together,' she wheedled. 'Uncle Edward said we could live at Trevowan.'

Adam sighed. 'Are you so eager to leave your family and friends? Life in England will be very different from how you live here? Trevowan is quiet, so unlike Paris which has many entertainments.'

She pouted and withdrew to the far end of the settee. 'It is as Etienne says. You do not love me. You are marrying me for my money, that is all. Because father insisted.'

'If I was marrying you for your money, do you not think I would have wed you by now, so I could get my hands on it?' Outraged, he rose to stand by the carved marble fireplace. He had not expected to walk into an inquisition as to his intentions. He had assumed the wedding plans satisfactorily set aside until Lisette was eighteen.

He mastered his anger. She was only sixteen, an age where girls' heads were filled with dreams of romance and of knights on white chargers. That was hardly how he saw himself. The circumstances which had brought him to France and saved him from his imprisonment was not the fabric of heroes.

When he turned to face her, she had dried her eyes and they now flashed with indignation as she accused, 'There is another woman who has your love.'

'Good Lord, where did you get that notion? Etienne, I suppose. Your brother does not want us to marry. He is trying to poison you against me.'

She jumped up in alarm. 'No. Never that.' She threw her arms around him to hold him close. Her lovely face tilted to look up at him, her expression beseeching. 'Etienne is worried for my happiness. He knows I adore you. He thinks you do not feel the same about me.'

He put his hands on her arms and smiled down at her. 'Now I am no longer in the navy I have more time to visit France.'

'Two years is too long to wait for us to marry,' she pouted. 'Let it be next summer. All my friends are married. I do not want to be an old maid.'

'Sixteen is not an old maid.' He made light of her entreaty.

She flounced away from him. 'You are heartless.'

He moved to her side and tipped up her chin with his finger. 'I have given you my promise. I will not break it. And there is no other woman, if that is what you fear.'

He kissed her tenderly, knowing no better way of silencing her demands. She drew back breathless, but her lips remained parted, inviting another kiss.

Louise Riviere entered with a rustle of silk, having deemed the couple had been alone long enough to resolve their differences. She was determined that before Adam left, the date for the wedding would be set.

Adam extended his stay to ten days. It was good to see Claude Riviere looking in better health, but there remained a heaviness to his tread and a breathlessness which warned Adam he was far from robust. There had been one frosty meeting with Etienne and his imperious bride. The name of the Marquis de Gramont and his interest in Lisette was constantly mentioned by Etienne.

On the Sunday before Adam was to leave, the family strolled in the Tuileries Gardens. Etienne and Vivienne had joined them. Vivienne was no beauty. She may have fine blue eyes but too often they flashed with scorn. Her long hooked nose was prepossessing and the wide mouth turned down in disparagement. Adam had given up trying to make polite conversation with her. She answered curtly as though deigning him a great favour.

'The Marquis de Gramont is an ardent admirer of Lisette,' Etienne provoked. 'Another month of your neglect and I declare Lisette would have found consolation in his arms.'

'I would not,' Lisette blushed. She was walking with her arm linked through Adam's and had been happily introducing him to any acquaintance they met. 'How can you say such things, Etienne? I love Adam.'

'But you like it when such an eminent man pays you attention, do you not, little one?'

'Stop teasing her,' Uncle Claude snapped. 'I will not have her in the company of that man.'

'Can I help it if Lisette meets him when we attend the theatre?' There was an oily smoothness to Etienne's voice. 'He is an important man and has brought much business to us. To insult him would be a grave mistake.'

'You insult your sister by allowing him to believe she may return his affections one day,' said Aunt Louise.

Lisette giggled. 'Etienne, you must inform the Marquis that Adam and I will marry next year.'

The agreement had been drawn from Adam for the wedding to take place in September next year after pressure from his aunt and uncle. Since their marriage was inevitable, he had complied. Lisette had matured since their betrothal and was accomplished at flirting. She was less shy and enjoyed taunting him so that he would kiss her. Her wit had sharpened and she often made him laugh. Her response to his kisses was unrestrained and, although out of respect he curbed the desire she could rouse in him, he was aware of the passionate side of her nature. He no longer considered the prospect of marriage such a burden. In time he believed they could find happiness together.

'Then you must be sure not to neglect her,' Etienne jeered.

'Your words are offensive, cousin. If Lisette did not wish our marriage I would not stand in the way of her happiness.'

Lisette looked appalled. 'I want to marry you, Adam, as we planned.' Her voice rose with passion. 'I love you.' Suddenly Lisette tensed. 'I am glad you are with me, Adam. The Marquis de Gramont approaches.'

Adam suppressed a shudder of shock. Gramont was the nobleman who had been at the bordello and whose bestiality had cause the young Monique to take her life.

He cursed that he could not unmask the libertine for the monster he was. How could he without revealing how he had come by that information? The work he did for Penwithick had to remain a secret, especially from his French relations, who may see it as treachery to their country.

Chapter Twenty-Three

'The child is breech. Ask the husband if he wants us to save his wife or the baby,' Dr Chegwidden ordered. He had removed his bagwig long ago and his shaven head glistened with sweat.

Meriel gave a hoarse scream her voice weak from the long hours of ordeal. The room was stifling in the late July heat. It was three in the afternoon and the sun streamed through the window Dr Chegwidden ordered kept closed. Three women, drenched in their own sweat, wrung their hands and murmured encouragement to the woman in labour. Each was staring at the stooped figure of the doctor working over Meriel.

Ginny Rundle, the midwife, shook her head. 'She's been in labour for three days. The child won't turn. I've tried all I know.'

Jenna Biddick groaned, wishing they would give her duties anywhere but in this room. It was the first time the maid had attended a birth and she looked terrified.

Another scream from Meriel sent Elspeth hurrying from the room. St John and Edward were closeted in the study.

'Chegwidden says you must chose between the mother or child.'

Edward whitened and rubbed a hand across his sweating brow. It was obvious he was reliving the agony of his own wife's death at the birth of the twins.

'There will be other children,' Edward commiserated.

Another tortured scream made both men flinch. St John nodded. 'Chegwidden must do all he can for Meriel.'

As Elspeth opened the door to leave a scream echoed chillingly around the house. It was cut short, the sudden silence ominous. All three sped towards the stairs and then paused to stare at one another. The faint cry of an infant carried to them.

Jenna was running towards them, her round face flushed with excitement. 'It be a girl, Mr Loveday.'

'And Meriel?' Elspeth demanded, already on a level with the maid despite her hip.

'Doctor be tending her now. Says for you to wait outside till he's done.'

'Nonsense, I will not be so ordered in my own home.' Elspeth limped into the bedchamber. The smell of sweat and blood hit her afresh. Dr Chegwidden was bent over Meriel, who was unconscious. Her face was whiter than the sheets and there seemed an alarming amount of blood.

Elspeth turned away from the scene and nodded to Ginny to show her the child. Ginny was washing the baby. It was capped with a riot of dark hair and was red-faced with what looked like bad temper. 'Looks like a skinned rabbit.'

Ginny tutted. 'She is a bonny thing.'

'Should she be crying like that?'

'Poor mite.' Ginny bit her lip. Her arm and leg were broke when Chegwidden delivered her. Once he's dealt with Meriel, he'll do what he can for the baby.'

A closer inspection showed a knee joint discoloured and the lower leg at a twisted angle. A hand also seemed to flop unnaturally and her arm was blue and oddly twisted.

'Little chance the child will live,' Dr Chegwidden said wearily, 'but I will bind her in swaddling which will give her bones a chance to mend.'

'And the mother?' Elspeth demanded.

'She has lost a great deal of blood and was badly torn. Still, she is young and strong. I have stopped the haemorrhaging. If she gets through the next day without another, or getting childbed fever she will pull through. I will stay on hand for an hour or so in case I am needed.'

A half-hour later Dr Chegwidden was downstairs devouring a vast plate of fish pie. Edward and St John were drinking brandies. Edward looked worried. 'I suppose the baby should be christened without delay if she is that weak.'

'Yes.' Chegwidden scratched at his wide side whiskers. 'Bad business, a breech birth. Her arm and leg may never be right.' He addressed St John. 'Your wife will need six months before she can be a proper wife to you again. And I cannot be sure if she will be capable of bearing more children. I'm sorry.'

St John broke away from his chair and stood in front of the fire, his head resting on his hands. 'Are you telling me that after all I have gone through she will not give me a son?'

'That is in God's hands.'

'No woman can inherit Trevowan while a Loveday male lives.' St John slammed his brandy glass down on the table and stormed from the room.

Edward recovered from his own anger at St John's outburst. 'Forgive him. He speaks out of shock. Naturally a man wants his own son to inherit.'

Chegwidden frowned after St John. 'He should be thankful his wife survived. But you are not yet old yourself, Edward. It will be

172

many years before St John becomes master here.'

Upstairs, Elspeth sat with Meriel until St John would visit her. Meriel remained deathly pale and her breathing was shallow. When her nephew did not appear after two hours, Elspeth was angry at his neglect.

Meriel stirred, opened her eyes, and let out a painful groan. 'Jesu, never again,' she vowed.

'You were very brave. You have a lovely daughter.' Elspeth gestured for Jenna to fetch the baby. She had not stopped squalling and had been taken out of the room to the nursery to allow Meriel to recover.

When the screaming baby was held before her, Meriel turned her head away. 'I am too tired. Where is St John? Why did no one wake me when he came in?'

Meriel saw the expression in Elspeth's eyes before she could avert them. The baby screamed louder as though sensing her rejection. 'The bastard didn't come, did he? He's disappointed it be a girl.'

Her lapse into common speech was forgiven by Elspeth in the circumstances.

'Poor mite be hungry.' Jenna held the baby closer.

Meriel shuddered and closed her eyes. 'Take her away. Get a wet nurse for her. I can't stand that mewling.'

Jenna turned her shocked stare upon Elspeth, who nodded for her to remove the child. Dr Chegwidden had been insistent that Meriel rest, as another haemorrhage would kill her.

The maid hesitated then blurted out, 'Ginny said her son's wife, Nell, has milk enough if we need a wet nurse. She'll come over from Penruan.'

'Send word to her. Give me the infant.' Cradling the baby, Elspeth felt a tightening around her heart. She tried to rally the mother's spirits. 'She is strong. Many eight-month children do not survive. That fall down the stairs which brought on your labour could so easily have killed you both. What will you call her?'

Meriel did not answer. She closed her eyes, the tears pushing through her lashes to run down her cheeks on to the pillows. 'Without a son, St John will never accept me. He will find a way to put me aside. He hates Adam too much to see him as his heir.'

Elspeth went cold. 'You exaggerate. Your ordeal has weakened you. St John will not put you aside over this. If ever there was a man in love with his wife, he is. At first I thought it was an act to save face, but I have seen the way he watches you. He loves you.'

'I had thought so too. The child has ruined everything. And if I cannot have another . . .'

Elspeth's dislike of the woman mellowed. The baby brought so brutally into the world was fighting for survival. She awakened a response of warmth and love lacking in Elspeth's life and she felt a need to protect the child. 'Meriel, you must concentrate on regaining your strength. Once you are recovered you will be received by our neighbours. What does Chegwidden know of women's matters? You must never give up hope.'

The light kindled behind Meriel's closed eyes. She would not be discounted. She would regain her strength and then the Lovedays would realise she was a force to be reckoned with.

Neither Meriel nor St John seemed able to decide on a name for the child by the next day when Joshua Loveday arrived to perform a hasty christening.

'What does a name matter, the child will die anyway?' St John flared. He had been drinking heavily since the birth. He looked haggard and avoided Meriel's entreating gaze.

'She reminds me of Rowena.' Elspeth wiped a tear from her eye. 'Your little twin sister, Edward, was so tiny and so helpless. She was only a month old when she died.'

Joshua and Cecily were taken to Meriel's chamber where the christening was to be conducted. Meriel was too weak to sit up and with the infant's name undecided, Elspeth claimed her as her goddaughter and named her Rowena. She stared down at the frail baby, who had been silenced by an opiate tincture prescribed by Dr Chegwidden and vowed, 'You will live.'

Rowen had carved a place in her heart denied her since the loss of her own baby. After the child was baptised Elspeth took her to the nursery. As the rest of the family filed from the bedchamber, Meriel held out her hand to St John.

'Go to her,' Edward commanded. 'Be grateful she is alive and, God willing, Rowena will be spared.'

Alone with his wife St John still could not look at her. He fiddled with a tassel of the bedhangings and stared across at the fire in the hearth.

'I have failed you. I am sorry,' Meriel sobbed. 'You must hate me now I may not ever give you a son.'

An anguished groan was torn from him. 'Have you any idea what I went through listening to all those hours of your screaming? I put you through that torture. It was my fault. I could not bear it. I was convinced you would die as my mother had done. Then to learn it was all for a girl . . .'

He slumped on the bed, the abruptness of his descending weight sending a jolt of pain through her body. She controlled a wince but the tears would not be dammed.

Immediately he took her hands and smothered them with kisses. 'What a monster you must think of me, my love. Yes, I ranted that you had produced a girl; it was the only way I could express my anger at how you had suffered.'

'You are lying, St John. I do not doubt your love but at least be honest with me. You will come to hate me because unless I give you a son, Adam will one day inherit Trevowan. All you work for will be his.'

'He has to outlive me.' St John attempted to make it sound like a joke. 'Forgive me for all you have suffered.'

He had allayed her fears, and a measure of her power over him returning was evident in the pleading in his eyes. He was fumbling in his pocket and drew out a leather jewel case. 'Papa, gave me these for you. They were my grandmother's.'

Meriel stared in delight at the beautiful amethyst necklace and matching bracelet and earrings. She put her hand to her ears in dismay. 'My ears are not pierced. I will get Jenna to do it immediately so that I can wear the earrings during my lying-in. Do put the necklace on and bring me a mirror.'

She smiled into the mirror to see the amethysts gleaming at her throat and turned her wrist from side to side to admire the bracelet. They were not the diamonds she had craved, but they were proof of her acceptance into the family. Elspeth was right. She must recover her strength for now she would be included in the social entertainments attended by the family. For her first ball she would wheedle a diamond necklace from the Loveday bank vault. She was on her way to being accepted by the society of the county. And she was determined that all her dreams would come true.

After the baptism Joshua walked with Edward through the orchard of Trevowan, Sabre and Barnaby foraging for rabbits ahead of them.

'I shall pray the child recovers. Such a sorry affair . . . Is it likely she will be a cripple?'

Edward sighed. 'Chegwidden believes she will die and that Meriel will bear no more children.'

Joshua put his hand on his older brother's shoulder. 'Then it will eventually be for Adam to carry on the Loveday line.'

'It is early days to think of that.'

'Quite so, but what of Adam? I heard of his arrest but when I went to the gaol last month they said he had been released.'

'Penwithick intervened, but felt in the circumstances that Adam should cool his heels for a while. He has gone to France to visit his fiancée.'

'Our erstwhile squire has the ear of our Prime Minister. Is it on government business Adam is engaged?'

'Penwithick did not say. He gave the impression it was better not to ask. I am grateful he got the boy off of those ridiculous charges.'

'What happened to the other man involved? A bounder called Lieutenant Beaumont, was it not?'

'Cashiered. Though I heard he is now with the excise service and in charge of a revenue cutter.'

'When do you expect Adam home?'

'He has been gone several weeks. Before all this happened he spoke of becoming more involved in the yard. But he will not work with St John. Adam is a born shipwright. He loves the yard and has a great knowledge of ships. St John has no interest nor aptitude. Yet Father and Grandfather were always adamant the yard and estate remained linked together.'

Joshua nodded. 'But you must do what is right for your family. How did your negotiations go in London?'

There was a secretive smile about Edward's lips as he answered, 'Very well. I secured a favourable loan and orders for two brigantines to be built over the next two years. They are to be built to Adam's plans.'

'Then I think it is right that Adam should inherit the yard. When the present brig is finished the final payments should secure the yard's future.'

They walked to the edge of the cliffs and stared out across the cove. The sun was hot in a cloudless sky and the waves lapped against the shore. A cormorant was perched on an outcrop of rock and they watched it beat its wide wings and take flight. Edward did not speak for some moments.

'The *Pegasus* is Adam's ship, built from a legacy left him by Uncle Amos. There is a restlessness about Adam. I see him on the open sea rather than spending all his days as a shipwright.'

Joshua laughed. 'He is young. Give him a few years of adventuring at sea. If I know Adam his head will always be full of the ships he wants to build. But Adam should know your plans for his future. And so should St John. Though I can guess it will cause dissent with him.'

'That is what I prefer to avoid. But when Adam returns it must be resolved.' They both turned back to regard Trevowan House. Edward became reflective. 'There's a wildness in our blood. Take our brother Hubert, and William will never settle down. And what of Japhet?'

'I despair of the boy. He has never done a decent day's work in his life as far as I know, but he is never short of money. I suppose he has been living off the proceeds of his share of Amos's legacy. He is talking of going to London. That place was nearly my undoing.'

'It was the making of you. Did you not come home vowing to take the cloth?'

'I had much to atone for. Not least a man's life. A worthless vagabond of a highwayman to be sure but still a life. And too many other men injured in duels. I do not want that for Japhet.'

'You must trust that Japhet will see the error of his ways as you did. You were a rakehell in your youth, Joshua.'

'And you were never so innocent. Though you changed after marrying.'

'I still miss her, you know,' Edward said heavily.

Joshua nodded. 'She would not have wanted you to be alone for the rest of your life.'

'You sound like Elspeth.' They laughed. Edward was easier in his mind. There was much to be resolved and many difficulties to overcome. Not least his own plans for the future.

Chapter Twenty-Four

Nell Rundle continued to wet nurse the baby when Meriel protested she was too ill. Neither did Merial show any inclination to hold and comfort the infant. Each time she was brought to her, Meriel ordered Rowena taken away.

'That screaming goes straight through my head,' she wailed. 'How can I bear it? Rundle will nurse her. She does not need me.'

'Every child needs its mother,' Elspeth urged.

Meriel turned her head away, refusing to acknowledge the presence of her daughter. With two young children of her own, Nell Rundle trudged with them from the village every morning and stayed at Trevowan all day.

At the end of the second week, Elspeth was worried about Rowena's health. She started screaming as soon as she awoke and was only quietened by the doctor's medicine. She then slept for hours in an unnaturally long and deep slumber. Most worrying was her lack of interest in suckling. She was becoming weaker by the day. Dr Chegwidden had been called out several times.

'There is nothing more I can do, Elspeth,' he declared with a shake of his whiskered head. 'It is in God's hands if she lives or dies.'

Elspeth spent hours each day in the nursery. She was determined that this Rowena would live. One morning Nell picked up the baby to suckle her and she no longer screamed but whimpered and would take no milk at all.

'She'll not last the day if you want my opinion.' Nell looked despairing.

'She will not die.' Elspeth took Rowena from her and held the baby close. 'Tell Japser Fraddon to saddle two horses immediately.'

She mounted her mare and Jenna handed Rowena up to Jasper. 'Do not jostle her,' Elspeth ordered. 'I am taking her to the Polglase cottage.'

Leah and Bridie were working in the garden. The ugly mastiff stood growling at the door.

'Good day, Miss Loveday.' Leah wiped her hands on her apron.

'Good day. Is Senara at home? I need her help. The child is dying.'

There was a wariness in Leah's manner. 'Dr Chegwidden should tend her.'

'Chegwidden says he can do nothing more. Senara helped me. Please . . .' Tears filled her eyes. 'If there is anything your daughter can do . . .'

'Best come inside.' Leah turned to Bridie. 'Put Angel in the stable.'

Senara was finishing a clay jug and continued her work at the potter's wheel as Elspeth entered the cottage. But at hearing the pitiful cries from the baby she stopped the wheel.

'The child is dying,' Elspeth repeated. 'Please, she seems in such pain and now will not suckle.'

Without speaking Senara washed her hands in a basin and threw the dirty water away. She took Rowena and stared down at the baby. 'What does your doctor say? The Lovedays can afford the best of physicians. Why come to me?'

'Chegwidden says it's in God's hands. But you helped me. And my mare. You have a knowledge . . .'

'I am no physician. I have a little knowledge of poultices and herbs, that is all.' There was a harshness in Senara's voice.

'So you would let this baby die without trying?' Elspeth accused.

Leah came forward to look at Rowena and her expression was grave as she regarded her daughter. 'Perhaps you should at least see if there is anything—'

'You were the one who said I should stop. Look at the trouble it has caused in the past.'

'She is an infant.' Leah shrugged. 'You save so many woodland creatures. We can trust Miss Loveday. She is not like the others.'

As though in acknowledgement the barn owl flapped its wings in the rafters.

Senara laid Rowena on the table. 'What is wrong with her?'

Elspeth explained the difficult birth while Senara unwrapped the foul-smelling swaddling. She threw it on the fire with a moan of disgust. 'It is a barbaric custom. No wonder the child is crying. Her skin is raw. Her leg seems to be healing but it will grow twisted if it is not bandaged securely. But no more swaddling bands. It is her arm which is causing the problem. It looks dislocated at the shoulder, probably from the birth; also the nerves may be damaged. I will do what I can, but I fear she will never have the proper use of her left hand.'

'But can you save her life? She is so weak.'

Senara lifted her green gaze from examining Rowena. 'I can make no promises.'

'Come back to Trevowan. Stay until she is well,' Elspeth declared.

Senara ignored her plea and worked in silence. Once her leg and arm had been carefully bandaged Rowena stopped whimpering.

'I will make up an infusion to be given to her at night and morning but it will take some while to prepare.'

'I will wait.' Elspeth was impressed at the way the young woman

180

worked and the tenderness of her ministrations. Strange as it seemed, her presence alone had seemed to calm Rowena. 'I am much obliged to you. How much do I owe you?'

'There is no charge but you must tell no one that I have tended her.'

'But surely if you can help Rowena, you can help others?'

Leah interrupted. 'You must tell no one. People are frightened of anything they do not understand. Senara uses knowledge she learned as a child. Her father was a gypsy and I travelled with his family for many years – until he and his brother were arrested for poaching and hanged. Senara was taught the use of herbs by her grandmother, who was a wise woman. Living with the gypsies taught us much about prejudice and persecution towards any who are different.'

'Is that why you live in seclusion?' Elspeth asked.

'That and Bridie. She too has suffered.'

'She is a charming girl and seems very bright.' The girl was outside chatting animatedly to Jasper Fraddon.

'Little good it will do her. We prefer to keep ourselves from prying eyes.'

'Yet do you not fear being two women alone?'

'We have Angel for protection.' Leah cleared away the basin Senara had used, angry at her indiscretion. She usually guarded her tongue well.

It was not easy living alone as they did. And none more than she was aware of the dangers. She had been raped by three soldiers when she had gone to Bodmin to hear her lover's trial. With no money she had slept in the hedgerow the night before her lover was hanged. That was where the men found her. She was helpless against them. Bridie was the outcome of that horrific ordeal.

Leah added with emphasis, 'Our needs are simple. We prefer to live alone.'

'Here is the child's tincture.' Senara placed a small bottle in Elspeth's hands. 'It will help strengthen her. She will need less of the opiate prescribed by your physician. The leg should be bandaged for another month.'

'And her hand?'

'There is little to be done. I have reset the shoulder and wrist but if a nerve was damaged there is nothing even a skilled surgeon could do. A gentle massage along her arm and fingers three or four times a day will keep the blood flowing and lessen the effects of the damage. The hand does not appear to be giving her pain. A little honey in water will also help her strength.'

Elspeth placed several silver coins on the table. Senara shook her head. 'I take no payment. The herbs are in the woods or grown from gathered seeds and cost nothing.'

181

The family had so little; the house although neat and tidy, was no better than a hovel. Life could not be easy for them. Yet the dignity of the younger woman put many of those in Elspeth's class to shame.

Returning to her mare, Elspeth was startled by the flapping of wings and a magpie flew in to rest on Senara's shoulder. It wobbled precariously and Elspeth saw it had only one leg.

Leah called Bridie and the three females stood together. None of them could read or write and yet there was about all three of them a wisdom beyond Elspeth's education.

Senara shivered as Elspeth and Jasper Fraddon rode away. 'That family will bring us trouble, I sense it.'

'We cannot keep running away. I am too old to spend another winter on the road. Bridie is happy here. We are left in peace.'

'But for how long?' Senara looked haunted.

'What do you mean, you have used a legacy which should have been mine to pay for the new dry dock in the yard?' St John shouted at his father. 'You had no right.'

'It is to secure your livelihood. It will be repaid in six months. What need have you for the money when all your needs are met?'

St John was puce with rage as he faced his father in the study. 'I have received no allowance since my marriage. Now you say I must wait another six months for this legacy. I have a wife and child to provide for. And unlike you, I am not so old I would moulder in Trevowan every day and night.'

'You would spend it on gambling,' Edward retorted.

'Perhaps I have investments of my own. This is outrageous.' St John almost wept with frustration. The legacy would have made a large investment in the smuggling trade. The return would be enormous. He had paid back the loan on the pewter and silver to avoid discovery by his father. It had left him only sixty pounds to invest in the last cargo. He had yet to receive the profits from that as it took weeks for the goods to be dispersed and paid for.

'I can let you have some on account. Say two hundred pounds.'

'And have you also spent Adam's legacy on the dry dock?'

'That went on the materials to build the *Pegasus*. I can understand your anger, St John, but you should have the interest of the yard at heart. Instead, this selfish attitude leads me to believe that you are not as committed to the yard as you should be. Would that you cherished it as does your brother, for then it would prosper.'

Suspicion filled St John with dread. 'You are thinking of breaking the trust. You want Adam to have the yard. He cannot. It is mine. I am the elder son.'

'I will do whatever is necessary to preserve the prosperity of the yard.'

St John stormed from the study. Edward lost his patience with his elder son. The atmosphere in his home since the wedding was becoming intolerable. He liked a quiet life, not all this arguing and turmoil. At least the next few weeks would be peaceful. He was travelling to London. Charles had found him a new investor willing to loan him the finance to expand the yard and enable them to build and repair the larger ships which would make the yard profitable again.

Chapter Twenty-Five

R owena did not die. No longer in her swaddling bands, she stopped screaming. A month after Elspeth took the baby to Senara, Meriel rose from her lying-in. Rowena was putting on weight and her broken leg was straight and strong. A long-sleeved nightgown covered her left hand. A hand she never moved.

Meriel stood naked in her bedchamber and ran her hands over her stomach. She was horrified at the sagginess of the muscles. Dr Chegwidden had told her it was unlikely she would conceive another child. She refused to believe him; she needed a son to secure her place at Trevowan. During her lying-in she had been busy plotting ways to establish herself with the local gentry.

Feeling stronger, she summoned Jenna to help her dress and ventured downstairs to the parlour. Edward was again in London and St John had taken advantage of his father's absence to make a smuggling run. Adam had returned two days ago and had spent all his time since at the yard. She had gone downstairs for the first time for the evening meal yesterday. Adam had looked more handsome than ever. He had scarcely spoken to her, merely congratulating her on the birth of Rowena and her recovery. Her hatred for him grew. One day he would suffer for all the insults and indignities heaped upon her. In the meantime she was alone in the house. With Elspeth out riding she was free to indulge her fantasy of ousting Elspeth from her role of mistress of Trevowan.

It was market day in St Austell and Senara had walked the dozen miles to sell her pottery. It was only her second visit. It was not a town where she felt comfortable. She loved the wildness of nature, but here the surrounding landscape was blighted by plunder. Unlike the tin mines, which left little outward signs, apart from the pump housings, of the ore scavenged from below ground, the land here was scarred by the china clay workings. The greyish white spoil heaps rose high as hills but were barren of plant and animal life.

Senara hurried past the desecrated land, her eyes averted. She hated to see such wanton destruction of land, even as she acknowledged that the china clay served an industry which benefited mankind.

Wilful, the donkey, carried two wicker panniers of pots. At the end of the month it was Bridie's birthday. Leah wanted some dimity or linsey-woolsey to sew a new dress for her. As Senara approached the town more people were on the road and she tied a rope leash around Angel's neck, the other end fastened to the pannier straps.

She was always apprehensive when she entered a place as a stranger. A woman alone could attract unwanted attention from men. She made a point of keeping her hair covered, and a wide-brimmed black felt hat was pulled low over her eyes. Angel may be protection, but he drew attention with his scars. Months of training made him obedient to her commands and he would doze at Senara's feet while she sold her wares.

The day had started with drizzle. By the time she reached the coastal town, the clouds had cleared and the late August sun was hot on her face. She set out her wares, also displaying some calendula-and-lavender-scented soap made by Leah, which was popular with the gentlewomen.

By mid-afternoon she had sold most of the pots and only a few bars of the soap remained. She had enough money to purchase more clay for herself, the material for Bridie's dress, plus flour, salt and other necessary provisions. If she was to reach home before dark it was time to make her purchases and leave St Austell.

Halfway up the hill by the Holy Trinity church there was a disturbance outside a tavern.

Japhet Loveday was standing with his arms around two women, who were hugging him and laughing at his words. A fisherman was shouting at him and lurched at one of the women to try to pull her away.

'That be my woman,' the fisherman yelled.

Japhet put both women behind him and in a lightning movement drew his sword. 'The lady chose my company.' He laughed, the sword flashing inches from the fisherman's nose.

The woman screamed. 'No, sir, don't kill him.' She ran to her lover and pulled him away, saying, 'It were nothing, Davey love. Just a bit of fooling.'

Senara urged Wilful on, keeping a nervous eye on the scene. Japhet had a reputation for attracting trouble. She had seen in the past how fights could escalate and did not want to be anywhere near one.

'Feckless jade,' Japhet declared as he sheathed his sword and kissed his other companion.

The woman giggled and nestled closer in her triumph. 'Good riddance to her. We don't need that slut Mary. I be woman enough for you, my fine buck.'

The fisherman dragged his woman across the street and into an alley where they began to shout at each other.

Wilful was being stubborn and had halted and refused to move.

'Wilful by name Wilful by nature, will you move yourself?' Senara gave him a shove, impatient to be home. He stared back at her with a look of hurt pride while still refusing to move.

'My word, I recognise this beauty. Where was it we met?' Japhet was suddenly beside her, his hand on Wilful's bridle. 'It was not in St Austell. Where do you live, my pretty?'

His companion gave a howl of displeasure. 'What you be playing at? I thought you was with me, Japhet Loveday.'

'All in good time, sweet lady,' Japhed called over his shoulder, but his eyes were hot upon Senara.

She found herself gazing into dark twinkling eyes. He was a handsome man, with his black hair unpowdered and tied in a queue. The thin moustache gave him the air of a dashing, devil-may-care adventurer, which many women would find mysterious and exciting. To her it proclaimed danger – a man to be avoided. She distrusted the bold appraisal she had met in Japhet's eyes. At Trevowan he had flirted with her, his attention unwanted.

He grinned. 'I never forget a beautiful face. Tell me who you are?'

'You are mistaken, sir.'

'I think not.' He fingered his moustache and there was mischief in his eyes as he continued to regard her. 'I remember now. It was at Trevowan. You promised me a dance but disappeared.'

'You are mistaken, sir. I promised nothing. I was not at Trevowan to dance, but to work.'

'I have not seen you there on other visits.'

'I am no one's servant, sir. Now please allow me to pass. I would be on my way.'

'I would be churlish to allow a beautiful woman to remain unescorted.' He put his hand on her arm and Angel growled.

Japhet removed his hand and glowered at the dog. 'That is an ugly brute.'

'He is a loyal and obedient friend.' A hand signal silenced Angel but the mastiff remained with teeth bared, his large body braced and ready to spring. She glanced at the red-faced woman bearing down on them. 'Your companion is becoming impatient.'

'But you hold the greater fascination to me.'

She side-stepped to move past him. 'I do not spend my time dallying with strangers. Good day, sir.'

He countered to block her passage. This time there was a challenge in his dark eyes. 'And if I say I would like us not to be strangers? That I would be honoured to call upon you?'

'You would find I am a poor companion. I do not receive callers.'

'Now I am intrigued. How can I resist a woman of such beauty and mystery?'

187

She lost her patience. 'There is nothing mysterious. I simply wish to be left alone!'

His companion thrust herself between them, her arm possessive on his. 'Japhet, what you be playing at? Who is this doxy?' Her eyes then widened and she screamed, 'Japhet run! Those men will kill you!'

Senara glanced in the direction she pointed and saw the fisherman lover of Mary had returned with three friends, all armed with stout cudgels.

'How will your sword stand up to four of us?' the fisherman yelled. 'At him, men!'

Japhet spun on his heel. His white teeth flashed beneath his dark moustache. There was no fear, only mockery on his handsome face. 'Were you gentlemen, I would fight you with pleasure. I do not indulge in common street fights.'

'Don't look like you have much choice,' the fisherman snarled and the four of them sprang forward.

Senara used the diversion to escape. But before the road twisted taking her out of sight, she turned to see how Japhet fared. He was holding his own. One man was sprawled on the cobbles and another was nursing a sword cut to his arm.

She hurried on. It was not her concern. Yet before she had walked a mile her thoughts had returned to Japhet Loveday and his cousins. St John had been the talk of the district when he married the tavern keeper's daughter. She had heard of the rivalry between St John and Adam, which was rumoured to be at the heart of St John's seduction of Meriel Sawle. They were all men of high passions. Adam, who had shown such kindness to Bridie, had seemed different. More caring. But the same reckless blood was in all their veins. The same wildness which had been in Ross Malone's blood.

A more handsome or charming rogue than Ross had yet to roam these shores. The youngest son of an Irish lord, he was a captain in the dragoons who had been stationed in Bristol. Leah had been engaged as housekeeper to a merchant who lived close to the inn where Ross had taken quarters. Senara helped her mother with light duties in the house and cared for Bridie, who had been three. Senara was fifteen and Ross twenty at the time.

How easily she had fallen in love with him, beguiled by words of love and undying devotion. Leah had forbidden Senara to see Ross, saying he was too old for her. It was too late, Senara had been too in love to obey her mother and within three weeks of their first meeting they'd become lovers.

Love had blinded her to wisdom. It had not been easy for her to get away from Leah's vigilance. One evening she'd stolen into town to his rooms and found Ross in bed with another woman.

He'd laughed at her outrage. 'Little fool! What an innocent you are to think I would wed you.'

'But you said you loved me.'

'How else was I to bed you?'

Her heart feeling trampled on, Senara had run home. He had been her first and only lover and her experience had made her suspicious of men like the Lovedays.

'Your report is excellent, Adam.' Squire Penwithick nodded with approval. 'It not only confirms information already received but has brought a new insight into the current political situation in France. Also, Manigault will be dealt with. The Prime Minister will be pleased.'

'Thank you, sir.'

'Your disguise as a native Frenchman was not questioned?'

'No. I explained I was from St Malo, which I have visited on several occasions when sailing to France.'

'Would you undertake another similar task?'

Adam had enjoyed the excitement of his work in France. 'I will always serve my country in any way I can, sir.'

'What excuse would you give to these revolutionary friends, if you had to return?'

'That a death in the family forced me to spend some months in St Malo.'

Penwithick nodded. 'You have a natural aptitude for this work. It is possible your services will be required again. I need not say that nothing must be mentioned of such work. Even to your father you must be circumspect. He is aware of my work for the Prime Minister and will not question you if he knows you have to leave Cornwall on my instructions.'

Adam felt his blood warm with anticipation. The reckless streak in his nature had always made the edge of danger an exciting prospect.

Chapter Twenty-Six

If this was meant to be the pattern of his life then Adam was content. In the last two months Edward had visited London three times and also other ports. There had been several enquires for merchant ships to be refitted for the long South Seas or Caribbean voyages. It meant another loan was needed to expand the yard and now in October his father was again in London arranging the loan.

Adam shut himself away in the yard office, working on the redesign work of a ship which needed adjustments for the weight and distribution of cannon on the lower decks and a swivel gun on the poop deck. He wanted his calculations and ideas on paper by his father's return. The atmosphere at Trevowan was not conducive to work. St John was constantly sniping at the hard work imposed on him by the management of the estate. Also, he never lost an opportunity to deride Adam for the idealism which had been rewarded by his court martial. Several times Adam came close to fighting with his twin. But if he was ever to have any place in the shipwright's yard, he knew he must control his anger and live amicably with St John.

He also found it hard to tolerate Meriel's proprietary air, as though she was already mistress of his home. Elspeth appeared not to notice the way Meriel ordered the servants, but then his aunt was besotted with her great-niece, spending far more time and attention upon her than either of her parents did.

When Adam saw the baby his emotions were strangely stirred. She was his niece and at two months old had a winning smile for anyone paying her attention. It saddened him to see her paralysed hand, which Elspeth massaged and gently manipulated every night and morning. But Rowena was Meriel's child and a sour reminder of the fickleness of the love she had so ardently declared for him, a love he no longer returned. But the memories of her passion were too recent and made her presence in his home as St John's wife intolerable.

It was easier to live and work in the yard, using the excuse of the urgent need to complete the refit plans.

The sound of a sea shanty being sung made Adam break off his work to gaze out of the window. The general labourers were working on the scaffolding around a fishing smack, painting the hull. The carpenters were constructing the cradle under the keel of the *Pegasus*,

191

fixing supports between the hull and the cradle to hold the ship upright before the original scaffolding could be removed. Then the cradle would slide on to a specially prepared launchway – a shallow trough well greased with tallow. The masts would be added once the hull was afloat.

Ben Mumford sauntered into the office. 'Should I put some extra men to work on the dry dock? After last week's rain we are behind schedule. It will mean taking them off the *Pegasus* and delaying her launch.'

'It cannot be avoided. The dock must have priority. *Pegasus* will be launched in a month, even with the delay.' He controlled his impatience. Seth Wakeley had completed the carvings on her stern and the figurehead would be ready to be mounted in a day or so. Then she could be launched into the river and work started on the final fitments, masts and rigging.

At the sight of the *Pegasus* Adam's heart swelled with pride. His ship. A ship any captain would be proud of. Upon her was set the path of his destiny.

At two the following afternoon Jasper Fraddon rode into the yard on a lathered horse. Adam climbed out of the dry dock where he had been inspecting the work.

'Mr Loveday is expected home from London by four this afternoon.' Japser was breathless and did not dismount. 'He sent a messenger on ahead to say he wants all the family at the house for a matter of the most importance.'

'Did he say why?'

'No. Just you and Master St John must be appropriately dressed. I'm off to summon the Reverend and his family.'

'Did Father not want you to take his horse to meet the London stage at Liskeard?'

'Apparently he is arriving in a private coach.'

Reluctantly Adam put away his plans and pens. As he walked to the stable to collect Solomon, he called out to Ben Mumford, 'Father has visitors. Important ones by the sound of it. Make sure the yard is shipshape in case it is investors and they will visit tomorrow.'

He arrived at Trevowan in time to shave and change into cream knee-breeches and a long cream waistcoat edged with gold braid. At hearing the pounding of hoofs and the rumble of carriage wheels, he looked out of his window to see a large fashionable coach pulled by six grey horses.

He snatched up his burgundy coat and ran down the stairs to greet them. Aunt Elspeth was in the hall. He had never seen her look so animated.

'We must go outside to greet our guests. This is a most uncommon

192

occasion.' She called to St John and Meriel. 'Do come along. We must greet Edward's guests in style.'

Adam raised an eyebrow in query as he saw Winnie Fraddon, and Jenna Biddick emerge from the kitchen, both patting their hair into place under their mobcaps. They were wearing their Sunday best clothes, as were Jasper and Isaac Nance, who followed them, both looking uncomfortable in their finery.

Before Adam could question his aunt, the coach drew to a halt and Elspeth ushered them all outside. Edward Loveday thew open the coach door and stepped on to the flagstones. His face registered surprise as the family and servants filed out, and then pleasure.

He laughed. 'I see Elspeth has anticipated the occasion.' There was a gleam in his eyes and an air of suppressed excitement in his manner. He turned back to the coach and handed a red-haired woman down, who was dressed in a grey silk travelling dress.

'Adam, St John, may I present you to Amelia, who has greatly honoured me by becoming my wife.' He raised the hand of the woman to his lips. 'Amelia, this is my son St John and his wife, Meriel.'

St John was rooted like a statue, too shocked to speak. Meriel looked equally stunned but in her eyes flashed a hostility which was quickly hidden under lowered lashes. She contrived a false smile. 'Welcome to Trevowan, Amelia.'

Meriel nudged St John in the ribs and he similarly responded but with a curtness which lacked warmth.

His father shot the couple a look of displeasure before introducing Adam. Adam had no reservations about his father's hasty and unexpected marriage. He recovered quickly from his surprise. The woman was striking in both looks and stature. She was only a handspan shorter than his father. When she held out her hand to Adam, he bowed over it.

'Madam, you must forgive our surprise. I had no idea Papa was planning marriage. But I am delighted for you both. Welcome to Trevowan and may you always find happiness here.'

She laughed in a soft infectious manner. 'Thank you, Adam. It happened very quickly. One moment I was agreeing to visit Trevowan as the sea air would be beneficient to my son, Richard. Next thing it seems we are planning our wedding. Your father is a very persuasive man.'

Edward grinned. 'I could not face returning to Trevowan alone. We married last week.'

Adam regarded the couple with amusement. He had not realised his father could be so impulsive. Their happiness was obvious. St John and Meriel remained in the background, their manner unwelcoming. Adam hoped Amelia had not noticed. Their shock was no excuse for their rudeness.

Elspeth limped forward to hold out her arms to Amelia. 'I am so happy for you both. It is long past the time when Edward should have remarried. But to win such a lovely bride has been his reward.'

Amelia drew a nervous and pale young boy from the carriage. 'This is Richard. He is eight. Richard this is your stepbrother Adam.'

Richard bowed self-consciously to Adam. 'P-pl-pleased t-to m-meet you, s-s-sir.'

The lad was small for his age and sickly, but his eyes lit up as Barnaby and Sabre appeared from the side of the house and ran to greet Edward, who ordered the boisterous Sabre down.

Richard stooped to fondle the ears of the more docile spaniel and when Sabre was still, he put a tentative hand on his head. The big dog licked his face with his long pink tongue. Richard laughed and looked shyly at Edward. 'They are grand d-dogs, s-sir. M-may I m-make f-friends with them?'

Amelia said, 'He has always wanted a dog, but it was not practical in London.'

'They are family dogs,' Edward replied, 'but Elspeth does not like them in the house during the day.'

'We can make an exception until Richard settles in,' Elspeth surprised Adam by announcing. She then kissed Amelia's cheek. 'My dear, you are mistress of Trevowan now. It is your will which we must all obey.'

'I have no wish to interfere in how you have run Edward's home in the past.'

Adam saw Meriel whiten and suck her lips in with displeasure. There was hatred in her eyes as she glared at Amelia's back. St John was not looking pleased either. How typical of the couple to only think of how the marriage affected their own lives and plans, and not the happiness and companionship it could bring Edward. Happiness their father deserved after so many years as a widower.

'Do you like ships, Richard?' Adam attempted to put Richard at ease.

'I've n-never b-been on one, s-sir.'

'That will change at Trevowan. And you must call me Adam. Am I not your brother now?'

'Stepbrother,' St John said with cool pointedness.

Adam concentrated on the young boy, who was overawed at meeting so many new people. 'I have my own small sloop. I learned to sail her when I was your age. I will teach you to sail if you like. It is also important that you learn to swim as we live and work so closely with the sea. Papa insisted we learn. You will find it fun.'

Richard looked less certain. The sea was calm as a millpond today and Adam added, 'It will only be on a day as hot and calm as now. I promise you will love it.'

194

Richard studied Adam and then put a thin, blue-veined hand out to him. When he spoke his nervous stammer had subsided. 'I always wanted a brother. I never dared hope to have one who could teach me so much.'

Adam took his hand and clasped it warmly, feeling a genuine affection for the boy.

Amelia put her arm protectively around her son's shoulders. 'Thank you, Adam. The doctors have said the country air will be good for Richard. He is also to have a pony and I hope he will ride.'

'Every boy should have a pony,' said Elspeth.

Annoyed at St John's reticence and sour manner, Adam stepped forward to kiss Amelia's cheek. 'I wish you and Father every happiness.'

'Thank you,' Amelia answered. 'That means a great deal to your father and me. It is not always easy for elder children to accept a stepmother in their lives. I have seen the petty jealousies and resentments amongst the children of my friends who have remarried.'

'There will be none of that from my sons,' Edward directed at St John.

'We are delighted at your marriage.' St John had a roughness to his voice at the effort his insincerity cost him.

Edward nodded with satisfaction and smiled at his wife. 'Did I not say my sons would welcome you with open arms?'

A covert glance by Adam at St John and Meriel showed them looking far from welcoming. Amelia smiled sweetly at them, her voice warm as she passed Meriel. 'I always wanted a younger sister; I hope we will be friends.'

Meriel did not answer but managed to incline her head as though in sullen agreement. Edward took Amelia's arm and led her into the house, introducing her to the servants who had lined up in the hall to greet their new mistress.

Meriel stood back, her face pale and harshened by her venom as she spat out, 'If that madam thinks she is going to lord it over us, she can think again.'

Adam saw his father stiffen. He had heard. He hoped Amelia had not. Why did they feel threatened? Amelia seemed such a charming and delightful woman. But then Amelia would be the new mistress of Trevowan. She was bound to bring about changes.

Chapter Twenty-Seven

The tension in the study rose with the virulence of a striking viper as Edward Loveday finished addressing his sons.

St John shot from his chair to bang his fist on the ancient desk. 'So all this time the yard has been working on Adam's ship. I have been slaving to provide a future for him. I was told it was for a customer. You made me work for a pittance.'

'The yard had to look prosperous to attract customers.'

'I should have been told. And by what right was his legacy used in this way, when he should not have benefited by it until he was twenty-one?' There was hatred in his eyes. 'Why could I not have had an advance on my money? I have a wife and child to support. What responsibilities has Adam?'

Adam sat in silence. He had known that when St John learned the truth about *Pegasus* he would take it badly. He could see no reason to add fuel to the fire.

St John blazed on, pacing the room in angry strides. 'All Adam has done is throw away his career in the navy by fighting a duel. Hardly a responsible action. Yet he gets a ship as a prize. I get nothing. Even while I slaved on the estate my allowance was stopped.'

'You were working for your future security, but you are too blind and self-indulgent to see it,' Edward fumed. 'We have responsibilities to the people we employ. Many of the families have worked on the estate and in the yard for generations.'

Edward made a visible effort to control his anger at St John's manner. He continued more calmly, 'No naval ships have been built since England has been at peace with the colonists and our age-old enemies, France and Spain. It is the same in every yard. We have to compete for work with much larger yards who can afford to do the work more cheaply. We have also suffered bad harvests in recent years.'

'Anyone would think we were paupers,' St John scoffed.

Adam could no longer contain his own anger. 'And what have you done to improve our finances? Where is your loyalty to Father and to our people?'

'I have worked as hard as any labourer. You are the one who left home to make your fortune at sea.'

197

'That is enough, St John.' Edward leaned forward over his desk, a vein pulsating in his forehead. 'Adam left home because of the rivalry between you. It was his plans we used to build *Pegasus* – his plans which have been innovative enough to attract new customers to our yard. The navy is no life of luxury.'

St John remained antagonistic. His father's marriage had been a shock. Meriel had complained all yesterday evening when they were alone at the damage it had done their status and he agreed with her. It was beyond tolerance to learn also how Adam had been favoured by his father. 'I should have been given my legacy on my marriage.'

Edward lost patience, his dislike at his son's petulance and greed intensifying. 'Now you have your legacy, St John, I counsel you to invest it wisely.'

St John toyed with the ruffle on his cuff. 'It is my money and I will do with it as I damned well please.'

'Which is precisely why I did not consider you responsible enough to be in charge of it before this. You would have gambled it away.'

'I needed money for investments of my own.' There was a belligerent glitter in his eyes.

'Which investments are these?' Edward sat back in his chair, his hands folded across his slim waist.

'That is my affair.' St John refused to meet his father's stare. He sat down on the far side of the room.

Anger thinned Edward's mouth. 'Clearly you have no intention of using the money to improve Trevowan.'

'Why should I? You have a rich wife now. Isn't that why you married her?'

'I did not marry Amelia because of her money. You expect to reap the rewards of all Trevowan and the yard to yield to you, without any effort on your behalf to work towards those ends.'

St John glared at him, his hands clenching and unclenching in impotent fury.

For Edward it made his next announcement easier. 'Your manner is regrettably what I have come to expect. You show no interest in the yard, neither have you any aptitude for the business. I have consulted Mr Blythe, our family lawyer. The yard and estate were never bound together in trust. It was my grandfather's wish that the land and yard go to a sole heir. As you know, annuities from the joint ventures go to William, Joshua and Elspeth. Indeed, I doubt Joshua could survive without it. I have decided that the yard will eventually go to you, Adam. St John, you will inherit Trevowan.'

'I will see him in hell first,' St John raged. 'The yard is my birthright.'

Edward marched across the room and slapped his son's face. 'Talk like that will see you without a penny. Each of you will be responsible to any annuities needed to support family members.'

For a moment St John looked stunned. Then, as the imprint of his father's hand became a fiery brand on his cheek, he stood up with such violence his chair scudded across the floor. His feet hammered across the polished boards as he stormed from the room and slammed the door.

Adam expelled a harsh breath. 'He took that badly. But I am delighted with your decision. I will not fail you, sir.'

Edward rested an elbow on the mantelpiece and put his hand to his brow. 'It will not be easy. St John will not forgive either of us.'

'Then I must move out of Trevowan. I shall take one of the empty shipwright's cottages.'

'No.' Edward turned his face, strained with worry. 'This is your home. One day Lisette will live here. She cannot live in a cottage. The house is large enough for us all.'

'As soon as I have the funds I will build a house to make her proud; until then I am content to live at the yard.'

Edward shook his head. 'St John does not approve of my marriage. I will not have tension in my house. The dower house has been empty for years. Elspeth spoke of moving into it as she wanted Amelia to feel at ease taking over the role of mistress here. Amelia would not hear of her moving out. The dower house will be made ready for St John and Meriel. Meriel has wanted to be mistress of her own home. She will have her wish.'

'I doubt her plans were for the dower house,' Adam said with a wry grin.

Edward had a mischievous twinkle in his eye. 'I doubt they were. She is a fool and has not learnt her manners as I would have wished. She deliberately ignored Amelia's attempts at friendship last evening and again at breakfast this morning. That I will not tolerate. It is time she learnt her place in this household.'

Meriel paced her bedchamber with her hands resting on her hips. She spun round at each turn with an angry swish of her skirts. Her face was pale, her eyes glittering with a gathering rage. 'So Adam will inherit the yard and we are to be banished to the dower house. And that bitch Edward married gets to lord it over us all.'

Edward had informed them of his plans that evening after dinner. Meriel had held in her fury until she was alone with St John. She had only seen the dower house from the outside. It was to the rear of the property with a separate drive. It was grey-stoned and sixty years older than the newer house of Trevowan. It had been the original residence of the Penhaligan family before the new house had been built closer to the sea. It had five bedrooms, albeit rather small ones, and four reception rooms, a kitchen and buttery. A storm five years ago had blown a tree down, damaging the end turret and several panes of glass. The windows had been boarded up and it was likely the plaster inside would be peeling and the house decaying.

'Now I have had time to consider, the dower house may benefit us,' St John placated. 'I will have the freedom to come and go as I please. It is out of sight of the house. Papa has promised to spend lavishly to repair and redecorate. Amelia has offered to help you choose materials and furniture.'

'I do not want her help.'

'It is her money which is providing it. Cross her and you may find her less generous.'

Meriel remained mutinous and her voice was shrill. 'Then it will cost her dear. I will not live in a hovel. Because of her we have become outcasts from what is rightfully your inheritance. I hate her. And that snivelling little milksop of a son. Have you ever seen such a puny weakling?'

St John glanced towards the door. 'Keep your voice down. Do you want the whole house to hear?'

'You are taking this very calmly.' She narrowed her eyes. 'I thought you were at least man enough to fight for your inheritance.'

He sighed. She was fanning the flames of his anger and resentment. But he knew his father. There would be no moving him. 'Amelia is not our enemy. It is Adam. And he will not get away with stealing half my inheritance.'

'Yes, Adam must be dealt with in time.' Meriel was focused on their immediate problem. Her mind was racing. She did not relish living under the same roof as Amelia. Elspeth had been bad enough, with her petty rules and interference with Rowena. Providing they did not lose any social standing, were invited to family gatherings and included in invitations to neighbours, she was beginning to wonder if the move would not be to their advantage. True, the dower house would not be as grand as Trevowan, but it would be her own. Edward had promised her two servants. He would attend the next hiring fair to engage a cook, and Rachel Glasson, the fourteen-year-old sister of Tilda, who worked as a barmaid in the Dolphin, was looking for work. She would act as nursemaid and general housemaid. It would mean Meriel could be mistress of her own home.

'I want to see the dower house tomorrow. It will cost Amelia a pretty penny to get us from under her feet.'

The next morning, as she inspected the dower house with St John, she realised it was far grander than any house in Penruan. She could visualise its walls freshly painted and the floors polished. Several pieces of the furniture were impressively carved; the old dresser would look very grand with a fashionable porcelain dinner service on display. New furniture would need to be purchased for the parlour and she would have the very latest in design and style.

St John perched on a windowsill while Meriel made her inspection. He was brooding on his own resentments at the changes in his life.

Excitement had replaced Meriel's anger. 'This can be made into a house to be proud of, St John. We can entertain your friends. And have you seen the size of the cellar? It could store the contraband in an emergency. Now you have your legacy, think of the profits to be made.'

'It does not change the way Adam has cheated me out of my inheritance.' St John ground his fist against a tortoiseshell butterfly fluttering against the windowpane. 'Adam always was father's favourite. I will not stand back and lose the shipyard. It is the wealth which has supported Trevowan. It is mine. Mine!'

'Calm down, St John. We must bide our time.' She saw the danger signs. St John would do something rash and ruin any chance of triumphing over Adam. 'Adam will not get away with this. But we must be careful. The yard *will* be yours.'

'How?' he snorted.

'Now is not the time to act. We must take care not to rouse your father's suspicion. Trust me. I was right about the money earned from free-trading. I am right about this. I have a plan. But one step at a time.' She put up a hand at his gesture of impatience. 'This house will give us greater independence. Let us first put it in order. And you must play the part of an exemplary son. Edward must never suspect the hatred you bear Adam.'

Chapter Twenty-Eight

'What do you think of my family, Amelia?' Edward asked. They had retired for the night.

'I have still to meet William.'

'He is at sea and not expected home until next year.'

Amelia sat before her dressing table, half undressed, with a loose silk robe over her corset and petticoats. She paused in brushing her copper hair, which fell to her waist. 'There is also Japhet to meet. So much was said about him. He sounds quite a character.'

'More like a rogue. Joshua is worried about him. But he can charm a carrot from a donkey, which gets him out of most scrapes. But what of the others?'

She put down her hairbrush and her stare was candid. It was a quality which had struck Edward on their first meeting and one which he admired.

'Once you see behind Elspeth's sharpness to the vulnerability it disguises, she is not so intimidating. I am very fond of her. We became friends in London.' She paused before continuing. 'There is still the gleam of the rakehell in Joshua which is so refreshing in a parson. I think I shall enjoy his sermons.'

'He delivers them with great gusto, only raising his voice slightly if one is indiscreet enough to be caught nodding off.'

They laughed in easy companionship and Amelia continued, 'Oswald clearly adores Hannah. She is delightful, though I suspect spirited. Cecily is very doting, like a mother hen fussing over her family.'

'There is nothing she would not do to help a parishioner,' Edward explained. 'But she can be trying at times with her constant prattle.'

'That is just typical of a man,' she chided, with a teasing sparkle in her eyes. 'Despite her family around her she feels lonely. The men may love her but they do not listen to her. It makes her try too hard to win others' approval.' There was a note of censure when she added, 'Peter is rather intense. No wonder they call him Pious Peter. A little compassion would not go amiss in his nature.'

Edward chuckled. 'I must say I prefer Japhet's easy-going manner. Peter's piety does not ring true to me.'

'Let us hope it is merely the fervour of youth. I had an uncle who was a sanctimonious bigot and he caused much unpleasantness in his village. My father would have nothing to do with him. That did not stop him standing at our gate and shouting abuse and recriminations. He was quite mad, of course. Ended his days chained in a lunatic asylum.'

Edward lifted the weight of her hair away from her neck and kissed the warm hollow at its base. His love for Amelia was overwhelming. There were times when he could not believe that she had agreed to give up her social life in London to seclude herself away in Cornwall.

'And what of my own family?' he persisted. 'I regret the way Meriel has behaved. I thought she had learnt better.'

Amelia turned to face him. 'You must not worry on my account. Meriel is a creature of emotions and was not brought up to hide them. Yet in many ways she is like a child. She seemed happy enough to accept the dower house as her home.'

'Only because of your generosity. It was not necessary.'

She held out her hand to him and as he raised her to her feet, she leaned her head against his chest. 'She could be a disruptive influence. There will be more harmony in our home without her presence.'

'I cannot fault your wisdom there. I have done my best to accept her, yet there is a cunning in her nature which does not sit well with me.' He slid his arms around her waist. He wanted to make love to her but it was also important to him just then to know that she felt comfortable with his family. 'And my sons . . .? They have accepted you as I knew they would.'

'Adam has been so kind to Richard that I fear Richard idolises him. Adam took him for his first swimming lesson this morning. I had told Richard not to keep pestering him. Adam is busy at the yard.'

'Adam will not mind. He often swims in the early morning if the weather is fine. And often of an evening after work.'

Amelia smiled with pleasure. 'Adam has so much energy and ambition. You must be very proud of him.'

'Yes, I am. Adam will be a good influence on Richard.'

She put her arms around his neck and gazed into his eyes. 'Trevowan is a beautiful house and already the Cornish air has brought more colour to Richard's cheeks.'

'You do not miss the excitement of London?'

'No. I was born in Waltham Abbey and my parents moved to London when I was twelve. I loved the country. I learned to accept London when I married Gerald. My husband's business kept us firmly rooted there. Mother would have loved it here. After Father died she wanted to move back to Waltham Abbey to live with her sister, Abigail. Then Abigail died, so she spent her last years with me in London. She was a comfort in my widowhood. I still miss her.'

'She has been dead only ten months.' He kissed her with growing passion. 'So you are an orphan and as an only child you have no relatives. Sometimes I feel that there is an abundance of Lovedays. Trevowan is very much the central focus for our family. Margaret and Charles visit most summers. It is unusual they did not come this year.'

Amelia enjoyed teasing her husband. 'Margaret did not come to Trevowan because she was too busy playing the matchmaker. She wanted me to come here with them in July. I felt it would be too forward. And I knew you had business which would bring you back to London. I hoped that you would wish for my company.'

'I could not stay away. Business or not, I would have found an excuse to return. I could not stop thinking of you.'

Edward had been so self-contained when they first met. She had been instantly attracted to him and sensed the caring side of his nature – unlike the beaux who recently courted her, many of whom were more attracted to her wealth than her person. Edward was touchingly shy but had an easy wit which she found delightful. Courtship had not come easily to him after twenty years as a widower. That had endeared her to him even more. He could be enigmatic and she found him intriguing. She had sensed his attraction to her, but he had not spoken of his feelings. It had made him more appealing than the transparent men who showered her with meaningless compliments. It was after he'd left that she realised that she was in love with him.

On his second visit to London he had been more at ease, often seeking Amelia's company without Margaret Mercer's devious plotting. London had been so hot that Edward had hired a sloop to take them on the river to Richmond. Once the river traffic thinned Edward had allowed Richard to take the helm, and then later insisted that Amelia try it herself. He had sat beside her at the tiller with his arm around her as he'd helped to guide her movements. It had been so natural to put her head on his shoulder and she had felt the hard beat of his heart.

They had moored by a secluded bank and when Richard had leapt ashore to explore the reed banks for duck nests Edward had kissed her for the first time. It had been a short kiss, but contained more sweetness and passion than she had thought possible. As they'd drawn apart, he'd announced simply, 'I cannot bear to live without you. Will you marry me, my darling?'

Now she smiled up at him, her heart swelling with happiness as she saw the strength of her own love mirrored in his eyes. 'Oh, Edward I am so happy. So very much in love with you.'

Their passion banished further conversation. It was not until the next morning that Edward realised Amelia had not commented upon St John. He had also noted a reserve in her manner when his elder son was present. St John had not hidden his sullenness since he had been told that it would be Adam who would inherit the yard. Edward suspected that Amelia did not greatly care for St John although she was effusive about Adam.

It was a shock for Edward to realise that in recent years his own feelings towards St John had changed. He still loved him as a man will always love his son, but he was no longer sure he liked him. And as for trusting him . . . Since his father's marriage, St John could be secretive and evasive. No, Edward did not trust him and that was the hardest knowledge of all to accept.

Edward never made any reference to Adam's trial, and nodded in understanding when he explained he had travelled to France on behalf of Squire Penwithick.

'It is better that I do not know of that work,' Edward had dismissed the matter when Adam needed to explain. 'Suffice that I am proud you have undertaken it. And there is plenty to do at home. The new dry dock will enable us to take on larger ships and we have orders for another brigantine and two cutters which you said would become popular. We also have three ships booked for a refit when they return from the South Seas.'

'That is good news,' Adam was delighted. 'The *Pegasus* will be launched next month. Weather permitting she should be fully rigged by January. I shall plan her first voyage for March.'

'I wish I could spare more men to work on her.'

Adam shook his head. 'I shall be content to wait until March before I sail in her. The men are needed on other work. I already owe you so much, arranging to use some of my salvage money from the slave ship to buy me out of the navy.'

'In the New Year I will be taking on more shipwrights. Seth Wakeley is to repair the cottages ready for them. The carvings he did for the *Pegasus* are superb quality. He is an asset to the yard.'

'He has exceeded my expectations. It is good to see how the health of his family has improved.'

Edward and Adam walked over to the *Pegasus*, which towered above them in its cradle. The smell of tar lingered on its hull mixing with the scent of oak and pine. The hull had been sealed by pounding tar-soaked rope, known as oakum, into every seam. As a further precaution Adam had insisted that a thin strip of lead be tacked over the oakum which would lie below the waterline, making it more watertight than many vessels.

They climbed the scaffolding to inspect the finished work. Edward stood on the poop deck above the stern and scanned the yard before him. To hear the constant grate of saws, ring of hammers, and squeak of windlasses and capstans as the men worked was sweeter than any music produced by Handel or Mozart. Several stacks of lumber were piled in the yard. Already a cradle had been built to support the first of the new keels to be laid down. Once the *Pegasus* was launched another cradle would be erected on this site. The yard had not been so busy for twenty years, since the height of the war with France and Spain.

The sound of young children playing near the water pump made Edward smile. 'If there are to be more families living here perhaps I should engage a school teacher for the children. Actually Amelia suggested it.'

'The nearest school is four miles. It would be a good idea. Uncle Joshua will be happy to welcome more worshippers at Trewenna church.'

'I suppose I should consider having more cottages built if further orders come in. Much of this new success is due to you.' Edward placed a hand on his son's shoulder. 'I should have realised years ago that St John would never make a shipwright.'

'I do not regret my experience in the navy. It taught me how different ships handle in all seas and I have been able to study the newer designs and compare the improvements.'

Edward nodded. 'It is a relief to have the matter settled. St John has taken it better than I hoped.'

Privately Adam disagreed. St John had screamed abuse at him in the stables last week. It had ended in a fight. Adam rubbed a bruise on his ribs where St John had kicked him when he had been knocked down. Both had taken care not to mark the other's face. Edward would not have tolerated their fighting. They had fought hard and Adam had been pressed to counter St John's extra weight, which was aided by his anger if not his skill. They had fought to a standstill, both bruised and battered and breathing heavily. It had resolved nothing.

Their scraped knuckles could not be hidden. St John had avoided questioning by their father by taking Meriel into Truro to buy furnishings for the dower house. They had stayed away for three days. Adam had explained his injuries by saying some timber had fallen on his knuckles. His father seemed to accept that all was well between the twins.

The fight had been won by Adam but he had flinched from the hatred burning in his twin's eyes. It marked an end to their rivalry and the start of something much deeper and more dangerous.

Chapter Twenty-Nine

A downpour had brought an end to work in the yard. Tomorrow the *Pegasus* would be launched. It was the fulfilment of Adam's dream. Most of the cradle had been removed and two wooden tracks ran down to the river. To avoid damage to the keel a trench had been dug between the two tracks. Tomorrow the tracks would be greased with tallow so that the brigantine would slide smoothly into the river.

A hogshead of brandy and a large vat of ale had been provided in the yard by Gil Pascoe of the Ship Inn. Winnie Fraddon had been cooking all day for the celebration. Edward had insisted on making much of the event.

Adam hoped the rain would hold off tomorrow. The sky was still overcast but the southerly wind could soon clear the skies. With work in the yard finishing early, Edward had been glad of the opportunity to spend more time with Amelia. Adam, remembering a promise to Aunt Elspeth, rode to the Polglases' cottage.

Leah came out at the sound of his horse approaching, her wary stance vanishing as she recognised him.

'Mr Loveday, how fare you? What brings you to our cottage? The baby is not ill again?'

'Rowena thrives. Her leg has mended well, though her hand will never be right. It is Aunt Elspeth I'm here for. You may have heard that my father has remarried. His wife, Amelia, loves to ride and Elspeth has rather overdone things. Her hip is painful.'

'She'll be wanting some of Senara's balm and herbs. Tether your horse and come inside. I've some mead you will enjoy to refresh yourself.'

Bridie had heard his voice and hobbled outside in her awkward shambling gait. 'Mr Loveday, I thought it was you.' Her face shone with pleasure.

He dismounted and swung her up in the air and she gave a whoop of pleasure. 'How is my brave imp? Have you been behaving yourself?'

She giggled and laughed as he swung her round. Leah wiped a tear from her eye. No man had given Bridie the simple pleasure of being spun round like that. It saddened her that Bridie missed so much what other children took for granted.

Bridie held his hand as he set her down and they walked to the cottage. Angel was braced at the door, barring his entrance and gave a low growl.

'Your vigilant guardian,' Adam joked.

'Oh, get away with you, Angel,' Bridie said, giving the large mastiff a shove. 'Adam is our friend.'

The dog licked the side of Bridie's head as she hobbled past, and from inside the cottage Senara ordered the dog to sit. Adam bent his head to step inside and it took a moment for his eyes to adjust to the darkness within. Senara was busy at her potter's wheel. Her hands were covered in reddish clay and there was a smudge of it across her cheek. Several tendrils of earthy-coloured hair had escaped her white headscarf and coiled around her neck. Senara never wore a mobcap like most working women or servants. The white linen square and the thick single plait hanging down her back was a style which set her apart from other women. The head square was immaculately clean, but her large brown apron was smeared with reddish clay and water. She nodded a silent greeting to him, apparently too absorbed in her work to stop.

Adam watched in fascination as he saw her draw the clay into a chimney shape, then deftly place her fingers inside for the clay to curve out and then in again. Within moments a perfect quart jug was on the potter's wheel. Senara pinched the lip into a point for pouring and rolled a long finger of clay into a handle. When it was in position she took a knife and made a pattern of oak leaves around its base.

'It is a marvel to watch you work. You have great skill.'

'Thank you,' she answered simply, and with a longer knife sliced it under the jug and lifted it carefully to place it on a table with five others to dry by the window.

'I must go down to the stream to wash.'

'May I accompany you? You can tell me how you fire your work. How large is your kiln?'

She answered his questions as they walked, but kept her head lowered. He stood by a tree as she knelt on the stream bank to wash her hands and then her face. He handed her the piece of heavy flannel Leah had pushed in his hands for Senara to use as a towel. When she removed the apron Adam saw a smear of clay along the back of her neck.

'You have missed some.' He took the flannel from her and moistened it in the stream and wiped it across her neck. He was close enough to feel the heat of her. The warm scent of her body was mixed with the perfume of lavender. Beneath his fingers her flesh was hot, its texture silky and golden as the palest honey. His fingers fanned to spread across her neck. A *frisson* passed through him and his flesh tingled as though St Elmo's fire had danced across it, as it played in

210

the ship's rigging during a tropical storm.

Shaken he withdrew it. She had tensed at his touch. With another woman he would laugh and flirt. What was it about Senara which made him tongue-tied? His throat dried and every particle of him was aware of her.

She moved away from him, but he saw that her hand was shaking as she pushed the stray tendrils of her hair back under her scarf. He reached out to detain her. The need to pull her into his arms and taste the sweetness of her lips overwhelming. She was too fast for him, lifting her skirts to run nimbly back to the cottage.

'Have I offended you, Senara? Why do you run from me?'

She paused and half turned her head. 'You have not offended me. You came for some herbs for your aunt. I must prepare them.'

Revealing a glimpse of slender ankle, she ran into the cottage. Adam followed and met Leah's speculative stare when he entered. Senara was busy inspecting the bundles of dried herbs hanging from the rafters. She did not glance at him. Bridie was sitting on the floor by a wicker basket. Three puppies tumbled over themselves as they lapped at the milk in a bowl on the floor.

'Where did these come from? According to Aunt Elspeth you perform miracles with your herbs, Senara. But even you could not make old Angel produce these. Unless he is the father. From the black and white colouring they look like they have part sheepdog in them.'

'Sheepdog and spaniel,' Bridie announced. 'Senara saved them. They were in a sack in the river. Some wicked man tried to drown them. Senara rescued them and we have had to feed them every few hours. Through the night as well. They are six weeks old now.'

'And time homes were found for them,' Leah remarked. 'We cannot afford to keep more dogs. Angel would eat us out of house and home given the chance.'

'No,' Bridie wailed, hugging a squirming black and white body to her chest. 'Not Charity. She is mine. She loves me. She's my friend.'

'I suppose we could manage to keep Charity but not Faith and Hope. And you must have your own patch of garden so we can sell the produce to help feed her,' Leah said with firmness. 'Senara will take the others to market to sell.'

'But I will never see them again,' Bridie sobbed.

'I know it will be hard, but that is how life is.' Leah gave her daughter's hand a squeeze. 'Senara will make sure they go to good homes.'

'I will buy Faith,' Adam picked the fattest of the puppies up. 'My stepbrother, Richard, will adore her.'

'And you could have Hope.' Bridie was jubilant.

Leah shook her head. 'Mr Loveday does not want Hope. It is good of him to find a home for Faith.'

Adam saw Bridie wipe a tear from her cheek. 'It would have been nice for Hope and Faith to be together and then I could see them from time to time,' she said.

There was a noise outside and Hope shot up on his stumpy legs and ran barking to the door. Harriet the goat butted him with her nose and he rolled head over tail back into the room.

Adam laughed heartily. 'He is more hopeless than Hope.' The puppy picked himself up and continued to growl at the goat. 'He will make a fine guard dog. I will take him as well. I am living in a cottage at the yard. We could do with a guard dog. There have been some thefts of materials lately.'

Senara was bent over the kettle on the trivet over the fire. 'We do not want your charity, Mr Loveday.'

'I am not taking Charity.' He winked at Bridie. 'Just Faith and Hope.' The puppy Hope had stopped barking at the goat and was now chasing the one-footed magpie out of the dwelling. When the bird flew into a tree Hope was distracted by a flapping sheet on the washing line. He leapt at it, fastening his teeth on the hem and began to tug. Leah shouted at him and shooed him away.

Adam laughed. 'He has character and will make a good gun dog. There is more spaniel in him than sheepdog. I shall change his name to Scamp.'

'Will I be able to see Faith and Scamp sometimes?' Bridie pleaded.

'You can see Scamp whenever you wish. I am sure Richard would not mind riding this way with Faith from time to time. He is eight and has yet to make any friends.'

Bridie's lower lip trembled. 'He will not want me for a friend. No one does. I'm a freak.'

Leah opened her mouth to protest but Adam forestalled her. 'You were born different from other children. That does not make you a freak. That makes you special. People are superstitious and see your specialness as a threat to them.' He hoisted her up on to his shoulders and, ducking low to avoid the door lintel, ran with her outside and raced round until she was screaming with pleasure.

Senara came out as he finally put Bridie to the ground. She held out a hand-stitched calico pouch of herbs and a large clay pot of unguent. 'If Miss Loveday returns the pot to me I can refill it, otherwise I have to charge her for it.'

'My aunt is happy to pay whatever you ask.' He handed her two guineas.

'The pot is but a shilling and the herbs a few pence.'

'You must charge for your skill and your time. Dr Chegwidden would charge more than double that for a visit.'

Her eyes widened and he saw a spark of fear within their forest-green depths. 'No. I have no special skill.'

She held the guineas out for Adam to take back. He shook his head. 'Please keep them.' He lowered his voice. 'You have done so much to help my aunt I would like to help Bridie in some way. Use the money to take her to Joseph Roche, the cobbler in Penruan. He will make her special boots with a built-up sole to help her to walk more easily.'

'There is no need.'

'There is every need. One special favour deserves another in return. I would be deeply offended if you did not do as I ask.' When she was about to protest he said more sharply, 'Pride is all very well if you forego luxuries for yourself, but is it worth denying Bridie this necessity? It will make her life easier.'

'You are very kind, sir. But what do you want from us?'

He sensed her wariness. Her beauty and grace greatly affected him. He had not been entirely altruistic in his generosity. He had wanted to gain this woman's confidence. He had not expected her pride to be against taking help from him. Yet as he studied her, he saw the faint flush to her skin, the dilation of her pupils. She was not immune to him. Far from it.

'Who said I wanted anything?' he was stung to defend.

The candidness of her stare was disconcerting. 'You are the only outsider that Bridie trusts. I do not want her hurt.'

'I would never hurt Bridie.' Indignation roughened his voice.

'Indirectly she would be hurt if I am put in a position when I must ask you not to come here.'

His gaze caressed her and within him stirred something far deeper than desire. His throat worked and he found it difficult to swallow.

'I hold you in the highest admiration, Senara.'

She blinked and he saw a tear glisten on her lashes and she put her hand to his mouth to stop any further words. 'Please say no more. It is impossible. We are too different and you are promised to another.'

He pressed his lips to her palm. 'I do not love her.'

'Then I pity her if she loves you.' She snatched back her hand. 'I will tell you this, then you will see how very unworthy I am of your attentions. There was a man, a captain in the army from a family as revered as your own. He said he loved me and I believed him. He promised me marriage and I was too young to know that a man can lie to win the favours of a woman he desires. I loved him, believing in his promises. He betrayed me with another woman. I later learned he was betrothed to the daughter of a baronet. When I found him with the other woman, he laughed at my pain and called me a fool for having such pretensions.'

'It would not be like that between us.' He lifted his hand to her face but she side-stepped and evaded him. There was no coquetry in her action and her eyes were sad.

213

'I am not like the Sawle woman your brother married. I know my place. No man wants a used woman for his bride. I have faced the abuse of village matrons and still carry the scars too freshly to wish to live anything but quietly and out of public gaze. It is the woman who pays the price in any scandal. If your aunt wants any more of my herbs she may send a servant to collect them. And for the two guineas, you must have the dogs. I will accept no more money from you. Goodbye, Mr Loveday.'

'Senara.' The hoarse whisper was heavy with his longing. She hesitated, her lower lip trembling as she turned her stare back upon him. Again he felt a current of emotion swirling between them like the charged air on a Caribbean island before a hurricane strikes with all its devastating violence.

He pulled her to him and his lips claimed hers. There was the briefest of response. Her body swayed, melted against him, he felt desire ripple through her. Then immediately she stiffened. His cheek flamed from her slap.

'You are no different from my captain.' Her scorn smote him and she ran into the woods.

He cursed his stupidity. He ran after her, but she was nimble and fleet as a doe. The undergrowth was thick and he soon lost sight of her. He could hear no sign of her passage. He called her name twice. The only reply was the wild thudding of his heart and the empty longing in his breast.

'Senara. Forgive me,' he called again, and leant his brow against the rough bark of an oak tree when she did not reappear. He returned to the cottage to collect the two puppies which he placed safely inside his leather jerkin after he mounted Solomon.

Leah stood by his bridle. Her knowing eyes on the woods where Senara had vanished. 'If it is in the stars she will be yours,' she said, 'but it will cause great upheaval. It is better for you both if you forget her.'

Chapter Thirty

A cheer went up as the last of the props were knocked away from *Pegasus*. At first nothing happened. Ben Mumford shouted at the men lined along each side of the wooden runway to gently rock the hull. Her timbers creaked, then gradually she inched forward along the greased tracks, gathering momentum as her bow splashed into the river. Water dripped from the figurehead as the horse seemed to buck then rise steadily up to settle high above the waves. The white body and outspread wings glistened in the sunlight and the gilding on its hoofs was dazzling.

Amelia clapped her hands and Richard cheered as loudly as any of the shipwrights. She hugged her son, her cheeks flushed with pleasure. 'It is a glorious sight to see a ship launched, is it not?'

'Adam designed her.' Richard moved from his mother to stand by the side of Adam and Edward.

Edward raised a glass of wine in salute to his son. 'May she be the first of a new fleet built in this yard.'

Further cheers drowned Adam's reply. When they died down Edward asked, 'So now she is built what have you decided for your future? In another month she will be ready to set sail.'

He could see the struggle Adam was having with his emotions. Finally he said, 'My place is in the yard. We must build on our success, but . . .' He looked with yearning at the *Pegasus*.

'But you want to captain her on her first voyage. That is natural enough. And why not? We have men enough to work in the yard. It is your plans which earned us the new contracts. The yard will be yours one day, Adam. Since I have no intention of retiring for many years, make the most of this time. Captain your ship. If that is what you wish.'

Adam clasped his father's hand. 'Thank you for understanding, sir.'

Edward nodded. 'Once your first voyage is behind you, you must marry Lisette.'

It came as a jolt for Adam to realise that it was not Lisette he longed to make his own but Senara.

Amelia came to his side. Edward was chatting to Ben Mumford and Seth Wakeley. Adam smiled at her. 'You have made all this possible, Amelia. Father said you had already arranged through Uncle Charles's bank to loan him the money to improve the yard and pay off Thadeous Lanyon before Father asked you to marry him.'

She gave him a conspiratorial smile. 'Your father is a proud man. He is no fortune-hunter and would never have asked me to wed him if he was in financial trouble. I wanted to help him as a friend. Then that friendship became something very special.'

Meriel stood to the back of the family, feeling excluded from the immediate circle. So did St John from the way he was glowering. It was Adam's day and that woman had also inveigled herself to be the centre of attention. She scowled at Amelia. Sometimes her hatred for the woman who had ruined so many of her dreams burned like poison in her stomach.

'Do not show your displeasure,' St John snarled in her ear. 'Smile. Next week a cargo arrives from Guernsey. In a month we shall be wealthy. No more dresses from the attic altered to fit you. You shall have three new gowns, all in the latest fashion.'

Even though the prospect thrilled her, she frowned. 'I wish you had not put all the money from your legacy into one voyage. That is too risky.'

'Nonsense. We have few storms this time of year. The fine weather should hold until the cargo is safely landed.'

'It is not just the weather. Clem warned you about the new revenue officer. Lieutenant Beaumont has been vigilant in these waters. He captured a free-trader last month and five men were imprisoned, the goods and ship seized.'

'That was over St Michael's Mount way.'

'He gave chase to the Mevagissey men a sennight past. Only the sea mist saved them – and then because he has yet to learn all the inlets and coves where a smaller vessel can hide. You were unwise to risk all your money on a single venture. You are too greedy. We could lose everything.'

'You will not be complaining when we make our fortune. Neither will your brothers,' he blustered. After the deed was done, he had doubted the risk of gambling all his money on one shipment and had suffered many sleepless nights. But the lure of a fast profit had been too much of a temptation

The payment of his legacy had enabled him to take a half-share in a ship of his own, the *Merry Maid*, and a three-quarter share in the contraband aboard it. He had sacrificed his evenings with his friends at the gaming houses to plough all his earnings into the smuggling trips. After this voyage it would all pay off. He could again afford to take up his old lifestyle, spend lavishly at his tailors and rejoin his friends of an evening.

He contemplated the fortune which the profits from the voyage would earn. He would be his own man, independent of his father's accounting. The freedom would be sweet. Yet with so much at stake, the queasiness brought on by fear churned in his gut. Lieutenant Beaumont aboard the *Deliverance* had been like a man possessed in his quest to eradicate smuggling in this area. He had achieved more success than his predecessors. And Beaumont had a grudge against his family. Not St John personally, but Adam.

Would his twin always be a bane? Yet Beaumont could not be so smart if Adam had bested him on several occasions. What Adam could do, St John could achieve with equal ease.

He rubbed his hands together. He felt confident. Almost omnipotent. They had planned well. He would rise supreme. The uncontested victor over his twin. Adam's days of glory were numbered.

A week later St John stood on the cliffs above the moonlit cove. It was an isolated landing place several miles from Penruan. To the west, on the next headland, the chimney of the workings of a tin mine was silhouetted against the night sky. There was a leaden beat to his heart as he strained to hear sounds of the *Merry Maid* approaching. His palms were moist with apprehension and his nerves were stretched taut so that he jumped at the slightest sound.

Clem Sawle snapped at him, 'You be as jittery as a virgin when a man puts his hand on her knee.'

'I have more to lose than you,' St John retorted.

'Never did reckon you had it in you, Loveday. Money bain't everything. This work takes guts.'

'Are you saying I am a coward?'

'If that is how you want to take it. One weak link is all it takes to destroy the strongest chain.'

The antagonism between the two men had increased during recent runs. Clem resented St John's involvement. After Reuban, Clem considered himself in charge of the smugglers. But St John's shares had given him more say.

St John swallowed the insult. One day Clem would go too far, but for now St John needed his experience.

'There she be,' Harry announced.

'Get the landing boats launched,' ordered Clem.

St John saw the twin masts of the *Merry Maid* outlined in the streamer of moonlight on the water. He ran with the rest of the men to the shore and was in the lead boat as it was rowed through the breakers. A half-hour later his boat was back on the beach and about to return for another load. The second boat was running ashore when a larger vessel appeared around the jagged cove headland.

'Ahoy there! Heave to. This is the King's ship *Deliverance*. What is your business?'

217

St John leapt ashore and drew his pistol. The revenue cutter was on a course to block the *Merry Maid*'s escape. He heard the clang as the rope of her anchor chain was cut. There was still time for her to get away. He scanned the sky, praying for clouds to obscure the moon and aid her flight, but the heavens were jewelled with stars. No clouds would aid them tonight.

He shouted, 'Get the packhorses away. Save what you can.'

'Leave the boat, men,' Clem ordered as the second boat was beached.

As the *Merry Maid* began to head for deeper water another shout came from the *Deliverance*. 'Heave to or we fire.'

A volley of musket shots spurted yellow flames from the *Merry Maid*, their discharge lighting up the gloom shrouding the vessel.

An answering cannon shot fell short of the *Merry Maid*'s stern. She was a fleet ship and her crew knew the waters well. It was rare for a revenue cutter to sink a smuggling ship. If they seized her, she would either be auctioned and the revenue ship's captain and crew would receive a share of the money, or she would be publicly broken up as an example of the fate of smuggling vessels. There was still a chance they could reach the Helston river and hide in one of the inlets.

The next cannon shot from the cutter destroyed that hope. The rending of wood was followed by screams from a wounded man. Figures ran in confusion on the *Merry Maid*.

'Cap'n Brother's been hit.'

'Get yourself away,' St John screamed. 'Save the ship.'

'Little chance of that,' Clem scoffed.

St John watched in horror. If the ship was lost, his fortune went with it. Only part of the cargo had been landed and that would yield less than a tenth of his original investment. There would be no riches. No independence from his father's purse. No freedom to take up his old life.

The revenue officer in charge was visible on the quarterdeck, his white waistcoat and breeches of a naval type of uniform marked him clearly. St John snatched the loaded musket from Harry Sawle and aimed it at the officer. As he pulled the trigger Harry knocked his arm.

'Idiot. Kill him and we all hang.' The bullet whizzed harmlessly into the water yards from the cutter.

Pandemonium had broken out on the *Merry Maid*. Several of the sailors jumped overboard to escape.

'Surrender or we continue our fire,' Beaumont shouted.

A longboat was being lowered from the *Deliverance*. St John flushed hot then cold in panic. 'We've got to save what cargo we can.'

An oath rumbled in Clem's throat and sudden pain shot through St

John's face, the impact of the punch knocking him to the sand. 'It's our men who need helping. I'm finished with you, Loveday. No man from Penruan will work any runs with you again.'

Clem loaded his own musket and ordered the men to provide covering fire for the sailors who were swimming to the beach. The first longboat was in pursuit of them and another was being launched. The cutter was closing on the *Merry Maid*. She could not escape.

St John stood upright and saw the Penruan men pulling their accomplices from the sea. They ran to the protection of the rocks as intermittent musketfire from the longboat raked the shoreline.

Clem and Harry yelled orders. On land the smugglers were making their escape. A glance at the *Merry Maid* showed the *Deliverance* now level with her.

St John staggered. He had gambled and lost. Any profits made from the night would be minimal. From Clem's words he knew no amount of money would allow him to work with the Penruan smugglers or their contacts. The lucrative trade had turned against him. He ran to Prince, tethered at the cliff edge. Already the revenue men were swarming over the beach. He was not hanging round risking his life. He had lost enough this night. It was a disaster. His legacy, which should have provided him with a comfortable lifestyle, was gone.

He had lost his ship. The thought which burned in his brain was the unfairness which gave Adam the *Pegasus* while he had lost so much. Again with effortless ease Adam emerged triumphant from the proceeds of his legacy, while the ashes of failure were choking in St John's throat.

The next morning the village was reeling from the effects of the midnight attack. Three of the smugglers had been shot and one had died from his wounds in the night. The other two remained seriously wounded and it would be months before they could fish with the fleet.

Reuban had sent a demand to St John to attend a meeting at the Dolphin that morning. He had gone with bad grace. He wanted nothing more to do with his wife's family, but unless he obeyed Reuban's orders, the old man might default in payment of his money on the ill-fated cargo.

All of the smugglers were assembled and they stopped talking as St John entered the dark interior of the inn. No one greeted him and there was a menacing set to their roughened features.

'What you be doing about our men who were wounded, Loveday?' Reuban challenged. 'There's doctor's fees need paying. He usually takes a keg of brandy per patient. Their families will need support until they can work again and there's also the widow with seven children to raise.'

Outrage stung him. 'They are not my responsibility. The men knew the risks.'

'We stick by our own, Loveday. Would you see three families starve through your greed?'

'They can go to the devil.' St John glared at Reuban. He glanced round the assembled men and at their surly expressions; swallowed against his throat dried by fear. 'How are they my responsibility? Did I not lose the cargo? There'll be no profits from that run.'

Reuban's gnarled hand snapped over St John's stock and dragged him across the bar. St John felt the iron talons grip his windpipe and began to choke. 'You had a three-quarter share in the cargo. That means you have a three-quarter share in responsibility.'

St John clawed at Reuban's hands to free their hold. It was useless. The grip tightened, blocking all air. His eyes were inches from Reuban's demonic gaze and he saw no mercy. Reuban would kill him without hesitation. He managed a nod of acceptance and was released. He straightened his stock, aware of the hostility emanating from every man present.

'That's settled then.' Reuban turned from him. 'The families will be paid and I'll settle with you. What we need to know now is if you've got the money for the next cargo.'

'I've only what profits there are from this run to invest.'

A rumble of dissent rose from four men seated round a beer barrel. Reuban gave a deprecating snort. 'They bain't sufficient. Looks like we'll be working for Lanyon again. He knows my men are the best to be had in these parts.'

'Lanyon learned of the landing, didn't he?' St John raged. The smugglers' banker had got his revenge for losing Meriel as his bride. 'He informed the customs.'

Reuban shrugged. 'A man as powerful as Lanyon has got his spies. But he has no love for the customs men.'

'But he had nothing to lose this time, did he? Damn you all.' St John marched to the door. He could feel the smugglers laughing at his misfortune. They had never accepted him as their leader. Confound them, they had never even accepted him as their equal. 'And you can forget any future handouts from Trevowan when times are hard.'

Clem scowled. 'We be well rid of him. It be our Meriel who wears the trousers in that marriage.'

'Are you satisfied now you've lost everything?' Meriel had worked herself into a fury. It was the middle of the night and St John had been away from Trevowan all day and he had not come to bed last night either. Now, drunk and maudlin with self-pity, he had confessed the truth. Meriel continued. 'You stupid fool. Why wouldn't you listen to me? I told you the risks.'

'Keep your voice down,' he warned. 'You'll wake Rowena, and it would finish me with Father if he learnt what I have done. He would use it as an excuse to disinherit me. Adam can do no wrong in his eyes at the moment.'

St John had woken Meriel when he'd stumbled against the end of the bed. He had drunk half a decanter of brandy to wash the taste of failure and fear from his throat. She had lit a candle and, taking in his haggard expression, black eye and wild appearance, had guessed the truth. Her tongue was as virulent as a fishwife as she berated him, her beauty vanishing as her face contorted with loathing.

'Hold your tongue, woman.' St John had been goaded too far. He had been humiliated by the night's events and Clem's scathing attack: he would not tolerate her contempt.

'The truth hurts does it?' she continued with scorn. 'We could have lived in comfort, but you had to be greedy.'

'I could be living in comfort if I had not burdened myself with a scheming guttersnipe for a wife. Whose idea was it to become embroiled with the smugglers? Yours.'

'There are risks as well as rewards. You were too stupid and greedy to see them.' Her eyes blazed at him with disgust.

Venom rose in him. 'Stupid, am I? I must have been stupid to fall for your false wiles. And greedy, am I? Who urged me to go in with the smugglers? Who tricked me into marriage? You succumbed fast enough to my attentions and not through love. You married out of greed for what you believed my name and family money could give you.'

'And what a mockery that has turned out.' She came up on her knees to scowl at him. 'No wonder your father favours Adam. You're not one-tenth the man your brother is.'

He saw her mouth hurling abuse at him but his ears were closed to it. A red haze formed in his brain. Meriel and Adam were the focus of his hatred – the cause of everything which had gone wrong in his life. 'It was him you loved, not me, wasn't it? But he could not give you the riches you craved – or so you thought. Why did you marry me?'

'I was carrying your child. I did not give myself willingly to you. You raped me.' She picked up a vase of flowers from the side of the bed and hurled them at him.

'A child which came after only eight months. Did you think I was so stupid I could not count?'

There was a flicker of fear in her eyes, then they hooded. 'I tripped on the stairs.'

'You were found at the foot of the stairs but no one saw or heard you fall. Rowena is not my child, is she?'

'Of course she is . . .'

His slap sent her sprawling across the bed. He flung himself at her

221

and she screamed. He stifled the sound with his hand. 'Whose child is she?'

She pushed his hand away. 'She is yours. I swear it.'

St John was not convinced. 'She's Adam's, isn't she? You could not take your eyes off him during the leave he became betrothed to his cousin. A betrothal he did not want. He could not stay away from the Dolphin. It was him, wasn't it? She has his colouring and your eyes.'

She shook her head, her own eyes wild. 'Fool, she has your grandmother's colouring, your mother's. Is that so surprising?'

The blood was thundering in St John's ears. Jealousy robbed him of reason. He had thought he had triumphed over Adam by winning Meriel. Had he instead been taken for a fool?

He caught Meriel's wrist and twisted it behind her back. 'The child is Adam's. Tell me the truth or I will break your wrist and every bone in your lying, cheating body.'

Where Reuban's beatings had not cowered her, the anger in St John's eyes terrified her. If she lost her power over him, she would lose everything. 'I swear Rowena is your child.'

He relaxed and his breathing slowed, but there was a strength of purpose in him she had not witnessed before.

She knew when to retreat. 'How can you think such vile things? Have I not been a dutiful wife?'

He sat back and there was anguish in his stare as it swept over her. 'I love you to distraction, Meriel. If ever you were unfaithful . . .'

She took him in her arms. 'Have I given you any cause to doubt me since our marriage? You wrong me. I want no one else.' She smoothed the hair back from his brow, her voice coaxing. 'Why do you doubt me? I love you.'

His passion was swift and with little care for her pleasure. She bore it stoically, feigning enjoyment and murmuring endearments. Her body may never stir at his touch but the satisfaction of regaining her power over him was immensely satisfying. When he slept she lay sleepless.

For now she had averted his suspicions. She prayed his pride would make him believe Rowena was his. She had never been so frightened as when he had come so close to discovering the truth.

Chapter Thirty-One

A dam was content living in the cottage situated to one end of the Loveday yard. The original dwelling had a single room downstairs and two bedrooms above. Edward had insisted that it be renovated. A wing was added containing a bow-windowed parlour, a study and kitchen and two further rooms above.

'It must befit the status of a Master Shipwright,' Edward had insisted. 'Though when you marry I shall expect you and Lisette to return to Trevowan. Such a humble abode would not be fitting for her. Neither will the constant clamour and noise from the yard.'

'In time I shall build her a grand house.' Adam had no wish to resume living at Trevowan. He had loved his home in the past but his future was elsewhere. The more distance placed between himself and St John the better for family peace. Even with St John and Meriel installed in the dower house there had been many encounters between the twins and St John never missed a chance to rile Adam. He called Adam a thief for stealing the yard which he regarded as his birthright. He was even worse if Meriel was present. And the one time he had enquired of Rowena's health, he thought St John was going to strike him with his riding crop.

Their arguments angered Edward. Adam was content with his life at the yard. He spent most evenings working on the plans for the refitment of ships.

The yard was prospering. All the cottages were repaired and inhabited, and his father was considering building another four to house the families of the extra workmen he had employed. At Amelia's insistence there was now a schoolroom set up in the back room of the Ship Inn for the children. She was providing the funds for a separate school to be built once the cottages were completed. Other children attended from some of the isolated cottages nearby, including Bridie.

Every day Leah walked the two miles to the school with her daughter. If Senara was not at a market selling her pots, Bridie would arrive on the donkey, otherwise she had to undergo the painful long walk. Aware of their straitened circumstances, Adam paid Leah to clean and cook for him during the school hours. Yet he had been unsuccessful in seeing more of Senara.

Several times he had called at the cottage but it was always empty.

Twice he thought he heard her calling Angel or Charity from the distance, but when he rode in that direction she was nowhere in sight. It could not be coincidence: Senara was avoiding him. It made him want her more but of one thing he was certain: he would never force her. He did not want her to fear him. He wanted her to acknowledge the love for him he had seen in her eyes.

He was never lonely. Scamp was always at his side. Adam mixed easily with the men if he joined them to enjoy a quart of ale at the Ship Inn of an evening. Twice a week his father insisted that he dine at Trevowan.

Richard often accompanied Edward to the yard, and Adam kept his promise to teach him to sail the small sloop beached in Trevowan Cove. Richard was tutored four days a week by Donald Trott, a distant cousin of Oswald Rabson, who rode over from St Austell. In the new year he would board at the twins old school in Bodmin.

Once a fortnight Henry Traherne rode over in the evening. There were also invitations for Adam to attend functions given by neighbours and which were attended by his family.

With the *Pegasus* almost fully rigged and fitted out, he had planned his first voyage to Boston in March; where despite her independence, America was eager for goods and provisions from England. The remainder of the salvage money from the slave ship, he invested in cargo. He had come to terms with the fact that money from the slave ship was somehow tainted. Yet their timely intervention had saved many of the slaves' lives and that helped his conscience. He would ship out of England furniture and oriental fabrics and return with cotton for the northern mills.

The pattern of his future was set. The yard would one day be his, and around him ships of his own design and by his own craftsmanship were being built. Yet an underlying discontent threatened his happiness and left him sleepless at nights. His inability to get close to Senara or banish her from his thoughts robbed him of his sense for fulfilment.

He had taken to riding of an evening, pushing Solomon and himself to the brink of exhaustion in his need to find peace. Far too often he found himself in the woods close to the Polglase cottage, but the hour would be too late to call, the cottage in darkness.

He would veer Solomon away, sometimes pounding along the sea's edge if the tide was out, or riding inland to an ancient standing stone which stood alone on an expanse of craggy moorland. Scamp, who accompanied him, was often carried home across the saddle.

Tonight he had given Solomon his head and after an hour found himself close to the moor. The outline of the great stone rose majestically ahead of him, bathed in a shaft of light from the full moon which had broken free of cloud. He drew near and tethered Solomon to an oak, which from its vast girth could have been a seedling at the time when King Arthur and his army protected this land.

Many locals feared the stone, linking it with demons, witches and ghosts. Adam knew there were hidden shafts from tin mines in the area which had been worked out centuries ago. They made ideal hiding places for the free-traders to store their cargo. It was in the smugglers' interest to promote sinister stories about the stone to keep intruders away.

He walked to the top of the tor. Scamp flopped down panting. Several miles to the south the sea sparkled in the moonlight. A breeze lifted the shoulder cape of Adam's greatcoat. Far across the moor were dotted sparks of light from farmhouse windows. The bleakness of the empty landscape had a serenity he found calming. In a distant wood a dog fox barked and Adam's gaze rested upon the standing stone, a tall proud sentinel, once the focus of ancient rituals. The moonlight cast shadows around it and he thought he saw movement, too quick for a moorland pony. Then a human form glided into the clearing.

Adam crouched on the rocky outcrop, watching. Surprise quickened his pulse. The animal was the mastiff Angel and it could only be Senara or Leah sitting alone by the stone. He put his hand on Scamp's collar and waited, wary that some tryst had been arranged. The notion angered him. It was madness for a woman to be alone on the moor at night. Angel was growling and there was a whinny from Solomon. The mastiff had discovered his horse.

He walked down from the outcrop. Angel streaked across in front of him to stand in defence of his mistress. His growls turned to snarls.

'Do not fear, it is I, Adam Loveday.' He kept Scamp close to him, concerned for the puppy. Angel ignored him.

Senara's voice commanded the dog to silence. 'Adam, what are you doing here?'

'I could well ask you the same. Have you lost your mind? The moor is a dangerous place for a woman at night.'

'And not for a man?' There was sarcasm in her voice. 'I often come here. It is only a mile from the cottage. You are the first person I have met.'

'Then you have been fortunate. Smugglers use the old tin workings to hide their cargo. Had you come across them I fear for your fate.'

'Packponies are never completely silent, even if their hoofs are tied in sacking. I would hear them coming and hide. I have seen you ride this way twice before. You never knew of my presence.'

Her calmness provoked him. 'You would hide from me? When have I ever harmed you?'

'I saw only a lone horseman and it was not until you passed close by that I knew it was you.'

'You did not reveal yourself.'

225

She did not answer but held his stare. Angel sat at her feet and her hand rested on his head. It was a regal pose. A dark hooded cloak covered her hair and figure.

'And what of vagabonds sleeping in hedgerows? The crags here provide shelter.'

'Those you can usually smell long before you stumble upon them, and would they not have lit fires?'

Adam could not believe her naivety. 'That great lumbering beast will warn others of your coming. They could lie downwind in ambush.'

'I travel many roads alone to sell my pottery. I feel safer by night than by day. But it is all in the hands of fate.' She turned to leave. 'I have herbs to gather which must be collected at the full of the moon.'

'Do not go.' He held a hand out in entreaty. 'I have wanted so often to see you again. You made it clear my company was not welcome at your home. But I hoped you would look kindly upon me.'

She stood with her head bowed. 'It is better if I go.' The catch in her voice betrayed her.

The moonlight silvered her face and Adam saw the glisten of a tear on her lashes. The silence of the moor held them captive; even the wind was still, its breath bated.

'Senara.' Her name was spoken with a sigh of longing.

She gazed up at him. The stone had always been a magical place for her, a place where she felt at peace with herself and her place in the world. That he was here with only the moon to shine its blessing upon them could not be a coincidence. It felt more like destiny.

She had begun to fall in love with him the day he had treated Bridie as an equal. The attraction of his handsome looks, raven dark hair and sea-blue eyes, which could reveal depths of tenderness, or be as stormy as the ocean, had been irresistible. Each time they met, her feelings had intensified, until her love for him pierced her dreams and brought an ache of emptiness to her days. Knowing that such a man could never be for her, she had erected barricades of indifference as protection. She had deluded herself they were built of stone. The day he had kissed her, she had found they were no more than a flimsy wattle.

The scar on is cheek showed as a thin white ridged crescent in the moonlight. Her hand was drawn to it, the contours creating an ache within her. The sensitive tips of her fingers tingled and burned.

With a gruff moan he drew her close. His lips were warm and demanding upon her own. When she offered no resistance, his tongue parted them to fill sweetly the hollowness which had become a craving. Her arms wound around him, sliding under the open greatcoat to feel the fine wool of his jacket and the play of hard muscles beneath. The touch of his hands on her breasts released a millstream of desire in her loins. It rose like a fountain through her veins and cascaded down

226

through her limbs, leaving her weak and breathless.

Abruptly he broke away, his expression haggard as he gazed down at her. 'I love you, Senara. But I can offer you nothing but my love and adoration.'

She silenced him with a kiss, then purred softly, 'You are bound to another, but you have not wed her. Let this be our time. I ask or expect nothing of you, but your heart.'

Adam shrugged his greatcoat from his shoulders and, in the shelter of the great stone, laid it upon the grass to protect them from the dew, and drew her down to lie beside him.

She responded with an ardour which came as natural as breathing. There was no sense of wrong, only of the inevitable. A union sanctified by this ancient holy place.

His consideration as a lover brought her to a pleasure that Ross Malone, in his selfish quest for lust, had never achieved. She cried his name over and over as the waves of exquisite sensation exploded through her body. Only then did he allow himself release and with a harsh groan withdrew from her, his seed pumping on to her thigh. He eased his weight to one side and held her close until their breathing slowed.

'My love, you have brought me such joy,' he murmured against her ear. 'If I were free—'

She broke away and straightened her clothes. 'No, Adam, talk not of a future. You have a betrothed. There is no future for us. We have the present, that is all.'

'I will not give you up.'

'And I cannot share you.' She stood up. She had thought she could love Adam and relish the present time they had together. The future mocked her. She loved him too well and that alarmed her. 'This is why I asked you not to seek me out. Why I did not want to meet you again. There is no place for me in your life. If you have any feelings for me you will stay away. Life is hard enough without you complicating it further.'

She was tensed for flight and he took her arms, preventing her. 'Do not run away from me again. You know this is right.'

Her throat was too constricted with unshed tears to speak. His touch was destroying her sanity. Her eyes silently pleaded with him to let her go – to forget her.

He stared down at her for a long moment. A part of her wanted him to crush her to him, a saner part held her stiff and terrified as a cornered doe. His hands fell away.

'How can you dispute that this was not meant to be? I have never felt this way about any woman. I love you. If I was free to offer marriage I would.'

She took retreat in outrage. 'I am no Meriel Sawle, to use wiles to

227

trick a man into marriage. I know my place. It is not as the wife of a Loveday or any man of your station.'

'Who you are matters not to me.'

'It matters to me. Forget tonight. Forget me, I beg you. My mother and Bridie are settled here. If I continue to see you there will be scandal and we shall have to leave. I will not condemn them to that. We have run so often from the past already. Promise me you will not seek me out again.'

'How can I? I love you.'

'Then we must leave.' She backed away.

'Can you truly deny what happened between us tonight?' There was a terseness and disbelief in his voice which harrowed her.

'I do not deny it. But it would be madness to repeat it. My world and your world cannot mix. I have no wish to put on silk gowns and ape those of your kind. I had found contentment in my life in the cottage.'

'Senara, you cannot mean what you say.'

'I do. Go back to your life, Adam Loveday. There is no place in it for the half-gypsy bastard Senara Polglase.'

She turned and fled into the shadows, Angel running beside her. Several times she stumbled, her eyes blinded by tears and her heart feeling it had been crushed by millstones. When she heard the pounding of Solomon's hoofs behind her, she ran towards a shallow cave covered by a gorse bush. Heedless of the needle-sharp leaves scratching her face and hands, she dived into its sanctuary, silencing Angel with a whispered command.

Horse and rider cantered past, a frantic note in Adam's voice as he continually called her name. Scamp was sniffing close by, threatening to reveal her hiding place. Then a fox rustled in the undergrowth and with an excited bark Scamp disappeared to chase it.

Adam searched for an hour. Senara had gone to ground and did not want to be found. He had seen the resolution in her eyes and known this was no womanly prevarication to sharpen his interest. She had meant every word.

Chapter Thirty-Two

To banish thoughts of Senara, Adam worked longer hours in the yard, involved in strenuous labours so that, at nights, he was too tired to think or dream.

Sir Henry Traherne visited him one evening at the yard. 'You have become a recluse.' There was a heaviness about Henry's manner and his teasing was forced. 'I thought now you were no longer at sea we would see more of you.'

Adam had been composing a letter to Claude Riviere from whom he had received disturbing correspondence that day. He had spent the evening in much heart-searching and Henry's appearance provided a welcome diversion.

'You have married life to occupy you,' Adam grinned.

'I am married but not shackled to my wife. Though there are times when it feels like it.'

From his slurred speech it was obvious Henry had been drinking earlier. He stood with his back to the fire in Adam's parlour. The room was sparsely furnished with a table, wooden settle and two wooden Jacobean chairs whose seats had been reupholstered in burgundy brocade. There was no carpet on the floor nor hangings at the window.

The four candles which lit the room cast saturnine shadows over Henry's face. He had lost weight, which made him appear taller than ever. He ground out, 'Roslyn is never content. Always I must do more for her; be at her side. Her shrew's tongue is wearying.'

'I have been so engrossed in my work I have neglected our friendship. Shall we go to the Ship for a drink?'

Henry waved a brandy bottle. 'No need.'

Adam found glasses and as Henry filled them, his friend sighed. 'You were wise to defer your marriage. Lady Druce and Gwendolyn seem a permanent feature at the Hall. They chatter like starlings every evening. I get no peace. They expect me to dance attendance on their whims. Roslyn even resents the time I spend at the mine.'

'Is the mine not prospering?'

'Yes, and Roslyn never stops harping that it was her money which saved it.' He sprawled on the wooden settle in front of the fire and stared disconsolately at his dusty boots. Perhaps after Easter, when

229

the baby is born, Roslyn will be more content.'

His words reflected Adam's doubts about his own forthcoming marriage. Henry had married for money and was miserable. St John had supposedly married for love and was more sour-tempered and bitter than Aunt Elspeth. He could not shake the feeling that his marriage to Lisette could never be more than tolerable.

But what honourable choice did he have? He must sacrifice his feelings and love for Senara, and make the best of his life with Lisette. He shook off his cynicism. It appeared that his father was happy with Amelia and she doted on him. When Adam visited Trevowan, laughter was never far from any conversation. If his own marriage failed it would be his fault, for Lisette's frequent letters were filled with her longing for their marriage and how wonderful their life would be together. She also spoke of Etienne's kindness in including her in any invitation to the opera or to balls.

'It does not look like my marriage can be put off much longer. Uncle Claude is ill again. And I am worried about the company Etienne forces Lisette to keep. The Marquis de Gramont is often mentioned in her letters.'

'Is the man a problem?'

'He is not the type whose company I wish my fiancée to associate with.' Adam chewed his nail in growing agitation, aware he must be discreet, but wanting to confide in Henry. 'There were rumours in Paris that he was responsible for a girl's suicide in a brothel after his brutal treatment.'

Henry looked shocked. 'And your cousin encourages this devil.'

Adam let out a harsh breath. 'Etienne is dazzled by his title. He was against my betrothal to his sister.'

'But a monster such as this man . . . Etienne should be horsewhipped.' Henry voiced Adam's own fears. 'Surely your uncle has no wish for her reputation to be endangered.'

'I received a letter from Uncle Claude today. He has been ill and is concerned for Lisette's welfare. He urges our speedy marriage. He wants me to marry her before I embark on the *Pegasus*' first voyage next month. I begin to think I have no choice.'

'Clearly Lisette could be in danger. But she does have her family to protect her.' Henry reasoned. 'The Rivieres are not without influence. And is it wise to marry and then be at sea for several months? It would be unfair on the girl, would it not?'

Adam was wrestling with duty and his reluctance for this wedding. He loved Senara. He wanted to spend his life with her, not Lisette. 'Father agrees with Uncle Claude. What if my uncle dies while I am at sea? Lisette would be at the mercy of her brother. I do not trust him.'

'Quite a dilemma, old boy,' Henry consoled. 'And knowing you, you will do the honourable thing.'

After the barest hesitation, Adam nodded. 'I have no choice. I will leave for Paris next week. The wedding will be a small affair. The crossing can be bad this time of year so my family will not be attending.'

St John flew into a rage when he learned of Adam's plans.

'Is this not typical of Adam's fortune? He will be a wealthy man once he marries Lisette.'

He had sought out Meriel in the dower house where she was rearranging the new dinner service on a dresser in the red and gold dining room. Since they had taken up residence in late January, she was constantly changing round the furniture.

'Adam has a charmed life,' Meriel goaded. Her own anger at him for his rejection of her advances was never far from the surface. She would never forgive him that insult.

A glance at her husband showed her his flushed face and white knuckles as he clenched his fists. With his own fortunes in decline, St John's hatred for his brother festered. While he had lost everything with the seizing of the cargo, Adam prospered.

'It is not to be tolerated,' he raged. 'The yard should be mine. Adam's scheming stole it from me. There must be a way to discredit him. Then Father will make me his heir.'

'I agree he should not get away with it. But Adam is wily. While he lives he will always be a danger to your inheritance.'

St John picked up a silver spoon from the table and examined it sullenly. Meriel watched him covertly. Her hatred for Adam was as strong as St John's, but in his weakness and fear of his father's censure, he would never take the initiative to put an end to their problems. She had approached Clem, but her brother, although he had beaten men half to death for crossing him, had been surly, declaring, 'I've got no grudge against Adam Loveday. St John is another matter.'

'St John is my husband. Harm him and where does that leave me?' she had raged at him.

He had laughed at her. 'As a widow you'd have no standing in the community, would you? But for all your scheming you married a weak man who will never amount to much.'

Her brother's ridicule had fanned her anger. St John was far from the answer to her dreams. Then he had only been second best to Adam as her choice of husband. Adam had wronged her. But she would make St John triumph over his twin and therefore wreak her own revenge.

St John had been a fool to alienate her brothers. If they would not help her get her vengeance on Adam there was another family who would. They would sell their own mother to the devil for a price.

'You could pay the Jowetts to teach Adam a lesson.' She used St John's anger to plant the idea.

'The Jowetts are not a family to tangle with.'

'But they will do your bidding with no questions asked. For a price.'

'I do not want Adam killed.' St John looked so appalled she knew she had to tread carefully.

'Who mentioned murder? A good beating will teach Adam a lesson that's long overdue.'

'But the Jowetts . . .'

She threw up her hands in exasperation. 'If you are too afeared to approach them, then Adam gets away with stealing your inheritance. Clem would not let Harry get away with it. And if the tables were reversed do you think Adam would sit back and allow his birthright to be stolen?'

That hit a nerve. His head jerked forward with belligerence. 'So you think Adam is more of a man than I?'

'Look at the way he stood up to Beaumont. I admire courage in a man above all else.' She sidled up to him and slid her arms around his waist. 'I know a beating will change nothing. Adam will still get the yard, but it proves you did not allow him to walk all over you.'

'I defied my family to wed you.' He became defensive and held himself away from her.

She summoned her most bewitching smile. 'You were magnificent that day. Of course it would be foolish to punish Adam yourself. If your father ever suspected you could lose Trevowan. If you want Adam to pay for the wrong you have suffered, then the Jowetts will extract the vengeance you seek.'

Still he did not seem convinced but she was not disheartened. St John always came round to her way of thinking, she made sure of that. It was just a matter of time.

Two weeks later, after evensong at Trewenna church, St John excused himself from joining the family who were to dine with Squire Penwithick. 'I have a headache and feel feverish,' he informed Edward. 'I will return to the dower house.'

'Indeed, you must stay in the warm.' Amelia was all concern.

'It will rain this evening,' Elspeth remarked. 'My hip is agony.'

Amelia cast an anxious glance at Richard, who, to her relief, looked pink-faced and healthy. 'A fever at this time of year can be dangerous.'

Elspeth regarded St John over the top of her pince-nez. 'You are looking pasty of late. It does not look like you have a fever.' She tried to feel his brow but St John evaded her.

'I am shivery and my head is pounding.'

Meriel took his arm. 'Shall I stay with you, my dear?'

232

'I would not deprive you of your entertainment. I am tired and will probably sleep all afternoon.'

'A wife's place is by her husband's sickbed.' Elspeth surveyed Meriel with displeasure.

'Yes, of course,' Meriel demurred, her irony lost on the doting aunt. 'Let us hope it is nothing contagious. It would be too terrible if Rowena contacted a fever.'

St John rubbed his brow. 'You act as though I am about to be smitten by the plague. It is a headache. A slight chill, nothing more.'

Elspeth continued to mutter to herself until St John feared he had overplayed his hand. Her lower lip thrust forward stubbornly. 'I shall give instructions to Winnie to bring you broth and to check that Rowena has not become feverish. You cannot be too careful with a young child.'

'No. I shall stay with my husband,' Meriel snapped.

Amelia reached across to squeeze her hand. 'I know how you were looking forward to this evening. We will have a special evening next week and invite the neighbours to dine.'

'That will be pleasant.' Meriel bit back her frustration. She was angered at missing out on an evening's entertainment and she hated it when Amelia played the benevolent lady of the manor. Why had St John insisted on playing on illness to escape his family? He should have known Elspeth would make a fuss. The old dragon interfered interminably if the baby so much as sneezed, though in fact she was growing into a healthy and strong child despite her difficult start in life.

There was nothing wrong with St John. Meriel had finally persuaded him to contact the Jowetts on Bodmin Moor. His visit must be kept secret from his family. If Winnie Fraddon came snooping round she would ruin everything. Meriel had already taken the precaution of giving the servants the day off.

When the family departed, Meriel followed St John into their parlour. 'That is one hurdle out of the way. No one must see you leave. Unfortunately it looks like rain. Bodmin can be dangerous if a mist closes in.'

'I will be home before dark.'

'Take care, my love.' She had a sudden misgiving that harm would come to St John. The Jowetts could not be trusted.

Her fears mounted as the hours past and St John did not return from Bodmin Moor. Elspeth visited late that evening and Meriel allowed her to look in on Rowena to see she was well, but not on St John, of course.

'He has only just managed to get to sleep. I would not want you catching his chill.'

'Should Dr Chegwidden be sent for?'

'It is but a cold. You know how men make such heavy weather of illness. I am sure he will be recovered by the morning.'

'Umph, knowing St John his malaise is caused by a heavy night's drinking.' Elspeth sniffed her disapproval.

Now in her nightrobe Meriel paced the parlour. St John should have returned hours ago. The weather had worsened. She tried to convince herself that St John had taken shelter somewhere. Bodmin could be treacherous. Many a traveller who had strayed off the road had never been heard of again.

And how far could they trust the Jowetts? They were a family who acknowledged no laws. Rough and unkempt, they were as feared as any medieval war barons and as capable of stealing another man's property, raping his daughters and, if only half the rumours were true, murdering without conscience or reason.

When she heard a stumbling step on the stairs, anger trampled her fears. St John was drunk. How dare he put her through such worry?

She wrenched open the door, a candle held high. Her tirade shrivelled at the sight of him. Water oozed from his boots and his greatcoat was dripping streams on to the floorboards and down the stairs. It was the sound of his wheezing which alarmed her.

'Good God! They have shot you!'

He slumped against the wall. A trembling hand fumbled with the fastening of his greatcoat and it slipped with a sodden thump to the floor. 'No. They agreed to our plan. On the way back my horse cast a shoe. I have had to walk the last four miles. Get me a brandy.'

He was shivering violently and there was a livid flush to his cheeks. He tossed back the brandy and coughed. It turned to a spasm which left him weak and shaken.

Meriel helped him to the bed and removed his wet clothes. She threw three more logs on the dying fire and prodded some life into the embers. He coughed several more times and slumped back exhausted on the bed.

As the logs began to catch St John had pulled the covers to his chin but she saw him shivering beneath the heavy quilt.

By the time dawn brightened the room, his breath was a harsh rasp and he was gibbering in delirium. Dr Chegwidden was sent for.

Two days later his fever was at its height. Chegwidden had purged and bled him to excess and still his fever raged. Frequently he called out his brother's name. Meriel sat hollow-eyed, her fear mistaken by the family as concern for her husband. When his delirium grew louder, she held his head against her breast, muffling his voice and talking above his words as though to calm him.

Dr Chegwidden stepped back from the bed, having just removed several bloated leeches from St John's chest and plopped them into a jar with a stopper. He met Edward's worried gaze and put a consoling hand on his shoulder. 'The fever shows no sign of abating. He should be left to rest now. I will return in the morning.'

The sheets had been changed before the leeches were applied and already they were wet from his sweat. His face had all the fire of a crimson midsummer sunset.

'Adam!' he called. Meriel reached for him, her own brow stippling with sweat at the thought of what his fevered mind could reveal.

Edward remained seated in a corner as Meriel tended her husband. 'You should rest, my dear. You have been two nights without sleep.'

'I would never forgive myself if anything happened. If he should need me . . . when I was asleep,' she evaded.

'You have proved a worthy wife. But I would not like to see you become ill.'

She was saved from replying when St John cried out again, 'Adam!' He thrashed and pushed her away, his voice hoarse but clear. 'Forgive . . . forgive me.'

'Hush, my love.' She gathered him close. 'Adam forgave you long ago for your childhood rivalry.'

She glanced fearfully at Edward, but he placed no significance on the words and walked to the door. His voice was weary. 'I will send for Adam. His presence may calm him. The squabbles of their childhood weigh heavily on him. I have long prayed for them to see sense and be at peace with one another.'

Adam stared at Jasper Fraddon with disbelief when he opened the door at nine in the evening to the servant's pounding.

'Mr Loveday says for you to come at once. Master St John has taken a turn for the worse.'

'I thought he just had a chill.'

'Fever of the lungs. Delirious, he be. He be asking for you.'

Adam raised a brow in surprise. 'I will go at once.' He looked sharply at Jasper Fraddon, who did not look well himself. There was a dark bruise on his jaw and that side of his face had swollen to twice its size. 'What ails you?'

'Damned horse was skittish when I saddled her. Swung her head round as I was putting the bridle on. The bit caught my face and broke a tooth. Feels like a pickaxe is being hacked at it.'

'Call on Seth Wakeley. His is the last cottage on the right. He did some tooth pulling in the navy when the surgeon was too drunk to be any use. There's a bottle of brandy in the cupboard. Drink all you need and sleep here tonight. I will tell Winnie what happened.'

'I couldn't do that, sir.' He eyed the brandy with hunger. There was a time when Jasper had been more often drunk than sober. When he courted Winnie, she agreed to wed him on condition he gave up

235

the drink. Her father had been a brutish drunkard who spent all his wages in the tavern, leaving his family to go hungry.

'The brandy will dull the pain,' Adam urged. 'It must be agony.'

'Aye, it be terrible indeed. But there be the horses to be fed and mucked out come morning. Happen the tooth bain't so bad.'

Adam insisted on inspecting it and shook his head. 'It will have to come out. It is broken in half. Why suffer when Seth can help you?'

Jasper visibly squirmed. 'Don't fancy no tooth puller hacking at me. Happen I'll be fine come morning.'

'The pain will not go until the tooth is pulled. Father will make allowance if you are late to work in the morning. Ned can feed and water the horses.'

Jasper eyed the brandy and weighed the pleasure of drinking it against the agony of the tooth puller. He shook his head. The movement caused his face to twist in agony and he emitted an animal howl of pain. Adam shoved him outside and went across to rap on Seth's door. By then Jasper was clinging to the brandy as though his life depended on it.

The waning moon was hidden by cloud. Adam lit a lantern to give him light in the blackness. Solomon was sure-footed on the familiar track. The horse had not been ridden for two days and when they approached the crossroads he fought Adam's control to turn away from the direction of his old stable at Trevowan. He wanted to gallop across country to the moor.

Scamp had taken off over the fields. Concentrating on keeping Solomon to the lane, Adam did not hear or see the men rising from the hedgerow. Without warning Solomon reared up. There was a flash of orange flame from a pistol, then pain punched into Adam's chest with the force of a charging bull and pitched him backwards out of the saddle, one foot still caught in the stirrup. His head struck the ground and he was unconscious before Solomon plunged up the bank and through a break in a patchy hedge to gallop across the field.

When the horse took off, the Jowetts ran after it, firing three more shots at Adam's disappearing figure. Their shouts frightened Solomon further and the gelding bolted in terror, spurred on by the unfamiliar burden dragged behind him.

'That were easy money and we only had to lie in wait two nights for him to leave the yard alone.' Emmanuel Jowett chuckled. He was as thickset as a pumpkin and his short legs were not used to walking. 'He'll be black and blue and saved us giving him a beating.'

Gabriel Jowett, tall and willowy, with a long hatchet face, led their horses out from their hiding place and flung the reins at his elder brother. 'Pity, nothing I like more than a good fight.'

Zachariah Jowett rubbed his groin, his bovine face devoid of

236

expression. 'That warning shot hit him when his horse reared. He be more than black and blue. Reckon Adam Loveday will get more than the comeuppance his brother planned. No man's gonna survive being dragged across the moor.'

Chapter Thirty-Three

At the sound of a whinny and slowing pace of a trotting horse, Senara flattened herself into the shadows of a gorse bush. She held Angel's collar, silencing his growl with a whispered command. As the horse came closer she saw it was riderless. Although it was too dark to see it clearly, the three white stockings on its legs were visible and she glimpsed the white star on its copper head. Those were the markings of Solomon. If he was riderless then Adam had been thrown.

'Whoa, boy!' She approached him. 'Whoa there, Solomon.'

The gelding was streaked with sweat and was breathing heavily. If he had not been tired she doubted she would have caught him. He backed away uneasily, wary of her scent, with which he was only vaguely familiar. She spoke softly to reassure him and reached for the reins. He reared, wrenching her arms but she hung on. 'Whoa, boy, that's it. Be still.'

His hoofs came down and the smell of crushed grass rose from his feet. She found a small apple in her pocket and held it out to him. He took it and began to settle.

'Now we must find your master.' Her voice shook as she ran her hand along his flank and it came away sticky with blood. Fear ground through her that Adam was seriously hurt. 'Seek, Angel.' She walked Solomon back the way he had been running. The mastiff ran ahead, sniffing at the ground, and she was forced to heave herself on to Solomon's back to keep up with him.

They had covered so much distance she feared Angel had missed the scent and was now hunting a rabbit or fox. The clouds had thinned and the moonlight was enough for Senara to follow the outlines of hedgerows but the dark impeded her progress. Then she heard a distant whining. Was it Scamp? It was in the direction Angel was heading.

Ahead she saw a patch of white on the ground. It moved as they neared and began to bark and circle an indistinct shape in the bulrushes at the side of a stream.

Senara dismounted to investigate and saw Adam's still form. There was no sign of life in his face, his eyes closed and skin torn and bruised. Blood was clotted in a large lump and gash above his ear. She opened his thick greatcoat and when she put her ear to his chest, there was no sound of breathing or a heartbeat. Sobs tore from her and her hands shook as she frantically sought for some sign of life. His jacket was also soaked in blood, but on the wrong side to have come from the head wound.

She could not believe that he was dead. She pulled off his gauntlets and held his icy fingers. Tears spilled over their joined hands. She had struggled so long to deny her love and now it burst from her like a dam. 'Oh Adam, no. No! Come back to me.'

There was the faintest twitch of a muscle in his hand. It was enough to convince her that he was alive. Barely.

She cursed the weak moonlight which made it impossible to see the full extent of his injuries. She suspected several ribs were cracked and from the angle of his leg he had broken his ankle. Her hands shook as she tore at the buttons of his jacket and ripped open his blood-soaked shirt. To her horror she saw the black hole of a bullet wound which had entered his body below the shoulder and missed his heart by some three inches. This then had been no chance accident. Someone had tried to kill Adam.

The extent of his injuries meant it would be dangerous to move him. If his wounds were not so serious, or his life did not hang by such a fragile thread, she would risk leaving him to fetch help. The night dew had chilled his body. If he was left the cold would kill him. He had to be in the warm as soon as possible or a fever would set in.

Trevowan was out of the question. It was too great a distance – some three or so miles. The shipyard was the closest place to go, closer even than her own home.

Pulling off her petticoat Senara ripped strips from the hem to bind the splints which would secure Adam's ankle. She wrapped the remainder of the garment tightly around his ribs, relieved that none had fractured and could cause internal injuries.

She prayed for strength. It took her several minutes to heave him over the saddle of Solomon. The task took all her resilience and, close to exhaustion, she leaned her brow against the gelding's side to recover her breath. Weak groans from Adam spurred her on. He may be unconscious and suffering shock, but he *was* still alive.

'Don't you dare slip away from me now, Adam Loveday,' she gasped as she staggered over the rough ground, leading Solomon by his bridle.

Their passage was agonisingly slow, the darkness making it difficult for Senara to keep her bearings. After his long flight, Solomon's head was drooping and it was instinct to return to the food and shelter of his stable which guided his steps to the Loveday yard.

When she banged on one of the darkened cottage doors it was less than an hour since she had found Adam. An upper window was flung open.

'Who the devil is making that row?' Ben Mumford bellowed.

'I need help. It's your master. He's seriously hurt.'

The head disappeared from the window and moments later the door was thrown open. The man had pulled on his breeches and was tucking his nightshirt into the waistband. He carried his boots. His nightgowned wife, with a shawl wrapped round her shoulders, followed behind him.

'Help me get him into his bed and send for a physician,' Senara demanded.

Ben knocked on another house to rouse Jacob Pengilly, his neighbour. The couple led the way to Adam's house. Lucy Mumford lit candles inside as Ben and Jacob carried Adam to his chamber and laid him on the bed.'

'He be a gonna,' Jacob pronounced.

Senara placed two candles beside the bed and eased the greatcoat from Adam's shoulders. 'One of you fetch a doctor. I need help to cut his boot from his ankle. It is broken.'

Jacob Pengilly volunteered. 'I'll fetch Chegwidden. Then I'll ride on to Trevowan.'

As Jacob left a figure staggered into the room, his hair wild and dishevelled. 'What's going on?'

Jasper Fraddon swayed drunkenly. There was a bandage round his swollen jaw. He focused blearily eyes on the figure on the bed. 'That be Master Adam. He were summoned to Trevowan.'

'His horse threw him—' Ben started to explain.

'Actually he was shot and probably dragged across the ground, from the state of his clothing,' Senara cut across their speech. 'Now will one of you help me? Before he dies.'

Ben Mumford thrust his hands in his belt. 'Look 'ere, miss. We don't know who you be. We thank 'ee for saving the master, but his chamber bain't no place for a woman.'

Her stare was forthright. 'I am Senara Polglase, Leah's daughter. I've experience of tending the sick, especially broken bones. If your master does not receive urgent attention he will be dead before the physician arrives.'

Jasper Fraddon groaned. 'It be my fault the master be hurt. I should have ridden with him.'

Senara continued to examine Adam. She feared the shock and chill would soon turn to a fever. 'If you know the old Polglase cottage I need someone to ride there. My mother will give you my medicine casket with herbs to ease his pain and prevent any infection.'

'Chegwidden will tend him.' Ben Mumford took her arm to pull her away from the bed.

'Best not be so uppity, Ben.' Jasper put his hand over the other man's. 'Miss Elspeth sets store by the woman's potions. It could be a while before Chegwidden attends. He left Trevowan to go to Polgarra

241

where a family were sick of fish poisoning. And what with Master St John laid so low . . . I'll go fetch what she needs.'

Ben glanced anxiously at Adam, who lay pale and unmoving. Senara wrenched her arm away. 'I shall do what I can until the doctor arrives.'

Lucy Mumford hovered by the door and introduced herself. 'Can I help?'

Senara nodded. 'I shall need hot water to bathe his wounds, a sheet ripped up into bandages, brandy to dull his pain and a sharp knife to cut away his boot. This fire should be lit and hot bricks wrapped in towels to warm the bed.'

'I can see to them and the fire.' Ben set to work. With the fire lit he returned with the heated bricks and gave a shocked gasp to see Senara removing Adam's clothing.

He pushed her aside. 'I'll do that. It bain't fitting for a lass.'

Senara stood back. 'Just remember I need to tend his torso and leg.' She curbed her impatience while Ben protected Adam's modesty. A sheet was laid across Adam's midriff.

At intervals throughout her ministrations she dribbled small quantities of brandy mixed with honey into his mouth. If it was administered carefully a few drops at a time it trickled down his throat. Once the boot had been cut away, the broken ankle seemed to swell before their eyes.

Jasper Fraddon returned with her medicine casket.

'Lucy, I need vinegar and sage poultices for his ankle and head. They will take the swelling down.' Senara handed her the dried sage leaves. 'Soak these in a little hot water. Then saturate a cloth in vinegar and bring it to me.'

Adam remained unconscious. Already a faint colour had returned to his lips and although his breathing was shallow it was at least now perceptible. But the danger was not over.

Senara applied the sage leaves and vinegar-soaked bandages to his head and ankle. The swelling in his ankle had to be reduced before she could apply a splint. While he remained unconscious it was easier to deal with the wounds which caused him greatest pain.

Senara fretted that Dr Chegwidden had not arrived. She was competent in dealing with Adam's injuries, but doctors rarely trusted the ancient skills taught her by her gypsy grandmother. It undermined their own importance in the community. More than one doctor in the past had been outraged by her remedies and, even though they had been successful, his persecution of her had forced the Polglase women to move on.

For now, the broken ankle wrapped in the poultice was supported by a pillow, and it was the chance of infection from the bullet wound which concerned her most. Fortunately the bullet had passed through

242

his body, but a poultice was needed to ensure there was no secondary infection.

Jasper Fraddon brought some more hot bricks to warm the bed. At seeing him wince and cradle his jaw, she sprinkled some comfrey and ground cloves into a cup. 'Add brandy and hot water to it and sip it. It will ease your toothache.' Jasper eyed the concoction suspiciously but Senara had already turned away to select from her casket a balm which she applied to Adam's battered back and hips. The heavy greatcoat had saved him from any abrasions but most of his back, buttocks and thighs were turning purple. She could only pray that there was no internal bleeding and damage. When she examined his ribcage, none of the ribs were fractured. With tender manipulation she ensured the ribs were not displaced, though there was the chance one or more could be cracked. She then applied a healing balm across them before binding them tightly with more bandages.

What worried her most was the bruising to his liver and kidneys. It could affect their function, making his recovery slow and painful. Any internal bleeding could kill him.

The sound of footsteps on the stairs made her straighten. Edward Loveday approached the bed. His face was ashen in the candlelight.

'Dear God, what have I done that both my sons should be struck mortally low?' He turned a stricken stare upon Senara. 'I understand we owe his life to you. Pengilly said you found him. And clearly have ably ministered to him. Chegwidden has sent word he cannot come until morning as he is delayed in Polgarra. What are Adam's chances?'

Senara outlined the details of his injuries, finishing in a shaky voice, 'It is an ill omen he has been unconscious so long. But his heartbeat is stronger now. I have no way of knowing if he has internal injuries. As for his leg, I suspect he was thrown from the saddle and dragged for some distance. His ankle is broken but the knee and hip joints are severely bruised and there is damage to the muscles or tendons. He really needs a splint to keep the entire hip and leg in place to ensure no lasting damage is sustained.'

'But who could have shot him?' Edward sank on to a chair by the bed and dropped his head into his hands. 'Adam was no threat to any smuggler. Those engaged in the trade hereabouts know him too well.'

'Poachers, smugglers, horse-thieves, even wreckers could be at work on a night like this,' Ben Mumford pronounced.

'The Lord Lieutenant of the County shall investigate this,' Edward declared. 'But what concerns me now is that my son should live.'

'Have I your permission to place his leg in splints?' Senara was uneasy in Edward's presence. 'It's important that the leg is bound and secured as soon as possible, especially if Dr Chegwidden cannot attend for some hours. Were Adam to gain consciousness and thrash about in pain he could cause further damage to his leg.'

'We are grateful for your knowledge, Miss Polglase. Please do all you can. You will be rewarded.'

'I expect no reward. Your son saved my sister's life when some young boys attacked her. It is how he came by the scar on his cheek.'

Edward grimaced at the effort it took to keep the pain from his voice. 'He never said how he came by the scar. I believe I gave him a tongue-lashing for fighting.'

Exhausted from his vigil at St John's bedside, he cursed Chegwidden's absence, which he feared could cost Adam his life. But the woman was competent as she bound the damaged leg in splints which Ben Mumford had planed to a smooth finish.

Edward stared at Adam's bandaged head and torso and held his breath, releasing it only when he saw the faint rise and fall of his son's shallow breathing. He willed him to draw in strength, and that each breath would be more forceful. As Senara laid his leg upon the supporting pillow, Adam groaned.

'Is he coming round?'

Senara felt the heartbeat and lifted an eyelid. The eyeball was no longer rolled back into the head.

'He is stronger. Perhaps the sound of your voice would rouse him.'

Edward gripped Adam's hand. His own knuckles were white with tension. 'Adam, can you hear me? Wake up, son.'

There was no response. Senara swayed with weariness. Now she was no longer occupied in caring for him, her own anguish formed a tight lump in her throat and she felt nauseous with fear.

'It is two in the morning,' Edward announced. 'Mrs Mumford has made a bed up for you in a spare chamber. You must be exhausted. It is some distance to your home, I believe.'

'You also look tired, Mr Loveday.'

He sighed. 'I have had little sleep the last three nights. My elder son has a lung fever. In his delirium he called out for Adam. If I had not summoned Adam to attend him, Adam would not be in this sorry state now.'

Her heart went out to the proud man. 'I will stay here until Dr Chegwidden arrives. But when your son recovers consciousness he will need careful tending for some weeks.'

'Please stay, Miss Polglase. Adam will be moved to Trevowan once Dr Chegwidden has examined him.'

Edward tore himself from the bedside to stare out of the darkened window. From the rigidness of his stance and the way his head bowed, Senara guessed he was close to breaking down.

'Dear God, this is more than a man can endure.' He spun round to face Adam's battered figure on the bed. His throat worked in a spasm. 'He cannot die.'

'He has much to live for.' Senara poured Edward Loveday a glass

244

of brandy. 'He is strong. But I fear it would be dangerous to move him for some days. It is not until his wits return that the extent of his injuries will be known.'

She took a cup of buttermilk from Lucy and thanked her. Ben had carried a chair into the bedchamber for her to sit on. She folded herself into it; her body ached from bending so long over Adam, but her mind was sharp and attuned to any change in her patient.

The room brightened and outside a lone blackbird sang. It was joined by other birds in their dawn chorus. Edward Loveday stretched out his legs and flicked open his fob watch.

'It is almost five.'

At the sound of his voice Adam gave a shuddering breath and his hands clenched.

Edward was on his feet. 'Adam! Wake up, Adam!' His tone was sharp, a command.

The eyelids fluttered and Adam seemed to be fighting to force them open. They flickered and a slither of blue was visible before they again closed.

'Adam. Can you hear me?' Edward squeezed his son's hand and his voice, no longer controlled, was raw with desperation. 'You were thrown from your horse. Adam!'

'S-s-sir,' the cracked voice slurred. The eyes battled to open and slowly the blue-green stare focused upon his father. 'Fell, sir. Sorry, sir. Feel like . . . hell.'

Senara held to his mouth a cup of water containing herbs to dull his pain, and he managed to gulp a mouthful down.

'What are you doing here . . .?' he dragged out.

'No questions,' she said with a smile. 'You must rest and regain your strength.'

'Who shot you?' Edward demanded.

'Was I shot?' Adam slurred, his voice was weak and confused.

'Please, no questions.' Senara looked at Edward. 'He must rest, not tax his mind.'

With great patience she managed to get Adam to swallow the rest of the contents of the cup. His eyes closed and his chest rose and fell in the steady breathing of sleep.

There were tears in Edward Loveday's eyes when they turned upon her. 'I can never thank you enough for what you have done this night. You have saved his life.'

'The danger is not yet over. But if no further infection sets in he will recover.' She wiped a tear from her own cheek.

Chapter Thirty-Four

D r Chegwidden finished his examination of Adam. Senara had protested when he insisted on removing the splint from the patient's leg. She had already vigorously shaken her head to signal to Edward to prevent the doctor opening up a vein in Adam's arm. He had lost too much blood already.

'If the injury is as serious as you say, then it needs expert attention.' Chegwidden's manner was gruff, and so far he had snubbed Senara throughout the examination.

Edward Loveday intervened. 'I saw Senara align the bones. I see no reason why Adam should suffer further. Does the splint look adequate to you? Senara used a poultice to reduce the swelling before applying it.'

Adam was awake but drowsy and his face was deeply grooved with pain. 'I trust Senara.'

'Then it seems my opinion is not wanted.' Chegwidden puffed out his chest with affront.

'Adam would have died but for Miss Polglase's skill,' Edward retorted. 'As our family physician your diagnosis is important.'

'Dr Chegwidden, your expertise is far superior to mine.' Senara humbled herself for the sake of Adam's welfare. 'I fear there could be internal damage. But there was no blood in his urine so I am optimistic that is not the case.'

'Thank you for your opinion, Miss Polglase.' Chegwidden's sarcastic tone whipped her. 'I suggest, since I intend to remove the bandages around his ribs, that as you are not a family member you wait outside until I am finished.'

Senara retreated though she was shaking with anger at his arrogance. The door to the bedchamber was left open and she positioned herself so that she could watch the doctor. Chegwidden continued his examination and his derisive remarks.

'Medicine is a precise science. These women who follow the old wives' remedies are all very well dealing with a cold or a simple ailment, but when a man's life is in the balance . . .'

It appeared to Senara that he was rougher than necessary in cutting away the bandages on Adam's ribs. The sweat broke out on Adam's face as the doctor prodded and poked. The splint was also removed and she saw Adam's body arch in agony when Chegwidden made a show of resetting his broken ankle and the suspected break to his upper thigh. He replaced the splints without the poultice to ease the swelling. Instead he placed two leeches on the flesh which Senara accepted would reduce the bruising.

'You would not want him a cripple, would you, Edward?'

Edward Loveday did not reply and Dr Chegwidden called out, 'You may rebandage the ribs, Miss Polglase. There is no need for that foul-smelling poultice, and the bandages should be much tighter upon the ribs.'

She disagreed: tighter bandages would constrict his breathing, and if any organ was inflamed increase the pressure upon it, even cause greater damage.

Chegwidden walked outside the room with Edward but his voice was loud enough for Senara to hear. 'The woman has some little knowledge. Be on guard, Edward, that a little knowledge can be more harmful than beneficial. I will send over an elixir and some liver pills. And a strong opiate for his pain. If there is any sign of a fever I must be summoned immediately. I cannot counsel strongly enough that he should be at Trevowan and tended in the loving bosom of his family. I will visit him in three days.'

'I would be happier if he were stronger before he was moved,' Edward replied.

A loud hrmph showed the doctor's displeasure. 'I have a wide practice, Edward. It is another two miles for me to come out as far as the shipyard.'

'And I would expect your fee to reflect the extra time and trouble.'

'Indeed, sir. Indeed it will.' Chegwidden did not hide his displeasure. 'I shall now call upon St John. Do you ride with me?'

'Yes. You must stay to dine with us.' Edward soothed the doctor's pride.

'That would be my pleasure.'

Senara busied herself tending to Adam. There was a tightness about her lips which showed her anger.

Adam dragged his hand across the covers to close over hers. Every effort took all his strength. His voice was laborious. 'Do not let Chegwidden upset you. I trust you.'

'And last night proved your worth, Miss Polglase,' Edward announced from behind her. 'I will rest easier with Adam recuperating at Trevowan, but he is not yet strong enough to be removed. Would you continue to tend him?'

She hesitated but when she glanced at Adam, who had again fallen asleep, she knew she could never abandon him until he had recovered.

Later that morning Edward stood beside St John's bed. The fever had

248

gone but his son lay weak and listless.

'Chegwidden informs me you should be up and about in a day or two.'

St John turned his head away.

'You have not asked after Adam. Did Meriel not tell you he was shot by smugglers or some such lawless band? He was lucky to survive. The bullet would not have killed him, but Solomon bolted and Adam's foot was caught in the stirrup. He will be laid up for some weeks.'

St John was failing miserably to master his emotions and Meriel feared his manner would arouse his father's suspicions. There was guilt written on her husband's face as he groped for words.

'The Lord be praised, Adam has been spared,' she gushed to divert Edward's attention. 'Such a terrible accident. And so worrying for you, sir. You must be exhausted after spending so long at both your sons' bedsides. Had I not been so fearful of St John's own recovery I would have offered my services to nurse Adam.'

'That is kind of you.' Edward turned to her with a deeper respect. 'But, of course, your place is at your husband's side. Miss Polglase will tend Adam.'

St John had put his hand across his eyes and shuddered. 'Thank God he was not killed.'

Edward touched his shoulder. 'Rest. It heartened me that in your delirium you called for Adam. I always knew that beneath the rivalry you cared for your brother. I have written to the Lord Lieutenant and there will be an investigation. I will not rest until an example has been made. We turn a blind eye to the smugglers too often, but after this I shall be vigilant in supporting the excise men in stamping out the trade.

'Could Adam not have been shot by poachers?' Meriel stated.

'He was no danger to a poacher, daughter. No more illicit goods will be stored or purchased by my family.'

When he left the room, St John turned an agonised stare on his wife. 'Dear God, the Jowetts could have killed Adam. What if Father ever suspects we were behind the attack?'

'He will not. It has gone in your favour that you kept calling out Adam's name in your delirium. Only I know it was through guilt. Edward blames the smugglers. So it is as well you are out of the trade.'

'And what if the Jowetts talk?'

'They have too much to lose. If no cattle were rustled that night they have nothing to fear from the law. I am sure they have an alibi as to their whereabouts. And your own alibi could not be more perfect. You were surrounded by your family and near to death yourself.'

Adam was too weak to be moved to Trevowan.

During Elspeth's first visit with Edward, she took one look at her semi-conscious nephew and declared to Edward, 'The boy has suffered enough. Senara tells me that moving him could risk his internal injuries. I trust her judgement. He will come to no harm under her care.'

Senara moved into the house in the shipyard. To preserve the proprieties, Leah, who was already Adam's housekeeper, and Bridie occupied another bedchamber. Depending upon Adam's condition either Leah or Senara returned twice a day to their cottage to feed the livestock. Wilful was given a place in the yard's stable and two wine vats were adapted as kennels for Angel and Charity. Both dogs were restrained by a long chain as, running loose, they had caused havoc amongst the workers.

For the first week Senara slept on a truckle bed in the corner of Adam's room. He had developed a fever which, although it was not dangerously high, was a complication to his recovery. By the second week he was stronger and able to sit up in bed but he made a poor patient. The splint ran from his ankle to hip and made movement difficult. He was bored by the enforced activity.

At the end of the second week the weather was mild and the Reverend Joshua Loveday and his wife arrived one day shortly after Adam's father and stepmother.

'Could I ask you to keep your visit short?' Senara said as she made a respectful curtsey. 'Henry Traherne was here earlier and the family have been here an hour. Adam is still weak.'

Joshua, who despite his holy orders, still appreciated a pretty woman, smiled at her. 'We will not overtax your patient.'

'Such wonders you have performed,' Cecily proclaimed. She had not followed her husband upstairs. 'Is the Polglase cottage not within our parish? I have not seen you at church. Apart from your spiritual comfort you will meet new friends. The cottage is isolated, is it not?'

'We are content with our own company.' Senara shifted uncomfortably. She did not want to offend this woman but she had as much distrust of the Church as she did of strange places and people.

After her gypsy father had been hanged the Polglase women had left the tribe and lived on the outskirts of a village. When she was fifteen she had been accosted by the parson's son while gathering wild herbs in the woods. She had fought him off but not without scratching his cheek. The next night he and a friend had tried to burn their cottage down while they were asleep. They had escaped but the fire destroyed half the cottage. Leah had reported him to his father and the son had denounced Senara for bewitching him. The parson's wife and five other village matrons had stormed on their cottage. Their goods which had survived the cottage fire had been broken up and the

250

good women of the village had stoned Leah, Bridie and Senara out of the village.

'Be gone daughter of Satan,' the parson's wife had screamed. 'We will have no witchcraft here.'

Their accusations had terrified her. Senara still bore a long scar on her shoulder from a sharp flint thrown by the parson's wife. It was not the first time her simple possets and balms had been hailed as a witch's brew. Women who sought her out to procure a love potion, or rid themselves of an unwanted child, muttered curses and threats when she refused to aid them.

There was the sound of excited barking outside and Richard Allbright, Scamp and Faith bound into the room. Bridie hobbled in and flopped on to a stool. Both the children's faces were flushed. This was Richard's third visit and gradually his and Bridie's shyness had dissolved and they had formed an easy companionship.

To Senara's relief Cecily laughed and was diverted from her questioning. 'Richard, you are looking hale. The country air agrees with you.'

'He is well.' Amelia held her cornflower silk skirts to one side as she descended the stairs. The lace from a half-dozen petticoats frothed like sea foam around her buckled shoes. 'For that I must also thank Senara. She prepared a tisane for him which has eased a cough he had developed.'

The two dogs chased one another round the room, upsetting a stool. Senara turned to her sister: 'Bridie, there are too many people here for the dogs to be inside. Take them outside.'

Richard jumped up. 'Let's go look for that badgers' sett you told me about.'

'I don't think so, Bridie.' Senara's expression was anxious as she regarded Amelia. Mrs Loveday may not wish her son to play with a servant's daughter, especially one with Bridie's deformity.

Amelia was frowning. 'You must not overexcite yourself, Richard. How is your cough?'

'I am fine, Mama. Bridie knows of this badgers' sett. It is in the woods behind the stacked timber. It is not far.'

'Then take care you do not tire, Bridie.' Amelia laughed as the children ran out. Richard adapted his pace to Bridie's shuffling gait. 'How bravely your sister manages, Senara. She has a sweet temperament. I've never known Richard take to another child so.'

'He is very kind to her, but I told Bridie not to expect him to play with her. She forgets her place.'

But Amelia did not appear displeased with her son's friendship. 'Richard sees few children his own age. It must be lonely for him at times.'

Amelia studied Senara. From their first meeting she had been struck

251

with the quiet dignity of this woman. She had been impressed by the way Adam was recovering and was grateful for all Senara had done to improve Richard's health. Yet she had been concerned at noticing the way Adam's gaze followed Senara whenever she was in the room with him. Neither had she missed the tenderness in Senara's eyes when she ministered to her patient. It was obvious that Adam was in love with Senara, and Amelia had wondered whether to speak to Edward of the matter. Edward had enough worries over the health of his sons. From what she knew of Adam he would not sway from his duty, but the sooner he was married to his French cousin the better.

The family had scarcely left the yard when Dr Chegwidden's figure darkened the window. Senara found Adam asleep and touched his shoulder to tell him the physician was here and helped him to sit up. Before she left the room she saw the doctor lift his jar of leeches from his bag.

She glanced anxiously at Adam and saw the grey tinge on his skin and the droplets of sweat. His body tensed as the first leech was placed upon his torso where the marks of faint bruises were still visible. For a moment she thought he would retch from the revulsion the touch of the leech roused as it fastened its greedy mouth to his skin.

'Must I endure those?' Adam appeared to shrink from the physician.

'Leeches are greatly beneficial.' Dr Chegwidden blithely applied another to his cringing flesh.

Senara suppressed the urge to take Adam's hand and reassure him. She avoided such intimate gestures. The leeches were the best means to reduce swelling and bruising; she often used them herself. He shuddered and she knew how hard he had to battle against his revulsion and irrational fear of the bloodsuckers. His muscles contracted as though ready to flee as he fought to control a rising nausea. Many people were the same with spiders or vermin. She left the sickroom, aware that Adam was embarrassed that she should witness this fear.

Throughout the hours she spent tending him she had put a shield around her emotions, forcing herself to see him as a patient and nothing else. To witness this chink in his armour, when he had borne so much pain in silence, had shown the shield to be made of spun sugar and not steel. Each day it was harder to keep her emotions at bay, her love for him all-consuming.

When Dr Chegwidden left, Adam called for her. The dressing around his head had been removed yesterday but as he sat propped up by pillows his shoulder and ribs remained bandaged. Adam refused to wear a nightshirt and she was acutely conscious of his half-naked torso.

'Chegwidden says I will be strong enough in four or five days to journey to Trevowan to complete my convalescence. Will you come with me?'

She shook her head. 'You have your family to tend you. I can prepare some herbs for a servant to administer.' She was straightening the sheet and he closed his hand over her arm.

'I owe you so much. I want you there.'

'It is not my place.' She tried to draw back her hand but it was held too tightly.

'Why do you deny what there is between us?' The words were a caress. 'No, please. Do not pull away. You know how I feel about you. And being thrown together in this way—'

'You must not say such things,' she interrupted. 'It changes nothing between us.'

'It changes everything!'

The gentle pressure of his hand increased. As she gazed into his eyes, he drew her towards him and with a sigh she sat on the bed.

He touched her hair. 'Senara, you know that I love you.'

'Please, if you talk like this I must leave.'

'You would never desert your patient.' He was teasing her, playing with her in a way which made her feel breathless.

'Soon you will not need my care.' She stood up quickly and pulled away from him. She had always known that once he began to recover there was danger in their close proximity.

He frowned and shifted uncomfortably. A pillow slipped sideways and when he reached to retrieve it, he winced. She took it from him, noticing again the lightning-shaped scar on his arm. He had told her how he had come by it. To her it was a reminder of his betrothal to another and the commitment he was bound to.

When she replaced the pillow, he moved quickly, capturing her in his arms and kissing her. Her instinct was to resist but the play of his mouth was pure enticement and her lips parted.

He was surprised at her response; throughout her tending him she had skilfully avoided any attempts he had made to kiss her. Now her lips moved in ardent supplication. Her body was poised above him the full curves of her breasts touching the bare skin above his bound ribs. Encouraged, he stroked her back, his hands circling under her arm to explore the heaviness of her breasts. The ties of her low-necked blouse above her bodice parted to his fingers.

At the touch of his lips on her breast, Senara gasped. She surrendered to the sweetness of his caress, the warmth which spread through her body and the tight nub of longing in the pit of her stomach. Then as her fingers brushed against a bandage it was like a dousing of cold water. She pulled back and drew a shaky breath.

'This is madness! You are on your sickbed.'

He gave a low seductive laugh and placed her hand over the hardening tumescence under the covers.

She blushed and withdrew her hand. 'Shame on you, sir,' she teased,

253

but her voice trembled with desire. 'I will not be responsible for a relapse. Behave yourself.'

'The pain of wanting you is more unbearable than my ribs or leg.'

Her gaze was serious. 'While I am tending you I will not be your lover. It would not be right.'

'Spare me from the workings of a woman's mind.' He wiped a hand across his brow. 'You are right, especially if you are to tend me at Trevowan.'

It would be too easy to agree. But the complications crowded like hurdles in her mind. 'I would not feel comfortable at Trevowan.'

'Then I shall stay here.'

'You need to recuperate with your family. To stay here would cause gossip.'

He let out a juddering breath. 'I would not have you the butt of gossip.'

When she tried to rise, he held her tight. 'I will find a way for us to be together, Senara. I will not lose you.'

Tears filled her eyes. She knew it was an impossible dream but the moment was too precious to spoil it by denial. When he drew her head to lay upon his chest she did not protest. She savoured the warmth and security of his arms around her and stayed with him until his even breathing told her he was asleep.

When he called out in the night it was Leah who went to him. 'Senara has returned to the cottage. The livestock needed attending and she had an order of several pottery items to be made and delivered to a house in Fowey before the end of the week. Her work has been neglected. She will be back tomorrow at midday once the pottery is firing in the kiln.'

The next morning, when Dr Chegwidden rode into the yard, Edward stopped preparing his list of materials to be ordered and left his office to attend the doctor's examination.

Chegwidden nodded with satisfaction. 'Adam is strong enough to be moved to Trevowan.'

'That is splendid news.' Edward smiled with relief.

'I would rather stay here,' Adam protested.

'I will not hear of it.' Edward was firm.

'But I can see how things are progressing at the yard. I will be able to leave this bed in a week. Seth has made me some crutches.'

Chegwidden folded his arms across his chest and rested his double chin on his waistcoat. 'You will push yourself before you are ready. You must rest to recover. Your father is right. You should be at Trevowan. In another week your ribs will be healed enough that you can safely walk with crutches. Another month and we can remove the splint.'

Adam continued to protest. Edward took the doctor's arm. 'If you would give me a moment with my son . . . There is an excellent claret downstairs to partake while we talk.'

When they were alone Edward turned a stern expression upon Adam. 'There is already talk about the Polglase woman living here. She has her own work and besides . . .' he frowned before adding, 'there is news from your Aunt Louise in France. Claude is dying. As soon as you are well you must marry Lisette. Fraddon will bring the coach for you to travel to Trevowan tomorrow morning.'

When Senara returned Adam told her his plans.

'Then I will not come to Trevowan. It is better that we part now.'

'You do not mean that. I love you, Senara. There must be some way we can be together.'

'Your world and mine are very different. We can never meet as equals. Our love is not meant to be. I could not share you.'

Nothing he said would change her mind. She left before he woke the next morning.

Adam railed against her stubbornness. During his convalescence there were times he cursed her. Yet he missed her. She was the only woman he would ever love. There must be some way they could be together.

Chapter Thirty-Five

It was late June before Adam and his father could sail to France. Adam's leg had been slow to heal and it was only now that he could undertake such an arduous journey. He was still unable to walk far without the aid of a stick. Edward had insisted on accompanying Adam, for the latest letter from Louise Riviere which arrived last week had been alarming.

Claude died last month. I could not write before. Please come quickly. There is so much danger. I fear for Lisette. I no longer know my son and he frightens me.

Louise had always written long chatty letters filled with family gossip. The shortness of this missive and the strangeness of its wording filled both men with dread. Most distressing was that Louise's letter had taken three weeks to reach them.

'There is no vessel sailing to France for another ten days,' Edward announced on his return from Falmouth. 'Then there is only one which will dock at St Malo and we will have a week's journey by coach from there to Paris.'

'Why not take the *Pegasus*?' Adam was impatient to undergo her sea trials which had been delayed for his recovery. 'We could sail her for a short run tomorrow and then set sail for Dieppe the following day, if all goes well.'

Edward looked uncertain. 'We keep the sea trials for a new vessel close to shore.'

'We are not sailing the Atlantic. We can keep inshore as far as Plymouth and then cross to Cherbourg. That is not so far. Then we can tack inshore to Dieppe. It will save us two weeks. Is it not worth the risk? We both know the *Pegasus* is seaworthy. The sea trials are a formality.'

'Very well.' The decision made Edward brighten. 'But we will need a day or so to raise enough men to sail her.'

'I'll ride into Penruan,' Adam suggested. 'There will be a dozen fishermen eager to sail. The pilchard fishing has been poor this season. Between Fowey and Falmouth there should be no trouble raising hands.'

Ominous storm clouds were chasing each other across the English Channel as Amelia stood beside the carriage to bid her husband farewell.

'You will take care, Edward?' she urged. 'Squire Penwithick has been talking of unrest in France for months. Are you sure it is safe to travel?'

'You must not worry. We will be home in ten days. There is a wedding celebration for you to start planning, and Elspeth is determined that Rowena's first birthday must be made a grand occasion.'

'The only occasion I want to celebrate is your safe return.'

He kissed her cheek and there was great tenderness in his eyes as with secret smiles they both remembered the passion they had shared on waking. 'I shall miss you, my darling,' he whispered.

'And I you.'

He glanced across the lawns to where Meriel was hurrying with Rowena in her arms.

'I thought I had missed you,' she called. 'Safe journey, sir.'

Edward waved and said in an undertone to Amelia, 'Do not let that minx upset you while I am away.'

Amelia smiled. 'Meriel has been pleasant company since St John was taken ill. Her manners are impeccable now. She is a credit to St John. They do seem very much in love and happy together.'

'St John too seems to have mended his ways. If that is her influence then the marriage may not be the disaster I feared.'

He entered the carriage to sit next to Adam. Japhet, who had been eager to join the expedition, winked at Amelia. 'There is no need to worry, Amelia, we will take care of him. The Lovedays are an invincible breed.'

A storm broke as they boarded *Pegasus*, but it had fortunately passed by the time they weighed anchor and sailed out of the Fowey river into the Channel. The wind was brisk and stayed with them so that the passage to Dieppe was made in record time. Adam was jubilant. The new sleeker lines of the ship's hull had proved superior to others of her class. 'Just think of the time she could take off an Atlantic or African run. She will never be as fast as the great South Sea clippers but she is a worthy opponent.'

The thrill of sailing his own ship had suppressed the worries concerning his aunt and cousin. But now that they were in France those fears returned and magnified. There was still a three-day coach ride to Paris.

During Adam's illness Penwithick had kept the family abreast of the news in France. The mood of the people was ominous and unstable.

The hatred of the monarchy and all the *ancien régime* was more violent than ever. With the price of bread rising and with so many of the poor starving, street-corner revolutionists were more open.

'It is a dangerous time to go to France, Edward,' Squire Penwithick had warned. 'Especially to Paris.'

'I cannot desert our family if they are in need of help. Now Claude Riviere is dead Adam must marry Lisette. She will be safer in England. Perhaps her mother also.'

'Then I advise you to travel well armed, my friend. And with the protection of others.'

It had been decided that Jasper Fraddon would accompany them. As their gamekeeper as well as groom he was an excellent shot. Japhet had arrived unexpectedly.

'Father said you were leaving for France and that the situation there could be dangerous. I always planned to visit Paris. I could not let my favourite uncle and cousin go on such a jaunt without offering my sword.'

'It will be no jaunt, Japhet,' Edward had advised.

'But it will be an adventure,' he'd answered, undeterred. 'Is St John to join us?'

'St John is too ill. He has again taken to his bed. His lungs were weakened by the fever. The slightest chill inflames them.'

Japhet had stared pointedly at Adam's leg and the stick he was leaning on. Adam had limped into the room. If anyone should not be undertaking such a venture with the explosive political situation in France it was Adam. Japhet had winked at his cousin and whispered, 'St John always knew how to protect his own hide when danger is around.'

Now the unrest in France was obvious as the coach took them towards Paris. Homeless, starving peasants wandered the roads, their bodies hunched and skeletal. There was bitterness and anger on many of their ravaged faces. It was the children which affected Adam most sharply. Their eyes were overlarge and peering out from hollowed, unsmiling faces. Often the smaller ones were crying, a pitiful litany of their suffering.

On Penwithick's advice the Lovedays dressed in their plainest clothes. Any show of wealth could attract the anger of the French peasants. Japhet found the necessity for disguise a source of amusement, though he was disgruntled at having to leave his sword behind. To compensate, he secreted a dagger in his boot. Another, together with a pistol, was tucked into his waistband beneath his jacket.

'Now you are armed like a cutthroat,' Edward reprimanded. 'Can not some of those weapons be packed away? We have no wish to attract undue attention.'

'They would not do us much good hidden in our luggage if we are set upon,' Japhet returned. 'Besides, I feel quite naked without my sword as it is.'

'That is because you have used it to get out of so many scrapes,' Adam taunted.

'And in to them.' Edward eyed his nephew sternly.

Japhet laughed and the coach lumbered into an inn yard. 'Finally there is a chance to chase the dust from our throats and stretch our legs. This coach is like a furnace.'

'And no dallying with the wenches, Japhet,' Edward warned as his nephew strode towards the taproom. Edward removed his hat and wiped his sweating brow with a kerchief. 'If we are delayed the coach will not reach Paris tonight. It has already taken a day longer than expected. It is now nearly five weeks since Louise wrote to us.'

They arrived at the Riviere house at dusk, footsore and weary. They had a half-mile walk across Paris from the inn where the public coach had deposited them. Usually at this time of the evening the shops would be open and the streets bustling with life and vehicles. Today, only an occasional shop was not shuttered, any citizen on the streets the most uncouth and unkempt. Any cart in evidence was empty of merchandise, driver and horse eager to reach the safety of their stable and home. That no bourgeois were on the streets showed the extent that the rabble ruled the city.

Menace was tangible in the lengthening shadows. Surly men huddled in groups, their stares belligerent as they watched the Lovedays pass. Ahead of them, on a street corner, a man stood on an upturned barrel and began denouncing the King as a tyrant. Within moments a crowd gathered, their mood volatile as they punched the air with their fists and joined in the tirade.

Japhet sucked in his breath. 'This has the stink of anarchy and rebellion. Did you see the knives some of those men were carrying in their belts?'

'It is not far to the Riviere house,' Edward answered. 'Do nothing to incense these men; they are spoiling for a fight. I doubt Adam's leg will hold up to us running through the streets.'

'I shall manage.' Adam was already gritting his teeth against the pain. The mood of the people was worse than he expected. Where were the guard to protect the citizens if a riot broke out?

The atmosphere made the hairs on Adam's neck crawl. More angry voices drifted out from a tavern. As a precaution he placed his hand on the pistol hidden in his jacket and he noticed Japhet did the same.

Twice they had been challenged, once by six men in uniform patrolling the streets. Adam, whose French was more fluent than his father's explained, 'We are newly arrived in Paris from St Malo. Our

260

uncle has recently died. We are here to pay our condolences to his widow.'

During the coach journey from Dieppe they had experienced the suspicion and antagonism which a group of foreigners could arouse and had decided that Adam would be their spokesman and they would pass themselves off as French.

'There is a curfew,' the thickset leader informed them. 'Be inside by dark or you will be arrested. There are many agitators causing trouble.'

At the next corner they had to push past another large group. Surprisingly, there was no National Guard attempting to disband them. As they were swarmed around by the crowd, an orator standing on a bale of straw proclaimed, '*Vive Mirabeau* and the Third Estate! He is the voice of the people. We will not be disbanded until we have fulfilled the wish of the people and a constitution is granted.'

Another shouted, 'Aye, the King had no right to try and dissolve the States-General. The Third Estate is a national assembly for the good of all the nation. A constitution must be made showing the King how much power we will tolerate.'

'*Vive Mirabeau! Vive Robespierre!*' Others chanted.

These were the men Penwithick had informed Adam were the leaders urging the country to rise against the monarchy. Many of the men around them wore red, white and blue cockades in their hats.

Pamphlets were handed out and the words *Liberty and the People* were boldly proclaimed.

The Englishmen kept their hands on their pistols as they edged through the menacing crowd and it was a relief to pass into another street without incident.

'What does all that mean?' Japhet cast a wary glance over his shoulder. 'Sounds like they are hatching a revolution.'

'I fear that is exactly what they are planning,' Adam increased his pace. His knee and hip were throbbing from the long walk.

'No wonder Louise sounded so distraught in her letter.' Edward's tone was anxious. 'We must get Louise and Lisette out of Paris at once. They will be safe in England until this madness blows over.'

The streets were quieter close to the Riviere house. They were too quiet. Many of the grand houses which belonged to the lesser nobles were in darkness with the shutters barred. As the Lovedays drew closer there were no lights visible at the windows of the Riviere house. No servants answered their knock. On closer inspection the pale moonlight revealed that several of the windowpanes had been smashed.

Adam rapped on a neighbour's house which showed a light in a first-storey window. He introduced himself to the servant and they were shown into a candlelit parlour. A wizened man, his grey tufted hair sticking out of a velvet skullcap, sat dwarfed by a highbacked chair.

'Forgive our travelling attire, Monsieur,' Adam said. 'We are relatives of Madame Riviere. We have just learned of her husband's death and have come to pay our respects.

'She has gone. Three weeks ago at least. Moved in with that upstart son of hers.' The man spoke with contempt. 'Since he has ingratiated himself with so many nobles I would think they have taken flight to the country. The mob broke into the house some days ago and there was looting before the National Guard arrived.'

Edward was appalled at these events. 'Where is her son now living? He would not leave Paris and the silk warehouse.'

'If you are family that is what you should know, not I.' The man lifted a glass of claret, his gnarled hands shaking with palsy. He sipped it and smacked his lips but made no effort to offer them refreshment.

'We will try at the warehouse,' Adam suggested as they entered the street. 'Voiron, Uncle Claude's chief clerk, lives at the back.'

'How far is this warehouse?' Japhet grumbled. 'These boots are intended for riding, not a walking expedition across Paris.'

'It is not far,' Edward informed him.

The warehouse was equally dark and forbidding. Edward knocked for five minutes before a querulous voice demanded who was disturbing his peace.

'I am Edward Loveday, open up, Voiron.'

'Monsieur Loveday?' The wrinkled clerk squinted up at him and held his candle higher. 'There is no one here but myself.'

'We have come from the Riviere house. Louise is not there. A neighbour said it had been ransacked. Are Louise and Lisette living with Etienne? I do not know his address.'

The old man shrank and made to shut the door in their faces. 'I know nothing.'

Japhet bound forward and stopped the door shutting with his foot. 'What the devil . . . ! Is this any way to greet your master's relatives? We have come from England and my feet are killing me.' He pushed the clerk aside. 'We will have some wine. There must be something to eat and drink in this place. Then you can send a servant to Etienne to send his coach to convey us to his home.'

Voiron flinched as though Japhet had struck him. He shook his head and muttered in rapid and incoherent French.

'Speak up, man,' Japhet bellowed. 'You try my weary patience too far.'

'The man is terrified, Japhet,' Edward intervened. 'There is something very wrong here. We will get nowhere by frightening him.'

Japhet swung himself up on to the mahogany counter and lay down with his hands behind his head and ankles crossed.

'Voiron, I am sure that you can understand how worried we are about Louise and Lisette.' Edward struggled to sound conciliatory. A cursory glance around the warehouse had shown him the shelves bare of materials. Usually the warehouse was packed to the rafters with exotic brocades, velvets and silks. Something was indeed very wrong.

'I know nothing, Monsieur. It would be more than my life is worth . . .'

'Ah, so the little French Frog does know,' Japhet expounded.

Adam lost his temper. His leg ached abominably. The long days of travelling had sapped his strength. He had spent weeks anguishing over his contract to wed Lisette when he was in love with Senara. Family duty had prevailed. To be confronted by this mystery was too much to tolerate.

He grabbed the neckcloth of the clerk. 'Lisette is my betrothed, where the devil is she? I am tired. I am hungry. I am thirsty. I am rapidly losing patience. And above all, I fear something terrible has happened to my aunt and fiancée. He lifted the man up by his neckcloth so that he was poised on his toes. 'Now tell me where the Riviere family is!'

There was a glint of silver in the candlelight and Japhet stood beside Adam, his dagger pressed to the clerk's throat. 'Tell him. For I, too, am a man of little patience.'

'Japhet, this is not the way,' Edward said in English.

To the terrified Voiron it must have sounded like another threat. He blinked rapidly and he shook with terror.

'They have gone to the warehouse in Marseilles. Look around you; this warehouse is all but empty. With the unrest it has been impossible to transport rich materials across land. Master Etienne sold our goods to London, Amsterdam and Belgium. Marseilles is the warehouse to which most of the precious silks are imported from the East.'

'Then why did Louise not tell us this?' Edward demanded.

'Because there is more, is there not, little Frog?' Japhet menaced.

Voiron cringed. 'Do not harm me. I will tell you. Take your dagger away.' It was withdrawn a couple of inches but still hovered close to his throat. 'Madame Riviere was distraught at the death of her husband as you will understand, yes. She collapsed. Next we hear that Mademoiselle Riviere has married the Marquis de Gramont. He has taken his wife to his château in the Auvergne.'

'This is outrageous!' Edward shouted.

The clerk's gaze darted from Japhet to Adam as though he feared his throat would be slit.

263

'I cannot believe Louise allowed this marriage,' Edward fumed. 'Is she in Auvergne?'

'I heard she had gone into a convent outside Rouen.'

'Good God!' Japhet thumped the counter with his fist. 'There is infamy afoot. It's Etienne. He is behind this.'

'What of Lisette? I cannot believe this match was of her choosing.'

Voiron cringed. 'I am a humble clerk. I've told you all I know. Madame Riviere was angry. There was a scene, I believe. But this is gossip. Monsieur Riviere told me only that I must take care of the warehouse and that he will be in Marseilles for the rest of the summer.'

'Etienne cannot get away with this,' Japhet raged. 'We will go to Marseilles and show him how a Loveday and an Englishman responds to his treachery and this insult.'

'It is Lisette and Louise I am concerned for,' Edward remonstrated.

Adam had been stunned by the revelations. Now he spoke. 'At least Louise is in no danger with the nuns. Not so Lisette. Yet what can we do, if she is already married?' He should have realised that Etienne was capable of such a devious scheme. He had wanted his sister wed to Gramont for his own elevation and importance. Anger ploughed through Adam. 'I fear for Lisette. The man she has married is evil.'

Edward leaned against a wooden post supporting the ceiling. 'I will consult with Claude's attorney. But though it grieves me that Etienne could have placed Lisette in an unhappy marriage, he is now her guardian. There is also Louise to consider. What possessed Etienne to have his mother shut away in a nunnery? That is barbaric. We must investigate that as well. It will take time. If Lisette is married the matter is out of our hands. What point is there in going to the courts for breach of contract? The scandal will only harm Lisette's reputation.'

The relief which had momentarily coursed through Adam that he was no longer bound to wed his cousin was replaced by his genuine fear for her safety. Yet what could he do? Lisette was now Gramont's wife and therefore his property. He felt guilty that he had not loved her more. Had he not been so insistent that they wait until she was eighteen and he able to support her, she would not now be in this danger. And she *was* in danger. He could not shake that from his conscience.

'Lisette is so young and innocent,' Adam protested. 'It will destroy her being wed to a lecher such as Gramont.'

'That is upon Etienne's head, not ours.' Edward was terse as he contained his own anger.

'If Lisette is harmed I swear he will pay for this,' Adam vowed. 'He has dishonoured his father by disregarding his wishes.'

'Had we not better find ourselves an inn for the night?' Japhet yawned and stretched his arms, rapping his knuckles on the low beam of the ceiling as he did so.

Edward nodded. 'Tomorrow I shall consult Claude's lawyer. I will not leave France until I have spoken with Louise.'

Chapter Thirty-Six

Senara woke from a nightmare. The gloom of the tiny cottage was filled with the red of her dream. Red from gutters gushing torrents of blood. She flung back her coverlet and pulled on her green woollen gown. Adam was in danger.

Leah stirred from the pallet bed they shared as she answered her mother's call. 'I need to walk.'

'Not on the moor, Senara, promise me. It is too dangerous.'

'I will have Angel.' The mastiff was padding silently at her side as she closed the cottage door. The night was dark and dense as obsidian; not even the trees were outlined against the sky.

Senara took the familiar path to the stream. The moon was full, but veiled by cloud. That some stars were visible gave her hope that the moon would soon appear to guide her steps to the moor. She had no fear of the desolate place for here she felt close to Adam.

She pulled the hood of her cloak over her unbound hair and sat on a boulder, waiting for the moon to illuminate her path. The dream haunted her with all its harrowing intensity. Blood and terror: screams and an all-pervading fear of evil. These images and feelings would not leave her.

It was not often she had such dreams but when she did they were always a portent of danger. She had dreamt of blood the week before her father was arrested, and again several years ago, a week before a shipwreck when thirty souls were drowned. But this seemed on a greater scale and was of man's own making.

When the moon broke through the cloud, she stared up at the silver orb, allowing its pure light to cleanse her fears. The unease stayed with her. Her restless steps were heavy, the dew from the bracken soaking into her long skirts and petticoats as she walked. Angel stayed close, neither distracted into hunting the fox which barked from a coppice, nor into investigating the snortings of the rough-coated moorland ponies. The moon was now poised above the craggy tor, and the circle of stones was bathed in a bluish-grey light as they soared skywards like the pillars of an ancient temple. Their foundations were surrounded by a swan's-down ethereal mist which expanded and subsided like a living breath.

Senara climbed to the crest of the tor. Here she sat until a duck-egg blue line on the horizon heralded the dawn. The sea was calm, the sun's golden and pink aureole radiating heavenwards. A flock of honking geese were a dark V as they flew overhead. Three tall-masted ships were tacking towards Falmouth with the rising tide and the triangular sails of the fishing sloops from Penruan were rounding the bay on the trail of a pilchard catch.

Outwardly all appeared as normal, but within her the turmoil remained. She had deliberately avoided Adam since his recovery, learning of his visit to France through Leah. Also, Elspeth Loveday kept drawing her into dealings with Trevowan. If one of her mares was ill Senara was the first person she called on to tend it. Leah was comfortable with her new life working as Adam's housekeeper. It was good that her mother was settled but for Senara it was hard. How could she bear living close to Adam when he returned with his French bride, knowing he was for ever out of reach? She loved Adam too much to share him. It would be better if she left. Leah, with Bridie, could then move into Adam's house as his permanent housekeeper. From what Senara had learned of Lisette Riviere, she had not been brought up to soil her hands with domestic duties.

Her hand clenched over her heart as the pain of loving him engulfed her. It was time for her to move on and make a new life for herself.

She stood on the tor with the stiffening breeze whipping her hair and cloak behind her, her eyes straining for a sight of the *Pegasus*. There was no sign of any twin-masted brigantine. Whatever her feelings about his marriage, she could not leave the district until she knew Adam was safe.

She shivered. The ring of stones below her were turning from grey to a dusky pink, and as the sun rose higher the clouds which were over the horizon towards France were smudges of crimson blood.

'May God have mercy on them,' she sobbed and, careless of her twisting ankles, ran from the tor. The largest of the stones, where she and Adam had made love, drew her. She threw herself on the ground, her body consumed by the feathery mist. 'Let him be safe,' she prayed. Her tears spilled into the earth and Angel lay down beside her, his rough tongue licking the salty trails from her hands.

The vagaries of the French people seemed intent on thwarting the Lovedays at every turn. Nothing was made easy for them. The office of Monsieur Bauchet, Uncle Claude's lawyer, was closed.

'He has gout,' a barrow boy pronounced as he continued shovelling the excrement from passing horses into his cart. His clothes were as foul-smelling and the same colour as the ordure he cleared from the streets. 'Suffers badly with it. The office has been shut all week. He'll be back in a day or so. Usually is.'

'Where does he live?' Edward demanded.

The barrow boy shrugged. 'No point in searching there. He lives with his spinster sister. The woman is deaf as a post. She never answers the door. Best try again tomorrow.'

They did and the next day and the two following. Finally the lawyer was available. His office was dark, dingy and cluttered with files which were spread across Monsieur Bauchet's desk and the floor. The man himself was short, bespectacled, bald and continually ringing his hands, his manner as ingratiatingly humble as it was false. His foot was bound in a large bandage and he kept it raised on a worn tapestry-covered footstool.

He declared Lisette's marriage as legal but would not divulge her whereabouts.

'We must assume that my niece is safe in the custody of a loving husband,' Edward said, his sarcasm lost on the Frenchman. 'I am concerned for the welfare of Louise Riviere. Why was it necessary for her to be put into a convent?'

'For the nuns to care for her, of course.' Monsieur Bauchet stretched his lips to a waspish smile. 'Madame Riviere suffered an apoplectic fit shortly before her daughter's marriage. The poor woman is partially paralysed and cannot speak. The nuns at Rouen will care for her. In these cases it is possible for the patients to recover some of their faculties and use of their limbs. Her husband's death was a great shock to her.'

'So no doubt was her son's perfidy,' Japhet snorted in disgust. 'Boiling in oil would be too good for that knave.'

Bauchet ignored Japhet's comment, which had been spoken in English. The lawyer continued, 'Madame Riviere is safe in the care of the nuns. You have seen the unrest in Paris. It is of grave concern to us all. Each day the rabble become more demanding and unruly. It is no wonder that the Marquis has taken his bride away from these troubles. Her brother and his wife accompany them.'

'I thought they were in Marseilles?' Adam was instantly suspicious.

The lawyer shrugged. 'Monsieur Riviere has a warehouse there. It is possible. Anything is possible in these troubled times. Had I a quieter place in the country to retreat to, I would not remain in Paris. Each day the weather grows hotter and the people more unstable.'

Bauchet rose from his chair and rummaged through a pile of papers on the floor by the grimy window. He drew out a folded parchment with a large red seal intact. He handed it to Adam.

'Etienne Riviere instructed that this be given to you should you arrive to claim his sister as your bride.'

Adam opened it and frowned as he read Lisette's large childish writing.

269

My dearest cousin,

My heart bleeds with shame that my affections have been won by another. The Marquis de Gramont is an honourable man and has been ardent in pursuit of my admiration. It would be unworthy of me to marry you when I love another. I believe Papa would have forgiven me, as I pray you will find it in your heart to forgive this wrong I do you.

Lisette

He handed the letter to his father, saying. 'This does not ring true. Lisette was frightened of Gramont when I was last in Paris.'

'That was some months ago, was it not?' Bauchet pursed his lips in recrimination. 'A young maid does not like to feel neglected. They can be fickle. Their feelings change.'

Edward turned a stony face upon the lawyer. 'This is my nephew's doing. Have you seen my niece? Was she under duress?'

'You are mistaken, monsieur. She is now a marchioness, the mistress of two châteaux, in the Loire Valley and Auvergne, plus a grand maison here in Paris. Why should she be other than happy?' He looked at Adam's practical travelling clothes and allowed a sneer to twist his lips. 'Now if you wish to contest the marriage contract that is another matter. One for the courts. However the Marquis has been most generous. He has offered to compensate Monsieur Adam Loveday with the sum of two thousand livres.'

'I want none of his tainted money.' Adam stood up, his face suffused with anger. 'Come, sir. There is nothing we can do here.'

Once out in the street it was immediately obvious that the atmosphere around them was charged with tension.

'We will leave for Dieppe early tomorrow,' Edward informed Adam and Japhet. 'The sooner we are out of here the better. It feels like there is a powder keg about to blow and I would rather not be close to it. I must consult an attorney of my own. There were business dealings with Claude which I do not trust Etienne to honour. I shall meet you back at the inn. There is no coach for Dieppe for another four days. We shall have to hire one.'

'Then I intend to enjoy my last night in Paris,' Japhet clapped Adam on the back.

'Yes, you two enjoy yourselves.' Edward said, distracted. 'But I warn you, Japhet, I intend to leave early tomorrow. A hangover makes a poor travelling companion.'

Adam was in no mood for drinking. Despite his relief that he was no longer bound to Lisette, he was worried for her safety. There was also more to this if Etienne had needed to consign Louise to a convent. It was nothing short of barbaric. They could not leave France without learning the truth.

Japhet was flirting with a tavern wench and making an assignation with her, his French remarkably fluent when pursuing a woman. Adam left his tankard half full and stood up. 'I am poor company. I will return to our inn.'

Japhet lifted his tankard. 'You should be celebrating your release from matrimony. You are a free man again.'

'And what if Lisette is in danger? She is still my cousin. She is little more than a child. When I think of her, so young and innocent, married to that man . . .' He bunched his fist. 'And what of Aunt Louise? She was so full of energy and life. To be struck so low. How can I celebrate?'

With a groan, Japhet rose and patted the tavern wench on her buttocks to send her away. 'This is not turning out the exciting adventure I had envisaged, but I will not desert my family. I may have many faults but that is not one of them. Besides, the French women are so dour. They are more interested in complaining about the price of bread and the injustice of the taxes, than making love.'

'If that is so, then either the situation here is far worse than we imagined, or you are losing your touch.'

Japhet looked astonished. 'Never, my cousin. Sex is a universal language. There is nothing wrong with me. That wench was agreeing to meet me later.' He pulled at his moustache. 'Though she did mention money. I may buy a wench the odd trinket but I never pay for their services. Mercenary lot, these Froggies.'

'Or desperately poor.'

Adam entered the street and was perturbed by the large number of men he encountered carrying makeshift weapons of pokers, cudgels and pitchforks. The mood was more dangerous than earlier. Events were moving swiftly, the dam of pent-up fury finally breaking through to wreak havoc and destruction in its wake.

A man shouted, 'To the Invalides. We join our brothers. The guard is on our side and the armaments we need shall be ours.'

Japhet glanced at Adam with a gleam in his dark eyes. 'Looks like someone has already lit the powder keg.'

Adam was reminded of his work for Penwithick. There were other English agents in Paris but this was the information the squire had asked Adam to report upon. He could see that Japhet was eager to investigate.

'Just remember this is not our fight,' Adam warned.

When they reached the domed barracks it had already been overtaken. Soldiers mingled with the mob. Some had discarded their uniform jackets and hats. Many now sported the red, blue and white tricolour cockades or ribbons. The mob were holding their plundered muskets and pikes aloft and chanting, '*Liberté!*' There was blood on clothing and hands, proclaiming that not all the guard had capitulated to the mob.

'To the Bastille!' The chant changed.

'The Bastille! The Bastille!'

The immense turreted walls of the ancient fortress represented oppression to the people. It was a place of incarceration without trial for those who had offended the King or nobles. Though in truth scarcely a half-dozen prisoners were lodged there.

They reached the Bastille as de Launay, the governor, made his surrender. The mood of the crowd remained menacing, pressing in around the governor. De Launay tried to stab himself with his sword stick as the mob marched him away.

The baying for blood began as a snarl and rose, swirling around, increasing volume to become a deafening roar. 'Kill him! Death to de Launay! Hang him!'

There was a scuffle as some of the old guard tried to protect the governor. Adam glimpsed the man's stricken face, the terror in his bulging eyes. The mob spat at de Launay, and Adam was horrified when several figures launched themselves at the now defenceless man. They were savages: clubbing him to the ground and screaming abuse as they kicked and beat him. For a moment de Launay managed to struggle upright with blood streaming from his head. Then a bayonet was thrust into his stomach and with a scream of bloodlust more weapons were fired or thrust into him. When someone held up the severed head, Adam veered away, repelled by the violence. Japhet followed him equally shaken.

'Paris is ours.' One bold insurgent raised his cockade in his hand. 'On to Versailles. The King will hear our voice. He must bow to the will of the people.'

Behind them a bellow of approval chilled Adam's blood.

'The sooner we leave Paris the better.' He shouted to make himself heard above the mob who were baying for more blood and the heads of any who opposed them.

Chapter Thirty-Seven

Trevowan was resplendent in all its summer glory. Hollyhocks, gillyflowers, lavender, roses and honeysuckle coloured the garden and scented the air. The orchard was laden with ripening pears and apples and the songs of blackbirds and thrushes trilled in competition with the skylarks.

Meriel stood outside the dower house and tilted her face to the harebell-blue sky. Life was good and she had found a measure of contentment after the havoc of last winter.

Beyond their garden, the two fields of corn and barley planted by St John rippled like golden ponds in the breeze. The harvest promised to be abundant and the fields were bejewelled with necklaces of red poppies and blue cornflowers. Not that Meriel registered their beauty, she calculated the yield and profit to be made. Her gaze scanned the hill where the Loveday sheep were tended by old Silas Tonkin and his son Paul. She was proud that the fifteen ewes she insisted St John purchased out of the last of his legacy, had all produced lambs and their own flock had expanded to thirty four. Without her guidance St John would have gambled the money away.

Not that her husband always appreciated her advice, but Meriel had learned the value of patience and guile. Along with her carefully cultured manners she had mastered her jealousy and resentment.

Meriel had insisted that Rowena's birthday celebration was to take pace in the dower house. It had not been easy to accept the change in her status when Edward Loveday married, but her new-found caution warned her that she needed the goodwill of Amelia and Elspeth to be accepted by Cornish society. Rowena had helped to smooth their relationship. Elspeth was devoted to her and Amelia was equally enchanted. To her delight, in recent months St John had become a doting father. Because of Rowena's hand, which Elspeth insisted that Rachel Glasson manipulate every day to encourage the circulation and muscle growth, the child did not crawl. Instead she pulled herself up and walked around the furniture and had taken her first steps last week.

Edward had not returned from France for the celebrations so it was to be a dinner dominated by women.

She had prepared the menu with care. There was beetroot soup spiced with claret and chives and served with cream; St John's favourite of jugged pigeons was accompanied by oyster loaves, a salamangundy salad of pickled herrings, apples, lettuce, anchovies and lemons served with nasturtium flowers and watercress; followed by bottled pears in rosewater syrup, and ending with marchpane and violet scented sweetmeats.

Rowena's birthday was an excuse to entertain. It was Meriel's first time as hostess to the family and friends. Apart from the Lovedays, Dr Chegwidden and his wife would attend. Also Sir Henry and Lady Traherne and Roslyn's sister, Gwendolyn Druce, had accepted their invitation.

Meriel had convinced St John of the need for Sir Henry's support and friendship. Lady Traherne remained cool towards Meriel, but not so her sister, who accepted Meriel without judging her background. To Meriel's delight friendship was blossoming between herself and Gwendolyn. It amused her that Gwendolyn's constant mentioning of Japhet's name revealed the woman's interest in St John's cousin.

Since Aunt Cecily was desperate for Japhet to settle down and marry, it was to Meriel's advantage to encourage the match. Gwendolyn would be forever grateful to her and she carried a lot of influence within society. Nothing would annoy the haughty Lady Traherne more than for her sister to wed Japhet. A few years earlier there had been rumours that Roslyn had set her cap at Japhet and after a summer of courtship and speculation, the rakehell had left her for another light of love.

Meriel knew Japhet's kind well. He would marry for money or not at all. His freedom was too precious to him. Gwendolyn was an heiress. Had not Roslyn's portion saved the Traherne mine and the estate from bankruptcy? Gwendolyn was far more biddable than her shrewish sister. Such a wife would turn a blind eye to Japhet's dalliances.

Meriel loved intrigue and what better way to repay Roslyn's insults than to be a matchmaker between Gwendolyn and Japhet? And would not Edward applaud such a match which would make Japhet more respectable?

Meriel dressed with care to greet her guests. Her golden curls were piled high and two fat ringlets hung down over one shoulder. She wore a rose-pink taffeta gown drawn back over a petticoat of pale lavender embroidered with red carnations. About her neck and wrists were proudly displayed the amethyst necklace and bracelet given to her after Rowena's birth.

Sir Henry, Lady Traherne and Gwendolyn Druce, were the first to arrive. Roslyn ran an assessing eye over Meriel's attire. Her long face was heavily powdered and rouged, emphasising her hooked nose and prominent teeth.

'How you brighten our existence.' Her tone was ridiculing. 'You are as colourful as a popinjay in your new-found splendour.'

Meriel sketched a mocking curtsey. 'Amelia chose it for me, and she has such discerning taste. She said that a plainer woman would find the colours threatening, as they would draw attention to their failings.'

Sir Henry cleared his throat and looked uncomfortable at the tension sparking between the two women. He lifted Meriel's fingers to his lips. 'You look charming. St John is justifiably proud of you.'

Seeing his stare upon the low neckline of her gown, Meriel gave him a seductive smile. 'You are to sit next to me when we dine, Sir Henry. St John has told me how well the mine is doing. I want to hear all about your success.'

'That will be my pleasure.' Sir Henry's freckled complexion had deepened to a vivid blush.

Roslyn dug her husband unceremoniously in the ribs and propelled him to the far side of the room. The early stages of her pregnancy had not been kind to her. Beneath the thick layer of powder, her cheeks were sunken and she constantly put a hand to her mouth, as though battling against nausea. Henry escorted his wife to a chair, but otherwise paid her little attention as he engaged St John in conversation.

A chorus of greetings heralded the arrival of the Loveday family walking over from the main house. St John was at his most affable, at ease with his family and friends. Meriel could not relax. She was always on guard that her tongue did not slide back into the rough dialect of her youth, or that a momentary lapse of manners betrayed her lowly birth. With a smile plastered securely on her lips, she was determined to triumph and become a hostess renowned for her entertainments.

Joshua and Cecily had arrived earlier in the coach sent for them by Amelia, and had spent an hour at Trevowan. Cousin Hannah looked in radiant health despite her figure being still swollen from her second pregnancy. The older woman smiled coolly at Meriel. Although Hannah frequently visited Trevowan with her parents, this was the first time she had entered the dower house since Meriel and St John had made it their home.

'The house is charming,' she said surveying the interior. 'Amelia has been very generous to you.'

Meriel smiled. 'She has. Yet it is nothing less than St John deserves. He is Edward's heir, is he not?'

Her defensive tone brought a glitter of amusement to Hannah's eyes. 'As is Adam,' she corrected her, before she moved on to claim Gwendolyn's attention.

Lady Traherne edged between the two friends, her shrill voice dominating the conversation. Oswald Rabson nodded curtly to Meriel and joined Sir Henry.

Meriel felt the sting of Oswald Rabson's unspoken censure. Despite his worn velvet coat and breeches, which showed how little spare money there was in his household, he came from an old family, and he had yet to accept her as an equal.

Before the farmer's censure could fester, Meriel was surrounded by Amelia, Elspeth and Cecily. Joshua gave her a hearty kiss on the cheek, and even Peter bowed graciously, his thin pious face flushing as his nose hovered inches above her cleavage.

Her chagrin forgotten, she played the hostess to perfection as the neighbours arrived. From across the room St John smiled at her, his pride in her appearance and manner increasing her confidence.

When Rachel Glasson appeared with Rowena, the focus of the guests centred on the child as she was admired and presented with her gifts. Her useless hand was hidden by a full sleeve, but it did not stop her delight in reaching out for each new toy. The older Loveday women cooed and fussed over her, until the child was hiccoughing with delight.

St John took her in his arms and placed her carefully on the floor. 'See how she walks.' He applauded at her four tottering steps, and scooped her up again to kiss her cheek. 'Is she not amazing and beautiful like her mother?'

Lady Roslyn placed a hand on her stomach, her expression patronising and her voice falsely compassionate. 'How well the child copes. One would scarcely note her deformity.'

Elspeth glared at Roslyn. 'To us she is perfect. She has the sweetest nature. A virtue lacking in so many others.'

Amelia was equally defensive. 'She is a beautiful girl. Edward says she is very like your mother, St John, with her dark hair and blue eyes.'

Meriel chewed her lip, alert for any hidden meaning in such comparison's whenever Rowena's dark colouring was mentioned. Fortunately St John had not heard the comment and before Amelia could repeat it the gong was sounded.

St John handed Rowena to Rachel to return her to the nursery, and the guests filed into the dining room. Meriel placed her hand through Sir Henry's arm as he led her to the table. His whispered compliments upon her beauty pandered to her vanity and pride. Lightly she tapped his forearm with her fan. 'Sir Henry, you will turn my head with such praise.'

'All justly deserved. There's not a man in the county who does not envy St John his lovely wife.'

She lowered her eyes. She knew the lechery of such men who would compliment her to try and bed her, then ridicule her lowly birth if she capitulated. 'I hold my husband in the highest esteem, Sir Henry.'

'No one doubts it, dear lady.' The glint in his eyes maintained their interest. Were rumours true that Sir Henry's eye had wandered upon several local maids to satisfy his passion in recent months? Yet she enjoyed Sir Henry's flirting. It was a long time since a new man fell under her spell, but she must be careful not to rouse St John's jealousy. He would not see her flirting as harmless fun, which was all it was.

'Amelia, is there news from Edward?' Joshua asked, as they finished the beetroot soup.

Lines of worry creased Amelia's brow. 'Nothing. Though that is to be expected in the circumstances. He had hoped to return before now. The house seems so empty, especially with Richard away at school.'

'Japhet will be loath to leave Paris,' Peter sneered. 'He saw their visit as an adventure. He will not want to leave the entertainments such a city can offer without sampling the pleasures.'

Gwendolyn Druce gasped and with a blush said, sharply, 'Why must you always be so unkind about Japhet, Peter?' Discovering several stares upon her she dropped her gaze to her lap and picked at a torn piece of lace on her gown.

'At least Japhet knows how to enjoy himself,' Hannah retorted. 'While you, Pious Peter, think a good time is haranguing the good people of the district with an impromptu sermon.'

'Frivolity is a sin, sister.' Peter puffed out his chest to continue.

Joshua was faster. 'No lectures today, Peter. And you would do well to remember that Japhet travelled to Paris out of family duty, as St John was too ill to accompany his father at the time.'

There was an embarrassed cough from St John. 'I curse the fever which keeps laying me low since my illness last winter. I should be with father.'

Meriel was drawn from observing Gwendolyn's discomfiture. 'You must not blame yourself, my dear,' Meriel smiled at her husband. 'Someone had to remain lest there were any emergencies or incidents here or at the yard.'

'How convenient for you, St John,' Hannah observed with a lift of her brow. 'You always did find a bolt hole whenever danger threatened.'

Fury simmered in Meriel at the insult to her husband. She curbed it. 'St John has family responsibilities now he has a wife and daughter. Unlike Japhet and Adam who are free to pursue any madcap venture they chose.'

'Adam will be returning with his bride,' Amelia reminded them all. 'And the situation in France is far from stable.'

'Let us not talk of politics,' Meriel took control. 'This is a day of feasting and celebration.'

Joshua leaned across the table and took her hand. 'How charmingly you remind us, Meriel.' He raised his wine glass. 'A toast to Rowena!'

The drinks sipped, Sir Henry raised his glass. 'And we must not forget the child's mother, who brings such beauty and grace to our gatherings.'

This was the realisation of Meriel's dream to be accepted in society and be worshipped by important and influential men.

The mood of the French people was too volatile for the Loveday party to risk travelling by coach. Any vehicle which had any trappings of wealth was being seized and overturned by the mob. Four disreputable nags were finally purchased at an extortionate fee and the party set out for Rouen. Edward refused to leave France without seeing Louise.

There was another long delay at the Convent of Poor Clares. The nuns were suspicious of them and of Edward's less-than-fluent French. Eventually they were granted an interview with the prioress. She regarded them with distaste, her distrust towards all men rather than their mission. She was a heavy-boned woman with buck teeth and a hair-sprouting wart on her chin. The house was not a wealthy one. Both the habits of the porteress and prioress were patched and frayed at the cuffs and hems. The buildings smelt musty from damp and there were several greenish-black patches on the walls, testifying to a leaky roof.

'Why did Etienne chose such an impoverished establishment for his mother?' Edward seethed. 'My nephew has a great deal to answer for.'

'What I would give to have him skewered on my sword,' Japhet muttered in English as he regarded the room with distaste. 'A man who treats his mother so shabbily deserves to die.'

'Such talk of violence is unseemly, young man,' the prioress reprimanded. 'You said you were from St Malo. Yet you speak English.'

'A ruse to escape the wrath of the mob,' Edward placated. 'Louise Riviere is my wife's sister. We intend no harm, Reverend Mother. I was shocked to learn that Louise was ill and placed here instead of being cared for by her family.'

He drew from beneath his coat a pouch of silver. Retaining a few coins for the journey, he placed the rest before the prioress. 'Please accept this contribution to the upkeep of your convent. The self-sacrificing work of the Poor Clares is renowned throughout England.'

The prioress dropped the pouch into a wooden casket. 'Only you, monsieur, will be permitted to speak with Madame Riviere. It will distress the other patients for so many men to be present in the infirmary.'

'Is it compulsory for the Poor Clares to be ugly?' Japhet commented as they waited and a cup of weak mead was presented to them by a young nun with the girth of a wine vat.

The infirmary was Spartan. There were six beds, five of which were occupied by women. Each bed had a wooden crucifix over its headboard, and a statue of the Madonna was in the corner with a single candle burning at her feet. Edward stood at the foot of Louise's pallet. There were no sheets, only a threadbare blanket to cover her. Her hair was now a pewter grey and was brushed back to reveal a cadaverous face, with the side of her mouth drawn down. Her hands lay across her stomach beneath the blanket and she did not move at his approach. The only movement came from her eyes, which filled with tears.

Edward knelt at her side. 'My dear Louise, it is atrocious that you should be treated so. I will arrange for you to be conveyed to England. You will stay at Trevowan and be cared for by us.'

Her eyes flickered a denial. There were such depths of emotion and pleading in her gaze but although her mouth worked to speak, no words formed. Her silent pleading tore at him.

'Surely you do not wish to stay here. Would you not be more rested at Trevowan?'

Again she looked worried.

'We know that Lisette is married. Is that what you fear?'

She seemed to be easier but her eyes continued their silent pleading for understanding.

A slender, middle-aged nun hovered at her side. 'Monsieur, she must rest. I am Sister Bernadette. You appear to be upsetting her.'

'I would like her to come to England. We will care for her in our home. No disrespect to your work here, but surely it is better for her to be with her family.'

'Madame is very ill. She can do nothing for herself. How can she travel? In a month or two she may be stronger. She is at peace here.'

He turned to Louise. 'Is that true, Louise? Are you at peace here?'

Louise closed her eyes. When they opened there was the faintest smile on her lips.

'She is content,' the nun said with compassion. 'We are a poor house but we have helped many cases like Madame Riviere. It takes time. Peace and tranquillity are great healers and we have an abundance of those here.'

Edward regarded Sister Bernadette, realising how impractical it was for them to travel with Louise in such a condition. 'Louise is very dear to us all in England. Will you write and let us know if there is anything we can do? Especially if she wishes to come to England when her health improves.'

'Of course, Monsieur. Leave your address with the prioress. She will contact you whatever happens.'

279

He had to be content with that. But his anger rose at the way Etienne had abandoned his mother.

Three days later they docked in London. Their stay was brief. Adam hired a carriage to deliver a written report of the escalating events in France to Squire Penwithick's London home. The storming of the Bastille and the murder of de Launay were the first acts of open revolution against the Monarchy. The information would be forwarded to the Prime Minister.

His duty done, Adam had returned to the ship to discover his father arguing with Japhet, who had decided to remain in London.

'You will return to Cornwall with us. Would you break your mother's heart by not taking a proper leave of her?'

'I will stay but a month or so,' Japhet's face was dark with anger. 'What point to endure the long journey from Cornwall again?'

'The point is a matter of decency and respect to your parents,' Edward raged. 'And what means have you to support yourself here?'

'I have the means.'

'Not honourable.' Edward became scathing. 'It is time you took up a profession. Amelia has many friends in business. They will find a position for you.'

Japhet gave a cynical bark of laughter. 'I would make a poor clerk and have not the patience to study law or apprentice myself to a guild.'

'Then find yourself an heiress and try not to fritter her fortune away within a twelve month.'

There was mutiny in Japhet's hazel eyes and his figure was stiff with affront as he held his uncle's glare. Then his manner changed. 'Do you hold me in such little regard, uncle?'

Edward shifted his own tack. He was fond of his wild and headstrong nephew. It was concern for Japhet which had caused the argument. 'You have the wit and ingenuity to succeed in any venture you set your mind upon. You also have a streak which could land you in trouble with the law.'

'Japhet could sail with me to America,' Adam offered. 'I would welcome his company on board.'

'I am no seafarer. I would go insane cooped up so long on a ship.'

'Then at least return to Cornwall before embarking on a life in London. I would not see my brother's son begin such a venture penniless,' Edward continued.

'I will not take your money, uncle. Though I appreciate the offer. I have funds. Little enough, but I will get by.' He rubbed his moustache and stared across the masts which forested the docks. Through narrowed eyes he scanned the river bank from the dome of St Paul's to the turrets of the ancient Tower. He sighed. 'I will return to Cornwall. I shall need my horse. There's Arab blood in her and she is the only possession I prize – though you condemn me to a sermon from Father and I shall likely half drown in Mama's tears.'

When he was alone with Adam, Japhet became unusually serious. 'The truth is, things are getting rather hot for me in Cornwall. Paris was a chance to let them cool down.'

Adam regarded his cousin with concern. 'Then take care, Japhet. You are too fine a rogue to end your days on Tyburn gallows, or rotting in Newgate.'

Japhet flashed him an incorrigible grin. 'I was thinking more on the lines of finding myself a lonely countess, or duchess, who will pay handsomely for my witty company.'

The following day they entered the Fowey river. With the cries of seagulls around them, the company of fishing smacks returning with their herring catch, and the last houses lining the Fowey estuary behind them, Edward stood at Adam's side as Adam steered *Pegasus* through the deeper channel towards the Loveday yard.

'She has proved herself a fine ship, Adam,' Edward remarked.

'She is indeed.'

'When will you be setting sail to America?'

'I cannot afford to delay further.' Adam's thoughts sobered. He was about to realise his dream of becoming a merchant adventurer and captain of his own ship. Yet there were matters still unresolved in Cornwall.

Optimism conquered his doubts. His future stretched before him like an uncharted sea to be discovered and explored. He had the *Pegasus* and his work in the yard. And now he was free of his obligations to Lisette.

He pushed aside momentary guilt that he had broken his promise to Claude Riviere. His accident had prevented his marriage. Such was fate.

Now he could pursue Senara. Although he loved her, she had proved no easy conquest. That was what made her so special. He was determined to win her and make her his wife.

He smiled at the memory of her stubbornness. She too was proud. It would be as hard to get her to accept him as it would be to win his father's approval for their marriage.

None of the challenges ahead of him would be easy. That was what made them so exciting.

The wildness in his blood soared with exhilaration. He could understand Japhet's hunger to experience all life had to offer. To do less was somehow to be only half alive. Life was a gamble and an adventure. No matter which way the vagaries of fate tossed him, he was eager for the challenge.

Newport Library and
Information Service

CENTRAL 24/11/ $99-

Z260647